Also by R.D. Lawrence

Wildlife in Canada (1966)
The Place in the Forest (1967)
Where the Water Lilies Grow (1968)
The Poison Makers (1969)
Cry Wild (1970)
Maple Syrup (1971)
Wildlife in North America: Mammals (1974)
Wildlife in North America: Birds (1974)
Paddy (1977)
The North Runner (1979)
Secret Go the Wolves (1980)
The Zoo That Never Was (1981)
Voyage of the Stella (1982)
The Ghost Walker (1983)
Canada's National Parks (1983)
The Shark (1985)
In Praise of Wolves (1986)
Trans-Canada Country (1986)
The Natural History of Canada (1988)
For the Love of Mike (1989)

THE WHITE PUMA

A NOVEL

R.D. LAWRENCE

Stoddart

Published in Canada in 1990 by
Stoddart Publishing Co. Limited
34 Lesmill Road
Toronto, Canada
M3B 2T6

Published in the United States by
Henry Holt and Company, Inc.,
115 West 18th Street
New York, New York 10011

BOOK DESIGN BY CLAIRE M. NAYLON

Canadian Cataloguing in Publication Data
Lawrence, R. D. (Ronald Douglas), 1921–
The white puma
ISBN 0-7737-2300-5
1. Pumas—Fiction. I. Title
QL795.P85L38 1990 C813'.54 C89-090626-2

Printed and bound in the United States of America

FOR MY GODSON,
CAIS CONSTANT JURGENS,
BORN AS THIS BOOK WAS BEING WRITTEN.
WELCOME. GROW WELL, BE STRONG.
"FOR THOU SHALT BE IN LEAGUE
WITH THE STONES OF THE FIELD;
AND THE BEASTS OF THE FIELD SHALL BE
AT PEACE WITH THEE" (JOB 5:23).

Can he who has only discovered the value of whale-bone and whale-oil be said to have discovered the true uses of the whale? Can he who slays the elephant for his ivory be said to have seen the elephant? No, these are petty and accidental uses. Just as if a stronger race were to kill us in order to make buttons and flageolets of our bones, and then prate of the usefulness of man.

—Henry David Thoreau, the Journal, 1853

ACKNOWLEDGMENTS

I want to thank Marian Wood for standing behind me and smoothing out the rough places of this book. I have contended for a long time now that a writer without a good editor is like a lawn without a mower—most untidy. I have been lucky; Marian is an excellent editor. I also must thank my wife, Sharon, who has again put up with me during those times when I have been, let us say, distracted and, as always, has given me encouragement.

THE PUMA

(Felis concolor)

The scientific name of this New World feline is derived from Latin. It means "uniformly colored cat." But this carnivore is known by a variety of other names. In Quechuan, the language of the Inca people, it is called *puma.* The Tupi natives of northern Brazil call it *cuacu ara,* and the name used by the related Guarani people is *guacu ara.* From these two native languages has emerged the name *cougar.*

When the Spaniards first saw the puma in Moctezuma's zoo in Mexico, they christened it *león*: lion. The early European settlers in North America often referred to the cat as *mountain lion,* a name that was later corrupted to *catamount.* Today, depending on the custom in the different regions of North America, the animal is variously referred to as *puma, mountain lion,* or *cougar.*

Historically, the puma had one of the most extensive ranges of any mammal in the Western Hemisphere. It was distributed from east to west right across North and South America and from Patagonia, on the southernmost tip of South America, to northern British Columbia and, more rarely, the Yukon Territory.

Today, because much of its range has been radically altered and, in addition, the puma has been unmercifully persecuted by man, this magnificent animal's numbers have been dramatically reduced. Until recently, the eastern species was thought to have become extinct except for a small population in Florida, but it appears that isolated individuals have managed to hang on in the forests of eastern Canada and the United States.

Although nowhere plentiful, the greatest number of cougars are now to be found only in western Canada, the western United States, and some areas of South America.

BIOLOGY

BREEDING: Once a year, but no fixed season.
GESTATION: Between ninety and ninety-six days.
NUMBER OF KITTENS: From one to six, usually two to four.
SEXUAL MATURITY: Females breed at thirty months; males are sexually mature at three years.

ADULT WEIGHTS AND MEASUREMENTS

FEMALES: Weight: 80 to 140 pounds. Length: 5 feet to 7 feet, 6 inches; tail 21 to 32 inches.
MALES: Weight: 148 to 227 pounds. Length: 5 feet, 6 inches to 9 feet; tail: 26 to 36 inches.
COLOR: The overall adult color is tawny brown to gray but can be yellowish or reddish. Chest and throat are white, the backs of the ears to their edges, tail tip, and muzzle stripes are black.

White pumas are extremely rare. The few that have been known to occur have all been killed for their skins.

THE WHITE PUMA

PROLOGUE

Although his coat was white, the puma was invisible against a background of evergreens. His lithe body was stretched full length on a flat-topped crag that stood some two thousand feet above the bottomlands. From this vantage, he had an uninterrupted view of the long, narrow valley that is located in the Columbia Region of west-central British Columbia, a vast wilderness within which the majority of tall peaks of the Coast Mountains range are perpetually covered by snow, or by glaciers and ice fields that shine like blued mirrors when highlighted by the summer sun.

High above the recumbent cat, a bald eagle sailed the azure sky, its great wings outstretched and immobile except for the tips of its primaries, which were spread apart, rather like the fingers of two wide-open hands, and quivered slightly each time the raptor used updrafts of land-warmed air to soar above the peaks. As the eagle circled over the wilderness, its white head moved from side to side, allowing its keen eyes to search for any fish that might be surface-swimming in the lakes and rivers that abound in the area.

The puma was aware of the eagle, but he ignored it. The big bird was neither a threat nor a competitor and was thus of no interest to the cat. Instead, his yellow eyes were fixed unblinking on two riders who were slowly guiding their mounts out of the western mouth of the Telkwa Pass, a narrow, sloping defile through which Limonite Creek runs to empty into the Zymoetz River.

Two black-and-tan hounds trotted ahead of the men, their tails held high and curving over their backs, their heads down as they sniffed at the trail. But the scent that they had been trained to seek was absent. No puma had trodden the ground in recent days.

The leading rider, a large, corpulent man of middle age, held his mount's reins in his left hand. His right arm hung straight down, but instead of a hand, a metal prosthetic appliance protruded from the shirtsleeve, a pincerlike, two-"fingered" device that could be activated by straps and springs built into a plastic sheath that encased the stump of the arm from just below the elbow. Because of his mutilation, the man carried his rifle on the left, its scabbard fixed to the saddle.

The second man was lean and dark haired; he appeared to be in his middle thirties. He slouched over the pommel of his saddle, left hand resting lightly on a thigh, the reins held in his right hand. A homemade cigarette rolled in brown rice paper dangled from a corner of his mouth, its smoke drifting backward.

When the trail led the riders to the stream bank, the big man called to the dogs, yelling "Back!" and then blowing two shrill blasts on a whistle suspended from a thin, silver chain that encircled his neck. The hounds responded immediately and were soon back and pacing around the horses. The man dismounted, speaking to his companion as he prepared to lead his mount to the water. "I guess the horses can take a drink without foundering, Steve? They ain't hardly lathered."

Steve Cousins frowned. He was a professional wrangler, and his knowledge of horses was far greater than that of his companion. After a long, sunny ride in early June weather, he knew that the mounts were hot and should not be allowed to drink until they had cooled down. "I'd wait a bit if I was you, Walt. Give 'em a breather first."

Walter Taggart nodded agreement as he turned his horse away from the stream. Clamping his metal pincers on the reins, he reached into a shirt pocket with his left hand, fished out a cigarette, and put it in his mouth; then he thrust his hand into his pants pocket to withdraw a wooden match. Igniting the flame with his thumbnail, he lit his smoke and tossed the match into the water. "If we don't pick up the varmint's trail by the time we get to the river, I reckon we might as well quit and head back."

Taggart was scanning the terrain as he spoke. His companion did not immediately answer. He was watching the hounds; they had quenched their thirst at the stream and were now sitting on the bank. "By the look of them dogs, I figure we might as well turn around now. They ain't excited none, that's for sure!"

Cousins sucked at his cigarette, drew smoke into his lungs, exhaled. "I reckon the cat's headed right out of this part of the country. We've done a good forty miles since we left the lodge, and we haven't hit even one patch of fresh scent since we left the cave . . . even the whiz spray we found there may not've been left by the white cat." As he spoke, Cousins lifted his field glasses and began to scan the surrounding mountains, moving the binoculars slowly from left to right.

"Hell, Steve, you *know* how much that cat's hide is worth! I ain't quitting just yet! If we don't get a crack at the varmint before sundown, we can camp out tonight and go back in the morning. Maybe then we should try south. Where it killed the pony."

The white puma kept his eyes fixed on the men and their animals. He knew them well. His sensitive ears recorded the sound of the human voices and the snorting and hoof stamping of the horses. When Taggart had blown the whistle to call back the dogs, the cat had flinched, the shrill blast assaulting his eardrums. He could also scent the group; in fact, his keen sense of smell even allowed him to recognize the individual odors of each of its participants. As he watched, listened, and sniffed, his emotions fired heavy charges of endocrine hormones into his bloodstream, especially adrenaline, the chemical that prepared his body for immediate and strenuous action.

The puma had good reason to remember Taggart and Cousins, their dogs, and their two horses. All were his enemies. They had collectively taught him to hate.

It was not in the nature of the puma to feel hatred, an emotion rarely experienced by any animal. The cat was inherently aware of this, although he was not given to conscious rationalization; nevertheless, he sensed that unbridled, single-minded odium was inhibiting and only rarely produced positive results. For the most part, and like all of the other mammals with whom he shared his range, the white puma responded most readily to a limited number of natural stimuli: the need for caution; fear; aggression when he had to hunt, or when he was given cause to defend himself; and courtship, and, of course, procreation when opportunity came his way.

Had he lived in a region undisturbed by human activity, the puma would never have been given cause to experience hatred. In his world, he became aggressively aroused only when it was necessary to kill in order to eat, but he hunted dispassionately. Similarly, if challenged by a male of his own species, he fought; afterward he did not hold a grudge. But he now hated, because he had been deprived of his family by the humans he was watching. He had been goaded by those men and their dogs. As a result, like other powerful predators before him, he had become a man-hater; and because he was strong and lithe and superbly equipped for killing, he was dangerous.

The puma continued to watch the hunters and their animals. He remained immobile, a statuesque being that might have been sculpted out of the compacted snow covering the higher slopes. He lay with ears pricked up, the silvery, tapering whiskers that adorned his muzzle curving forward, chin resting on one huge, outstretched paw. The only continuous movements of his body that might have been noticed—and then only by a near observer—were those made by his breathing: a slight twitching of his nostrils and the slow, rhythmic heaving of his sides. Occasionally, the tip of his outstretched, thirty-inch tail jerked from side to side for some moments, then became still.

The big cat's body suggested that he was totally relaxed, but his eyes signaled emotion. The vertical irises were mere dark slits, and the eyes, fully exposed by wide-open lids, had become sulfur yellow. The gaze that the cougar directed at the hunters telegraphed the hatred he felt for humans and for their dogs and horses.

The puma had started to trail his enemies not long after they had entered the pass early that afternoon. An hour before first light that morning, he had been asleep, curled up in a roomy cave located three-quarters of the way up Eagle Mountain and some fifteen miles southeast of his present location. But as dawn came, he had awakened and gone outside, soon to find a gratuitous meal when his nose led him to a mountain goat that had evidently fallen and killed itself. The goat was thin and aswarm with feeding flies, but there was more than enough meat on the carcass to satisfy the cat. He left the remains, which would soon be entirely consumed by a variety of other carnivores. Like all wild felines, the cat preferred fresh meat, and, knowing that prey was abundant in the region and he could easily make another kill when hunger drove him to hunt, he was willing to abandon the partly eaten carcass. So he had returned to his cave. Some time later, during full daylight, he was awakened by the distant baying of hounds.

Taggart's dogs had found the puma's old tracks. At first they bugled halfheartedly, but when they encountered fresh spoor they raised their voices, calling more rapidly as they forged ahead of the horses, pulling hard against their long rope leads. The two dogs were as worked up by the prospects of a hunt as were Taggart and Cousins, but whereas the hounds were motivated by inherent predatory urges and centuries of selective breeding, the excitement evident in the men was generated by the fact that they stood to earn a great deal of money if they could kill the white puma.

By now, however, the cat was wise to the ways of men and their dogs, and, unlike the majority of his kind, he refused to be brought to bay. In past encounters, he invariably sought alpine height whenever he was pursued, bounding up-mountain swiftly and agilely and always staying within the shelter of trees, underbrush, or boulders. Once out of reach and out of sight, he would circle and station himself on a point of vantage. From there he would watch the fruitless chase, his hatred of the hunters increasing with every new invasion of his territory. Of late, however, the cat had begun to hunt the hunters.

When he had first been alerted by the baying hounds, he had left his cave and started to climb, traveling in a northwesterly direction up the flank of Eagle Mountain until he was at five thousand feet. Then he began to descend, crossing a barren, scree-littered col in order to follow a narrow, barely discernible track that would eventually lead him to the tree line and to a well-used trail that, in its turn, would guide him to the Telkwa Pass.

Because of his detour, the puma had outdistanced his pursuers and could no longer hear the voices of the hounds, but he continued to travel, descending another barren slope, until he was just below the snow line and some three thousand feet above the west side of the pass entrance. Here, in an area dominated by tall, arrow-straight lodgepole pines, he concealed himself among the trees and shrubs in such a way that he was able to watch unnoticed the east entrance to the pass. Now he waited.

Several hours passed before he heard the sounds made when the horses' shod hooves struck echoes from the rocks. But he could not hear the hounds. Soft footed and silent since they had lost the cougar's scent, the two dogs loped along beside Taggart's black gelding.

Fifteen minutes later, the puma sighted the hunters. When they crossed over the divide and began to descend, the cat followed, maintaining height but keeping behind his quarry and always remaining concealed. Later, when Taggart and Cousins neared the Zymoetz River, the cat moved faster, shortcutting over rocks and through ravines in order to get ahead of the trackers. The river flows south there, running through a sloping valley that lies along the western flanks of the Hazelton Mountains.

At a point ten miles due west from the entrance to the Telkwa Pass, two creeks create a liquid crossroads; Nogold Creek flows in from the western slopes; Many Bear Creek trundles downward out of the eastern mountains. The two waterways meet almost head-on as they empty into the winding river. Here, flanked by Many Bear Creek to the north and the river to the west, Taggart and Cousins decided to spend the night. As the sun concealed itself behind the western peaks, they made camp.

While Cousins erected a small, two-man tent, Taggart led the horses to an area of open pastureland and hobbled them; on his return to the campsite, he fastened the dogs to short, individual chains, staking each in a different location to prevent them from becoming entangled. Afterward, Taggart took a canvas water bag and went to fill it with creek water, while Cousins gathered wood for the cooking fire.

Soon after full dark, the mosquitoes attacked in force. Even the smoky fire created by the rotting pieces of wood that the men fed into it couldn't discourage them. The partners realized there was nothing for it but to call it a day and turn in. They crawled into the tent. After a hard day in the wilderness, they soon fell asleep. Outside, the darkness was relieved marginally by countless stars that sequined the blue-black skies and, near the tent, by the glowing coals of the dying campfire. The hounds slept, each curled up nose to tail. The horses rested, snorting now and then, or pawing at the ground to dislodge pestering mosquitoes.

The white puma traveled down-slope, moving against the wind as silently as drifting thistledown, sliding from cover to cover as he approached the camp of his enemies. He was not hungry. He hated. He meant to kill.

1

Bleeding from her wound, the tawny puma limped into the cave, crossed a dimly lit, open area, and squeezed herself into a fissure that began several feet above the level of the rocky floor. Blood spots marked her trail, giving away her hiding place, but once inside the crevice she knew that she was safe.

Flattening her body, she began to crawl, following a rapidly darkening, upward course that after some forty yards ended at a right-angle bend. Making the turn with some difficulty, the lion entered a short, roomy tunnel that continued to rise steeply. Here she stopped to lick at her left thigh, where the 30.06 rifle bullet had creased her flesh, ripping a rough furrow that bled profusely, but missing bone and tendons. For some moments the mountain lion licked her wound; her saliva, with its natural healing agents, somewhat stanched the flow of blood. Finished, she followed the tunnel to where it ended at a sheer face of rock in which a second crevice led her into a natural nesting chamber that was about six feet in diameter and perhaps four feet in height at its central point. The lion lay down, grunting from the pain while keeping uppermost her wounded thigh. Once more she began to lick her injury.

Outside, down-slope from the lion's cave, five hounds ran

in single file, each sliding occasionally on patches of scree that littered the flanks of The Eagle, a seven-thousand-foot, snow-capped peak that forms part of the Hazelton Mountains. Following the excitedly baying hounds, two horsemen pushed their mounts up the grade. The lead rider, a burly man, tried to force the pace by quirting his gelding.

Stumbling on the treacherous surface, the horses snorted as they did their best, the black shaking his head each time the leather quirt connected with his rump; but, despite the whip, he was unable to move faster than the same shambling walk attained by the trailing palomino. The hounds, more surefooted on such terrain, outdistanced the hunters, soon disappearing among the evergreens that grew in profusion in the area surrounding the entrance to the cougar's refuge.

Only the clear, bell-like sounds of the dogs guided the riders, the leader of whom, a man in his early forties, now red faced from exertion, reined his panting mount and turned to his companion. "The horses aren't going catch up with the dogs any better than we can on foot, Steve. Guess we oughta tie 'em up here and walk. I *know* I winged that cat. It can't go far with a thirty-ought-six in it."

His partner seemed glad to get off his palomino. As he set foot on the ground, the only answer he gave his companion was a nod, delivered briefly as he tied the split reins to a sapling birch. The big man, dismounting heavily, slapped his horse in the face with a huge hand, a hard blow that made the black rear backward and snort loudly. As he was about to hit the horse again, controlling its lunge with his left hand, his partner intervened. "Cut it out, Walt! Beating your horse isn't going to get us up there no quicker. Let's go, or that cat may get clear away. Listen . . . the hounds are still running."

Taggart grunted an unintelligible answer and tied his horse to a young poplar. Each man slid his rifle out of its saddle scabbard and began toiling up the grade, but they had taken only a few steps when the baying of the hounds changed, becoming noticeably more excited. It was now obvious that the dogs were barking from a stationary location.

"We got it! Bet the lion's treed. Or maybe it's climbed up on a rock someplace." Taggart almost shouted, his face alight with pleasure. "That's soon going to be one very dead cat, and you and me, Steve, we're going be two, maybe three hundred bucks better off when we sell the hide to that pilgrim at the lodge."

Steve Cousins, a man of few words, merely nodded again. The two moved faster, scrambling over areas of scree, grabbing at saplings and bushes. The higher they climbed, the louder were the voices of their dogs. Soon, because the baying continued from the same place, the hunters slowed down, confident that the wounded cat would remain at bay in its place of refuge, kept there by the noisy hounds.

After the men had climbed about one hundred yards, Cousins, who was now in the lead because his companion was winded, was the first to see the blood; it had stained carmine a large area of rock and grass, telling the hunters that this was where the bullet from Taggart's rifle had found its mark. The big man preened himself visibly. "That was some shot, hey? From two hundred yards . . . and uphill, at that. I tell you, that cat's hurt bad. We're going to get it for sure, and *that's* a fact!"

"Not if we stand here jawing, we won't," Cousins replied.

Without another word, Taggart shouldered his companion aside, taking the lead, his adrenaline flowing, fanned by the nearness of the quarry.

Twenty minutes later, the men reached the cave. Both were sweating copiously after their long, steep climb under the June sun. Only their eagerness to make the kill had carried them this far. Inside, the hounds were milling around the crevice through which the lion had disappeared, pawing at the rock, alternately baying and whining, their breeding urging them on and making them as anxious to be in on the kill as the men were to execute it, a right that the hunters considered theirs by holy ordinance.

When the hunters saw the crevice into which the puma had squeezed herself and realized that even if the dogs managed to enter the confined space, the wounded cat would tear them to pieces one at a time, their disappointment turned into rage. Taggart, swearing loudly and calling down imprecations on the puma, kicked at one of the hounds, sending it rolling over and over. Seeing the fate of their companion, the other dogs scuttled away, whining, tails between their legs. They had all experienced the edge of Taggart's temper on many an occasion.

Cousins was more controlled but equally angry at the lion. He thumbed back the safety catch of his rifle and walked to the crevice. Thrusting the barrel into the dark interior, he fired two shots in quick succession. The reports were muffled within the roomy cavern, but, in the confines of the crevice and in the lion's den, the concussion was a physical thing. The cat bunched her muscles and sprang to her feet; her wound, which had stopped bleeding, opened anew and gushed blood.

Taggart and Cousins worked as hunting guides for a British Columbia big-game outfitter with headquarters in a valley within the Telkwa Range. The hunting lodge and its attendant cluster of log buildings had been erected on the southeastern shore of Moose-skin Johnny Lake and so were located about ten miles, straight-line distance, from the puma's impregnable refuge. Catering to rich men and women from a number of countries, who paid high prices for the privilege of killing animals, the business was prosperous despite its short season—just a few weeks in autumn. In fact, Andrew Bell, the owner, now had bookings, including substantial down payments, that guaranteed his continued prosperity for the next three years at least. During the long off-season, Bell's camp operated as a fishing resort, the patrons at these times being mostly Canadian and American businessmen, the majority of whom were picked up by Bell's wheel-and-float-equipped aircraft at the Smithers Airport, located twenty-five miles to the northeast of Moose-skin Johnny Lake, and flown to High Country Safaris, as Bell had named his operation.

When Taggart and Cousins were not guiding, they did odd jobs around the resort, keeping the outboard motors and boats in running order, caring for a stable of fifteen horses, and drinking the free whiskey provided by "the pilgrims," as they thought of Bell's patrons, entertaining them with tall tales of their hunting abilities. Sometimes they dangled a bait in front of a patron whom they thought would not object to some poaching. For a fee, they engaged to go into the mountains and return with the skin and head of a trophy animal that the guest could ship home. Later, each of these illegal spoils would be preserved and taxidermied, the skin turned into a rug to go in front of a fireplace and the head, properly mounted on a polished wooden plaque, fashioned into a nice trophy to hang on a wall or over the hearth, becoming conversation pieces that testified to their owners' hunting prowess.

Smuggling such trophies out of Canada was not difficult. Taggart or Cousins would take them to a taxidermist in a regional community, there to be preserved for shipment. Afterward, wrapped in polyethylene and crated, trophies would be shipped to a Canadian airport, usually Vancouver or Toronto. Trophies for American clients could then be flown or driven across the border and declared to U.S. Customs officials. European clients had no difficulty shipping theirs, for, apart from security checks, which look only for weapons or explosives, outward-bound luggage is rarely searched.

Because none of the illegally killed animals were listed as endangered or threatened, their importation into the United States and Europe was not restricted.

During the second week of June 1984, while boasting to an obviously rich New York City stockbroker, Taggart had talked about the lion he had seen briefly the week before in the vicinity of The Eagle. The cat, he explained, was not actually protected by law in that region, although it was not legal to hunt at this season. "But they're pests, those cats. They take sheep and calves and even our own horses. And they kill a whole lot of game. So nobody really gives a darn if one of them gets to eat a nice lead pill, you know?"

The bait was taken. It was agreed that if the lion was a particularly large one, Taggart and Cousins would receive three hundred dollars for its head and hide, provided the skin was not badly mutilated by bullets. If it was a small cat, the fee would be two hundred dollars. The bargain was struck and toasted with Glenfiddich, a supply of which the stockbroker had brought in his private aircraft, a float-equipped four-passenger Cessna flown by a pilot who was employed full-time by the New Yorker.

The next day, while the stockbroker was catching rainbow trout from the well-stocked comfort of a small but roomy cruiser, and thus free of any legal responsibilities that the poachers might incur, Taggart and Cousins set out at first light, accompanied by the eager hounds.

By dusk they had failed to sight the lion, although the dogs had found several old scent trails. One of these led them to the remnants of one of the lion's kills, the stripped carcass of a deer that was already decomposing. Examining the terrain, the hunters noted a number of coyote and bobcat tracks converging on the leftovers—evidence that when a predator kills large prey, many other animals eat of it also. Searching carefully, Cousins found lion tracks. They were medium-sized impressions, which suggested that the cat was not very large. But Taggart refused to believe the evidence of his eyes. "Those tracks were probably left by another cat. The lion *I* saw was big—a two hundred pounder and more than eight feet long. And *that's* the truth!"

"Maybe," Cousins said as he straightened himself, distastefully wrinkling his nose at the carrion odor.

The next day was almost a repeat of the first. The poachers did not find another kill, but they were led to a relatively fresh set of lion tracks along the sandy bank of a creek. According to their estimate of the spoor, the cat had made the tracks the previous night and was working its way up-mountain. But it was too late in the day to continue the search.

That evening, drinking with the stockbroker on the screened porch of his chalet-style cabin, Taggart explained the difficulties of finding a mountain lion in that kind of habitat, at the same time making his pitch for a higher payment if they did manage to kill the animal. In this he was unsuccessful, but since he was treated to a number of large malt whiskeys, the big man left the cabin well satisfied with his evening.

The next morning, riding up-mountain, the hounds questing excitedly ahead, the poachers at last spotted the lion. All they saw was a flash of tawny body and a long tail as the animal darted into the concealment of the evergreens. But that one glimpse of the quarry galvanized them into action. Quirting their mounts and yelling encouragement to the hounds, Taggart and Cousins dashed up-slope in pursuit. The rise was gentle, but the furious pace soon had its effect on the horses. Both mounts began to slow almost in unison, despite the repeated quirting and the maledictions the men yelled in their ears. In the end, realizing that if they continued to force the pace the horses would flounder, Taggart pulled up his black gelding. Cousins did the same. The men dismounted.

Scanning the mountainside, Taggart thought he saw movement at a place where the evergreens had been thinned by logging. He grabbed for his rifle and had just worked the breech mechanism to place a shell in the chamber when the puma stepped into full view. The cat's attention was riveted on the charging hounds, which were only about one hundred yards away from her, but running slowly because of the climb. Momentarily disoriented by the baying dogs, the quarry paused, one big front paw held off the ground, in the act of taking a step. She was facing down-slope, her golden body at a three-quarter angle to Taggart, who was even then taking aim. Had she moved a split second earlier, she would have got away unscathed. But she stayed still, a tawny statue framed by the evergreens and the gray rocks of the mountain's flank.

The 180-grain soft-nosed bullet hit the puma's thigh at a velocity of 2,250 feet per second, packing an energy punch of more than one ton. Although the bullet delivered only a glancing wound, the force of its impact knocked the lion off her feet, actually causing her to spin in a complete circle. Bleeding profusely, shocked by the impact, the *spanging* echo of the shot, and the fast-approaching, barking dogs, the puma was yet quick to recover.

As Taggart ejected the spent cartridge, the cat sprang upright and streaked into the shelter of the trees; despite her handicap, her rate of travel was at least twice that of the dogs. The hounds disappeared from view as the guides remounted and clattered upward in pursuit, but even before the men were forced to tether their horses and continue the chase on foot, the lion had entered the cave and found sanctuary in her impregnable den.

Leashing the hounds and leaving the cave, Taggart and Cousins stood outside and did some planning. Then Cousins mounted his palomino and rode to High Country Safaris, where he picked up a large-size leg-hold trap, a twenty-five-foot length of three-quarter-inch chain, a handful of heavy fence staples, and an ax with a three-pound head. Tying these items to his saddle thongs, he remounted and returned to the cave, arriving in late afternoon. The poachers now set to work. Taking turns with the ax, they chopped down a spruce tree that had a twelve-inch diameter where the trunk emerged from the soil. This was limbed; then, twenty feet from the butt, it was chopped again. The result was a twenty-foot length of green spruce that was too heavy for one man to carry.

Grunting with the effort, Taggart picked up the butt while Cousins lifted the other end. They carried the timber into the cave, set it down about ten feet from the crevice into which the cat had gone, and wrapped one end of the chain several times around the center of the log, fastening the last four links to the wood with half a dozen staples. Next they securely wired the other end of the chain to the trap before forcing the ax handle between the tooth-studded jaws, using the oak haft as a lever that counteracted the pressure of two heavy leaf springs. In this way they opened the trap's semicircular jaws, afterward holding them down against the pressure of the springs while they set the pan trigger. The trap was now armed. If the lion stepped on the round central pan, the trigger would be sprung and the jaws would snap shut on its leg or foot.

Taggart lifted the trap carefully and placed it about five feet in front of the crevice, judging this to be the correct distance to catch one of the cat's front paws when it jumped down on leaving its hiding place. Cousins collected some of the spruce boughs and lightly covered the trap with them.

The poachers had used the standard techniques for catching and holding a large animal. The toothed jaws of the trap made it impossible for the captive to pull itself free, while the chained log acted as a drag, moving each time the frantic prisoner lunged against the biting steel. Heavy as the timber was, it would give sufficiently to prevent the chain from being broken. Employing this method, Taggart and Cousins had trapped black and grizzly bears. They were confident that if the lion stepped on the pan, it would get caught.

Although she had been badly shaken by the concussive effects of the rifle shots echoing within the cavern, the puma took only moments to settle down again. She knew from past experience that she was safe within her deep shelter, just as she understood the relationship between the sounds of exploding shells and her injury. She was three years old, and had once before been wounded by man. The injury, a minor nick on the lower portion of her left ear, was received when she was a yearling, when she and her sister accompanied their mother on a hunt in a region some miles away from her present territory. The wound had been more startling than painful, for the ears of mammals are largely composed of cartilage. She had bled a little, but the injury had soon healed. The memory of it, and the events that had accompanied it, however, would never be forgotten.

During an early evening in autumn, the pumas were stalking an aging woodland caribou that was browsing in a small mountain valley. Because the cats had not eaten for three days, the predominantly nocturnal hunters had abandoned normal caution when they scented the quarry from their place of concealment in a shallow cave.

Following the odor trail, the mother had led her daughters down-slope and into the valley, soon afterward sighting the prey. But as the adult cat began the stalk, she collapsed suddenly. Split seconds later her daughters heard the report of the rifle shot. Even as they did so, the smaller of the two young pumas collapsed, and the survivor felt the sting of the bullet that nicked her ear. The sharp reports of the shots came almost instantly after her sister's death and her own injury. The puma was quick to connect the explosions with these events. But by then she was already traveling downhill at full speed, her body alternately bunching and stretching as she bounded into concealment, each prodigious leap covering between twenty and thirty feet. There were two more shots, but both missed.

Panicked and confused, the cat ran at full speed until she reached an area where a landslide had occurred many years earlier. Here, well concealed by tightly packed evergreens, she found shelter between two enormous slabs of rock that had come to rest leaning against each other, forming a narrow, A-shaped cave. During the next two days she lay inside the den, fearful and unable to understand the absence of her mother and sister. By evening of the second day, ravenously hungry after five days of fasting, she left the shelter.

For the first time in her life, the cat was going to have to depend on her own skills in order to eat, for, until she had been shot, the mother had found the prey and killed it while her daughters watched and learned from her example, not yet being sufficiently experienced or developed physically to bring down anything larger than mice and an occasional marmot.

The cougar had been born in late December of the previous year; now, in early October, she was nine months old. From the tip of her nose to the end of her tail, she measured just slightly more than five feet, the tail itself being eighteen inches long. She weighed sixty-five pounds, about half the weight she would attain when she became fully adult.

As she traveled whisper-footed through the rapidly darkening wilderness, the cat did not know that now, being alone, her chances of survival were small. Apart from her limited hunting skills, she was herself potential prey. Wolves, working in a pack, would not have much trouble killing her, and, should she encounter a grizzly bear—a very real possibility in her territory—she would be killed if she was unable to escape quickly. Additionally, neighboring adult mountain lions might well invade her territory, terminating her occupancy of a range with which she was familiar and forcing her to wander through unknown country until she found a region that was not occupied by a resident cat but contained sufficient prey animals for her needs. Meanwhile, she somehow had to keep herself fed.

Not being human, and thus not having a brain that preoccupies itself excessively with the future, the lion was not intimidated by the dangers and trials that lay ahead. The immediate present was all that mattered to her as she padded along a well-used game trail. Like all of her kind—indeed, like all wild animals—she lived in the *now* and was entirely free from the negative effects of fear of or worry about the future. Instead, she fully committed herself to her quest for food, remaining in constant touch with all the other influences of her environment as a matter of course. She had been inherently equipped with acute senses of hearing, sight, and scent, and she relied on them to guide her to possible prey and to warn her of the presence of enemies.

In the absence of humans, whose scent she had now cataloged with all those others that had special meaning for her, the lion was confident that she could elude natural enemies, just as she was inherently aware that her mother and sibling were no more. She did not think of them as being dead, however. Death held no meaning for her. An animal, or a tree or rock, was either present or absent. If present, an object held tangible meaning, either negative or positive; if absent, it was no cause for concern. Nevertheless, the abrupt separation from her mother and sibling had upset the lion's emotional stability. She missed them, and she realized that she needed them, especially her mother. But apart from uttering an occasional low and husky call, she concentrated fully on her quest for food.

After traveling for more than an hour, during which night

had set in, she at last managed to catch several white-footed mice, mere tidbits that made her even more conscious of her hunger pangs. But soon afterward luck came her way. She detected the odor of coyote. The scent was faint, yet easily noticed by her keen nose, despite the fact that the quarry was still too far away for her to hear its movements.

The puma positioned herself in the deep shadow of a downed tree. She crouched, her hindquarters bunched, ready for a spring, her front legs stretched forward, the big paws pressing against the mat of leaf litter that covered the soil to a depth of several inches. In that position she remained statue-still, her breathing shallow and silent, but her nose and ears fully alert.

Minutes passed before she heard the first faint sounds of one or more animals that appeared to be traveling in her direction. The odor became stronger. She was familiar with the scent of coyote, for she had eaten the meat of several of the small wild dogs her mother had killed.

Salivating and hardly able to control her impatience, the cat tensed, the muscles on her haunches rippling smoothly as she put pressure against the ground. With ears pricked forward, her amber eyes fixed on the dark trail ahead and her front claws already extruding, she forced herself to wait. Presently, from the slight difference in the odors, she was able to establish that two coyotes were approaching.

Traveling at an easy lope along the well-trodden trail, the coyotes remained unaware of the lion's presence because the slight breeze was at their backs. They were returning to their home base after an evening's hunt, during which they had killed and eaten three snowshoe hares and a number of voles.

The dog, slightly ahead of his mate, stopped suddenly when the pair were about forty feet from the mountain lion's hiding place. His keen nose had alerted him to the presence of the enemy, but, before he could turn to escape, the puma charged. From the crouch, she leaped into space, traveled fifteen feet, touched down with her large front paws, and launched again, all in a matter of seconds. The coyotes panicked. The female darted behind a tree and sped away, but, as the male moved to follow, the cat leaped again, and her outstretched front paws hit the coyote on the shoulder. The sudden jolt, backed by sixty-five pounds and a speed close to thirty miles an hour, flung the coyote against the trunk of a large spruce. But the wild dog died before his body struck the tree, his neck broken as it was whiplashed when the puma's paws struck his shoulder.

Turning around after she landed, the cat padded to the carcass and picked it up in her mouth. The coyote weighed thirty-five pounds, but she carried it away easily, taking it to the deadfall tree in the shelter of which she had waited for the quarry. There she began to eat. After she had ingested six or seven pounds of food, she cleaned herself meticulously, licking a front paw and reaching up with the dampened pad to scrub her ears and the side of her head before doing the same to her muzzle, wiping away the blood that had stained her fur. Last, she licked her paws, spreading the toes in order to get her tongue down into the creases. Finished, she stood and began covering the remains of the carcass with leaves, twigs, and duff from the forest floor. This done, she walked away, searching for a nearby place in which to lie up until she became hungry again. From such a location, she could also guard the remains from scavengers.

Ambushing and killing the coyote on her own gave the cat confidence in her hunting abilities. She had learned from her mother's behavior but had not until that night put her skills to the test. Apart from the fact that her inexperience made her timid, the discipline exerted by their mother had been such that the young lions had not dared take the lead when the trio was hunting. But that night hunger and loneliness had forced the young lion to attack an animal that a few days earlier she would have avoided had she met it in the absence of her mother. Now she knew that she was ready to take her place in the mountain wilderness, to pursue the solitary life that was her destiny.

Two and a half years later, when she was fully adult and had become an efficient huntress, the mountain lion entered her first breeding cycle. Made restless as her sex hormones increased, she strayed out of her territory, searching for a male. As she prowled, hunting less and not finishing the kills that she made, she wailed a great deal, her high-pitched screams echoing through the wilderness and putting to flight the deer, caribou, and other prey animals that were within sound of her voice. The time was late April.

Five days after the cat had started to wander, she entered the range of a large male lion, knowing of his presence by the debris-covered scent mounds that pumas and other members of the cat family construct over their wastes in order to mark their territories. The cougar sniffed at one of the mounds and at a grassy area that had been sprayed with urine. Her body tense, tail lashing spasmodically, she lifted her head and uttered one of her bansheelike screams.

The tomcat became immediately interested. From half a mile away, within the shelter of a tight-packed clump of evergreens where he had been dozing, he leaped to his feet and bounded forward, slowing down when he was within two hundred yards of the female, but striding purposefully toward her. Now he began to whistle, a sound not unlike the call of a red-tailed hawk, but softer. Responding in this somewhat odd way to the female's strident call, he advanced, lashing his three-foot-long tail and causing his facial whiskers to bristle forward.

The female heard the tom's whistle as she was emerging from the shelter of a jumble of moss-covered rocks. Her ears had been erect before the male replied to her courting screams, but she now laid them backward, almost as though pasting them to her broad head. Bounding down from the rocks, she broke out of the forested land and entered an alpine meadow in the center of which was a small, irregularly shaped lake six or seven acres in extent and rimmed by sedges, cattails, and ferns. The male's scent was strong in this area, which marked the westernmost boundary of the territory that the big cat claimed for himself. Somewhat like the spokes of a cartwheel, well-defined trails had been beaten into the grasses and sedges that grew in the valley, the tracks starting at the edges of the surrounding forests and converging at the shores of the lake, here and there intersecting one another between forest and water's edge. A number of fecal mounds were readily discernible at the junctions of intersecting pathways, the oldest almost flat, the newest standing out like molehills.

As the female entered the valley, she detected a number of other scents. Grizzly bears had recently traveled the male puma's trails; so had wolves, and wolverines. All had left their identifiable odors as they had quenched their thirst with the crystal waters of the spring-fed tarn.

At any other time the female cat would have avoided a locality so redolent of danger, but the allure of the tom's odor aroused her to such an extent that she ignored the alien scents. Walking sinuously over the grasses, she stopped at the lake's edge and drank deeply; afterward, water dripping from her muzzle, she opened her mouth wide, revealing her formidable fangs as she launched one of her bloodcurdling screams.

Utter silence followed the primeval call. The cat stood by the water's edge, head held high and nostrils flaring as she siphoned the male's scent, oblivious of the fear that her wail had instilled in the smaller animals that lived in the area. Birds, many of which had been singing in the meadow and surrounding forests, were no longer heard. Even the bullfrogs stifled their bass voices. But a small, maverick wind could not be stilled. It continued to ruffle the treetops while the irrepressible biting flies droned and whined without pause.

The cat was still holding her stance when the tom's soft whistle was repeated. Much closer now. When the sound ended, the lioness moved forward, crossing the meadow in five fluid bounds and entering the forest. Within the trees, she stopped to listen. The sounds made by the velvet pads of the advancing tom were faint, but they were clearly audible to the waiting cat. She moved toward the male. As she did so, her throat worked, rippling the fur and skin along her lower jaw as she began to purr. Then she too whistled, the birdlike call similar to but softer than the male's.

The pumas met in a relatively open area a quarter of a mile west of the alpine meadow. The male, a magnificent animal more than eight feet long and weighing two hundred pounds, was standing on a bare, granite kopje when the female came into view. Brashly eager, the big puma leaped down from his perch and bounded toward her, but, despite the cat's own desires, she faced the male with gaping, spitting jaws, her tail lashing spasmodically and her right paw, toes spread wide and dagger-claws fully extruded, raised threateningly. The tom was not intimidated by the cat's hostile display. He came close to her, his lips pursed, a low whistle emerging from their rounded center. The cat screamed and struck at him with her paw, but the male leaped aside with quicksilver agility. He now began to purr, his tail held upright, its tip wagging jerkily. He approached again and met with the same behavior. Avoiding the cat's slashing paw for the second time, he backed off and sprayed urine against the hillock upon which he had been standing moments earlier.

Afterward, he moved away, standing clear of the female and purring loudly. The cat now approached the kopje and sniffed at the urine intently, then she turned, sat on her haunches, and began to wash her face and neck. Presently she lay down, her golden eyes following the restless pacings of her would-be mate, a pose that she held during the remaining hours of daylight and that was altered only when the tom approached her too closely and she felt impelled to threaten him.

By nightfall, under a full moon and amid much screaming and hoarse snarling, the lions mated. They were destined to remain together for the next ten days, until a hunter's bullet found its mark in the tom's brain. Otherwise, they might have continued courting for five or six weeks before going their separate ways to resume the solitary life of adult pumas.

Because the pregnant cat was some distance from her mate when he was killed, she escaped unseen. The shot, and the hated scent of man and of his gunpowder, drove her away from the area and kept her traveling until she found a new home range in the Hazelton Mountains, on the east flank of The Eagle, and located the cave.

2

The puma remained in her den for the next forty-six hours, alternately sleeping and licking the injury inflicted by Taggart's bullet. At the end of that time, although her wound had stopped bleeding and was starting to scab, she was tormented by a raging thirst. She was also hungry, of course, but, like all carnivores, she was inured to periods of famine. Water, on the other hand, she *had* to have—and soon—if she hoped to survive.

During the morning of her second day in the den, as she tried to lick her wound, she found she did not have enough saliva to do so. Now she knew that she must leave her shelter. Yet she hesitated, made fearful because the men had returned the previous afternoon. She had smelled and heard them, their horses, and the one hound that had accompanied them. And she knew the men and the dog had entered the cave. These memories made her indecisive.

Half a dozen times in as many hours the cat got up, left her den, and walked along the tunnel to the crevice, only to stop and return to the shelter. By four o'clock that afternoon, however, she could endure no longer. Limping at first, but limbering up with each stride, she crossed the tunnel and entered the narrow shaft. Rain was falling outside, and a brisk wind was keening through the trees and echoing inside her shelter.

The din of the storm masked the sounds made by Taggart and Cousins when they arrived. As on the previous day, they had brought Taggart's best tracking hound with them, a large male who would immediately detect the cat if she was caught in the trap, or who, by his disinterest in the weak scent of the old tracks, would tell the men that the quarry had not yet emerged.

Riding to within thirty yards of the puma's sanctuary, the poachers dismounted and secured their horses to nearby trees. Then, with Cousins holding the eager hound's lead, they walked toward the cave, entering it when the cat was within twenty feet of the opening.

"If that varmint ain't come out by now, I reckon it's dead. No way can it hold out this long without food or water," Taggart said.

"Maybe there's water inside," Cousins offered, allowing the hound to be the first to enter the gloomy cavern.

"Hey! Don't let the dog off his lead. He could stick his paw in the trap," Taggart ordered.

The cougar, her emotions oscillating between fear and hatred, crouched inside the fissure, invisible from the outside and herself unable to see what was going on in the cavern. Like a furred sculpture, she remained totally still, only her nose and ears working as she tuned in on the sounds and scent-tasted the various odors.

When the men and the dog walked up to the trap and paused beside it, the cat knew exactly where they were, despite the fact that she could not see them. Her tail began to lash, making short swishes in the confinement of the crevice. Like her ears, which were laid back against her head, the spasmodically lashing tail advertised her aggressive mood. As though she were stalking prey, she began to move slowly toward the cave.

When she had almost reached the entrance to the crevice, she stopped, her head and shoulders less than three feet from the opening.

Bunching her hindquarters, she launched herself suddenly, a deep, throaty snarl issuing from her open mouth as she moved. Dropping toward the cavern's floor, her front legs outstretched so she could break with her spread paws the shock of landing, she hit a yielding object. Its movement caused her to stumble slightly as she landed on the rocky floor. Recovering agilely without losing any of her forward momentum, she dashed to the cave mouth followed by Taggart's agonized scream and by the excited baying of the hound, which pulled its leash out of Cousins's hand the instant that the lion's blurred shape appeared outside the crevice. Closely pursued by the courageous but foolish dog, the puma jumped through the cavern's entrance, veered to the left at speed, and was about to bound toward a jumble of rocks and deadfall trees when the hound caught up with her. The cat whipped around in a trice, her enormous right front paw flashing, its talons fully extruded.

Even if the claws had not ripped out the dog's throat the instant that they connected, he would have died split seconds later from a broken neck, his body thrown through the air to land near the cavern's mouth as the cat bounded into shelter and continued running up-mountain, being careful to keep to the cover of the trees. As she ran, Taggart's screams of agony continued to pursue her.

Inside the cave, the big man thrashed and screamed, while Cousins searched frantically for his cigarette lighter, cursing because the flashlight he had brought remained in his saddlebag. The younger man was so badly scared that when he at last found the lighter, it took him several tries to ignite it. The sight that met his gaze was horrifying.

Taggart writhed on the cave floor, his right arm caught in the trap. The jaws had clamped shut several inches above his wrist. Blood spouted in fountains, turning into spray whenever the arm was moved by the big man's contortions. Momentarily immobilized by shock, Cousins was yet able to notice that each time his partner jerked at the trap, that part of his arm that was imprisoned below the jaws remained still, a ghoulish tribute to the efficiency of the device, which had broken both the bones in Taggart's forearm and appeared to have nearly severed the limb's lower portion.

It took a supreme effort of will for Cousins to pull himself together. Yelling at Taggart, ordering him to remain still, the younger man dashed out of the cave to his horse, passing the mangled body of the hound. From his saddlebag he collected the flashlight and the first-aid kit that he always carried; then he ran back to the cave. Taggart was still screaming, but his cries were weaker now. He no longer moved.

Crouched beside his partner, Cousins used the blade of his heavy hunting knife to pry the trap's jaws slightly apart, relieving some of the pressure, but causing the blood to gush out of Taggart's arm in torrents. Realizing his error, he allowed the jaws to close again and hastily broke open the first-aid kit, taking from it a length of surgical tubing that he carried for use as a tourniquet. After wrapping this tightly above the injury and securing it firmly, Cousins again ran outside and looked around until he found a dead branch that appeared to be strong enough to pry the trap's jaws open and free Taggart's mangled arm.

The trap was an old model that required two screw clamps for depressing the springs if one man was to open it safely. In the absence of such a tool, it became necessary to step on the springs, placing one foot on each, or, as the poachers had done earlier, to pry the jaws apart by leverage. Cousins was unable to step on the springs and at the same time free his partner's arm, so he twisted the knife blade with one hand, forcing the jaws to open sufficiently to accept one end of the stick. In this way he was able to free Taggart, but it took several minutes to do so. Meanwhile, the big man had lost consciousness.

Outside again, Cousins collected three short, half-inch-thick branches, then hurried back to the cave and bandaged Taggart's lacerated arm, using the sticks as makeshift splints, which he firmly secured with strips of adhesive tape. By now twenty minutes had elapsed since the tourniquet had been applied, and it had to be loosened to restore circulation. As soon as the tubing became slack, blood soaked the bandage, and Cousins was forced to reapply the ligature. During all this, Taggart remained unconscious.

Cousins was now in a quandary. His partner was in urgent need of medical attention, but they were more than a two-hour ride from the Moose-skin Johnny Lake headquarters. Had it not been for the need to loosen the tourniquet every fifteen minutes, the younger man could have ridden back alone and summoned help. As matters stood, he had no choice but to hoist Taggart's one hundred and ninety pounds onto his mount's saddle and lash the big man in place before leading the horse downslope.

The needs to go slowly and to stop every quarter of an hour to loosen and refasten the tourniquet would at least double the time it would take to reach help. Meanwhile, Taggart might die. The man was in shock and had lost a lot of blood. And he would probably continue to hemorrhage every time the tourniquet was loosened. To make matters worse, rain was coming down hard, and the temperature had fallen noticeably. The cold and the wet would aggravate Taggart's condition, and the muddy, slippery trail would cause further delay. But there was no alternative. The injured man had to be taken to safety.

Cousins left to get the horses. Moments later he led his palomino and his partner's black gelding to the cavern entrance. After unfastening the large water canteen that was lashed to the big man's horse, Cousins entered the cave and doused

Taggart's face with water. Groaning, the injured man opened his eyes.

"You're hurt badly, Walt. Listen, you've got to help me get you to your horse. I can't leave you here and go for help alone, OK?"

"No! You can't leave me, for God's sake!" Taggart's voice was weak, but there was no mistaking the urgency in his tone. Lifting his head off the pillow of boughs that Cousins had fashioned for him, he paused for breath before adding, "If you leave me, that cat will come back and kill me."

In his shocked condition, Taggart had misunderstood his partner's words. Cousins wasted no more time on talk. He positioned himself behind Taggart, stooped, placed both arms under his partner's shoulders, and began to heave upward. At first Taggart's body was a dead weight, but when he understood that Cousins was trying to lift him, he gave some help by pushing with his legs. Moments later he was on his feet, though unable to stand without assistance. Waiting until they had both recovered from their exertions, Cousins led the tottering man toward the cave entrance, their pace agonizingly slow and punctuated by a number of stops when Taggart seemed about to collapse.

Reaching the black horse, Taggart was barely able to hang on to the saddle horn with his left hand while Cousins heaved him upward, a task that required all the younger man's energies. Lashing his partner's swaying body securely to the horse and saddle was no less difficult than hoisting him onto the gelding's back. Taggart slumped over the animal's neck, his left arm hanging limply, his injured right limb fastened to his chest by a sling. Cousins had to hold on to Taggart with one hand while he worked with the other until he had secured enough lashings to make sure the injured man stayed in place. But at last the job was done. Taggart was only semiconscious as Cousins mounted his horse and led the black down-slope.

Because the mounts were experienced, Cousins knew that his palomino could be left to follow the trail home without guidance and at a safe pace. Rising on his stirrups, the younger man swung his right leg over the pommel, twisting his body around so he could watch the injured man. It was only then that he began to reflect on the events that had led to his companion's dreadful injury, trying to piece together what had happened.

He recalled that just before the puma leaped out of the crevice, Taggart squatted in front of the trap and was reaching down with his right hand to remove some of the evergreen boughs with which they had covered the set. Then, without any warming, the puma emerged, her shape a ghostly, terrifying blur. Despite the shock and confusion of the moment, Cousins had seen the cat jump almost clear of Taggart's stooping body. But, at the last instant, as her front paws were about to land on the cave floor, her back feet struck his partner's shoulders, pushing his torso downward. Now, watching his wounded companion as the horses traveled slowly along the winding trail, Cousins concluded that his partner's reaching hand must have been forced into contact with the pan, releasing the trigger and snapping the trap's powerful jaws on Taggart's arm.

The journey back to headquarters lasted almost five hours, a nightmare ride during which Taggart's condition deteriorated steadily. At the lodge, the injured man was loaded onto the company aircraft and flown to the hospital in Smithers. After receiving emergency treatment, he was sent by air ambulance to Vancouver. That same day, his arm was amputated four inches below the elbow.

Late the next morning, a corporal of the Royal Canadian Mounted Police arrived to interview Cousins. The policeman had spent four hours driving a four-wheel-drive station wagon over the bumpy, narrow bush road that led from Smithers to Moose-skin Johnny Lake. This was the only land route to High

Country Safaris, and it meandered for more than forty miles, almost doubling the straight-line distance between the town and the lodge.

Before setting out from the regional RCMP detachment headquarters, the corporal had radioed ahead, notifying Andrew Bell of his visit and asking that Steve Cousins be made available. Nevertheless, Cousins was not at the lodge when the policeman arrived.

Hot, fly-bitten, tired after his rugged drive, and aware that he must face the same route on his return to Smithers, the policeman was considerably put out to learn that the witness had gone fishing with a client and would not be back for another hour or more. He was only slightly mollified when Bell gave him a tall glass of chilled orange juice and followed this with a meal of freshly caught trout.

As he ate, the corporal told Bell that Taggart's condition was no longer considered critical, but that he remained in intensive care and was only semiconscious. "We haven't been able to talk to him yet, and the only information we have comes from the hospital authorities. That's why we're anxious to talk to Mr. Cousins," the Mountie explained.

Cousins arrived in time to hear the report on his partner's condition, but as he was about to ask for more details, the policeman pushed away from the table and spoke first. "Are you Steven Michael Cousins?"

On receiving a nod, the corporal continued, his manner correctly formal, if somewhat abrupt. "Why didn't you report the accident immediately after you obtained medical help for Mr. Taggart?"

Cousins frowned at the question and was silent for a time. "Figured the hospital would've done that. It wasn't none of my business to call you guys. Was it?"

"Yes, Mr. Cousins. It *was* your business. All accidents must be reported to the police. They must be investigated."

Cousins merely nodded.

"Well, now. If we've got that straightened out, I'd like you to tell me in your own words just what happened on that mountain."

As he spoke, the corporal took a notebook and pen out of his tunic pocket, opened the pad, and waited, ballpoint poised.

Cousins scratched his head and looked at Andrew Bell, who had been about to leave the room when his employee arrived but had stayed when asked to do so by the policeman.

"Well . . . it's like this. Walt and me, we have our own mounts, you know. And Walt's got a mare what had a foal. Well, a couple nights before Walt got hurt, that cat came down the mountain and tried to get the foal, but Walt's hounds made such a racket that he came out with his rifle and took a shot at the varmint. It was dark, you know, but there was this bit of moon to see by and Walt figured he'd winged the cat. Next morning he looked around and, sure enough, there was blood near the corral and more of it trailing up mountain. We reckoned we should go and track the varmint and put it out of its misery, you know?"

This lengthy sentence was uncharacteristic of the laconic man. To the policeman, the words and tone sounded rehearsed. He felt there was more to the story. When Cousins fell silent, the policeman looked up, waiting for more. When Cousins did not continue, the corporal's impatience registered in his voice. "And *then* what happened? I need a full statement from you, Mr. Cousins. Please continue."

Rambling, his remarks often interrupted by lengthy silences, Cousins concocted his fiction. He told how the two men had ridden up the flanks of The Eagle, their hounds following the spoor and the bloodstains until they sighted the cougar in the area where Taggart had actually shot her. But now Cousins claimed that Taggart had fired and wounded the cat for a second time. After this, he told how the men had followed the hounds and located the animal's refuge.

Thus far, the account was one that he and Taggart had long ago agreed upon as their excuse should they ever be caught poaching any of the large predatory animals—a series of lies he was sure his partner would back up more or less when he was eventually questioned. Cousins was on less practiced ground when he came to the trap and to the events that had led to his partner's injury, but he was quite sure that Taggart could not unwittingly contradict his spurious account because the big man, his attention fixed on the trap, had not the slightest idea of what had really occurred.

"We couldn't get the varmint out of that crack in the rock, and since it'd been wounded two times, we figured it would probably die in there. But, because we didn't want the animal to suffer any more'n necessary, we figured that just in case it weren't going to die, we'd best set a trap. And if we caught the cat, why . . . we'd shoot it and put it out of its misery. You know? Course, we'd've reported it to the wildlife guys if we'd killed it. You know?

"Well, we were just checking the trap. Walt had bent down. I reckon he was going to give up and take the trap out of there, figuring the cat was done for. I was standing nearby, holding the hound's chain. Then, you know, that cat just came out of nowhere. It charged Walt, and I'm sure it would've killed him if the hound hadn't pulled his chain out of my hand and charged it. Then the cougar killed the hound, and I guess by then it was scared an' ran off. An' that's how it all happened, you know?"

Although far from satisfied by the account, the Mountie had to accept it. Later, the report he wrote would reflect his doubts, but when Taggart was questioned and told a nearly similar tale, the various discrepancies it contained were assumed to be the result of confusion caused by his injury and by the fact that eyewitness accounts often differ in detail if not in substance. The investigation was closed.

The next morning, an exaggerated report of the affair appeared in a leading daily newspaper under the headline SAVAGE LION ATTACKS MAN. The story was quickly picked up by the wire services and flashed across the continent. The attendant notoriety turned Walt Taggart into something of a heroic figure, with Steven Cousins lauded as a "daring rescuer."

After television cameras filmed Taggart in the hospital, several television reporters and their crews were sent to High Country Safaris, there to film Cousins on horseback accoutred with his Stetson, hunting knife, and rifle while surrounded by Taggart's remaining three hounds. Cousins was later interviewed in the main lodge, sitting in the bar enjoying whiskey bought by the reporters.

Andrew Bell, delighted with so much publicity, took one of the television reporters and his crew for a flight over the country, circling the area where the cave was located and flying a wide search pattern over the puma's presumed territory.

Filming and recording in flight, the fast-talking, deep-voiced commentator concluded his report: "Somewhere beneath our wings skulks the vicious mountain lion that cunningly ambushed Mr. Walter Taggart and mauled him so savagely that doctors had to cut off his right arm. Even as we are flying over this limitless wilderness during what has turned out to be a hopeless search for the killer cat, the few hardy people who live scattered across this inhospitable country are keeping to their homes, their doors locked and their guns at the ready, fearful for their lives."

After her escape from the cave, the injured puma ran at full speed for several hundred yards, working her way up-mountain and having to bound from rock to rock while taking care to remain within the cover of the evergreens. Like all members of the cat family, she could not maintain such exertion for long because of her narrow chest and relatively small lungs. Only minutes after she had made good her escape, the cat was forced to slow down, her breathing stertorous and her heart racing.

Presently, as she walked slowly and painfully, for her wound had again opened and was bleeding, she encountered a trail that coursed erratically between the north flank of The Eagle and a neighboring mountain. Working her way along this trail for some distance, she at last became satisfied that she was no longer being pursued. She stopped, sat on her haunches facing in the direction of the cave, and listened attentively while testing the air for the odor of her enemies. After some moments, convinced that the hunters had given up the chase, she tried to lick her wound, but her saliva had all but dried up. She turned around and continued to follow the trail, keenly aware of her thirst and moving as quickly as she could. Half a mile later she encountered Scallon Creek, a small stream that owes its origins to meltwater that leaks down from The Eagle's snow-covered peak. Crouching low, she slaked her thirst. Afterward, still in a recumbent posture, she attended to her wound. Then she dozed fitfully, her ears ever on the alert and causing her to lift her head to check her environment every time a sudden noise disturbed her.

An hour later she stood up, drank again from the stream, licked her wound, stretched, and became very conscious of her need for food. Yet her desire to find a new sanctuary overruled the pangs of hunger. Moving on, the puma forded the narrow, shallow creek and picked up a trail on its far side. She followed it.

Ignoring the constant demands of her empty belly, she walked through the afternoon, into the evening, and all night, stopping occasionally to rest briefly or to drink more water from a succession of mountain streams encountered along the way.

By first light the next morning, having traveled almost continuously for thirteen hours—a time during which she averaged three miles an hour—the wounded cat had placed almost forty miles between herself and her persecutors. Her journey had been prodigious. First, she had climbed straight up and over Eagle Mountain, making the crossing through deep, crusted snow at an elevation of five thousand feet before descending once again into the trees to encounter Elliott Creek, a tributary of the Telkwa River that led her to the Telkwa Pass and thence, during the middle of the night, to the Zymoetz River. Like most cats, she disliked water, so she next traveled northward, following the river's east bank until some fifteen miles later she encountered a number of sandbars at the junction of Red Canyon Creek. Using the sandbars, she forded the river and followed the creek along the relatively wide canyon from which it derives its name.

As the eastern peaks began to glow pink, the puma was loping tiredly beside the stream when she reached the end of the canyon and entered a relatively large, flat valley. This region, in the middle of the Bulkley Range, is entirely devoid of human habitation. But after she had walked along the stream bank for a quarter of a mile, her fine sense of smell told her that the well-treed bottomlands were home to a number of animals. She soon noted the odors left by the passing of such predators as wolves, bears, coyotes, and wolverines. They put her on alert; yet the scent that would have most affected her future, that left by a member of her own species, was not evident.

Exhausted as she was, the lion's great hunger denied her the comfort of rest. Siphoning the scent trails, she detected the fresh spoor of marmot before long and followed it to an area of grassy land that was interrupted in a number of places by large, moss- and fern-covered boulders. This was the home of the marmot, a large male whose burrow was deep under one of the granite blocks. The cat had eaten marmot on many occasions, and she knew the ways of this rodent, a relative of the groundhog.

Aware that it was yet too early for her quarry to venture out of its den, the puma climbed on the boulder beneath which the marmot's main doorway was located. She knew this was the entrance by the heavy scent that lingered around it.

The sun, which had to breast the high mountains before its rays could be reflected into the lowlands, did not begin to clear the eastern peaks until an hour after the huntress had positioned herself atop her point of ambush. Presently, the first orange light beamed into the valley; coincidental with its arrival, the cat heard the slight, stealthy sounds of the marmot as it approached the mouth of its burrow. Soon afterward, a high, piercing whistle broke the stillness of the morning. The puma bunched her muscles, knowing that this was the quarry's way of checking for enemies. From the safety of the den entrance, the big rodent whistled again, the note long and carrying, reverberating within the confines of the cirque. The call, emitted suddenly, is intended to startle a would-be enemy, at the least causing it to flinch, and even such a slight movement is immediately noted by the keen-eyed whistler. Hunters such as wolves, bears, coyotes, and foxes are often confused by the call, which echoes simultaneously from so many different places that it is difficult to locate its point of origin. But feline predators—cougars, lynx, and bobcats—are less likely to be taken in by the echoes because they so often lie in ambush, whenever possible selecting dense cover as close to the marmot's den as possible. Because it is screened in such a way, any slight, involuntary movement that a feline predator might make in response to the marmot's sibilant call is unlikely to be detected by the wary rodent.

Certainly, on that morning of famine, the puma was not fooled. She knew precisely where the marmot was hiding, and although her body twitched briefly in response to the first whistle, she did not move so much as a whisker when the second call was made. Instead, she waited, ready to spring.

Minutes passed. The marmot whistled again. And waited. Presently, driven by his own hunger and reassured by the absence of predatory movement, he emerged into full view. Sitting upright, firmly planted on his back feet, arms and front paws pressed against his chest, he inspected the terrain for several minutes before dropping onto all fours and trundling forward, aiming for a nearby patch of lush grass.

When her quarry was in full view and about twenty feet away from its den, the cat sprang. Fatigued, her flank made stiff by the injury, and weakened by hunger, she moved more slowly than usual and lacked the magnificent coordination that is normal for her species. She landed short. The marmot veered away in a flash, dodging as it ran at full speed. The cat turned, tried to capture the animal with one of her front paws, missed. She lunged forward, missed again by a fraction. Then, making a supreme effort, she leaped and landed just short of the quarry. Again one of her massive front paws lashed out, this time trapping the marmot. Seconds later the animal was dead.

Carrying the prey in her mouth, the exhausted puma returned to the rocky area and settled herself in a depression between several boulders. There she fed off the plump animal, which weighed almost thirteen pounds. There was not much left when the cat had finished eating. Some of the smaller bones had been chewed and swallowed; sections of skin, the fur casually pulled off by her flat incisor teeth, had also been eaten, and the major bones were scraped clean of meat by her rasp-like tongue. Even so, she was far from replete. This was her first meal in almost four days. But at least now she was partially sated and could afford to take a much needed rest. First, however, she had to quench her thirst. She left her shelter and walked to the stream, where she drank deeply, crouching at the water's edge while sunlight burnished her tawny coat. Afterward, she returned to the rocks and licked her wound before stretching out.

3

The puma rested until nightfall. She slept peacefully among the rocks behind the marmot's den, oblivious of the hysterical clamor that her leap to freedom had aroused in man's domain. Occasionally she awakened to lick her wound, and twice she got up and padded down to the stream to drink, on her return to shelter during both of those trips stopping to spray nearby vegetation with her urine, in this way announcing her claim to the territory.

By evening, when she was fully rested, the puma stretched lethargically and sat up on her haunches, not yet in a hurry to leave her shelter. She yawned, her mouth opening wide, revealing four great fangs and a thick, arched tongue. Afterward, she listened to the sounds and smelled the essences of her new range; some odors were days old and barely noticeable, others had been left a few hours earlier. Listening intently as she sniffed, she detected a badger in one area and in another a band of black-tailed deer. The badger was north of her location and no more than one hundred yards away; the deer were more distant and to the south. Like a person who makes a shopping list before going to buy provisions, the cat took inventory in her brain of all those sounds and scents that told of the presence of prey animals, but, unlike a supermarket shopper, she also cataloged the messages left by her competitors.

The bears and coyotes did not greatly concern her. Bears are too slow to offer much competition to a large, agile feline; besides, they feed largely on wild fruit, grasses, roots, bulbs, insects, and carrion, although they do take some prey animals. Coyotes compete with the more powerful carnivores, but they are also preyed upon by those hunters. Wolves are strong competitors for prey, but they well know the risks of an attack on a puma. Wolverines, however, are formidable hunters of smaller prey and notorious robbers of kills made by other predators; for the cougar, they are rivals to be reckoned with. As the cat knew from past experience, wolverines are hard to deter and harder still to subdue, lightning fast, extremely powerful, and daringly aggressive. Even the lordly grizzly will if possible avoid a confrontation with a wolverine. Because it has been endowed with an exceptionally fast metabolic rate, the bantam warrior is nearly always hungry. Once it has appropriated a kill in the absence of the rightful owner, even pumas and wolves are likely to avoid an argument with the pugnacious thief, although this animal, while the largest member of the weasel family, rarely exceeds forty-five pounds in weight or a total length of fifty inches.

The respect awarded this audacious raider by larger and more powerful carnivores does not entirely stem from its fighting prowess. It is a result also of the wolverine's habit of spraying appropriated kills with a foul secretion produced by two well-developed anal glands, a musk carried by all members of the weasel family, including the notorious skunk. Usually, remains tainted by this noxious discharge are palatable only to another wolverine, but should a large predator be reduced to a state of famine, it will reluctantly partake of wolverine-sprayed leftovers.

Caution made the cat ignore her hunger as she monitored

her environment while remaining seated on her haunches, not moving except for the frequent occasions when she brushed mosquitoes from her face and ears with one of her front paws; similarly, she would jerk small areas of her skin, a reflexive twitching that would dislodge pestering bloodsuckers, a cloud of which whined continually around her. The insects were bothersome, but she did not allow their bites or the monotonous susurrus of their wings to distract her. She was fully aware that her survival depended upon a thorough knowledge of her environment, so for an hour she continued to check her surroundings with her ears and nose before venturing out to hunt.

It was full dark, and countless stars sequined the blue-black sky when the puma at last arose, stretched, and padded out of her rock-studded resting area. First, she went to get a drink; then, with water dripping from her muzzle, she followed the stream against its flow, traveling in a northwesterly direction. As usual when she was not charging to attack, or running to escape, her pads made hardly any sound and her sinuous body elicited only vague whispers as it brushed delicately against low-hanging tree limbs or bushes. Her progress was slow, methodical, frequently interrupted by stops during which she would stand on three legs, one or the other of her front paws poised in midair and bent at the wrist, its great pad hanging vertically. In that pose, she would swing her head slowly either to the left or to the right, and she would look, listen, and smell. Then she would turn her head in the opposite direction, repeating her checks; in this fashion she monitored an arc that encompassed 180 degrees.

The puma was not as famished as she had been before she killed the marmot, yet she was in need of food. Weakened by loss of blood and still tired from her long trek through the wilderness, she was often tempted to abandon her cautious exploration of the new range and to concentrate instead on a hunt. But she persisted, following a well-defined trail and paying meticulous attention to the contours of the land and to the trees and bushes and rocks, at the same time monitoring the scents and sounds she detected. Aware of the presence and location of the badger that she had identified from her resting place, she left the trail and began to approach the animal's lair, guided unerringly by her nose. But she had traveled only a short distance when she realized that the badger had left its den.

Changing direction in response to the scent trail and moving with extreme caution, she presently saw the quarry. The badger was digging energetically in the vicinity of a large boulder that was about fifty feet to her right and visible as a shadow darker than the rest. The cat stopped and went into a crouch, remaining immobile while she continued to smell and listen. Moments later, as she was about to creep toward her objective, a gibbous moon edged above one of the western peaks. The puma remained still, waiting for the light.

When the moon cleared the peak, it highlighted the more open areas and created long, dark shadows in heavily timbered locations. The puma slithered forward, advancing slowly and soundlessly until she was only thirty feet from the badger. The chunky, long-clawed carnivore, a male, was busy excavating the burrow of a pocket gopher. He was at first completely unaware of the cougar's presence. But as the cat moved closer, he scented her. Startled, he whirled around and backed himself quickly into the hole he had been digging, protecting his back and baring his quite formidable fangs while hissing almost like a snake.

The puma stopped. Had she been able to surprise the quarry and kill it with one swift blow from a powerful paw, she would have done so, but experience had taught her that badgers, like their wolverine relatives, are doughty fighters capable of inflicting serious wounds. In her weakened state, the cat could not afford further injury, so she ignored the spitting animal, padding past him with but a sideways glance in his direction. As adept as the cat at reading all the signals of his environment, the badger became immediately aware that the puma now had no intention of attacking him, so he turned around and resumed digging.

The cougar returned to the main trail, padding along it slowly and, as before, pausing often to investigate her surroundings, but, especially now, looking for deer. Several times during the next hour she disturbed small animals and roosting birds, but although the grasses and soil over which she passed were impregnated with the odor of deer, the scent trail was weak.

By midnight, when she was famished and getting desperate, a sudden change of the breeze brought her the strong scent of deer. Nostrils quivering, she turned off course and followed the fragrant spoor, moving with the utmost stealth and holding her body low to the ground.

Ten minutes after she had first detected the scent, the puma sighted her quarry. Three young black-tailed deer were grazing near a small stream that emerged from an isolated, mesalike formation of layered slabs of granite and feldspar that rose to a height of fifteen feet, its northern face sheer and fractured, its southern extremity and its sides somewhat sloping. The blacktails, all of them two-year-old bucks, were feeding near the clifflike northern face. Two of them were sleek and obviously in good condition; they stood together near the little stream. The third buck was cropping grass about thirty feet from the mesa. It was thin and seemed to have trouble breathing, for it stopped eating at frequent intervals and inhaled and exhaled noisily.

The puma, almost dragging her stomach on the ground, moved to the sloping side of the crag, her progress slow but soundless. Yard by yard she advanced, stopping often and flattening herself among the underbrush while scent-checking the quarry. She was eager for the kill, but too disciplined to allow hurry to alert the blacktails. As a result, it took her fifteen minutes to reach the top of the mesa, there to flatten herself on its edge. The deer were unaware of her presence. Eyes fixed on the thin buck, the cat bunched her hindquarters, her long tail lying straight, only its tip jerking from side to side.

The deer took two steps away from the rock face, stopped, and lowered his head toward the grass, as if he were about to eat. Instead he coughed violently, mouth agape, his breath whistling out of his nostrils. The animal's distress was great. It was caused by a severe infestation of the larvae of the botfly, a pest that lays its eggs within or at the edges of the nostrils of members of the deer family, and also attacks horses, cattle, and sheep.

When botfly eggs hatch, the tiny larvae migrate into the nasal passages and sinus cavities of their victims, there to attach themselves with a pair of hooks that emerge from their mouths. Firmly anchored, they spend ten months inside their victims, feeding on the tissues and fluids of the host animals while growing into fat, inch-long maggots. If an animal is not heavily infested, it is not greatly affected by the bot larvae, but when many maggots are present, they weaken a deer or moose and make it vulnerable to other parasites, disease, and predation.

The young deer's nose passages and sinus cavities were filled with the whitish, black-banded parasites. Weak, unable to breathe properly, and tormented by the wriggling, feeding worms, he was in great distress.

The puma launched herself from the mesa. As she did so, the two bucks near the stream took alarm and wheeled away, alerting their ailing companion. He turned as the cat landed ten feet from him, but even before he was ready to get into stride, the puma launched herself anew, her outstretched paws hitting the quarry's shoulder. As she had done to Taggart's hound and to the coyote, she broke the deer's neck through whiplash.

Afterward, she dragged the carcass to a brushy area, and there she opened the stomach and ate first of the intestines, liver, and kidneys; she was genetically programmed to do this because the visceral organs of herbivores contain special nutrients, including vitamin C, that are essential for the well-being of carnivores. When she had eaten her fill, the cougar stretched out in a secluded area near the remains, prepared to guard them against the inroads of large carnivores, but unconcerned by the petty thievery exercised by small mammals and birds.

As summer aged, the pregnant mountain lion started to search for a den more suitable than those she had already located in various parts of her new range. She was by now thoroughly familiar with the whole of the territory that she considered her own, and she was prepared to defend it, if need be, against any other member of her species. Yet, heavy with the young in her belly, she had become somewhat sluggish and would probably at that time have retreated from a confrontation with a puma had one wandered into her domain. She also tended to avoid hunting large prey, feeding instead on the smaller animals of the wilderness. Hitherto, she had only rarely moved out of shelter during full daylight, but now, in her anxiety to find a good birthing den, she began to travel a great deal during the early afternoon and evening. By the end of July, when she was within days of bearing her young, she had not yet located a nursery that suited her.

Then, during early evening on the last day of the month, she wandered into an area where a stream emerged from a small, emeraldine lake that was fed by a number of creeks, each drawing its waters from mountaintop glaciers. The rivulets trundled lakeward from heights of between six and seven thousand feet. One of the rills, larger than the rest, ran down the east side of a dogtooth-shaped mountain and dropped over a cliff that had been made sheer by a landslide. As the crystal water shot into space, it spread like a fan and curved gracefully away from the rock face before dropping two hundred feet to feed the lake.

Drawn to the place where the frothy water became spray as it made contact with the rocks and scree deposited by the ancient slide, the mountain lion looked up as a number of quick, dark shapes sailed into the evening from behind the cascade. Bats. She was familiar with these flying mammals, colonies of which she had encountered in a number of caves. She immediately made for the waterfall, keeping to the drier rocks. A short time later she scrambled over a series of large, moss-covered boulders behind which she smelled the musky odor given off by the guano pellets that had been deposited on the cave floor by generations of little brown bats.

On the far side of a fairly roomy cavern, the terrain climbed upward. Following the slope to its end, the puma found a small chamber, its floor shaped somewhat like a basin. This was an ideal den. It had several advantages: the scooped-out nesting chamber would prevent her kittens from crawling too far during the early stages of their development; the entrance to the grotto, concealed as it was by the falling water, was unlikely to draw attention, and the noise of the cascade would discourage the kittens from wandering far from their birthplace until they were old enough to explore the outside world with their mother.

On August 4, the puma gave birth to three tiny kittens, two females and a male.

The birth process began in the early hours of the morning, and, from the start of her contractions, the mother spent seven hours in labor. The male kitten emerged first. He was soaked by uterine fluids and blood, and his eyes were glued shut. He weighed sixteen ounces and measured thirteen inches from his nose to the end of his stubby tail.

The tiny animal's only reaction as it emerged into the darkened world was to open and close its mouth, little gasping movements that ceased the moment the mother began to lick him dry, using her raspy tongue softly, so as not to damage his sensitive skin, and purring, her soft rumble echoing within the nesting chamber and in the outside cavern.

Because the kitten was still attached by his umbilical cord to the placental membranes, the cat paused during her licking. With one huge but gentle paw she held the wriggling cub on his back. As he struggled feebly, she lowered her muzzle and nipped off the cord at a place about half an inch from the kitten's stomach. The little tube that remained gouted a few drops of blood that the cat immediately licked up. She continued licking the minor wound for some minutes, stanching the flow before nosing her firstborn toward her six milk-full teats, which, as in all felines, were spaced in two rows of three on either side of the centerline of her stomach. The first pair, located on the left and right side of her groin area, held the most milk. The kitten quickly found one of these and began to suck, holding to the teat so tenaciously that he did not lose it when the mother's contractions began anew and she became busy dealing with the arrival of her second-born, who was appreciably smaller than her brother. The mother tended her daughter as she had cared for her son, except that the umbilical cord parted of its own accord during the final moments of this kitten's birth. And while the two kittens were nursing, their mother gave birth to the second female.

After she had washed her second daughter and the newborns were settled, each sucking her milk, the mother rested. She lay in a slightly curved posture, head on her outstretched paws but turned toward the kittens. The feel of her young nuzzling at her belly, the sounds that they made as they fed were new but comforting experiences. Her amber eyes were soft and loving as she watched the little cats.

The female kittens were covered by fawn coats of fine, woolly fur that was plentifully decorated by black-to-brown spots, rather similar to a leopard's rosettes. Each of their short tails was embellished by a series of dark rings not unlike those of raccoon tails. Inside their ears, long white fur was emphasized by pure black bands that edged the outsides of their ears, and their faces were decorated by dark etchings that began above each eye, traveled down the muzzle, and turned under the chin. Apart from their dark facial and head markings, the two female kittens did not at all resemble adult pumas, although their birth markings were normal for the species. The little tom's coloring, however, was different. He shared the dark spots, tail rings, and facial etchings of his sisters, but his coat was milk white.

By the time the noon sun beamed on the puma's valley, her kittens had finished the first feed of their lives and had gone to sleep, each pressed tight against their mother's underfur and one, the smallest female, still holding a back teat in her mouth. The puma, tired after her ordeal, now relaxed. Eyes closed, but ears held stiffly on the alert, the big cat purred softly, a hoarse sound that echoed within the nesting chamber. Presently, she too went to sleep.

The mother remained with her newborn kittens for thirty hours, leaving the den briefly on only two occasions to pad to the water to drink. But by sundown of the next day, not having eaten for two full days, she was ravenously hungry, and she knew that she had to go on a hunt.

The three kittens, having but recently sucked their fill of

their mother's thick, creamy milk, were asleep as the puma left the nesting chamber, her soft pads making no sound as she approached the cascading water that shrouded the entrance to the cave.

Outside dusk was beginning to descend over the valley, for as soon as the sun sinks behind western peaks, daylight becomes dimmed. Peering from the cave entrance, her tawny body partially hidden by spray from the waterfall, the puma used sight and scent to reconnoiter the wilderness; her ears were made useless by the thunderous noise of the falling, splashing water. Balanced on top of a wet and glistening boulder, she remained stock-still for several minutes; then, with but one backward glance into the cave, she stepped away from the cataract and loped purposefully in a southeasterly direction, at first walking through heavy forest, presently emerging into a more scrubby region, where underlying granite prevented large trees from holding fast in the thin soil.

Up to this location the cat had been moving silently, but in a relaxed way. Now she began to stalk, her golden eyes fixed on the way ahead, her ears erect, and her nostrils working to the scent of deer. The trail was weak, but as the puma kept her nose to the pathway, the odors rising from the tracks gradually grew stronger. Somewhere ahead, she now knew, there were four deer, each scent containing subtly different properties. The cougar continued moving with the spoor, but her progress was slower now, and she sought as much cover as she could find in the fairly open vale through which the scent was leading her.

When she had traveled somewhat more than two miles, the puma stopped, sniffed the trail, and flattened herself on the ground. In that posture she remained for several minutes, working with her nose and ears. Then she rose, but she kept herself in a semicrouch as she turned; the quarry was not far ahead of her. She was aiming to her left, toward a foothill-like region that lay about three hundred yards away, where white spruces grew tall and close together. She slid ghostlike from cover to cover, stopping often to turn her head toward the trail that she had been following. Invisible in the dusk and totally silent, she covered the distance to the forested rise in just a few minutes. Once she reached the trees, she stopped briefly to make sure that the slight breeze that existed blew in her face, bringing her the scent of the deer, but failing to take her scent to the quarry.

Satisfied, she straightened her legs and moved faster, intent on making a detour so as to get into a position from which she could charge the grazing deer, none of which she had yet seen but all of which she could now identify by scent. She also knew exactly where they were grazing. Had she been able to compute distances in human terms, she would have noted that 250 yards had separated her from the quarry at the point where she turned off course in order to place herself in ambush. Without the benefit of mechanical instructions or mathematics, her fine senses gave her the exact whereabouts of the deer and told her precisely how far she had to travel in order to put herself within striking distance of them.

After walking slowly and silently in a semicircle for several minutes, the puma stopped, sat upright, and oriented herself by scent and sound. She was now above the deer and only one hundred yards from them. She could hear the animals as they fed, cropping at the grass and pulling sharply at each mouthful; the slight noise made as the green blades were jerked loose reached her attentive ears. Once again she crouched, paused momentarily, and advanced, now moving with infinite care, her body so low that she was almost dragging her chest and stomach over the ground. She covered twenty yards and stopped. Lifting her head, she tested the air while listening. Reassured, she advanced about the same distance and paused anew. In this way, halting four times, she eventually placed herself in a position slightly more elevated than that of the quarry and only some forty-five feet from the nearest deer. Her vantage was surrounded by thimbleberry bushes, which grew to a height of three feet.

The deer that the puma had tracked were inexperienced young bucks that had not yet attained sexual maturity; each weighed about one hundred pounds. Many like them roamed the forests that year because the local deer were approaching the high point of a cycle of abundance that was in keeping with fluctuations common to all animals inhabiting the northern forests and the tundra. Such swings in numbers are not general, neither do they affect all the species that inhabit a particular area. Population highs usually occur among a particular species when abundant food is available to its members; conversely, when food supplies are insufficient, population numbers crash as a result of overcrowding and malnutrition. Such cycles of feast and famine occur at intervals of from a few years to thirty or forty years, depending upon the size of the animals concerned and the kinds of foods that each species requires. When numbers of prey animals are high, predator numbers gradually increase, but after a population of prey animals crashes, the numbers of those predators that are dependent on them for food will eventually crash as well, although carnivore numbers usually continue to increase for several years after the prey species have started to decline. Eventually, however, the predator numbers will inevitably crash. In this way nature, when undisturbed by humans, has been attaining the natural balance for untold thousands of years.

When the puma was born, the mule deer in her domain were starting to recover from a crash that had drastically reduced their numbers, and for this reason she had never experienced famine. Now, as she prepared to make her charge, she was not aware that a decline in the numbers of deer would lead to her death in the not-too-distant future.

One of the bucks was being especially pestered by biting flies. Every few moments he would stop grazing, raise his head, and shake it, at the same time twitching the skin on various parts of his body. While he was thus engaged, the puma leaped out of concealment.

The cat's first prodigious bound almost cut in half the distance that separated her from the quarry, but before the deer could do more than tense his muscles as a preliminary to his dash for survival, she leaped again. This time she landed just short of the target, because the buck was already starting to spring away.

The cougar lashed out with her right front paw, claws bared, but she missed the deer's rump by several inches. Instantly, tucking her hind legs beneath her body to recover her balance, the cat surged forward, reaching now with both extended paws.

Her left paw connected with the deer's rump. In a trice, with her claws embedded in the buck's tough skin, she dragged herself forward and secured a hold on his right flank with her other paw. A moment later she climbed on his back, kicked against his body with her hind feet, and, reaching outward with her right front paw, grabbed his nose, at the same time wrenching his neck sideways. The neck broke with an audible snap. Prey and predator crashed to the ground. The deer was dead. His companions were no longer visible; only the gradually fading sounds of their pounding hooves indicated that they had been there.

The puma had landed underneath her prey. Heaving, she got out from under the weight and stood, shaking herself to rid her coat of debris. Her tail lashed fitfully from side to side, her stiff whiskers jutted forward, her ears were flattened against her head. Now she stood quietly, a tawny statue that epitomized the power as well as the grace of the wild. She opened her mouth and let out a held breath as her long pink tongue spilled out on the left side of her jaws. Panting slightly, she lowered her head and sniffed at the carcass; then she licked at the blood that was seeping out of the top of the buck's black nose, droplets of crimson that emerged from the claw-inflicted wounds.

The puma opened her mouth and fastened her great fangs on the deer's neck. She began to drag its body to the thimbleberry shrubs, pulling the weight easily, her front legs straddling the carcass. With the sheltering bushes, she started to eat, first opening the stomach with one swift slash of a clawed front paw and thrusting her muzzle deep into the carcass. When her bloodied face emerged, her jaws were working and a length of greenish gut jutted out of her mouth, its other end still connected to the deer's intestinal tract.

Before the birth of her kittens, the puma would have satisfied her immediate hunger and rested nearby after covering the remains. But the need to return to her den to care for her young made the cat gorge. She ate twice as much as usual, not stopping until her stomach was actually distended and hanging low, the inner pressure even causing her back teats to leak driblets of milk after she abandoned the kill and started for home.

As the big cat left the area, seven ravens descended on the carcass and began to eat of it. Minutes later a red fox arrived, dislodged two of the ravens from their feeding places, and then started to rip off pieces of meat. The displaced birds went to another part of the kill and continued feeding, but when the shrubs parted and two coyotes trotted toward the carcass, the fox and the ravens left the scene. When darkness arrived, a number of other animals came to feed. Two weasels, each arriving from a different direction, slid out of the underbrush, one stationing itself at the head, the other near the stomach opening. Soon afterward a striped skunk arrived, causing the weasel that was feeding by the abdominal cavity to dart inside the deer's body, hissing as it went, but soon becoming silent as it devoured morsels of liver.

By first light the next morning there was little left of the buck. Even so, mice, shrews, and insects continued to feed off the remains, taking marrow and bits of flesh and sinew from the bones, which, in time, would also be consumed for the calcium that they contained.

4

Five days after her kittens were born, the puma needed to hunt again, but because the little cats required frequent nursing, she was aware that she could not go far afield. The enormous meal of deer meat she had ingested three days earlier had sustained her for forty-eight hours, but now she was ravenous. Yet she was loath to leave her young, all of which had gained weight and size and had become quite active.

At birth, the white tom had measured thirteen inches from nose tip to tail end and had weighed sixteen ounces. The first female to be born was twelve inches long and weighed fourteen ounces; the last to arrive was one inch shorter than her sister and weighed twelve ounces. During the intervening time, the male kitten had added two inches to his length and three ounces to his weight, while his siblings had each gained two ounces and attained somewhat more than one inch of length.

For the first few days of their lives, the kittens remained almost totally inactive. They mewed softly when hungry, but between feeds they spent most of their time sleeping, tucked tightly against their mother, or, when she padded out of the cavern to have a drink and to stretch her cramped muscles, they curled up together, forming a tight ball and sucking on each other, using a sibling's leg, foot, or ear as a comforter. When they were four days old, however, they began to move about, crawling awkwardly and slowly, mewling, and climbing on top of or over their companions.

The white tom was the most active. He often crawled toward the den entrance, sensing its location because of the cooler outside air that entered the chamber through the opening. When he did this, his mother would thrust out a gentle paw and trap him; then, curving her big toes around his body, claws well sheathed, she would drag him back. The adventurous kitten protested such treatment, at first by struggling and screaming; but after the third time he had been dragged back so ignominiously, he began to growl, a feeble imitation of his mother's loud snarl, yet a sound that clearly proclaimed his displeasure.

During the evening of the fifth day of his life, and soon after his mother had left the chamber to go outside to drink at the lake, the tom seized the opportunity to explore, again drawn to the entrance. Stumbling, crawling, now and then trying to actually walk on all fours but falling over each time, he persevered. Three feet from the den mouth, the rock sloped upward, at first inclined gently, but becoming steeper about halfway. The little tom reached this point after a lot of struggling, mewling, and grunting. Sensing the grade, he began to climb it. Pushing with his back feet, he slipped and fell, rolling over and over to land near his sisters. Now he was scared. Mewling loudly, he sought his siblings, guided to them by scent and by the heat of their bodies. He had just tucked himself in among the two females when the mother returned. She had heard his cries and had hurried back, tail lashing, ears held against her head, and lips curled in a silent snarl that revealed to the full her predatory teeth. She had thought that something was attacking her offspring, but, realizing immediately that all was well, she approached the kittens, lowered her muzzle, and licked all three at the same time. Afterward, she curled herself around them so that they could suckle from her.

One after the other, the two females became satisfied, releasing the teats from which they had been sucking and going to sleep. The white tom, always the biggest eater, continued feeding for a while, but at last even he became sated. With hunger causing her stomach to rumble, the mother puma waited only long enough to make sure that her young were settled before she rose quietly and padded out of the nesting chamber.

It was not quite full dark when she stepped away from the waterfall and put her nose to work, almost immediately detecting the scent of a lone coyote. This was not her favorite food, but she realized that, if she could kill it only a short distance from her shelter, she would be able to carry the prey home, where she could protect it after taking her first feed, and where it would be readily available when she was again hungry.

The puma had caught the first trace of the coyote's scent as she was about to enter the forest after crossing the more open, rocky area that led away from the cave. Pausing, nose down, she judged by the strength of the odor that the tracks were relatively fresh, perhaps only one or two hours old. She began to track, traveling quickly and easily through the deepening darkness with a prowess shared by all felines, which are the best nocturnal hunters, night-stalking specialists whose eyes can make use of even the most feeble light. The coyote that the puma was tracking also had good night vision, as do all wild animals, but the cat's round, light-intensifying eyes allowed her to move through the darkened wilderness almost as easily as she could travel through it in daylight, although, as a rule, she stalked more slowly and cautiously during darkness. Tonight, however, her hunger and her anxiety to catch up to the prey urged her to travel as quickly as possible.

The coyote was a large, unattached male whose quest for a

female had caused him to stray out of his home territory. The previous evening, not long before he'd entered the puma's range, he had killed and eaten two ruffed grouse and a number of mice. Later, well satisfied but tired after a long journey, he stretched out under a tree and went to sleep, awakening at dawn and rising with the sun so as to continue his quest. He spent the day traveling steadily eastward, sniffing at the ground, searching for the odor of a female coyote rather than for the scent of prey.

Trotting easily at about seven miles an hour, the coyote wandered aimlessly through the wilderness, covering a good deal of territory but, after a whole day of running, having traveled from his starting point only two miles in straight-line distance. By late evening he had scented many mammals and birds, but no coyotes. He was disappointed. He was also very hungry after trotting continuously and for so long through some very rough, mountainous terrain.

It was starting to get dark when he reached the area of the waterfall and the puma's den. He immediately scented the cat's presence, and he hurried away, following a well-defined game trail. After a time, thinking himself safe, and little knowing that the cat had already picked up his scent, he slowed down. He even paused occasionally to pounce on mice or voles, catching several and swallowing each at a single gulp.

Later, when he was about three-quarters of a mile from the puma's den, the coyote killed a pregnant snowshoe hare and ate her, leaving only some bits of skin and clumps of fine, brown-and-white fur. Well satisfied now that he had almost four pounds of fresh meat inside his stomach, he next sought the shelter of some bushes several hundred yards away from where he had made the kill. There he settled down to rest while digesting his meal.

The puma's sensitive nose, meanwhile, soon led her to the meager remains of the snowshoe hare. Sniffing at the blood and body fluids in the area of the kill, the cat immediately picked up the coyote's trail. His scent was fresh and strong. She began to stalk, adopting her customary half crouch and moving from cover to cover. As she advanced, the prey's scent trail became stronger. Ten minutes later she had a fix on the place where the coyote was resting within a clump of dwarf juniper that grew on the edge of an old rock slide.

The cat stopped and studied the terrain. She was about one hundred yards from her quarry, but, to get within striking distance of the coyote from her present position, she would have to cross a scree-littered, open slope that was devoid of cover except for a few clumps of fireweed. Experience told her that if she tried to do that, she would dislodge pieces of rock, sending them cascading down the incline to alert her quarry, which would escape long before she could strike.

Considering these things, the puma elected to make a wide detour. She was going to have to climb partway up the tumble-down slope, avoiding the area of loose scree, to get above the coyote. Once in position, and using the height of land to increase the momentum and the length of her leap downhill, she would reach the coyote before he had time to get away at his full speed, a rate that could exceed more than twenty-five miles an hour and one the cat knew she could not match. The puma was swift and agile in turning and twisting and dodging and climbing, but, like all cats, she was a bounder and a leaper rather than a long-distance runner. When going flat-out, she could attain a speed of slightly more than twenty miles an hour, but she could keep it up only for a short distance, perhaps for about one hundred yards.

Well aware that she could not win a footrace against the coyote, the mother puma started detouring. She moved slowly and carefully, angling toward an area where the rock slide had left a cascade of large boulders among which she would be entirely concealed. When she entered the trees, the darkness became intense, but she was able to see the way. Soon she was among the big rocks. Once she had climbed to a height of forty feet, she oriented herself. Her nose quickly pointed out the place where the quarry was located. She turned in that direction, continuing to detour, yet working unerringly toward her target.

Ten minutes later she left the boulders and stepped silently among the juniper bushes that almost covered the slope in the vicinity of the coyote's bedding place. From her vantage forty feet above the sleeping quarry, her sense of smell and her keen hearing combined to pinpoint the animal's exact location.

The puma crouched, remained perfectly still. Her ears pricked forward, listening to the quarry's soft breathing. Her black nostrils flared wide to siphon its odor. She moved forward to place herself on a relatively flat rock, where she stood in a crouch. She was ready.

Slowly drawing up her powerful haunches as her tail lashed from side to side, the puma tensed her muscles. Then, when her tail became suddenly still and rigid, she lifted off, a ghostly being sailing through dark space, yet knowing exactly where she was going to land. Her leap spanned thirty-five feet and brought her almost on top of the coyote. Startled, he leaped upright. But before he could run, one of the puma's huge, clawed paws hit his neck, breaking it instantly. The body rolled downhill for some yards before it came to rest against the bowl of a spruce. Padding toward it, the cat began to purr. Moments later she started to feed.

When she had eaten seven or eight pounds of warm meat, she picked up the carcass and started for home, carrying the inert burden easily. The coyote had weighed forty pounds when alive; now, with the amount that the cougar had taken from its body and the loss of a quantity of its blood and other fluids, there remained about thirty pounds of meat, bone, skin, and fur, enough food to satisfy the puma's needs for the next five or six days.

It took only half an hour for the mother cat to return home from the kill site, a distance of little more than a mile, which she covered at a good pace. Stepping behind the waterfall to enter the main cavern, she dropped her burden near the entrance to her den; then she climbed into the chamber and greeted her kittens by whistling softly to reassure them, immediately afterward licking them from a standing position for some moments. Presently she lay down, curling her body around the tiny cats and allowing them to drink her rich milk.

The next morning, just when the sun was starting to edge over the eastern mountains, the sleeping puma was awakened by a great roaring. She sat upright, tumbling her kittens away from her body as she did so. With her ears back, and mouth open in a silent snarl, she faced the den entrance, listening. The roar was repeated, a hoarse, short, but primordially savage sound that echoed within the cavern and inside the nesting chamber. The cat recognized the noise and became afraid, but when her kittens began to cry plaintively, each wriggling around her feet in frantic distress, her maternal emotions overcame her fear. She became aggressively aroused.

Before leaving the nesting chamber, the mother cat used her nose to nudge her kittens together. She purred softly as she worked. Afterward, forcing herself to remain calm and to ignore the threatening roars that sporadically reverberated within the cavern, she licked the kittens, continuing to purr. Perhaps thirty seconds later the little pumas became quiet; they had been lulled into a tranquil state by their mother's caresses.

The kittens would now remain huddled together and utterly silent, making their location more difficult for an enemy to discover. At this stage of their lives, their hearing was very poor, the channels within their ears not yet being fully open, but they were sensitive to sound waves and especially to the whistles and the purring of their mother. Alarmed at first by the roars and by the puma's sudden movements, they had become active and noisy, but as soon as they sensed the female's purrs and felt her caressing tongue, they were reassured.

The cat left the nesting chamber. Crossing the cavern, she stopped at its entrance, her body concealed by the cascading water. Here she waited, listening.

As usually occurs when the normal tenor of wilderness life is suddenly upset, those animals and birds nearest the source of the sudden turmoil had become immediately still. At first, while the savage cries were being uttered, the fear-inspired silence had not been readily apparent, but when the stentorian calls ended abruptly, the unnatural quiet was immediately evident. It was as though every living thing within hearing was holding its breath.

Despite the incessant gossip of the waterfall, the puma at once became aware of the uneasy calm; responding to it, she turned to her right and began to climb, her movements ghostlike as she aimed for a large, flat boulder that she habitually used as an observation platform, a lookout that was about forty feet above the cave entrance. Knowing every inch of the trail, she made the ascent in record time and was soon settled full length on the flat rock, her tawny body invisible against a brown-and-green background.

As the silence continued and as the puma studied the wilderness, the roars were suddenly repeated, issuing from across the rocky opening and within a dense screen of evergreens. But the uproar was accompanied by the loud crackling of brush. The din rose out of the forest and was repeated endlessly as it echoed within the mountain passes. Then, as suddenly as before, it ended.

As the puma watched, the shrubbery at the edge of the rocky opening began to move, parted, and allowed a grizzly bear to run into the lakeside clearing. Split seconds later, another grizzly emerged. The first bear was medium sized, probably weighing three or four hundred pounds; its pursuer was enormous, a formidable male that must have weighed twice as much.

Finding itself being overtaken, the smaller grizzly turned to its right and dashed into the lake, its bulk and speed displacing volumes of water that splashed to each side of the fleeing animal and made sudden, noisy waves that crashed against the shore rocks. The pursuing bear turned also, but when he reached the water's edge he stopped, his head moving from side to side like a great, hairy pendulum while he pawed at the shoreline and roared.

The two male grizzlies had met unexpectedly in the forest. Being largely solitary and quick to become enraged, they had immediately begun to fight, but the smaller of the two soon realized that he faced an antagonist that would kill him if he was unable to escape. Amid much roaring and brush crackling, fights had erupted whenever the big grizzly had managed to catch up to the smaller one. During each encounter, though, the weaker animal had managed to escape after only a few seconds of conflict.

Watching as the smaller bear swam vigorously across the lake, the large grizzly appeared satisfied with the rout of his antagonist. He grunted hoarsely, took one last swipe at the shoreline with a huge paw, and turned away from the water, evidently intending to return to the forest. But when he was halfway to the trees, he stopped and sniffed at the ground. He had found the puma's scent.

At first the bear followed the spoor in the wrong direction, continuing toward the trees at an angle, but as the puma's track odors became weaker, he turned around and sniffed his way toward the cave entrance. He was within one hundred yards of the cavern when the cat announced her presence with a series of loud snarls.

The grizzly stopped, looked up in the direction of the challenging sounds, and was just in time to see a lithe, tawny shape launch itself into space. As if mesmerized, the big bear remained still, one paw raised, mouth open, his small brown eyes trying to follow the puma's flying shape. An instant later the cat landed fifteen feet from the intruder. But before the startled bear could do more than set his paw on the ground, she charged him.

Spitting and snarling, ears flat on her head and her mouth open wide to reveal the full extent of her great fangs, the puma flashed forward, swung away from the grizzly's head, and raked his rear with her claws. The bear was well padded by his shaggy coat of coarse hairs, so the claws only scratched his skin, but the slash hurt, and warm blood flowed down his left thigh.

Astonished and outraged, the bear roared angrily as he turned agilely and rushed at the puma, trying to reach her with both front paws as he propelled himself forward. He was fast. But the puma was faster.

Before the grizzly had been able to react, she was already moving. Rising on her back legs, with both front legs stretched out wide and claws fully extruded, she leaped over the bear as he turned toward her. Whereas the grizzly's outstretched paws found only space where his attacker had been but a split second earlier, both the cougar's lethal front paws flashed out and gripped the bear's rear, five sharp, curved claws digging into each flank. Bellowing in pain and fury, the bear turned, throwing the cougar to the right and dislodging her grip, but not before her fixed claws cut deep furrows in his flesh.

The bear made to charge the dislodged cat, but she had landed upright, and she leaped to one side as her opponent again rushed at her. Slashing quickly with her left paw as she darted toward the bear's rear, she caught his nose with her claws, opening several deep cuts on his muzzle. The action so far had occupied but a few moments. During this time, the grizzly roared and the puma snarled while also emitting a hoarse, throaty scream. Now, the furious bear swung around, smashing out blindly with one of his front paws. Again the puma dodged out of harm's way, this time leaping right over her opponent and retreating several yards, there to crouch, ready to attack again, her mouth wide and continuing to give voice to her rage.

Brushing at his bleeding nose with a paw, the grizzly became silent. He stood undecided, glaring myopically at the puma, who held her ground and stared back, her yellow eyes telegraphing her aggression. The two faced each other for mere seconds, then the grizzly, no doubt deciding that he had taken enough punishment from his elusive antagonist, uttered one more ferocious roar, shook his head, scattering droplets of blood from his injured muzzle, turned, and began to amble toward the forest, perhaps intending to retreat in a dignified manner. But the enraged puma charged him, again raking his flanks with both of her paws.

Bellowing, the bear galloped away at full speed, now wanting nothing more than to escape the furious cat. Nevertheless, the puma was intent on chasing him far from her den. Pausing momentarily, she launched one of her great banshee screams; then she charged again, quickly catching up to the fleeing bear and raking his rear one more time.

The grizzly increased his speed. Once he was in top stride, he soon outdistanced the pursuing cat, who stopped suddenly. Standing still, panting, her tail slashing the air in sideways swoops, she watched the bear disappear within the trees, but she continued to stand vigil until she could no longer hear the sounds of his passage through the forest.

The kittens opened their eyes when they were ten days old, and with the gift of vision they became very active. The white tom was the first to attain sight. His eyes had opened slowly during midmorning, when his mother was out in the cave scraping clean the bones of the coyote that she had killed and dragged home five days earlier.

At first, the kitten did not realize what was happening when a corner of his left eye suddenly became slitted. He rubbed the eye with one paw, causing the lid to part a little more. Made restless and fearful by the new experience, the white kitten kept hiding his head against the bodies of his siblings, his behavior causing the lids of both eyes to part fraction by fraction. After an hour, he discovered that he could open his eyes fully, and, although only a meager amount of dim light penetrated the nesting chamber from the outside, there was enough for him to see his surroundings for the first time. He immediately became afraid and once again buried his face in the bodies of his sisters, but the temptation to repeat the new and mysterious experience soon caused him to lift his head so as to stare at the chamber's doorway, its brightest area. As he held his gaze steady, his eyes became gradually accustomed to the filtered glow. As soon as he was able to discern form, he became extremely curious.

Leaving his sisters, the little tom began to walk toward the opening. His legs were stronger now, capable of bearing his weight, but he walked very unsteadily, for he was not yet properly able to coordinate balance and movement, or to judge the effects upon his gait of inequalities in the level of the den's floor. But, because his sense of smell had by now considerably improved, he soon realized that he could guide himself by the odor left on the rock by his mother's feet, which, as in all soft-footed animals, were well supplied with scent glands. Despite the fact that the body odors of his mother and siblings, like his own, were distinctive, there was a particular scent genetically passed on by the puma to her offspring that united them as a family, a subtle essence imprinted on each kitten even before birth.

Guided by such reassuring odors, the little tom slowly advanced toward the den entrance. He tottered a great deal and he stumbled, but he was determined to reach the source of light, dim as it was. At times, tired and faced by a sudden rise in the floor, he would flop on his belly, reach forward with his front paws, claws extruded, and drag himself up the incline. In such ways he made progress, but it took him seven minutes to travel the twelve feet that separated the nesting chamber from the short, sloping tunnel that led to the den's rocky doorway, and, afterward, a further two or three minutes to actually arrive at his goal.

When the kitten poked his head into the cavern, balancing precariously at the edge of the slightly elevated opening, he was momentarily blinded by a shaft of light that reached him from the main entrance. At the same moment that the glare robbed him of his newfound sight, his ears were shocked by the rumble of the cascade, a sound that was considerably muted inside the nesting chamber. Startled, he fell out of the den entrance, tumbling onto the cave floor and screaming as he rolled.

The mother cat was at that moment turning away from the coyote's meager remains, actually intending to leave the cave and start a daylight hunt. But, on hearing her son's anguished cries, she leaped toward the sound, reaching the unhurt but terrified kitten in four lithe bounds. Uttering a single, hoarse purr of reassurance, the puma picked up her son and carried him back to the nest. After placing him with his siblings, she lay down and allowed the young cats to suckle. Later, when the kittens were asleep, she padded out of the den, sniffed at the coyote's clean bones, and then, ravenous, left the cave and entered the forest. It was now midafternoon, a bad time of day to hunt, for most prey animals were bedded down and alert to the passage of a large predator, even to the supremely stealthy movement of the big cat. But hunger drove her on.

The stresses of pregnancy, and now the demands made by her kittens, had caused the puma to lose weight and had dulled her once sleek and shiny coat; large patches of hair had fallen out, exposing skin that was unnaturally scaly. And her belly sagged, her abdominal muscles not yet having recovered their tone after being stretched while she carried her unborn young. Had she been seen by a trophy hunter as she padded across the valley following a well-defined trail, her shabby appearance would have saved her from a bullet. Yet her looks were deceptive. Although she was in need of food and had lost almost thirty pounds, she was still healthy, strong, and as agile as ever. Before her pregnancy, when she was sleek and well fed, she had at times indulged herself, remaining idle, perhaps sunning herself on a rock or snoozing in the shade during especially hot days, even when she had been hungry, inherently aware that she had more than enough fat on her body to nourish her while she was, in effect, putting herself on a diet. Now, however, she was lean and very much aware of her own needs and of her responsibilities to her kittens. She was keenly honed, all her senses tuned to fine pitch, a superbly efficient huntress who this day would not give up until she had made a kill.

As matters turned out, luck was with her, for only two hours after she had left the cave she scented the remains of a bull caribou that had been killed by wolves early that morning. The pack, consisting of four adults and three of that year's young, had eaten their fill and then, as is the habit of these hunters, had retired to nearby shelter, there to sleep or rest until hunger prompted them to return to their kill.

The puma turned off course, the scent of fresh meat strong in her nostrils as she bounded along, careless of the noise she was making. Soon afterward she also scented the pack. Now she slowed, stopped, sniffed, intent on locating the resting place of each wolf. Satisfied, she continued to advance, adopting her hunting stalk and intending to reach the kill before its rightful owners were aware of her presence.

The odor trail led her through a thick stand of cedar, large trees whose skirts hugged the forest floor. She slithered through this tangled barrier like a ghost, using the branches and foliage for concealment. Presently, as the cedars started to thin out, the trail led down-slope to a small, rocky area where a scattering of bushes and wildflowers grew. In the center of this glen lay the remains of the caribou. The cougar stopped about one hundred yards away. From that distance she could see that although the wolves had taken a considerable amount of meat from the large deer, they had left more than enough to satisfy her needs.

The wolf pack's leading male, a large, gray animal, suddenly became aware of the puma's scent. Leaping to his feet, he was about to burst out of concealment when the cat charged across the opening and in three bounds reached the prey, straddling it and snarling loudly, her great mouth opened wide. She knew that she had been detected. The wolf emerged at that moment. He was followed by his mate, the lead female, behind which came the other two adults; last, and with more hesitation, the young wolves appeared. The puma stood her ground, ears back, tail lashing, her growls turning to banshee wails.

The big wolf advanced stiff legged, growling, lips peeled back to show his formidable fangs, and, like the cat's, his ears flattened backward against his head. His mate copied his behavior, but she advanced on the puma from behind, while the two subordinate wolves, a male and a female, in turn approached from a different direction. The young wolves, inexperienced and nervous, alternately whined and growled, keeping together and standing off to one side, watching.

Hackles raised high, the wolf leader charged the puma. She crouched, spitting and snarling, one huge paw raised, claws fully extruded. But even as she centered her attention on the male wolf, his mate attacked from the rear. The cat whirled and met the wolf's charge before the wild dog could bite. Instantly the female wolf veered away. Her consort at the same moment charged and snapped at the puma's flank. The cat turned again, lashing at the retreating wolf with one paw, missing; but as she did so, the other adult wolves charged her simultaneously.

The male, a husky animal, actually managed to snap at her rump, but the bite left only some red marks. The mountain lion again whirled and chased the attackers away. Now there was a standoff.

The wolf leader retreated some yards and sat on his haunches, tongue out as he panted, his amber eyes fixed on the cougar. His mate sat on the far side of the cat; the two subordinates and the yearlings followed their example.

The puma stopped snarling. Her ears became upright, but her tail continued to lash and her yellow eyes blazed defiance. When the wolves remained sitting, the cat crouched and tore a mouthful of meat from one of the caribou's haunches. As she began to chew, the gray wolf charged at her. This time, however, the cat ignored him. Beyond raising a threatening forepaw, she remained in a crouch and continued to chew. The male wolf retreated. The cat swallowed, tore more meat from the carcass, and chewed; now the female wolf made a charge but stopped about three feet from the puma's flank.

The cat had experienced similar confrontations with wolves. In some instances, the wild dogs had sought to appropriate her kills; at other times, she had been the aggressor. When a pack had been large, the wolves had usually chased the lion away. But with small packs, or when, like the one that now faced her, the group consisted of only a few adults and some young wolves, the puma had been the winner. In either event, she had never been seriously injured by wolves and had herself never quite been able to hurt her antagonists. The present contest, as all the others she had experienced, was more like a ritual jousting. The wolves were not willing to give up their prey without some show of force, while the cougar was not prepared to relinquish what she now considered to be her property.

Ringed by the wolves, all of which drooled as they watched, the puma continued to eat, every now and then stopping between mouthfuls to snarl a perfunctory warning and otherwise showing plainly that she was not intending to leave the remains. Noting this, the leaders at last gave up. Turning away, they trotted into the forest followed by the other pack members.

Later, after the sun had fallen behind the mountains, the puma secured a firm grip on the back of the caribou and started dragging the carcass home, a task that required more than three hours of hard work, for the remains weighed almost as much as the cat. Often during the journey she had to stop for brief rests. During two such occasions she fed off the remains, so that when she at last reached her cave, and although she was exhausted, she was not hungry and was able to go directly to her ravenous kittens, all of whom had detected her return and had immediately combined their small voices in dissonant chorus.

5

The cougar's young grew rapidly and became increasingly active. In early September, when they were five weeks old, the tom, at six and a half pounds, exceeded the weight of his sisters by sixteen ounces. Apart from being the largest, he was also the most active and venturesome and the most difficult to control. Whereas his sisters were content to wander about inside the nesting chamber, the white kitten took to exploring the main cavern whenever his mother was away, knowing full well that he would be ignominiously carried back into the safety of the den if he sought to sally forth when she was home.

Except when morning sunshine struck its entrance, the cavern was always gloomy. Its floor contained only a few boulders and no plants, and it was covered by the droppings and urine of generations of bats as well as by the bodies of bats that had died of disease or old age. These tiny, often rotting, cadavers soon became the white lion's toys; indeed, as far as he was concerned, they were the cave's only redeeming feature. He usually played with them outside the den, but at times he carried a putrid little carcass into the chamber, whereupon his sisters would seek to take it away from him. A fight would soon follow, a sibling argument that was invariably punctuated by much juvenile spitting and growling but was rarely accompanied by injuries more severe than a scratch or two inflicted by the needlelike claws of the contestants, who were unable to damage each other by biting because their teeth were not yet much more than pinpoints emerging from inflamed gums.

The puma soon became aware that her son's unruly behavior stemmed from the sterile environment in which the kittens had been born; she also knew that her young now needed to be in a more challenging habitat, perhaps a den that was not quite as safe for them but one from which they could better hone their feline skills while developing a sense of independence.

During one early morning in midmonth, preparing to go and look for a new shelter, the puma carried into the den a clump of bloody deer rib bones, for recently the little cats had started to eat solids, chewing lightly with their emerging teeth and scraping off particles of meat with their rough tongues. As she entered the chamber with the offering, they mobbed her, each trying to appropriate the gift, which was too heavy for any one of them to drag away. While her young were busy squabbling over the ribs, the cat left on her search.

Soon after their mother's departure, the kittens realized that they could not on their own drag away the huge prize and for this reason, as suddenly as they had started to squabble, they stopped, settling themselves instead around the gory ribs and thereafter chewing and licking noisily and purring at the same time. An hour later the female kittens went to sleep, curled up one against the other, but their brother decided to do some exploring.

The white tom had always avoided going near the cavern's entrance, mostly because he was deterred by the constant roaring of the cascading waters; but that morning, with the sun positioned so that its rays streamed into the cave, he became fascinated. Nevertheless, he at first stood near the den's doorway and stared at the yellow light, excited by the shimmering reflections elicited by the mist that perpetually curtained the cave mouth, but needing a little more time to pluck up the courage needed to advance toward the waterfall's fearful noise. While he was thus undecided, a cloud slid over the sun. The light was dimmed. The tom had not before experienced such an event.

Apprehensive and almost ready to scamper back to the safety of the den and the comfort of his sisters, he became calmer as the sun slowly filtered back into the cave. For a few more moments he continued to stare at the entrance, but when no harm came to him, he started to move toward the light. He walked slowly, assuming the stalking crouch. His tail, somewhat longer now than it had been at birth, started to jerk from side to side; he held his head low, chin almost touching the rocky floor, and he flattened his ears. He progressed for ten feet in this manner; then he stopped, a miniature of an adult cougar. His eyes were focused intently on the target area, one front paw was raised, and his silver whiskers were curved forward on either side of his pink nostrils, which were moving in and out as he sniffed.

The noise of falling water grew louder, but, inasmuch as he could not detect any danger, he began to advance anew. This time he covered about twenty feet before stopping, his stance much as it had been before. But the allure of the sunlight and the absence of hostile signs encouraged him, and he straightened his legs, raised his head, and actually ran to the cave's entrance. Reaching it and blinking at the sunlight, he was hit by some of the waterfall's spray. He jumped, wailed loudly, and spat in fear-triggered aggression as he retreated.

When he had backed away to what he felt was a safe distance, he again studied the situation. He licked his lips, tasting water for the first time. He liked it. Encouraged, he went forward again, and on this occasion he did not stop when the spray landed on him. He started to play instead, batting at the water droplets with a cupped paw, stopping often to lick the water off his pads, then batting again. As he amused himself, he continued to advance. Suddenly, he found himself outside the cave for the first time in his life.

The roaring water, the drenching he was receiving from the spray, and the vast, strange world in which he now found himself terrified him. Wailing, he dashed back into the cavern and did not stop running until he reached the den. About to jump inside, he paused, stared back at the sunlight, and turned toward it again. Four times did the white kitten gain the outer world only to become afraid and run back to his den. But on his fifth attempt, he advanced beyond the waterfall's spray and climbed over a large boulder.

Poised on the rock, the little puma stared in wonderment at the wilderness. The trees, the waterfall and the lake, the great snowcapped mountains, the eye-hurting sunlight, and the enormous blue sky across which drifted a succession of small, white clouds all formed an awe-inspiring panorama that at first occupied his attention to the exclusion of the sounds and scents that filled his strange new world. Then, as he was watching the scudding clouds, the melodious call of a fox sparrow put his hearing in touch with the environment. Moving his head in obedience to his ears, he soon saw the songster, a sturdy, brown bird with a speckled chest and stomach that was perched in a nearby fir, on an end branch that was about ten feet from the ground. Ignoring the small puma, the sparrow continued to sing.

As the kitten watched the bird and listened to the melody, he became consciously aware of the bewildering number of odors that were reaching him. He could smell the sparrow, the soil, the water, the distinctive aroma given off by the various species of trees, the weakened spoor of a variety of animals. These, and a veritable potpourri of other scents—some reaching him as mere traces, others strong and acrid—were all gathered by his nose and registered on his cortex, but they could not be identified. He became confused. Had he been born in a more conventional den, and thus early exposed to the majority of the scents and sounds of the wilderness, he would by now have been familiar with all of them, perhaps even able to identify their origins. And had he left the cave for the first time accompanied by his mother, her presence and behavior would have reassured him. As it was, confusion led to panic. He scrambled off the rock and raced back to the cave, there to remain until his mother returned in the late afternoon.

The puma had found a new den, and she intended to move her young to it that same day. During her search she had wandered erratically, at times climbing to examine likely slopes, on other occasions searching the lowlands, but always confining her attention to areas dominated by rocks. At first she had traveled to the south of Red Canyon Creek, but, by the time the sun had reached its noon zenith, she forded the waterway and climbed to an altitude of two thousand feet.

She was then on the west side of the Hazelton Mountains at a point where the creek swings south to join the Zymoetz River. There, seven miles from the waterfall, she found what she was seeking: a shallow cave whose entrance was wide and about five feet high. Its roof was domed at first, but then it sloped backward quite steeply to an area supplied with crevices, boulders, and small dead-end tunnels that would offer excellent shelter to her young should a bear or a pack of wolves seek to attack them. The grotto faced southeast. It had been formed by an ancient landslide during which large boulders, scree, and earth had paved the slope for a considerable distance. Few large trees had been able to find roothold in such inhospitable terrain, and, as a result, while the entrance was somewhat concealed by shrubbery, it offered an excellent view of the country that lay above the river, which at that juncture was visible a mile downslope. The cave would make an ideal nursery for the kittens.

On her return to the waterfall den, the cougar was almost immediately greeted by the white tom. Pausing only long enough to lick her daughters, she turned to her son, grabbed him by the back of the neck, and turned to leave the nesting chamber. The kitten, having already been carried many times in the same manner, hung silent and completely relaxed. Because she was in a hurry now, it only took an hour for the cat to reach the new shelter. Inside, she liberated the kitten, licked him, and then spat at him, inducing fear that caused him to immediately seek shelter in the deepest part of the cave. The puma did not tarry. She returned to the bat cave and collected her smallest daughter.

By nightfall the three kittens had been installed in their new home, had sucked a full ration of milk, and had gone to sleep. The puma left to go hunting.

For the next two weeks the kittens explored their new range, practiced stalking birds and rodents, wrestled with each other, and grew rapidly. By the third week of September the white tom weighed ten pounds and his sisters each weighed eight pounds. Soon they would be large and strong enough to accompany their mother when she hunted, after which they would not again have need of a den. Now they were seven weeks old; their tails had lengthened, the dark birth spots on the coats of the females were starting to fade, and the slight blemishes that had adorned the tom's white coat had almost entirely disappeared, so that apart from the dark facial markings and the black tip on his tail, his coat was snowy white.

Each kitten had already caught and killed small prey animals, the tom being the first to do so, when he stalked and captured a red squirrel, but the female kittens soon afterward managing to trap mice and voles, all of which were particularly active now that autumn was descending on the mountain wilderness. Subdued but beautiful hues were slowly being painted on the leaves of deciduous trees, and the needles of the larches were turning butter yellow. Late-ripening fruits, such as saskatoons, bearberries, and blue elderberries, were plentiful and eagerly devoured by bears and by numbers of birds, many species of which were now massing in preparation for their southward migration flights.

Early one evening, soon after the mother puma had left the den to go hunting, the three kittens were romping down-slope about one hundred yards from their cave in an area that was densely covered by a large mat of bearberry plants. The low-growing, creeping shrub in places climbed over boulders and partly up the trunks of dead trees and everywhere showed off its bright red berries against the background of its evergreen leaves. The kittens stalked through this carpeting of leaf and fruit, sometimes pouncing on escaping mice, on other occasions playing tag or rolling on the ground during short bouts of mock combat.

After the kittens had been playing for half an hour, and as dusk deepened, the smallest of them wandered away from her brother and sister and began digging at a rotting log, exercising her already quite formidable claws. Busy gouging great chunks of damp, splintery wood, the small puma did not notice the sudden disappearance of her siblings, both of which had leaped up-slope and quickly gained the shelter of their cave, a panic move initiated by the white kitten when his nostrils detected a strong, rank odor that, although he had not smelled it before that moment, filled him with a sense of peril. His larger sister smelled it also, and, inasmuch as her brother was already running, she followed, not pausing to analyze his reasons for escaping.

The smallest kitten, engrossed, continued scratching at the log. She did not detect the new, powerful scent—perhaps because her nostrils were filled with the aroma of rotting wood. Mere seconds after her brother and sister had run away, however, she heard a heavy, shuffling step coming from nearby. Turning her head, she saw the black bear, a huge, autumn-fat male that was emerging from behind a large boulder, his small, brown eyes fixed on her. Before the kitten had time to run, the bear lunged, flashed out a huge paw, and struck her on the left side. The powerful blow sent her sailing, lifting her six feet off the ground and hurling her among a tumble of rocks, where she lay broken backed and concussed. The bear had resented the presence of the intruder in what he considered his exclusive berry patch.

Despite the fact that he was not actually hunting, the bear would almost certainly have eaten the kitten had he realized that she was lying helpless only a few yards away. But he had come here to eat berries, as he had done at this season for the past four years. Single-minded about such an objective, he was satisfied once the small intruder had been tossed aside, and he immediately switched his attention to the ripe fruit, for, like all of his kind, he had a sweet tooth. In any event, he needed the natural sugars to help build up the fat reserves that would sustain his body after he had found a hibernating den and gone to sleep for the winter.

An hour later, when it was almost full dark, the bear was still eating berries. The mother puma returned from her hunt, carrying in her mouth part of the hindquarters of a deer. This time it was the bear's turn to be caught unawares. He was greedily eating berries seventy-five feet from the cave when the puma came out of the forest.

The cat was down-slope. She could not actually see the intruder, but she could smell and hear him, and through these senses she was able to determine his exact whereabouts. Setting her burden on the ground, she stalked to a part of the talus where large boulders offered concealment. Then she climbed, hurrying, but making no noise while ensuring that she continued to travel against the breeze, so that her own scent would not be telegraphed to the bear. Moments later she had positioned herself on a boulder to the bear's right but some thirty feet above him. Crouching, and after settling her haunches into position for a spring and staring balefully at the large bear to fix his position and determine her trajectory, she lifted off the rock.

The bear did not become aware of the puma's presence until her moving shape, a shadow darker than the evening skyline, was almost on top of him. Even so, belying his clumsy appearance, he was quick to swing around to face the airborne cat, at the same time rearing on his hind legs, his huge mouth opened wide, his great fangs ready to repel the attack. But he was too late.

The puma's front paws, toes spread and claws unsheathed, hit his chest while her body was stretched almost horizontally, a living missile whose sinews, muscles, and joints were locked in rigid alignment. The blow that the cat administered was powered by the full force of gravity acceleration and backed by her entire weight and a speed of more than thirty miles an hour. The impact was devastating. It hurled the bear backward and whiplashed his neck forward, almost breaking it. At the instant the puma's back feet touched the ground, the bear somersaulted down-slope, an incongruous, uncontrolled shape.

The cat collected herself for another leap, but before she was ready to launch herself anew the bear managed to regain his footing. He had been taken so totally by surprise that he was not really sure what had struck him so powerfully. Made dizzy by the enormous strain that the whiplash had exerted on his spinal column, he turned away from the berry patch and ran down-slope, staggering as though inebriated.

The puma checked her leap, remaining where she was, listening and sniffing. When she was sure that the bear had left her neighborhood, she turned and started the climb toward her den. But as she was walking parallel to the pile of rocks among which her kitten lay unconscious, she scented her, knowing immediately by the intensity of the odor that the little cat was concealed in that location. She turned, walked to the rocks, and found her injured daughter. At first she licked her, but, when the kitten did not respond, she picked her up gently and carried her up-slope to the den. Inside, after being greeted by the white tom and his sister, the puma lay down, allowing her son and daughter to suck from her while she continued to nurse their injured sibling, holding her between her front paws as she licked the inert little body.

The kitten died during the night.

In early October, just before the start of the big-game hunting season, Andrew Bell took off from Moose-skin Johnny Lake and set his Cessna aircraft on a course for Vancouver. He was going to pick up Walter Taggart, who was now fully recovered from his injury, although he was still having difficulties operating his prosthetic right arm.

The proprietor of High Country Safaris had paid Taggart's salary during the weeks he had spent in the hospital and afterward during the time he was receiving physical therapy as an outpatient and being taught how to use his new arm. Taggart had been assured that he would get his old job back as soon as he was fit enough to handle it. The amputee was grateful to his boss, but he was shrewd enough to suspect that altruism was not responsible for Bell's generosity. Taggart was right in his thinking, although he did not know that, as a result of his injury, High Country Safaris had received so much publicity that Bell's business had doubled almost overnight and now, months later, was still growing.

Walter Taggart had become famous; so had Steve Cousins, although to a somewhat lesser extent. Quick to take advantage of the unexpected and totally free publicity, Bell had immediately applied for, and easily obtained, official permission to expand his licensed hunting area; he was also allowed to construct three new lodges strategically located in his new territory. As a result, he obtained exclusive guiding rights to a region of wilderness that was 150 miles in width and 250 miles in length. With money readily loaned to him by the bank, Bell set about expanding his wilderness empire. He hired building crews and bought another Cessna. Construction of the lodges had been started three weeks after Taggart was flown to the hospital.

While all of this was taking place, Bell had received so many applications from would-be clients that he had been forced to turn down many. All of the applicants were wealthy men and women who ostensibly wanted to hunt and fish, but who were just as eager to experience the vicarious thrill of visiting the region where lived the puma that the press had labeled a man-eater. Bell hated turning away customers, but he was delighted with the advance bookings and substantial deposits that he received from the majority of those who had been turned down for that year.

Switching from autopilot to manual control of his aircraft as he approached Vancouver, Bell went over in his mind his plans for the upcoming hunting season. All his lodges were now completed and staffed by cooks, cleaners, and handymen. He had also hired six extra guides. These, added to the six he already employed, including Walt Taggart and Steve Cousins, gave him three guides for each of his lodges. Added up, these things meant that he could now cater to sixteen clients at a time. At $5,000 a week from each, he would gross $240,000 for the three-week big-game hunting season. In addition, he was fully booked for next year's seven-month fishing season, at the same rate, and, during September, he had catered to two dozen waterfowl hunters. From the rough-and-ready arithmetic he had done before leaving his headquarters, he knew that his gross income for the next twelve months would amount to more than two million dollars. Whistling softly as he brought the Cessna in for a landing after receiving clearance from the tower, Andrew Bell was a happy man.

Two hours later, accompanied by Taggart, Bell lifted off again. As the aircraft circled before turning on course for Moose-skin Johnny Lake, the resort owner brought the one-armed man up to date on events at High Country Safaris and showed him topographic maps of the region in which the three new lodges were located.

Taggart was familiar with the country surrounding the first new lodge, which was located on the east shore of Burnie Lake and only fifteen miles southwest of the Moose-skin Johnny Lake headquarters; he also knew the wilderness surrounding lodge number two, which had been built on the north shore of McDonell Lake, twenty-one miles almost due north of headquarters. But he had never visited the region that surrounded the third lodge; this had been erected on the northeast shore of Gunanoot Lake, some six miles north of the meandering Babine River and ninety miles north of headquarters.

When Taggart finished scanning the maps, he folded them and returned them to the elasticized pocket set in the passenger door, fished a cigarette out of his shirt pocket, lit it, and puffed in silence for some moments. Then he turned to Bell. "You sure got things organized, boss! But . . . where do *I* fit in now?"

Bell had set his course and put the Cessna on autopilot. Before replying, he too lit a cigarette. "Well, I decided to make you and Steve my chief guides. You get a raise, of course, and you'll have to go on guiding during the busy times, but it'll be your job to supervise the others, to scout the country for game, supervise the work crews in making trails and building line shacks and so on. And another thing. A lot of the pilgrims have especially asked to be guided by you and Steve. So, I have added a ten percent extra fee for your services and five percent for Steve's. You and Steve get a third of the fee as a bonus."

Taggart was silent. Slow to compute sums, he took a little

time to determine that his one-third share of a fee would earn him $166. "Yeah, not bad, boss," he said at last. "Won't buy back my right arm, but that ain't your fault, I reckon."

At that moment Bell felt sorry for Taggart. The resort owner, busy with his plans, had not as yet given much thought to the big man's condition, but now, looking sideways at him and noting how he was clutching the prosthetic limb with his left hand while staring into space, Bell realized that Taggart had been deeply affected by the loss of his arm. The man had grown up in a rough-and-ready world, a wilderness milieu where a boy of ten was expected to work almost as hard as a grown man. By the time he was fourteen, Taggart was already a veteran logger who ran a trapline in his spare time. Then, too, his father having been killed during World War II, he and two brothers had to hunt for their winter meat, and if they took more game than they were legally entitled to, nobody, not even the game warden who policed the region, took them to task, for survival in their hinterland world was precarious during the 1950s.

Bell knew these things about Taggart. He knew also that the man put great store on personal strength and on his ability to hunt. Now, missing an arm, especially the right one, Taggart was bound to feel incomplete and self-conscious.

Walter Taggart had gone to work for High Country Safaris six years earlier, and Bell had soon recognized that the man's outwardly calm personality concealed a smoldering, angry being who felt, and not without reason, that life had treated him unfairly. The outfitter's shrewd assessment was correct, but it fell short of the mark, for, beneath his seeming confidence, Taggart thought himself a loser. He had acquired this inferiority complex when, as a boy, he showed kindly interest in animals.

Unlike his father and his older brothers, eight-year-old Walter was gentle with the hounds and was captivated by birds and mammals, often incurring parental wrath when he was caught watching squirrels or birds instead of attending to his chores.

What was worse, as far as his father and brothers were concerned, was that he showed no interest in hunting, was repulsed by the bloody carcasses that they brought home, and was reluctant to help butcher them. Because of these things, he was labeled a sissy, punished by his father, and teased unmercifully by his brothers.

In time, Walt adapted. He concealed what he thought of as a weakness and hunted as eagerly as his father and brothers. To prove himself, he started to trap furbearers, and, when he discovered that he could make extra money this way, he extended his trapline. In his late teens he hunted expertly and took pride in killing, especially so because his skills surpassed those of his brothers. Now he believed that his prowess had at last made him the kind of man that his dead father would have been proud of.

As an adult, Taggart presented himself to others as a tough, coarse, and unfeeling man who had long ago outgrown any childish weaknesses he might have had. Subconsciously, he continued to feel inferior. Such mixed emotions turned him into an angry man. Nevertheless, he usually kept his temper in check. He was not quarrelsome, but he somehow managed to remain aloof while seeming to be outwardly gregarious. With clients he became loquacious and boastful, but he did not allow them to get close to him, although he gave them the impression that he was their friend.

Reflecting about Taggart as the aircraft droned northward, Bell conceded that the man was an excellent guide. His knowledge of the wilderness was superb, and as a tracker he had no peers. His clients rarely went home without at least one trophy animal, and many of them returned to ask for Taggart's services. But Taggart refused to guide women on big-game hunts, although he did consent to take them on fishing trips.

One day, when Bell had asked Taggart why he was willing to take women fishing but would not take them hunting, the man had wrinkled his brow, stared into space, and then, spitting on the ground after clearing his throat, said, "I don't reckon women to be much good out there in the bush, let alone shoot good. And they talk too much. Always asking about animals and all like that. Fishing's different. You put bait on the hook, take the boat to a good spot, and let 'em go to it. If they make a catch, you just got to net the fish, take it off the hook, put on new bait, or a lure, and do it all again."

"But, don't women clients ask questions when they're out fishing?" Bell asked.

"Oh, sure. They ask questions. But there ain't much to ask questions about out there on the lake. Maybe they want to know about a bird, or the shore, or flowers, but they ain't asking all manner of damn fool questions about tracks, and how come I know what critter made 'em and like that."

Bell realized that although Taggart was not an out-and-out chauvinist, he was unconsciously prejudiced against females, seeing them as objects of sex, as wives and mothers or as housekeepers and cooks, but not as beings who could take their places next to men in the wild country through which he guided his male clients. But the guide's reply made Bell curious about one of Taggart's accomplishments: he knew a great deal about nature, details that no other guides or trappers seemed aware of.

"You know, Walt, I realize that you got your knowledge about big-game animals and about trapping through experience, but how is it you know so much about birds and flowers?"

Bell was looking at Taggart as he asked the question. The big man's face went red, and he frowned. "Hell, I don't know. Guess because I'm out in the bush a lot," he said abruptly.

Bell didn't press the point. Instead he asked Taggart if he disliked women.

"Hell no! I married one, didn't I? No. Women's OK, but not

out in the bush. That's how my Martha died, y'know? We'd gone out to scale timber, camping out. When I was away, she went to gather kindling and damned if she didn't fall down a slide and kill herself!"

That reply ended the conversation, but Bell had seen Taggart's eyes become cloudy when he spoke about his dead wife. The man had emotions, he just guarded them carefully.

6

While Andrew Bell was flying back from Vancouver with

Walt Taggart, the puma family was resting inside a shallow cave near Kitseguecla Lake, a body of clear, blue-tinged water one mile long by a third of a mile wide that was located twenty miles northeast of the puma's second nursery and only twelve miles north of High Country Safaris' McDonell Lake camp, both distances being straight line. On the ground, however, within the labyrinthine mountain wilderness, neither animal nor human can travel directly to an objective.

To reach the valley in which the lake nestled, the three cougars had covered some fifty miles of winding, up-and-down trails, at times climbing high as they followed narrow passes before descending steep defiles, on other occasions padding along well-trodden pathways through gently sloping, lush valleys.

The white tom and his sister were now eleven weeks old and had grown considerably since leaving the waterfall den. The female kitten weighed fifteen pounds; her brother was four pounds heavier. Both had developed the graceful tails of their kind and were approximately three feet long from nose tip to tail end.

Two weeks earlier, the mother puma had led her young away from the rock den and had started to teach them to survive in the wilderness. The young cats were by then extremely active, strong, and already capable of hunting small animals and birds. They had also become skilled acrobats and climbers and had earlier learned to take refuge high up a tree when danger threatened, or whenever they felt insecure. Nevertheless, the evening during which they left the den for the first time to pursue the wandering life of their kind, the kittens had yet to learn many lessons. The first of these was taught to them quickly and with considerable emphasis barely twenty-four hours after they had followed their mother into the wilderness.

The family had traveled through the previous night and had covered fifteen miles by dawn, when the puma led the tom and his sister into the shelter of a thick stand of evergreens. Here they remained for the day. The mother dozed, her body fully relaxed but her ears alert for alien sounds. The kittens slept peacefully throughout the morning but awakened in late afternoon and immediately began to amuse themselves, playing or hunting the underbrush for mice and voles.

The day had begun sunny but cool, giving relief from the biting flies, but two hours after the kittens awakened, the afternoon became gloomy as the sun hid itself behind the western peak. These conditions allowed the tom and his sister to romp and climb without becoming overheated.

Later, as a succession of rose and mauve tints glowed and faded behind the western snowcaps, the wind arrived; it brought a promise of frost. It was one of those round winds that are so common in alpine country, the kind that starts out by blowing from a particular direction and continues to maintain its trajectory while traveling the lowlands, but rises abruptly when it is confronted by the mountains. Thereafter it rides over the lower peaks until it encounters the passes. Swooping left and right at the same time wherever two openings intersect, it enters valleys, courses through them, and sweeps upward again to rebound off the flanks of the mountains. Then it begins to whirl, a capricious, invisible will-o'-the-wisp that dances circles while creating dust devils in dry places and making spinning funnels out of fallen leaves.

The wind awakened the puma. She sat upright, yawned, and stretched languorously. Finished, she purred loudly, the special purr that summoned her children. The kittens were playing tag some distance away, but on hearing their mother's call they instantly responded, galloping toward her and making a race of it, each trying to outdistance the other, but arriving at her side at the same time. Leaping on the puma, the white tom climbed up her back and started to play with one of her ears; his sister darted to the rear and sought to trap her mother's jerking tail. The cat continued to purr, but more softly now, a sound of contentment and enjoyment.

Suddenly, she stiffened, dislodging her son and turning toward the north, her tail now still. She had caught the scent of deer. But it was quickly gone, dispersed by the wind. Nevertheless, the aroma had been strong, a tantalizing odor that immediately fanned to high pitch her latent hunger. The kittens had not detected it, but they instantly recognized their mother's body language—her pose, her intensity, the way that her ears and eyes were fixed on the northern trees while her whiskers curved forward on either side of her nose. Moments later she was ready to go hunting. In the absence of a round wind, the cat would have allowed the young pumas to follow her, but the capricious air currents made it impossible for her to follow a scent trail. She was going to have to search carefully, quartering the territory and orienting herself when she obtained a brief sniff of the quarry.

Hunting during such conditions required more skill and patience than she could devote to the task while encumbered by her often clumsy-footed and irrepressibly curious young, who had already demonstrated that, when on the move, they could become so intent on their own affairs they would ignore their mother's commands, which, during a hunt or in the face of caution, were always given by means of body movements and eye contact.

Before setting out, the puma turned to look at the kittens, her tail rigid and her eyes fixing a stare first on the male, then on his sister, telling them in these ways to remain within the concealment of the rocks and emphasizing her command by growling softly, as she had been in the practice of doing each time she had left them in the den. The tom and his sister did not want to be left behind, however; for the first time in their lives, they were about to disobey their mother's direct command.

The puma, accustomed to immediate obedience from her young, turned away after uttering her growls, assuming that the kittens would remain in place. But the moment she entered the forest, they started to follow her. The big cat knew immediately that the tom and his sister were coming. She stopped when she was barely within the concealment of the trees, then swung around swiftly. Snarling loudly, she reentered the clearing, meeting the kittens as they were about to step on the forest pathway.

Continuing to snarl, the puma raised a front paw, toes spread, and threatened the recalcitrant youngsters. Startled but evidently not at all abashed, the kittens stopped and sat on their haunches. Believing they would now remain within the shelter of the rocks, the mother turned around and resumed her journey. But the young cats started to follow her almost before she had completed her first stride. The puma swung around anew. This time she charged them.

The white tom was leading, so he was the first to receive a good slap from the cat's huge paw, a blow that sent him tumbling head over heels and caused him to wail in anguish.

His sister, noting the fate of her brother, turned about quickly and started to scamper for the rocks, but her mother overtook her in a bound and slapped her rump. The blow was not as vigorous as that delivered to the tom, but it sent her sprawling. Both kittens wailed in distress, although they were not seriously hurt. They scrambled to their feet and ran for the shelter of the boulders.

Growling, the mother followed them a short way; then she stopped and, facing them, waited until they had crawled under an overhanging granite slab. The cat then repeated her command. Afterward, preparing to leave, she turned around, took a few steps, paused, and looked back over her shoulder. She growled again. The kittens mewed distress; clearly unhappy about being left alone, they nevertheless obeyed. The puma padded away.

Three hours later and two miles from where she had left her young, the puma killed a black-tailed deer buck. When she had eaten her fill, she cleaned herself and then raked leaves and debris over the remains. Last, she urinated nearby to mark her ownership of the carcass before returning to collect her kittens.

Night had enveloped the wilderness. A crescent moon hung over the northern peaks, coaxing silver reflections from the ice caps and from the snow-mantled upper flanks of the mountains, but only a glimmer of light reached into the heavily treed regions.

About half an hour after the puma had covered her kill and left the area, a male black bear was drawn by its odor. Myopic by nature, the intruder's eyes were further hindered by the darkness, so he had to rely most heavily on his nose and ears, senses that were exceptionally keen and that had also detected the still-fresh scent of the puma. The bear was not really hungry. In fact, he was already butter fat and almost ready to find a shelter in which to sleep for the winter. But the aroma of fresh deer meat was too tantalizing to resist. So he let his nose guide him toward the kill. Nevertheless, because his eyes could not clearly identify objects located more than seventy-five feet away, he advanced cautiously, made uneasy by the cat's strong scent.

Stopping often to sniff and listen, the bear took about ten minutes to reach the debris-covered mound. Standing some six feet from the carcass, he scanned the neighborhood with all his senses, until he became satisfied that the puma was not nearby. Now he approached the cache, scattered the covering debris, and dragged the remains to another nearby location, there settling to feed.

Unaware that a bear was feasting on her kill, the puma rejoined her young, greeted them with purrs and licks, and then led them away, retracing the more direct route that she had taken on her return from the hunt.

Half an hour later, when the family was still five hundred yards away from the kill site, the cat smelled the bear. She stopped, scented the atmosphere intently, and cupped her ears toward the odor. A low growl escaped her as a muffled but continuous sound reached her.

After the bear had taken his fill, he had dragged the carcass under the full skirts of a tall cedar. That done, and feeling sleepy, he'd settled down almost next to the remains, intent on guarding the food. Before the cougars had arrived in the vicinity, two coyotes had been lured to the cedar tree by the scent, but when the bear growled a warning, the small wild dogs wisely trotted away. Mice, shrews, and voles also arrived. The bear did not molest these tiny opportunists, aware that they could not take much of the meat. On two occasions, lone dog foxes approached, detected the bear's smell, and veered away before he was aware of their presence. Soon afterward, the puma picked up the bear's scent and tuned in to the sounds of his heavy breathing.

For a matter of seconds, the big cat stood absolutely still; then she turned to the kittens, both of whom were crowding her haunches. She growled softly—the alarm signal. Hungry, the young cats did not respond quickly enough, and the mother made as though to attack. Recognizing the intent of her posture, the kittens climbed a tall lodgepole pine, its trunk without limbs for the first thirty feet of its rise.

Making considerable noise as they clawed their way up the scaly bark, the young cats alerted the bear, whose ears were every bit as keen as the puma's, even at a distance of five hundred yards. The replete and lazy thief lifted his head, listened, and sniffed, but because the puma was downwind he failed to detect her scent. He continued to listen until the kittens had reached the tree's branches and settled down, each on one stout limb. Reassured by the ensuing silence, the bear went back to sleep.

The puma had heard the slight sounds made by the bear's movements. She waited, an immobile, umbral shape barely distinguishable from the many other amorphous shadows that filled the forest. After some moments, convinced by the sounds of the bear's even breathing that he had gone back to sleep, she began to advance. Crouching, using cover, she snaked her way forward, moving slowly but unerringly toward the bear and her rightful food.

Traveling at about two miles an hour, the cat took three minutes to reach a location some twenty-five feet from the bear's hiding place. There she flattened herself, scenting and listening, waiting to see if the bear had become alerted to her presence. His odor was strong in her nostrils but static; the cat's ears continued to monitor the animal's hoarse breathing.

Inching along, the puma advanced another ten feet. Now she knew exactly where the bear lay; she could actually detect his bulk, a shape darker than the prevailing shadows, and she could see that, although the tree's skirts were thick, the branches did not present a barrier to a charge. She crouched. Carefully, she positioned her strong haunches so that they would ensure a smooth leap. She was ready, yet she paused to study the bear one more time. Satisfied that she would be able to dislodge him, she launched herself.

The puma's takeoff was controlled, for she was near her quarry and did not want to overshoot it. She rose no more than six feet from the ground, her outstretched body remaining rigidly straight for half the distance to the tree, then curving, her front paws, toes fully spread, reaching forward, ready to cushion her landing. Touching down just outside the cedar's spread skirts, she immediately leaped forward again, a small jump this time that hardly lifted her off the ground. But the forward momentum was powerful; it thrust her body through the foliage like an arrow.

The bear awakened as the cat charged, but before he could do more than lift his shaggy head, she burst through the screening boughs and hit him a massive blow with her forepaws, her full weight behind her stiffened front legs impacting against his ribs, causing the growl that he was about to utter to emerge as an explosive *whoof* as the breath was suddenly expelled from his lungs. At the same time, the force of the blow knocked him over, and he rolled outside his shelter. Stunned by the impact of the powerful and totally unexpected attack, the bear was slow to regain his footing.

The puma, on the other hand, was swift in pressing her advantage. As the bear was rising, the cat burst from the foliage and hit him again with her front paws, causing him to roll sideways and to continue rolling as his body passed over a rise and was propelled into a steep declivity. The cat followed. Bounding downward, she reached the bear as he again was trying to get to his feet. This time she slashed at his face with her right front paw, her long, sharp claws opening three deep cuts on the muzzle.

Stunned by the swift attack, winded, and pained by the cuts on his nose, the bear turned swiftly and ran from the puma. She pursued him for a short distance, but it soon became clear to her that he was intent on escaping. Satisfied, she turned around and passed through the cedar's skirts to check the kill; then, intending to go back for her kittens, she exited at the same place through which she had charged, only to stop suddenly when confronted by her young.

The kittens, hungry and lured by the tantalizing smell of fresh meat, had descended from their refuge as soon as they had heard the commotion created by their mother's first attack on the bear. They ran through the forest without concern for the noise they were making and forgetful of the command that had sent them to safety in the tree, where they should have remained until their mother returned for them.

Seeing them as she emerged into the open, the puma snarled angrily. At the sound the kittens crouched, aware that they were in trouble. The cat strode to them and cuffed each in turn, two swift but controlled slaps that caused the young cougars to roll over and over and made them wail in distress. But their punishment was not yet over. The mother advanced, fastened her jaws on the back of the tom's neck, and lifted him off his feet. The young cat went limp, hanging as his mother carried him to the foot of a nearby pine. There she dropped him, straddling him with her forefeet. She growled. Needing no second bidding, the tom scrambled up the tree. As he was climbing, his sister ran to the same pine and began scaling it, hurrying so much that she caught up with her brother before he had reached the branches.

The puma looked up and saw that both kittens were settled, each on a branch; she growled at them again. Afterward she returned to the kill and dragged it out from under the cedar. In full view of her hungry young, she settled down to feed, completely ignoring their plaintive mews. Another lesson in survival had been learned by the young cougars. Henceforth, until they were old enough to participate fully in the hunt, they would remain in place when their mother ordered them to do so.

Later, after the chastened kittens had been allowed to feed, the cat led them in a northeasterly direction, abandoning the deer's remains. She was reluctant to leave so much food, but the lateness of the season made it imperative that she and her young find a suitable range in which to settle before the arrival of winter. They needed an area where there was good shelter and an abundant supply of prey, and for this reason the cat was anxious to claim the Kitseguecla Valley. She knew the place well, having spent the two previous winters there, and she intended to reach it before it was appropriated by another puma.

Snow arrives early in the northern mountains. At first, during mid-September, it merely dusts the lower peaks; then, week by week, it creeps downward, its time of arrival and rate of descent varying according to the annual vagaries of weather. In the region of British Columbia occupied by the puma and her kittens, the snow that year reached the low country later than usual.

By the first week of October, the blanketing white had descended only as far as the upper lowlands, leaving the valley bottoms green but frost nipped during the hours of darkness. Under such conditions, stalking becomes more difficult between sunset and sunrise because the ice-coated grasses and small plants produce subdued but distinct crunching sounds when trodden upon by even the lightest animals; each step taken by a large predator may raise an alarm.

For the fleet-footed wolves, which run down their prey, the crackling rime poses no problems, but for animals like the pumas, which predominantly hunt at night and stalk their food or lie in ambush, the frost becomes an impediment. Nevertheless, like all other mountain lions that survive into adulthood, the mother puma had already experienced such conditions and had adapted to them, at first learning from her mother, later honing her skills and developing her own tactics.

Despite her dislike of getting her feet wet, wherever shallow, running streams were available—and there were many such creeks in that region—the puma used the waterways as silent pathways when she was following the scent of a prey animal during frosty nights. If possible, she would not leave the water until she was relatively close to her quarry, at which time she would advance very slowly, setting down each foot with great care, at first barely touching the frost. This caused the heat of her pads to melt the rime, so that when she allowed the full weight of a step to rest on the ground, no telltale crackling sounds emerged.

On other occasions during frosty, snowless times, the cat hunted in late afternoon, before the ice had formed on the grasses and shrubs, often climbing up-mountain and scanning the lowland terrain. When she located moving prey, she would race ahead unseen and unheard. Placing herself in a position to intercept the quarry, she would lie in wait. If she had judged correctly, the prey animal eventually approached the ambush; she would then strike swiftly.

All of her tactics kept her well fed most of the time, although she had to work hard to secure a meal. She was an experienced and capable huntress, but the animals that she sought were also capable and forever on the alert. Indeed, on the average, she was forced to make five or six tries for every kill, quite often having to hunt nonstop for three or four days before she was able to eat, in the process expending much energy and becoming ravenously hungry by the time she was successful. On her own, the puma had always fared relatively well, but now, as a mother with two dependents and with the approach of winter, she hunted almost full-time.

Four nights after the puma's encounter with the black bear, the snow descended on the lowlands. Small, lazy flakes began to fall shortly before midnight, while the cougar family was resting on a long, juniper-covered ridge north of the Kitseguecla River. The cats had eaten well that evening, for the mother had earlier surprised and killed an aging cow moose, a huge animal that she would not have been able to tackle had it been in good condition.

The moose was afflicted by an infestation of brain worms, nematodes that commonly parasitize deer, settling in their lungs without, as a rule, causing them much distress. Deer so affected usually rid themselves of the parasites in the spring by coughing them up. In the larger moose, however, the minute worm larvae migrate to the nervous system and settle in the brain, eventually causing a condition know as the blind staggers. In time, a moose so affected will die—unless it is first killed by predators.

The puma scented this prey during late afternoon. Leaving her young, she followed the trail until she sighted the cow, which was wandering aimlessly, stumbling a great deal, and shaking her head almost continuously. From a vantage forty feet above the moose, the puma noted the cow's behavior and knew at once that she could easily attack and kill her.

Working her way downward, the cat got into position and charged, leaping on the cow's back and quickly working her way to the neck, biting into it. One of her fangs entered between two vertebrae, severing the spinal cord and immediately paralyzing the animal's body. The moose crashed to the ground, pinning the puma underneath her. Heaving, the cat managed to free herself. The moose was still alive, but the puma bit deeply into her throat and tore out the jugular vein. Blood gushed into the cat's mouth as the cow's body trembled in its death throes.

After feeding on the warm meat, the puma cleaned herself meticulously, then, without covering the remains, she went to collect her kittens and led them to the kill. Later the family settled on the ridge, concealed by the shrubbery but within sight of the carcass, now covered with debris.

Curled up near one another, the three cats were sleeping when the snow began to fall. But, secure and warm within the shelter of the evergreen shrubs, they at first disregarded the drifting flakes. Later, as the storm became more intense and a northwest wind arrived to howl through the valley, the puma led her young into the shelter of a cave that was midway up a hogback ridge. From inside the cavity, the remains of the moose were out of her sight, but the cat was not unduly concerned. She knew from past experience that when a mountain storm arrives in full bloom, most animals seek shelter, and, in any event, the snow would cover the kill.

The wind dropped during the night, but light snow continued to fall. At dawn, the flakes were still drifting down, each six-rayed crystal adding to the foot-deep white mantle that covered the wilderness. Only a small breeze stirred the foliage at ground level, but moderately strong air currents swept through the upper atmosphere, pushing the massed clouds eastward and leaving in their wake a green-blue sky in which a few late stars hung like polished emeralds.

Soon afterward, the pastel hues of sunrise bedaubed the eastern skies, promising a fine day. The last dark cumulus vanished beyond the western peaks, and small, white clouds took their place, each scudding in slow and stately parade across the now deep-blue ether.

The cats awakened at the moment that the sun edged its orange rim above the tallest peaks. Golden light rays, reflected in miniature from each white flake, slanted into the cave. The puma was lying with her head on her paws, facing the entrance; she blinked when she opened her eyes. Next, she stretched, remaining supine, and she yawned, her mouth becoming a small cavern in which her tongue was arched and deep red and her fangs shone like polished ivory. Closing her gape with an audible snap, she turned to look for her kittens. The young cats were just rising to their feet.

The tom's white coat attracted the light. He shone like a silver sculpture as he stood, stretched, and yawned. Finished, he raised himself on his hind legs, flexed his front paws, and scratched at the rock wall, his claws dislodging bits of granite. Dropping back to all four feet, he padded to his mother and rubbed his head against her face. His sister, meanwhile, completed her own awakening rituals and then scampered forward to join her brother at the puma's side. She too rubbed against the mother, selecting one of her large hips against which to scrub her head.

The three cats purred in unison, the mother's throat making a loud, motorlike sonance that almost drowned out the more subdued, thrumming sounds issuing from the mouths of the kittens. In these ways the cougars spent several minutes greeting one another; afterward, the mother led her young out of the cave.

The puma plunged into the snow, which had formed a deep drift around the cave's entrance, opening a pathway for her young as she plowed through the soft but impeding white mantle while unerringly making her way to the moose carcass. Soon afterward the snow leveled off, allowing the young cats to scamper through it. Intrigued by a substance they were experiencing for the first time, the tom and his sister frolicked, at times play fighting and rolling over and over in the fluffy, white material, but now and then stopping to eat a mouthful of it, surprised that what appeared relatively solid quickly turned into water when it met the warmth of their mouths. The puma, meanwhile, continued toward the carcass. Snow was no new experience for her, and she was hungry.

Arriving at the food cache, the cat soon cleared the snow from the remains, scooping it away with her cupped front paws and sending it flying like a miniature blizzard. This attracted the attention of the kittens, who abandoned their games and galloped to their mother, getting in her way, yet trying to help, although their ineffectual batting at the snow did little to uncover the food. Moments later, the puma hunkered down and started to eat. The kittens joined her. The family fed well that morning. When the last mouthful had been swallowed, the mother again covered the carcass. There was enough meat left on the dead animal to keep them well nourished for the next five or six days. But as the tawny cat began to move toward her shelter, she showed signs of nervousness. Her whiskers jutted forward; her tail lashed spasmodically from side to side.

On awakening earlier, lethargic from her long sleep and made eager by pangs of hunger, she had forgotten the disturbing sounds that had reached her the previous afternoon. Her keen hearing had distinguished two different kinds of noise, the one a steady droning, the other more rapid and crepitant; she had immediately identified them. The droning was made by aircraft engines; the sharp, explosive clattering came from the motors of snowmobiles. The noisy, mechanical objects themselves had no meaning for the cougar, but she well knew that the sounds were associated with those beings who had chased her with dogs and had wounded her. Several times during the past three hunting seasons she had been buzzed by aircraft and chased by snowmobiles. She was not likely to forget their cacophony, nor the pungent, unpleasant smell of their fuels.

After she had taken a dozen strides toward the cave, the puma stopped, lifted her head, and listened. When she detected no alarming sounds, she swiveled her head to the left, then to the right, sniffing intently but failing to pick up the miasmic odor of exhaust fumes. Somewhat reassured but still uneasy, she led her kittens back to their shelter.

The tom and his sister, replete and made torpid, immediately curled up and went to sleep, but their mother stretched out near the cave entrance and remained on guard.

On the morning the puma and her kittens breakfasted on the moose carcass, Walt Taggart, a bulky sack draped over his left shoulder and his rifle slung on his right, left his cabin at sunup and snowshoed to a nearby slide, an area of boulders above which an almost straight wall of granite formed an ideal backdrop for a shooting range. Here, three weeks earlier, in a location that was clear of large rocks and four feet above the ground, Steve Cousins had fastened a number of makeshift targets soon after his handicapped partner had exercised himself back to moderate fitness after the debilitating weeks in the hospital.

The laconic guide had willingly performed the task at Taggart's request, for, although the big man was by then able to manipulate his prosthetic limb with considerable skill, he was still having difficulty teaching himself to employ his left hand, instead of his right, when it became necessary to handle tools or to do other delicate work. Above all, Taggart was determined to learn to shoot left-handed. To that end, he had bought a new rifle in Vancouver, a five-shot, bolt-action Savage chambered to fire 30.06-caliber bullets, which was equipped with a left-handed breech.

Arriving at the impromptu range, Taggart set down the burlap bag, removed his snowshoes, and trudged to the rock face. Withdrawing from his pocket a roll of masking tape, he systematically covered the holes he had made on each wooden target the day before. When this task was finished, he returned to his shooting position, a large, flat boulder that rose to chest height. Picking up the sack, he walked back to the granite wall, staggering on the slippery, uneven ground. From the sack he withdrew a number of empty food cans, each of which he placed on a rock ledge or on top of nearby boulders. Now he returned to his shooting station, unslung the rifle, loaded it, and began shooting.

Taggart fired twenty cartridges within a few minutes, then, picking up the empty brass cases and putting them in a pocket, he went to check his targets. He was smiling with satisfaction as he made his way back to the shooting rock to collect his bag and rifle and strap on his snowshoes. His shooting, he now knew, was as good as it had ever been, perhaps even a little better, although he conceded that this might be because of the new rifle, a fine precision weapon that had cost him almost five hundred dollars. In any event, he was now ready to go back to doing what he most enjoyed, guiding hunters and, on the side, making extra money by poaching, a practice he did not consider illicit.

Walter Taggart, like quite a number of other men who grow up in the wilderness, had become convinced that his environment and the animals it contained were a part of his heritage and so could be used at his will. Poaching was a way of life; it put food on the table and money in the pocket. As he often said to Steve Cousins, he was damned if he was going to let "a bunch of city-slicker bleeding hearts" tell him what to do.

Neither Taggart nor Cousins was an evil man. Indeed, outside of their abuse of the environment, they were generally good-natured and always willing to lend a helping hand to people in distress. That they were also quick to anger and at times provoked into violent behavior stemmed more from their upbringing than from any conscious desire to inflict hurt. Taggart and Cousins still adhered to beliefs proven false by the advance of biological knowledge, but, living in isolation as they did and educated only to the grade-eight level in single-room hinterland schools in which biology formed no part of the curriculum, they were unable to understand the need for conservation.

They did, however, realize that animals are sentient beings who feel pain and sorrow and who are also entitled to their place in the sun. But whereas Cousins was not willfully cruel and was critical of Taggart or others who needlessly caused animals to suffer, his partner hid his feelings and at times deliberately committed brutal acts in order to prove that he was tough and uncaring, behavior that he justified when challenged by Cousins by pointing out how many city-dwelling hunters and fishermen entered the wilderness at least once a year in order to kill animals in the name of sport.

Taggart was not the only one to hold such a view; the majority of outfitter-guides held their clients in contempt, although they were all glad to take their money and to drink their whiskey. But they felt—and not without reason—that the "city slickers" were physically too weak and environmentally too ignorant to face the wilderness alone and on its own terms. They also resented the "pilgrims," as they so often referred to their clients, because, by and large, they killed only to obtain trophy heads or skins, usually leaving the meat to rot or to serve as bait that would bring other animals into their gun sights.

As he returned home that morning, Taggart was thinking about the forthcoming hunting season and about the clients who would soon fill all the lodges. More particularly, he wondered how many of the new arrivals could be induced to put up extra cash in order to hunt illegally once they had filled the quotas prescribed by their licenses. Musing in this vein, he decided that the time had come to take his partner into his confidence, to tell Cousins about the man who had come to see him in his private hospital room three weeks after his arm had been amputated.

Taggart had by that time become accustomed to visitors, the majority of whom were journalists, but one afternoon he received a different kind of visitor, a heavyset man who spoke with a pronounced American accent and who was much better dressed than the average journalist. At Taggart's bedside, the man thrust out soft, well-manicured fingers and delivered a perfunctory handshake. He then introduced himself. "Hi, fella, how're you doing? I'm Joe."

Joe then said that he had come from Seattle, Washington, especially to meet Taggart. He had watched a number of television interviews and read newspaper accounts about the injured man and had been impressed with his views. He had, in fact, become particularly interested in Mr. Taggart. What was more, he wanted to make him a business offer.

It turned out that the mysterious Joe—the man would not give his last name, and Taggart wondered if Joe was even his proper first name—was a dealer in animal parts for illicit export to the Far East.

Taggart was interested, but he had never heard of animal parts being exported to Asia. "What d'you mean, 'animal parts'? Why would anyone want to ship that kind of stuff to China?" he asked.

For centuries, Joe explained, some Asian peoples had been using certain parts of certain animals for medicinal or erotic purposes. The genitalia of bears and other large predators were prized aphrodisiacs; the gall bladders of bears were believed to have powerful medicinal properties; so were the antlers of deer, caribou, and even moose, which were ground to powder and mixed with other supposedly curative ingredients. For necklaces, bracelets, and exotic key chains, the claws of bears, lynx, and wolverines were also in demand, as were the canine teeth of all these animals.

There was a lot of money to be made exporting animal parts. The only problem, Joe explained, was that although Canada did not forbid the export of such items, because each province had the right to administer its own wildlife laws, the federal government of the United States had within its powers the right to control this trade and had done so.

"The feds in your country," said Joe, "they ain't got clout. They can only stop the *import* of those animals and their parts that are figured to be endangered species. But the Washington feds, they have got clout! The Fish and Wildlife Service has an enforcement outfit that's tough and spread all over the country, and those guys work with the customs at all the border crossings."

Joe paused to light a cigarette, then, exhaling smoke and smiling, he added, "Us now, well, we're *organized*! We've operated for six years and never been nailed. There's lots of poachers in America, you know, but most of them aren't organized. They get nailed, and the fines are big and the jail terms long. But they can't even get a *smell* of what we're doing. You guys, why, all you got to worry about is the provincial enforcement guys. And there aren't many of them in British Columbia, and they can only nail you if they catch you poaching."

The upshot of Joe's visit was that Taggart agreed to supply as many gall bladders, antlers, genitalia, claws, pelts, and heads as he and Cousins could gather. The bladders and genitals were to be sun dried between spring and autumn, or dried in a slow oven in winter. Joe would also buy the skins of bears, wolves, and, especially, pumas.

Joe then told Taggart that he would receive one hundred dollars for a bear bladder, twenty-five dollars for genitalia, and ten dollars for each antler. Bear and wolf skins and heads would net fifty dollars and good puma hides with heads attached, one hundred dollars.

"How do I get paid?" Taggart asked, his question showing that he was already committed to the scheme. "And how do I get the stuff to you?"

"First, pal, *we* come to get the parts. By helicopter. All you have to do is get to a phone and call this number." Joe handed Taggart a printed card bearing only a 206 area code and a telephone number.

"When you call, you have to have a topographic map and you have to find a good spot for a chopper to land. You give the coordinates to the guy who answers the phone. Just the numbers, OK? You don't say anything else. Like, you say: 'fifty-six-twenty-two-five and one-twenty-eight-forty-four-two,' or whatever numbers you figure out for the landing pad.

"The first set of numbers are for the north latitude, the second set for the west longitude. The coordinates have to be exact. I guess you know how to read a top map and plot the numbers?"

Taggart nodded yes. Joe continued. "As for getting paid, it's cash on the nail. After the pilot checks the stuff and gets it loaded, he gives you the dough. And, hey! This is important! When you call the number, no matter who answers, you say: 'This is Tag. I got a message for Joe.' Get it? Tag, that's you. You don't say nothing more. Just those words. Then you give the numbers. And when whoever answers the phone says 'OK,' you hang up."

Joe paused and gave Taggart a hard stare. "Another thing, pal. We fetch and carry and we pay, but you're on your own in this. You get nailed, you take the heat. OK?"

Taggart had readily agreed. He and Cousins had been operating outside the law for so long that he had little fear of getting caught in the mountain wilderness.

Now, as he neared his cabin, he was looking forward to planning this new enterprise with Cousins, who, Taggart was sure, would jump at the chance to make some extra easy money. The beauty of the scheme, he thought, was that they could save the bladders and genitals of bears and the genitals of other animals that were shot by clients, and they could also kill animals for their parts, hides, and antlers from early autumn to early spring, when their coats were in prime condition.

Soon after arriving home from the hospital, Taggart had picked out a good landing site for the helicopter, a small clearing some four miles south of the main lodge at the junction of the Thautil River and Denys Loljuh Creek. The coordinates were 54-7-0 north and 127-17-0 west. All he and Cousins had to do now was build a small shack in which to store the parts and hides. He planned a building with an almost flat roof on which, during sunny weather, they could dry the bladders and genitals. A small, gasoline-fueled camp oven that he owned would do for drying the parts at other times.

7

During first light four days after the puma and her kittens had settled in the Kitseguecla Valley and as they were returning to the cave after having taken their last meal from the moose carcass, the guns of autumn began to speak. The rifle fire was sporadic. It began with two closely spaced reports that came from the south and were followed only seconds later by a single shot that issued from the west. Several minutes of silence followed. Then, from different locations, at intervals, more reports disturbed the wilderness. Each staccato bark was immediately bounced off the mountains, channeled into the canyons, and pushed into the valleys, the concussive echoes becoming gradually weaker as they rose above the peaks and thereafter became lost in space.

The instant the first reports shattered the morning's stillness, the puma bounded at full speed toward her shelter. The kittens, made fearful by their mother's behavior, ran after her as fast as they could, mewing distress, but they soon began to lag. When the puma realized that her son and daughter were falling far behind, she waited for them. As they caught up, she galloped away, but at a slower pace. Soon afterward, as more distant guns echoed in the valley, they reached their shelter.

Once inside the cave, the mother comforted her kittens,

purring softly while licking them and at the same time making a determined effort to control her own fears, for she knew that her alarm had been immediately detected by the young cats. Although the tom and his sister were comforted by their mother's attention, they remained apprehensive as sporadic rifle fire continued. Eventually, however, as the sun was slipping behind the western peaks, the shooting stopped, and the kittens began to play.

In late evening, two hours after the last shot had been fired, the cougar rose, thrust her head and shoulders out of the cave entrance, and studied the wilderness, a statuelike being whose keen senses were fully alerted. Several minutes later, mollified by the silence, she backed into the cave and lay down again near the entrance. The kittens were now asleep in their dark bedroom.

The puma's cave faced northwest. From its entrance, Kitseguecla Mountain, some seventeen miles away, was visible. Fixing her gaze on the mountain's snowbound crown, its six-thousand-foot peak still slightly haloed by crepuscular light, the cat watched the coming of blue night, remaining prone within the shelter's entrance until Venus emerged green and winking in a cloudless sky.

As true night mantled the silva, the cat turned her head toward the cave's interior. She could not see her kittens, but their scent allowed her to aim her muzzle directly at them. She grunted once, a soft, throaty summons that awakened the tom and his sister and caused them to jump to their feet and gallop toward her. The puma rose to all fours. She lowered her head and purred. Now followed a short greeting ceremony, during which the kittens rubbed against their mother and the cat licked first one offspring, then the other.

Afterward, the puma moved out of the cave. The hunting guns had warned her that she was too close to her enemies, those beings who, noisily and from a long distance, had the power to inflict pain. So she had decided to leave the valley and to take her young toward a west-heading canyon that, she knew, led to a large and secluded alpine meadow five thousand feet above the lowlands.

Traveling at a leisurely pace through the relatively flat, easy-going valley, the cats took an hour to reach the mouth of the canyon. Now the going was harder. The route was wide and the slope gradual at first, but after half a mile the way became narrow and steep and was in places blocked by slides that only surefooted animals could negotiate.

When the cougar family reached the four-thousand-foot level, three feet of snow further hindered their progress, but the cat opened the way for her struggling kittens and paused often to allow them to rest before continuing the difficult ascent. In darkness only slightly relieved by the white mantle that covered the wilderness, the cats toiled upward, sometimes having to climb almost sheer escarpments, on other occasions needing to make wide detours to circumvent areas that were completely blocked by huge rock slides.

The tortuous route threatened to exhaust the kittens before they were halfway to their goal, but, by allowing them to rest at frequent intervals, the mother kept them on the go, despite the fact that she herself was tiring.

If the steep, obstacle-laden climb and the deep snow were trying for the kittens, what bothered them most was the oxygen-thin alpine air they were experiencing for the first time. This caused them to gasp during periods of extreme exertion. The young female had twice collapsed following especially difficult climbs. On each occasion it took her longer to recover. The white tom was equally affected. He had almost fallen to a certain death while leaping across a gap, barely managing to scramble to safety on the far side before he collapsed, gasping. Undaunted, however, the mother cat persevered. Her kittens had to follow.

Eventually the nightmare ended when, after a grueling five-hour journey, the family reached the alpine valley. The exhausted pumas were at last able to walk on level ground, and, although the snow was just as deep here as it had been during their climb, the going was much easier.

Pausing only long enough to get her bearings, the cat led her kittens to the far, eastern side of the meadow, where a rock wall rose perpendicularly. At the base of this granite scarp lay hundreds of huge boulders that many years earlier had broken away from the rocky matrix. Within this maze of tumbled rocks there was a deep cave that the puma had used as shelter in the past.

Picking her way between the monolithic blocks and slabs, the mother led the kittens to within fifty yards of the cave entrance. Here she stopped, growled, and climbed up a sloping rock that was some nine feet high. The tom and his sister followed, and, once they were settled on the elevated natural platform, the puma growled again, giving them the order to stay. Then she leaped down and made her way silently to the cave entrance, which was partially blocked by snow.

The cougar stood in front of the opening and sniffed intently, her ears pricked forward, as sensitive to sound as her nose was to scent. When she became satisfied that the den was not already occupied by a large and powerful animal—such as a bear or another cougar—she advanced, pushing through the snow and stepping into an antechamber that was almost oval. It had a low ceiling, and it led to a short passageway that was formed by two enormous slabs resting one against the other. Beyond the tunnel, at a somewhat higher elevation, was a second chamber. This grotto was almost perfectly round and had a diameter of somewhat more than nine feet. The roof sloped away from the tunnel entrance; at the near end it was three feet from the chamber's floor, but at the far end only eighteen inches separated ceiling and bedrock.

Inside the antechamber, the cougar again checked for scent or sound of occupation. When she was completely certain that the den was indeed vacant, she moved forward with assurance, padded down the tunnel, and entered the pitch black chamber, giving it a cursory inspection. Satisfied, she urinated near the entrance to stake her claim; then she left to collect her kittens.

Minutes later the three cats lay comfortably outstretched in the dark grotto. They were ravenously hungry, but their need to rest took precedence over their empty stomachs. The exhausted kittens went to sleep minutes after lying down, but their mother remained alert for a time, accustoming herself to those sounds and scents that were detectable within the den and outside, in the immediate environs.

Had the kittens not been so tired, the puma would have kept them awake so that they could monitor with her the signals in this new place. Thc cat was, of course, aware that the influences reaching her ears and nose were the normal and unchallenging signatures of a given home site: the smells and noises made by small animals, the sound of the wind passing through particular trees or over rocks, and a number of other detectable but harmless stimuli of which, she had noted years earlier, each den site had its own special medley. Some were usually encountered in all shelters: the body odors of mice, shrews, voles, and weasels, and the fetor of their droppings and urine. All were fresh and strong in this chamber, bespeaking regular occupancy. Somewhat less intrusive, yet easily detectable, was a hoglike smell, which told the cat that since she had last used this den, a grizzly had hibernated in it, probably during the previous winter. Then there was the distinctive odor of porcupine, which wafted most strongly from decomposing droppings, black and oblong pellets that were mounded in one corner of the chamber. On top of the pile of its own dung, the porcupine had sheltered during the past winter, the fermenting droppings releasing heat that warmed the sparsely furred, prickly animal.

The puma inventoried all the scents in her vicinity before turning her attention to the sounds that were immediately noticeable. The soft breeze that swirled over the outside world coaxed muffled notes from the craggy entranceway; intermittently, the cat heard the stealthy, scurrying noises made by the feet of mice and voles; occasionally, a muted squeak announced that two rodents had met and had briefly argued over the right-of-way.

Without conscious intent, the cat identified and memorized all the olfactory and sonic characteristics of this den, a task that would occupy her briefly every time she reentered the shelter. The odors were the most constant and easily recognized characteristics of the den. But sounds that reached the chamber from the outside varied constantly, according to the strength and direction of the wind and to the particular sounds made by the passing of animals.

The signals she monitored that night were familiar and long ago stored in her memory, but the puma did not relax until she had completed her inventory. She was not in any way apprehensive, but she was inherently prompted to take mental note of all environmental disturbances at all times, especially when she moved to a new territory, or settled herself and her young in any part of an existing range.

Unlike humans, who, by comparison, possess limited hearing and inferior olfactory powers and who almost certainly would have been daunted by the challenges implicit in the making of so many detailed environmental checks, the cat did not quail at the prospect. Indeed, she never ceased routinely to examine her world in such ways. Nevertheless, since the shooting, she *was* worried about her ability to detect in time those beings who had once wounded her and who had now again invaded her world. In the more recent past, they had chased her with dogs on several occasions, and they had buzzed her with their noisy aerial machines.

Those experiences had been terrifying, but, after she had escaped unharmed, she had profited from them, for they had caused her to realize that humans are poor trackers when unaccompanied by their hounds. She had also learned that even the dogs could not match her superlative sense of smell or her superb hearing.

Not long before her kittens were to be born, riders unaccompanied by dogs had on two occasions passed near where she had been hiding. She had detected the men and their mounts by scent and sound long before she had sighted them, but neither the hunters nor their horses had been able to smell her, and, on each occasion, they had not heard her movements when she shifted position as they were passing within yards of her.

Before she mated with the large tom, and despite the fact that it was relatively easy for her to survive on her own in the wilderness when not harassed by humans, she had already been in the habit of routinely checking every one of the environmental influences that she detected. Prudence, she had learned from her mother at an early age, keeps the body alive and the belly full.

After she had recovered from the wound inflicted by Walt Taggart's bullet, memory of the shock, pain, and fear she had experienced made her more cautious than ever. Now, as a mother with two dependents, she had to be somewhat reckless in her hunt for food, yet she was aware that if her kittens were to survive, they had to be taught to be cautious, to be keenly observant, and to exercise their memories, even while engaging in routine affairs. So, outside of those times when it was necessary to be venturesome to procure food, the puma led her kittens cautiously and taught them by example; patiently, and hour by hour, she demonstrated the skills that would make them capable of identifying and storing a veritable cornucopia of environmental signals.

The kittens were also taught that the present was the most

important time of their lives. The past was useful because it gave them experience; it was therefore subconsciously attended to; the future, however, was an abstract dimension that held little or no meaning for them or for the rest of the wild beings with whom they shared the wilderness. Only by being constantly attentive to the present—to the *now* of every moment—would the kittens be able to encounter their futures. Fortunately, the tom and his sister had already demonstrated a great fascination for the present time scale while showing an almost total disregard for the future. As to the past, they had been born with excellent recall, so they profited from their mother's teaching and from the experiences gained during the yesterdays of their young lives.

Although lacking their mother's stock of natural lore, the small cats were rapidly becoming acquainted with the hazards and profits of their world, their avid curiosity continually spurring them on cautiously to investigate every scent, sight, and sound that they encountered. In recent days they had become more daring and, before their trek to the alpine valley, had occasionally left their resting mother to play or to hunt rodents in the adjacent forest.

Nevertheless, like all young beings, they were at times forgetful and inclined to be willful if they deemed that they could disobey with impunity; this was a mild form of delinquency that the puma was always quick to correct. After their long and arduous climb up-mountain, however, the kittens were only too eager to rest, and, by the time the puma became satisfied that no threat lingered in the vicinity of the den, they were already snoring.

Yawning silently, their mother listened to them for some moments; then she walked quietly to the entranceway, there to settle herself within shelter, yet in a spot from which she was able to monitor the outside world.

The moon hung above the western peaks, a yellow-green,

gibbous light that was between the full phase and the last quarter. Adding to the lunar radiance, the aurora borealis swept across the starred firmament, at one moment spreading in phosphorescent waves, at the next and with dramatic suddenness, changing into coruscating spears that swept across the sky in ever-changing angles.

Perched in the naked branches of an aspen, a great horned owl called five deep and resonant *whoos* that echoed within the puma's den. The owl called again, this time giving three hoots, pausing, and then uttering six more husky notes. As though in answer, a lone wolf howled, its voice faint, for it was rising from the valley.

The puma looked up. Her eyes found the owl at the same moment that the night bird's huge orbs detected the cat's movement. On silent wings the night bird flew away. The cougar lowered her head, settled it comfortably on her outstretched front paws, and went to sleep.

The distant, ululating cry of the wolf was repeated. And then there was silence.

8

At first light the next morning, two guides from the McDonell Lake lodge set out on snowmobiles to scout for game, their route taking them northwest of Hudson Bay Mountain along the east bank of Passby Creek. One man carried a portable radio transmitter-receiver with which he could keep in touch with the lodge and report tracks or sightings. The scouts had no specific destination in mind. They followed lowland valleys and climbed gentle passes, working their way northward and stopped often at elevated strategic places to scan the terrain with field glasses.

Three hours after leaving the lodge, the guides entered the Kitseguecla Valley and almost immediately found the tracks of the puma and her kittens. Following the spoor, they were led to the cave and from there to the by-now-sparse remains of the moose. Excited by their discovery, they radioed the news to the lodge, reporting the moose kill and giving it as their opinion that unless the adult puma was not killed, she would continue taking ungulate prey, which, in the view of the guides, rightfully belonged to the High Country Safaris clients.

The consensus at the Moose-skin Johnny Lake headquarters, where Bell was monitoring the transmission, was that the cat should be located so that two clients who had bought licenses to shoot pumas could be taken to the location by air. Acknowledging the instructions, the senior guide put away his radio and, with his companion, began following the tracks on foot. The spoor was easy to trace in the snow. It led the men down-slope to where several alpine creeks joined their waters with the Kitseguecla River. Here it became evident that the pumas had crossed the shallow water and entered the pass. Its opening, only about five hundred yards away, was clearly visible to the guides, and the route to it clearly signposted by the cougar tracks. Scanning the col through his field glasses, the senior guide noted that the route was clear of obstructions, fairly wide, and gently sloping. He decided that the pumas could be followed with the snowmobiles.

Retracing their steps, the men returned to their machines, started the motors, and roared away. They reached the waterways in minutes, splashed across them, and soon afterward entered the defile. But after they had traveled up-slope for less than a mile, the pass became narrow and steep and was strewn with boulders and landslide. The snowmobiles could go no farther. Dismounting, the men tried to continue on foot but very soon had to give up, radioing headquarters to report the situation. Bell ordered them to return to McDonell Lake. He would dispatch a scouting aircraft.

Before the guides were halfway back to their lodge, Walt Taggart was being piloted to the scene. The big man cradled a rifle. If the puma was sighted, he had been ordered not to kill her but to shoot near her in an attempt to drive her to a location suitable for landing an aircraft, or at least to a place that was reachable by snowmobile.

At first, flying low between the peaks, the pilot followed the relatively straight defile while Taggart hung out the passenger window and scanned the ground. Despite the cold that lashed at his face and caused tears to flood his eyes, the guide had no difficulty detecting the trails left by the cougar and her kittens.

But after only five minutes flying time, the pass rose abruptly and became too narrow for the Cessna. Lifting the aircraft's nose, the pilot rose above the peaks and was not able to level off until he had climbed above five thousand feet. Taggart could no longer see the tracks. But inasmuch as no descending line of spoor had been visible, he and the pilot were sure that the puma and her kittens had continued to climb. They kept searching the terrain.

Half an hour after leaving the main lodge, the Cessna cleared the peaks and flew over the alpine meadow. Circling the bowl-shaped opening, the pilot descended to three hundred feet. Taggart immediately spotted the tracks and was about to duck his head back into the cabin to give the news to his companion when the puma burst out of a thicket of young firs and dashed across the open space. Before Taggart could lift his rifle, the cat disappeared into the cave.

"We got her!" he shouted as he ducked back into the cabin.

The pilot was an experienced bush flier. He had already noted that the meadow was too small and too uneven for a landing. "No, Walt . . . we *don't* got her! There's no way we can land down there, and there sure isn't any way to get up here with a snowmobile. We couldn't even *climb* up here, man!"

Taggart did not immediately reply. Staring into the valley as the pilot made another circuit, he realized that the flier was right. He had watched the cougar disappear into the cave and now, as he scanned the snow more carefully, the relatively few tracks to be noted made him realize that the cat and her kittens had only recently occupied the meadow. He was also aware that there were no large prey animals in the area, which meant that hunger would soon drive the puma out of this sanctuary. As the aircraft climbed over the peaks, he turned to the pilot. "I guess you'd better radio the boss and tell him what's up. I figure the cat and her kittens will stay holed up until dark, then she'll leave. If we come back early in the morning, we'll be able to spot their tracks in the snow."

Apprized of the situation, Bell ordered the pilot to return. Knowing that the puma was accompanied by kittens did not cause him to call off the hunt. To the contrary, he knew that his clients would be even more eager to go after the puma, for, if they shot the mother, the law allowed them to kill her young, because they would starve to death in any case.

Nevertheless, Bell decided that he would consult the clients. If they were willing to pay extra for one or two additional reconnaissance flights, the pilots could fly Taggart over the region the next day, provided new snow did not fall overnight and cover the exit tracks. His clients readily agreed.

Shortly before sunrise that same morning, driven by hunger, the cat had ordered her kittens to remain in shelter and had gone outside to reconnoiter the meadow. When she had last visited this location, it had contained a number of mountain goats, but now, apart from mice and voles, the open area appeared to be devoid of sizable prey. Still, she searched the valley. When her search yielded only a few scuttling voles, which she ignored, she turned her attention to the lower slopes, making a complete circuit of the precipitous terrain that surrounded the glen. When she was somewhat more than one thousand feet above the meadow, she knew that her search was fruitless; there was no food to be had in the place. She began to descend, moving slowly and stopping often to scent-check marmot burrows and hollow logs, just in case she had overlooked one of the medium-sized animals that usually abounded in her world.

By the time she had descended to a level five hundred feet above the valley, the puma had made up her mind; she would return to the cave, collect her kittens, and leave the barren refuge, it being imperative that she find a safe and productive range before the coming of winter. Having arrived at that decision, she stopped to quench her thirst with snow, gulping down several mouthfuls. Finished, she raised her head and was about to continue downward when she heard the aircraft.

The sound was faint and would have been undetectable by human ears, but the cougar immediately deduced from its line of approach that the machine was flying directly toward her range. Even as she listened, the motor's tone and pitch grew perceptibly louder. The aircraft would soon be flying over the valley. She began to hurry, bounding from rock to rock and on several occasions almost losing her footing on the snowy cover. She had not yet reached the bottom when the Cessna swooped low over the opening. Startled and fearful, she slipped and rolled into a clump of young firs, then, disregarding her bruises, she immediately leaped to her feet and dashed across the opening, disappearing into her shelter as the aircraft started to rise in preparation for another pass.

Inside the den, the kittens were huddled together, terrified by the engine's roar, which filled the valley and reverberated within the confines of the cave. Lashing her tail, the puma walked to her young, lowered her muzzle, and licked them. She grunted, giving them the order to stay; then she turned and padded to the opening, there to stand monitoring the noisy machine that continued to fly over the meadow. She remained on guard just inside the doorway until the noise of the Cessna's motor had faded to a low throb, then, dropping to the ground, she slithered out of the cave, moving into the open as slowly and carefully as she would have had she been stalking prey.

Using all her faculties, she next checked the meadow for signs of man's occupancy, but only the lingering odor of exhaust fumes remained to mark the passage of her enemies. Still feeling apprehensive, yet emboldened by the absence of hostile signs, she rose to all fours and took three strides into the open, there to stand listening intently. After some moments, she became almost entirely sure that no danger existed in the immediate vicinity of the meadow. The sound of the Cessna had by now faded completely; yet she remained still, ears pricked forward, nose twitching. Waiting.

Several minutes elapsed. Then, almost in perfect unison, the nuthatches and chickadees that inhabited the meadow began to call as they flitted from tree to tree while resuming their search for the dormant insects and larvae that sheltered under scaling bark or in the cracks of weathered branches. Like the cougars, the perky northern birds had become agitated as soon as the roar of the aircraft's motor had filled their world. They had immediately sought shelter in silence. The absence of their almost continuous melodies had been a signal to all the animals of the area, for during the daylight hours the tiny and extremely cautious songsters still their collective voices only when they are greatly alarmed. Now, half an hour after the Cessna had departed, the resumption of their songs, and the slight, scraping sounds made by their tiny claws as they returned to foraging, announced the end of danger.

The puma had been waiting for the birds to resume their calls. When they did so, she was totally convinced that all was well. She turned and reentered the cave, calling softly to her young as she approached the den.

The tone of their mother's throaty, almost purring mew immediately reassured the tom and his sister. They jumped to their feet and rushed to greet her as she emerged from the passageway, each eager to lick and to be licked and both purring loudly. The cat lay down and allowed the kittens to play with her, occasionally using a spread front paw to trap one or the other under it so as to give each of the youngsters a thorough, comforting licking with her raspy tongue. When she sensed that the kittens were completely relaxed, she rose and led them out of the cave and then set a course for the far side of the meadow, where the pass by which they had gained access to the place continued westward, dropping steeply at first, then widening and becoming less inclined. The kittens, hungry and impatient, padded behind their mother, now and then mewing plaintively. The cougar ignored them. Experienced in the ways of humans, she was anxious to leave the meadow as quickly as possible now that her hiding place had been discovered.

Moving with easy grace and at a pace that was fast enough to make the kittens hurry, yet slow enough to enable them to keep up with her, the cat picked her way down the tree-clogged, boulder-strewn pass, every so often having to climb one of the alpine flanks so as to bypass recent landslides, areas that had been completely filled with splintered trees, huge boulders, scree, and earth. Such obstacles, and the encumbrance of her young, slowed the journey and made the cat anxious. On her own, even if discovered within the confines of the pass, she would have been capable of escaping swiftly by going up-mountain until she could find a hiding place, or until she arrived at a location where neither the men nor their hounds could reach her. Despite the fact that the col was well treed for the most part, the absence of a good place in which to hide her kittens should the noisemaking machine return urged her to hurry. But she knew her young could not go any faster than they were already traveling, so she kept moving at the same pace, controlling her apprehension while remaining fully alert.

Two hours after the cats had entered the westward-bound pass, the sun slid behind the peaks, leaving an absolutely cloudless sky that was bedaubed with orange-red in the west and tinted deep blue in the east. Noting that they were in a wide, well-forested part of the canyon, the puma decided to spend the night there, which was something that she would not have countenanced had she been on her own. But her kittens were tired; they needed rest even more than they needed food.

Looking around briefly, the cougar led her young toward the shelter of a thick cluster of firs. On the way, the winded kittens stopped to eat snow, panting heavily between gulps and immediately afterward mewing at their mother, reminding her noisily that they were famished. The cougar turned back, licked each youngster, purred, and then continued into the evergreens. There the cats spent the night, using sleep to still the gnawing in their bellies.

The puma awakened just as the dawn was beginning to displace darkness. In the east, the blue-black of night was already diluted by an admixture of jade and lavender hues against which the tallest peaks were silhouetted, their snowy caps blushing faintly with the first roseate pastels of day. But the puma was unmoved by the poetic splendors of a new sun rising. As was her habit, she stood immediately after she opened her eyes, yawning noisily and awakening her kittens as she did so. Next, she stretched languidly, first bowing her front quarters, then stretching her legs backward, her spine arching downward somewhat like a half-moon when its horns point skyward. Before she had finished, her hungry kittens mobbed her, nibbling at her mouth, alternately purring their pleasure and mewling with hunger.

The cat licked her young briefly, token caresses delivered almost as she was moving forward to lead the way out of the sheltering trees. Closely followed by the kittens, she cut through the forest at an angle and entered the trail some distance west of the point at which she had left it the night before. Now, because young evergreens lined each side of the declivity, the cat kept within the trees, maintaining a relatively brisk pace until, an hour after leaving their stopover, she led the kittens into the wider, less steep part of the col, a passage that in the center was almost entirely clear of vegetation. Here the going was much easier, but the cat continued to travel within the cover of the trees, a somewhat more difficult route but one that would conceal her and her young should the noisemaking machine return.

The kittens were by now exhausted and ravenously hungry, but the cougar kept going, anxious to put as much distance as possible between herself and the meadow and perhaps even more anxious to find a range where large prey was to be had. Onward she plodded, and the tom and his sister followed, by some supreme effort of will managing to keep up.

As the sun showed its rim above the mountains, the family at last reached the bottomlands in a region that the puma and her kittens knew well, for they were only one mile east of the Zymoetz River and a scant three miles from the nursery, located northeast of Red Canyon Creek, to which the puma had transferred the kittens from the waterfall den.

The straight-line distance from the alpine meadow to the end of the pass that they had followed was only eight miles, but, not counting the time they had spent sleeping, it had taken the pumas more than seven hours of fatiguing travel to negotiate the winding, detour-full route, a time during which they had covered twenty-seven miles.

As she was leading the kittens toward the river so that they could all drink water instead of having to quench their thirst with snow, the puma stopped suddenly, ears pricked forward, head held high; her nostrils twitched avidly as she scented the breeze. She had picked up the aerial spoor of deer. So had the kittens.

The white tom stepped forward boldly to stand beside his mother, imitating her actions; his sister, somewhat less venturesome, remained a few paces behind, her own nose twitching.

Apart from those times when the young pumas had hunted small animals, they had hitherto shown little interest in scent trails released by large, distant prey. It was evident that hunger had sharpened their senses, had almost instantly transformed them. The insecure, highly dependent kittens now displayed for the first time the alert and eager sensitivities of true hunters.

The puma continued to monitor the deer scent, fixing her line of travel. Despite her intense preoccupation with the task that lay ahead, she became aware of the change that had so suddenly overtaken her young. As soon as she had oriented herself, she moved forward without ordering the kittens to stay behind. She was tacitly allowing them to be her partners in the hunt.

The scent of deer, the manner in which their mother was moving, and the fact that she was clearly allowing them to participate in the hunt further affected the behavior of the kittens. Hitherto they almost certainly would have been inclined to play, perhaps even to become distracted by the sounds or odors of mice, but now, sensing their mother's trust and disciplined by their inherent predatory urges, they moved just behind the puma as stealthily as she was traveling, their whiskers projecting forward, their ears fully attentive, and their nostrils twitching. For the next fifteen minutes the family moved in that fashion. Then the mother stopped; the deer scent had suddenly become stronger. It was reaching her nose from several directions.

Experience told the cat that a band of deer, which had hitherto been bunched together while grazing or resting, were now spread out and moving in her direction. The light breeze that traveled the lowlands was fanning the prey's scent toward the cougars, creating ideal conditions for an undetectable ambush. The puma's eyes searched her surroundings. The cats were in a relatively narrow valley that interrupted the north-south run of the Hazelton Range, and they had stopped at a location where the skirts of two in-line mountains emerged from the lowlands within yards of each other to create a sudden and acute narrowing of the flatlands.

Standing just outside the ravinelike cleft, the cougar noted a rock ledge that overhung the narrow path along which the deer would have to travel if they continued on their present course. The granite platform was on the south side of the opening; it was covered by shrubby clusters of dwarf juniper that offered excellent cover. Located ten feet above the trail and some thirty feet west of where the cats stood, the outcrop could be reached by scaling a series of smaller ledges that led upward rather steeply from the forest floor.

The mother walked toward the rock face followed by the kittens. Surefooted and almost as agile as the adult puma, and now powered by a rush of prehunt adrenaline, the tom and his sister had no trouble keeping up with their mother as she climbed. A few minutes later the three cats lay concealed within the embrace of the blue-berried junipers; the fragrance from the pungent fruit was so strong that it would mask any traces of feline odor that might filter downward to alert the quarry. Soon after, they heard the approaching mule deer.

Uttering a soft growl of warning, a signal that told the kittens to remain prone, the puma settled herself for the leap. She lay within the junipers at the very lip of the shelf, but invisible to the approaching prey. Her hindquarters were bunched, the thigh muscles already tensed and corded ropelike under her fur; her chin and her chest were pressed flat against the stone, and her front legs were wide apart, their paws spread and ready to push her front quarters upward the instant that the powerful hind legs jerked into action so as to propel the body forward. The kittens, although obedient to their mother's command, had also arranged themselves in the attack position. They crouched side by side four feet behind the puma, their stances identical to hers and their eyes fixed upon the black tip of her sinuous tail, which jerked swiftly from side to side and advertised her tension as well as her readiness to charge, just as their own, shorter tails were doing. Apart from such silent and undetectable movements, the three cats lay still.

The puma, her entire being concentrating on the nearing odor of prey, now ignored her young. Her yellow eyes were fixed on the trail; her ears were tuned to the slight noise made by the small, sharp hooves of the deer.

Suddenly, the puma's tail became still. A slight tremor rippled over her body. Seconds later the deer came into partial view as they rounded a bend in the trail at a point forty feet from the ledge where a number of young spruces broke up the solid outlines of each grizzled-brown body. There were seven of them. Because the trail continued to be wide at that point, they traveled spread out; but, as they neared the rising terrain and the runway began to narrow, they were forced into single file, a move initiated by their leader, a large and experienced doe who changed her pace as she entered the defile. Three younger does and two mature, heavily antlered bucks immediately got into line behind the old pathfinder, but the seventh animal, a young buck wearing only one antler, lagged in the rear. He traveled on his own along the very edge of the pathway and had to weave around the shrubbery and young trees.

The general behavior of the deer told the puma that the animals were not alarmed and were merely traveling from one part of their range to another. As she continued to monitor their advance, she fixed most of her attention on the straggler's behavior and condition.

Without consciously itemizing all the reasons she had become interested in the buck, the puma was aware that his gait lacked the fluidity of that of the others, that one of his antlers had been lost early and that the one he carried was small and deformed, that he was smaller and leaner than his companions, and, particularly, that he was being careless and dangerously inattentive in not responding to the example of the lead doe. Taken as a whole, these signals caused the cat to select the laggard as her target, for, like all predators when given the choice of several prey animals at a time, she invariably chose the one whose behavior and condition demonstrated physical weakness or emotional distress.

When the leading doe was close to the narrowest part of the trail, she stopped suddenly and stamped at the ground with one front hoof at the same time that she gave a single, sharp snort. She had become alarmed. Her behavior immediately halted her followers. But the lone buck continued walking.

The doe, her body quivering with apprehension, had detected the scent left on the trail by the cougars' pads. She was about to wheel around and make a dash for safety when the one-antlered buck squeezed past her to continue walking through the defile. Seconds later he had placed himself in range of the waiting puma.

Even as the cat sprang into space, the old doe wheeled around and led her followers away. The buck, startled by the sounds made by his fleeing companions, and panic-stricken by the appearance of the leaping puma, ran forward, unconsciously putting himself in mortal danger when he reached the exact place upon which the flying cat's body was about to touch down. A second later the cat landed right on top of the buck's back. Her weight and the force of the impact broke his spine.

The puma and the deer became locked together as they crashed to the ground, and, for a few seconds only, their two bodies became a single, struggling mass. Then, as they came to rest against a large boulder, the paralyzed buck tried to lift his head. As he was seeking to do so, the cat grabbed his nose with one front paw and broke his neck.

The attack and the kill had taken only a few seconds, the action being critically observed by the tom and his sister, who had leaped to their feet the moment their mother had leaped from the shelf. Rushing forward, the two kittens had evidently intended to follow the puma's example and spring into space, but they halted abruptly when they reached the edge and saw the extent of the drop. Waiting until their mother had killed the buck, they then scrambled down to her as fast as they could go, made eager by their hunger as well as by the excitement of the hunt.

Before her kittens could reach her, the cougar fastened her jaws to the deer's neck, close to its shoulders, and picked up the animal's forequarters, dragging the heavy carcass out of the ravine and into thick forest.

Within the shelter of the evergreens, in a small open space, she dropped her quarry and settled down to feed without waiting for her young. But the hungry kittens arrived moments later. As their mother had done, they pounced on the prey and began to feed, at first not bothering to remove the hair with their incisor teeth, but swallowing it and the hide and meat just as quickly as they could wrench each mouthful away from the carcass. Later, when partially sated, they copied their mother's behavior, pausing in their meal to clamp their flat teeth on clumps of fur and tear the hairs out by the roots, in this way being able to eat without ingesting large quantities of fur.

Amid much satisfied purring that was now and then interrupted by feline growls when one of the kittens sought to snatch a choice piece of meat from the other, the pumas fed to satiety. Later, sitting by the kill, the three cats cleaned the blood from their faces, paws, and chests. Afterward, the puma led the kittens away without covering the kill, an unusual failure, which was prompted by anxiety. She knew, of course, that she and her kittens had been discovered, and her past experiences with man made her believe that her enemies and their noisemaking machine would return to search for her. So, instead of lying up nearby and returning later to feed again off the carcass, she led her young westward, keeping within the heavy forests for an hour, then settling down under the wide skirts of a large cedar.

9

Soon after the puma and her kittens left the deer carcass, one of Andrew Bell's smaller Cessnas took off from Moose-skin Johnny Lake, its floats making crackling noises as they shattered the light skin of ice that had coated the water surface overnight. Sitting next to the pilot, Walter Taggart was drinking from a can of beer. A pair of high-powered binoculars hung from his chest, and around his waist he wore a gun belt, the holster of which, fastened on the left, contained a nine-shot, .45-caliber U.S. government Colt automatic, an illegal hunting weapon in Canada, but one Taggart had obtained from an American client, who had smuggled it across the border.

Taggart did not hunt with the Colt; the weapon's range was too short. But he did use it at times to finish off wounded game or to harry an animal from the air so as to drive it toward a more accessible location, something that he was hoping to do now if the puma and her young were sighted.

Taggart believed that the cats would be spotted, and, when they were, he was equally sure that he and the pilot would be able to drive the quarry toward one of the numerous lakes that dotted the region, preferably one on which Bell's large, six-seater Cessna could land, for this aircraft would be needed to carry the two cougar-licensed hunters, as well as Taggart and Cousins and two tracking hounds.

When Taggart and the pilot had returned to Moose-skin Johnny Lake the previous morning, the lodge owner had already obtained the agreement of the clients. The search would continue, and the hunters would pay four hundred dollars for up to three additional reconnaissance flights.

The hunters, wealthy German businessmen, were repeat clients. This was their fourth High Country Safaris *Jagdexpedition,* as they referred to the hunting trip. They had readily agreed to Bell's surcharges, because on their last three forays in British Columbia, they had failed to kill pumas, and bagging a "big yellow cat" was something they really wanted to do. As friends, they would share the extra charges, but as hunting rivals, each wanted to outdo the other.

Having come to terms with his clients, Bell discussed the next moves with Taggart and Cousins. Both were of the opinion that the puma, encumbered as she was by two kittens, would remain in her den until dark.

"I figure she'll stay holed up until maybe dusk. Then she'll hightail it out of there. Unless we're unlucky and get another snow squall, we'll be able to pick up the tracks come morning," Taggart stated.

Cousins nodded agreement.

It was arranged that Taggart would go out with the pilot in search of the pumas and try to force the mother cat toward a suitable landing lake. If successful, Taggart would stay behind to monitor the quarry while the pilot returned, switched aircraft, and flew back with Cousins, the hunters, and two of Taggart's dogs.

The distance between Moose-skin Johnny Lake and the alpine meadow where the puma had last been seen was only thirty-seven air miles, a flight that at ninety knots took less than half an hour. Taggart was already leaning out his window, field glasses ready, when the pilot nosed the Cessna into the open area. As the guide scanned the swiftly moving terrain, he at first confused the puma family's westward-bound tracks for those left by the cat the previous day, when they had seen her burst out of the trees and make a run for the shelter.

"You're going to have to make another pass," Taggart yelled at the pilot as he ducked his head back into the cabin. "It looks like that damned cat is still in the den!"

Rising, circling, and reentering the air over the meadow at a slightly lower altitude, the pilot dropped the plane's right wing, giving Taggart a better view of the snowy land. This time the guide noticed the twin set of smaller tracks and realized that the cat had entered the westward end of the pass.

"OK, Charlie, she's quit the meadow. Head west, over the pass!"

The pilot again circled the meadow, at first keeping the aircraft high so as to avoid the peaks, then dropping into the pass and flying one thousand feet above the trees.

Taggart, his parka zipped up to his throat, the hood fastened tightly about his already scarlet face, leaned out the window and focused the glasses, but after five minutes of wind-buffeted agony, his eyes flooded by tears, he had to duck back into the cabin. Closing the window, he asked the pilot to tip the right wing downward again, so he could look through the closed window without using the glasses. "If the cats headed down there—and they must've done—I'll be able to see tracks with my naked eyes. I just can't stand that freeze!"

Flying at a relatively low elevation down a twisting mountain canyon is risky business. Charlie, although an experienced bush pilot, did not like taking such risks. But he was being well paid, and he knew that if he refused Taggart and they returned to base without having sighted the cats, Taggart would be quick to blame him. So he did what was asked, but, before dropping the wing, he climbed another two hundred feet.

Four minutes after entering the pass, the Cessna was approaching the firs near the place where the puma had made her kill.

Taggart spotted the tracks almost immediately. "The damned cat! She's gone into the trees!" he yelled at Charlie. "Hell, we'd better keep following the pass, pal. She's got to hit one of the valleys sooner or later. She's *got* to show herself!"

Doing as he was told, the pilot continued westward, and, against his better judgment, he descended to within three hundred feet of the treetops and continued at that altitude for the next five minutes. Suddenly, there came a yell from Taggart. *"There! There's one of her kittens!* I told you, didn't I tell you, Charlie? I said we'd find her. Quick, drop the wing. For crying out loud, *drop the bloody wing!"*

As he yelled the order, Taggart hastily opened his window and pulled the .45 out of its holster. When the pilot dropped the wing, Taggart leaned out of the window and began shooting, aiming the weapon in the general direction of the frantically running female kitten and continuing to squeeze the trigger until the automatic's magazine was empty.

The pumas had heard the aircraft soon after it left the alpine meadow, while the cat was leading the kittens away from the deer's remains and into the trees, but staying near the edge of the valley, where the traveling was easier. As soon as the sound of the motor increased in volume, she turned to go deeper into the shelter of the evergreens. The tom followed closely on his mother's heels, but his sister became fearful and disoriented. Instead of keeping up with the puma's quickened stride, she stopped, hesitated, and, as the Cessna's clatter grew loud, she dashed away in the wrong direction, running into the open just as the aircraft was approaching.

The sound of gunfire, too percussive to be drowned out by

the roar of the engine, and the *spanging*, quivering whine made as bullets hit solid objects, caused the panicked little puma to turn back, but, as she was about to reenter the screening trees, one of the steel-nosed slugs hit a rock and chipped pieces off it. One of these struck the kitten's left ear, severing its tip. The young cougar, pumped full of adrenaline by now, did not feel pain and hardly noticed the blood that ran down the side of her head. She continued to run, frantically looking for her mother and brother.

The mother puma, hearing the shots, looked back, realizing for the first time that one of her young was missing. She growled the "stay" order to the tom, who was also in a state of near-panic. He dropped flat on his belly within the skirts of a fir. The cat, not tarrying to ensure that her son had obeyed her command, ran at full speed toward the sounds that her frantic daughter was making as she galloped away from the terrifying encounter with the Cessna, which by then had climbed and was circling in preparation for another pass.

Mother and daughter met within fifty yards of where the tom was hiding. Pausing only to deliver a couple of brief licks to the kitten's bleeding ear, the puma growled, ordering her daughter to follow as she ran back to the waiting tom. No ceremony accompanied the reunion of the three cats.

The puma led the way into the deep forest at a fast pace. Fear allowed the kittens to keep up with her.

When the pilot once again made a pass over the valley, the pumas were more than two hundred yards away, now traveling due south. At Taggart's urging, Charlie Turner made three more passes; then he turned back. As they flew home, Taggart maintained an angry silence, believing that he could have killed the small cougar if the pilot had "hugged the deck," as he later stated to Bell. But the owner of High Country Safaris agreed with his pilot. The aircraft was too valuable to risk. And, as Bell forcefully reminded his employee, he had been expressly ordered *not* to try to kill the pumas.

Leading her young south, but continuing to travel in the shelter of the forest, the puma quickly realized from the sound of its engine that the aircraft was searching in the wrong direction. She nevertheless kept moving at a good pace, a rate she maintained for another two hours, long after the Cessna had returned to Moose-skin Johnny Lake.

The cats were padding through the forest that lined the east bank of the Zymoetz River, the headwaters of which had for centuries gathered at the foot of the glacier-covered Seven Sisters Peaks, a succession of permanently iced alps that form part of the Bulkley Ranges. From its start as a series of frigid mountain streams, the ancient river had carved for itself a tortuous route through the soil and rock of the region as it followed slopes and passes for thirty-five miles before it was made to turn abruptly west, to empty its waters into the boisterous Skeena River twenty-five miles later.

The puma was not traveling aimlessly. She was determined to take her young to a range that she had first come to know as a kitten with her own mother, and later as a two-year-old. To get to her destination, she first had to cross the river, but she could not do so until she reached its western turn because for the first thirty miles of its course a series of turbulent rapids made the waterway too swift to ford.

Pressing onward at a rate of about five miles an hour, the puma family took almost six hours to reach the place where the river flowed west. Here, three mountain creeks became one, their combined waters entering the river. The puma led her kittens across one of the shallow streams and at last allowed the exhausted and again famished youngsters to rest within the dense forest. Leaving them asleep, she went hunting, unaware that she was now only fifteen air miles from Bell's Burnie Lake lodge.

Listening, alternately testing the air and ground for scent spoor, the puma wandered slowly westward, following the south bank of the river and traveling through riparian flatlands. Tall tussock sedges, cattails, and rushes dressed the wetlands near the water, while the less moist ground sustained aspens and poplars. Both types of vegetation offered excellent cover to the stalking cat, who took full advantage of it.

She moved like a phantom, her coloring blending perfectly with the trees and grasses, her pace slow, her huge, soft paws making no sound each time she set them down. After taking a step, the puma would stop briefly to listen and smell; sometimes, as she was about to move forward after one of her momentary pauses and had actually raised one forefoot, she would stop abruptly in reaction to some scent or sound suddenly noted. Having checked and dismissed as harmless whatever influence had caused her to halt, she would complete the stride and continue the stalk, shoulders lowered slightly, nose aimed at the ground, eyes directed ahead. Through all of this, her erect ears continued to swivel, turning almost imperceptibly as they encompassed a 180-degree arc.

Eighty minutes after leaving her kittens, but having traveled only two miles, the puma stopped and lowered her body to the ground, flattening herself within the surrounding vegetation. She had scented a moose. The odor was strong, suggesting that the animal was nearby. And it was evidently resting, for the spoor did not waver but reached her nostrils steadily from one location. The puma started to crawl, inching her way through the vegetation with only occasional whispers of sound. She had covered some ten yards, and the scent of the would-be quarry was strong in her nostrils, its taste filtering into her mouth, when a sudden crackling of the brush made her think that the animal was about to run.

From her prone position, the cougar leaped upright and almost at the same instant charged ahead, only to stop suddenly, using her spread front paws, claws extruded, as brakes.

Instead of rising to escape, a huge bull moose lay on the ground. The animal was moribund, bleeding profusely from a hole on the right side of its chest, and from a four-inch gash in its large paunch through which parts of its intestines were showing. As the cougar studied the moose in puzzlement, the animal's back legs kicked spasmodically, creating the sound that had caused the cat to charge. Immediately afterward the moose became still, its large, luminous eyes open, its long, thick, bluish tongue hanging out of one corner of its mouth. Before the cougar could move, a shudder ran through the huge, chocolate brown body; the eyes lost their luminosity and turned up in the head as the moose died.

The puma padded up to the carcass. She paused, her nostrils flaring as she sniffed at the head. Tentatively, she stretched forward a front paw and clawed the head off the ground. When the inert animal did not react, she backed away slightly and with one swift slash of a clawed paw she disemboweled it, opening the abdominal wound to reveal fully the steaming intestines and stomach.

Hunkering down, she began to feed, quite unaware that the moose had been shot by one of the Burnie Lake hunters, but, although mortally wounded, had managed to escape. One bullet had lacerated a lung, another had sliced across its paunch, opening it but not lodging inside the stomach. Ravenously hungry and eager to feed off the unexpected and easily procured prey, the puma did not at first notice the lingering smell of gunpowder. Later, when she was partially sated and about to swallow a mouthful of the animal's lungs, her sensitive nose picked up the odor. She immediately leapt to her feet and backed away. But she did not run. Instead, she began to check her surroundings, sniffing intently and examining the nearby vegetation with her eyes while her ears swiveled rapidly from side to side. Twice she turned around to check other sections of the wilderness. Failing to discover any traces of her human enemies, the puma went back to her meal. Afterward, her stomach bulging, she returned to her kittens and regurgitated for them. When they had consumed what she had given them, she led them to the moose, whereupon the young cats gorged while their mother snacked.

The cats remained near the moose carcass for the rest of the day and through the night, feeding twice more on the providentially offered meat. At first light the next morning, they continued their journey.

Ten hours later, in midafternoon, the puma reached her destination, a large, sheltered valley at the eastern edge of the Coast Mountains, the source of the Kitimat River. The cats had traveled twenty-four miles and had scaled a four-thousand-foot mountain to reach this valley. The region was surrounded by tall, glaciered peaks whose meltwaters maintained a network of creeks that fed the Kitimat River during thaw times. Winter temperatures were relatively mild in the area, being influenced by an arm of the Pacific Ocean that reached sixty miles inland to end at the mouth of the river, but snowfalls were heavier, the warmer oceanic air creating heavy and frequent precipitation when it encountered the freezing air from the glaciers. As a result, most experienced animals migrated to sheltered valleys in the autumn, knowing that in exposed areas here the amount of snow to fall during a winter could total up to fifty feet.

Within the range chosen by the puma, large prey animals

included moose, mule deer, and mountain goats, which were distributed over some one hundred square miles. Wolves and coyotes also frequented the territory, although these hunters tended to range over larger distances. The puma was not perturbed by the presence of the wild dogs, but as soon as she entered the valley she began to search for signs left by her own kind, which were her greatest competitors. As she herself did, members of her species invariably left markers that advertised their claim to a range. These included urine sprays on rocks and trees and fecal mounds, which were made by raking earth and debris over their droppings. Such mounds are always present at the junction of puma trails, a dozen or more being usual in such locations, the most recent giving off the most powerful scent.

A number of times in the past, the puma had been chased away from an already occupied territory, but no other cougar had yet claimed this range. Having made sure of this, she immediately set about establishing her presence and claiming possession of the valley. First she sprayed urine at a number of boulders and trees, then she defecated at the entrance to the lowlands, thereafter making her first territorial mound. Her kittens joined her in these tasks, adding their own odors to hers, although their mounds were small and rather flat and their urine was deposited on the ground.

In that well-sheltered setting, safe from the depredations of human hunters and provided with sufficient prey, the puma family settled itself for the long winter, which was even now starting to exert its first pressures.

The arrival of winter in early October marked the end of the hunting season in British Columbia. It was a time when Bell and his staff became busy closing down operations for the year. Foodstuffs and other perishables were removed from all the lodges, water systems were drained and protected from frost, and last-minute repairs to buildings and equipment were made. Afterward, all the guides except Taggart and Cousins were laid off and returned to their homes in Smithers, Telkwa, and Burns Lake. Bell, as was his custom, collected his wife from their home in Vancouver and flew with her to Escondido, in southern California, where the couple maintained a permanent winter residence.

Taggart and Cousins remained at the Moose-skin Johnny Lake headquarters as caretakers. Their official duties were minimal, but since the addition of the new lodges they had to make periodic snowmobile inspection trips to each camp, principally to ensure that the roofs of the buildings were not overburdened by snow. On such journeys they also had to check on the two dozen horses used as mounts and pack carriers during the hunting season, but, as soon as they were no longer needed, turned out to fend for themselves during the winter in the Burnie Lake valley. This practice was common among hunting outfitters in other areas of British Columbia and in the Yukon Territory and Alaska.

Each spring, when the mounts were rounded up, new horses had to be bought to replace a number of the unfortunate animals that had starved to death, a seemingly wasteful and certainly cruel practice ostensibly justified because purchasing replacement mounts was cheaper than stabling the horses and feeding them throughout the long winter. Hay did not grow in the region. It was expensive to buy and almost as expensive to transport to the lodges. In any event, Bell and other operators, claiming that wolves or pumas had killed the animals, were usually allowed to trap or shoot the predators without a permit. The lodge owners did not much care what happened to the carcasses, and, since they paid but minimum wages to the men who did the killing, these men, like Taggart and Cousins, often kept the pelts and heads and later made a good profit by selling them to licensed clients who had failed to make kills. More commonly, the salted skins and frozen heads were smuggled into the United States and sold at higher prices.

Inasmuch as Taggart and Cousins were now the only humans present in the region covered by Bell's licenses, their periodic journeys to each of the three new lodges and their regular visits to the horses served as ideal cover for their poaching operations in the unlikely event that a provincial conservation officer should enter their territory.

Before the expansion of Bell's hunting territory, Cousins and Taggart had had less excuse for roaming the wilderness. They had illegally killed a number of wolves and cougars, but their forays had been limited by a relative lack of purchasers. Now, however, with Joe's offer to buy animal parts, they were looking forward to a very lucrative winter. Hibernating grizzly and black bears were easy to kill once their dens were discovered; deer and moose, bands of which usually congregate in sheltered locations before the arrival of the really heavy snowfalls, were also vulnerable.

The morning after Bell set off for California, Taggart and Cousins sat in the lodge kitchen discussing their poaching plans. Each man was sipping from a mug containing strong black coffee, which had been poured, partly stewed, from a large enamel jug sitting on the wood-fired cookstove, a huge appliance that also served to warm the kitchen and the adjoining dining room when stoked to capacity. Taggart, as was his habit, had added a generous shot of whiskey to his muddy beverage, a concoction he referred to as his morning "gunfire." He was taking his third swallow as Cousins asked a question. "Did Joe say that he'd buy the hides and heads of deer and moose?"

Taggart, his mouth full of almost scalding liquid, nodded assent.

"Then I've got an idea. We skin the critters, cut off the heads, and leave the carcasses right where they lie. *Then* we set traps around them; maybe four, right up close and covered by snow. That way we'll get us some wolves and coyotes and maybe some wolverines."

Pointing the mug at his partner while a big smile split his mouth and revealed his even, very white teeth, Taggart replied, "Great idea, pal! I got a better one. We'll get poison, strychnine would do, but 1080 would be a whole lot better!"

"Sure," Cousins answered sarcastically. "Where're we going to get our hands on poisons, 'specially 1080? You can't buy that stuff here, you know that. Strychnine maybe, but even then we'd need a license, and we sure wouldn't get one from the game department guys."

"You're right," said Taggart. "But I'll bet you anything you care to mention that *Joe* can get 1080! I reckon that guy can get just about anything. Tell you what, after the 'copter makes its first run, we'll ask the pilot to give Joe a message and I'll be darned sure surprised if he don't bring us some 1080 on his next trip."

Sodium monofluoroacetate—1080—is a virulent, chain-acting compound generally injected into baits or whole carcasses. Any animal or bird ingesting 1080 dies in convulsive agony, usually up to six hours afterward, depending on its size and on the amount of poison ingested, and any animal that later eats the poisoned carcass dies in the same way, although it may take longer. The partners were not aware of the extent of suffering caused by poison baits.

After a winter during which the snow had piled deeply in open locations and the temperatures had often plummeted to thirty degrees below zero, the land of the pumas began to respond to the advance of spring. At first, as the sun showed itself earlier, climbed higher each noon, and remained longer in the evening sky, temperatures rose above the freezing point during the day, though they dropped quickly at night. These variations gave rise to two different climates every twenty-four hours. During daylight, the sun-warmed air caused the snow to become soft and wet, releasing water that swelled the streams and made them gurgle as they coursed down the mountains. Toward the end of day, as the sun began to arc downward, the temperature started to drop and the thaw slowed; when night arrived, the land was once again gripped by the freeze.

On sunny days, which were now the rule, the snow turned soft, but frost arrived during late evening to freeze its surface, making it hard enough for the pumas to walk on without breaking through. Sharp-footed animals like moose and deer and goats, however, punctured the icy crusts, and for these the going was hard.

At this season hunting was good for the predators, especially because many of the prey, the old and arthritic and the genetically unfit, were half starved, some actually moribund. A number of such animals had died during the winter, and their ice-preserved bodies were uncovered as the weather became warmer. These carcasses provided fresh food for the pumas, wolves, coyotes, wolverines, lynx, and small meat eaters like mink, weasels, and shrews. Birds also took advantage of the freely available meat: the big ebon ravens, the gray jays, woodpeckers, and tiny chickadees and nuthatches, all of these hardy northerners feasted upon the corpses. Even such predominantly vegetarian mammals as porcupines, snowshoe hares, squirrels, and mice fed on the remains, supplementing their restricted winter diets with animal protein.

Gradually, yet with marked daily effect, the spring advanced, the reluctant winter retreated, and the stubborn snows lost ground, although the thaw slowed during the hours of darkness, when heavy, frigid air from the glacier-covered peaks traveled downward. But temperatures remained slightly above the freezing point at midelevations and somewhat warmer in the lowlands. The high peaks, however, continued to be snowbound; some of them would never be free from ice.

Creeks that for so long had been imprisoned by the freeze-up became fully boisterous during mid-May. They overflowed their banks and cascaded down the slopes with enough power to cause landslides in some areas and in others to uproot large trees from their moorings. The sound made by the fast-moving water was loud and constant; it roistered through all parts of the wilderness, and its echoes were repeated endlessly whenever a waterway trundled through a steep-walled gorge.

Occasionally, when a rushing stream was unable to surmount a log-filled ice jam that blocked a narrow defile, it backed up. As the water accumulated behind the dam, the enormous hydraulic pressure could not long be denied. At the moment when force exceeded resistance, the dam would burst, emitting a stentorian roar of protest. The sudden breach immediately released a furious torrent that swept all before it; blocks of ice, shattered trees, boulders from the banks, and red earth were all carried noisily downward by the wild flume, which continued to gather debris as it traveled the high country. Animals caught in the path of these lethal torrents were almost instantly battered to death; later, their pulped and torn remains would be deposited downstream, providing food for many other wild beings. The fury of such cascades did not diminish until the lowlands were reached. As a watercourse began to assume its more normal springtime width and depth, the flotsam it carried was gradually deposited on the banks or left wedged on the bottom. Free from these obstructions, the water flowed more quietly, its volume considerably reduced.

In the valley of the pumas, five alpine creeks that fed the Kitimat River began to thaw rapidly and almost simultaneously. Two of these became jammed within hours of each other and, a few days later, the jams began to break.

The resulting cataclysmal roars filled the valley, terrifying the two young cougars. But their mother had been waiting for these sounds. Experience told her that the bursting dams signaled warmer weather and a drop in the water levels that had for almost two weeks flooded large areas of the bottomlands. Six days earlier she had led her young to the top of a foothill that rose from the south side of the lowlands to an elevation of two thousand feet. Here, on the broad and gently rounded peak, the terrain was clear of snow and was dry, except for small pools that had accumulated in a number of rocky hollows, each granite basin offering a convenient supply of crystal-clear drinking water. Dead grasses and sedges, brown and slimy from their time under the snowpack, could not quite conceal the green shoots that were already reaching upward for sunlight. Marmot burrows were open, although the fat, hibernating rodents were still sleeping inside their nesting chambers; the buds of aspens and cherries were starting to unfurl, and dwarf huckleberries, alpine fruit bushes that only reach a height of five or six inches, showed stems that had acquired the rusty red hue which announces the upward movement of root-stored sap.

Two major features had attracted the puma to this place: it was safe from floodwaters, and, more important, the white goats had returned to the adjacent mountains after spending the winter scattered in small groups over a range that encompassed some four hundred square miles. The hardy mountain goats were never easy to hunt after good spring forage had returned to them the vitality that a hard winter had sapped, but at this time of the year they were a major part of the diet of cougars.

The three cats had survived the cold season relatively well, although there had been times of famine, days and nights when the snow came down as a smothering white fog that kept all animals huddled within shelter. There had also been occasions when, try as she might, the cat had been unable to bring down prey. But, on the whole, the family greeted spring in a healthy, if somewhat thin condition.

The young pumas were now almost ten months old. They had grown considerably since leaving the barren alpine valley and escaping from the searching aircraft, and they could now hunt independently, although they did so only when hunger drove each cat to fend for itself.

The white tom was more than six feet long from nose tip to tail end; he weighed sixty-eight pounds. His sister was five and a half feet long and weighed fifty-six pounds. The tom's coat was pure white, its dark birth spots having long ago faded. The black markings on his face and the sable tip of his tail contrasted dramatically with his milky body, giving him a vibrant and regal appearance. The female kitten, dressed in a glistening rufous coat from which all but a few dorsal spots had disappeared, was beautiful in her own right. She was svelte and more finely built than the tom; her face, smaller and less angular than her brother's, was distinctly pretty. Her amber eyes usually sparkled with kittenish inquisitiveness, but at times her stare became meditative and mystical. Despite her mutilated ear, the young female's appearance was in no way eclipsed by the tom's extraordinary coat.

During the last month or two it had become evident that the white puma was destined to be exceptionally large; it was also clear that he was quick to learn and far more resourceful and daring than his rather timid sister, who nevertheless made up in sagacity what she lacked in aggression. Time and again during periods of shortage, the young female tricked her brother into relinquishing a cherished bone or the meager remains of some small mammal that he had caught. On such occasions she would approach the male directly, as if she were about to contest his ownership of the food. The tom would immediately growl, showing his now quite formidable fangs as he warned her off. His sister would then exhibit extreme contrition, and she would crouch submissively; at the same time she would reach forward with her neck and head, and lick his face. Mollified, the tom would return to his meal, whereupon the cat would flop down very near to him, turn on her back, her legs in the air, and, inch by inch, tip herself toward him.

Employing such wiles, the young female almost always managed to nudge the tom away from the food, which she gradually covered with her body. The tom, annoyed, usually jumped to his feet, whereupon the cat would spring upright in a flash, grab the food, and dash away with it, her speed greater than his. As a rule, she would either climb a tree or back herself up against a boulder, preferably one that had a space beneath it. Inasmuch as among carnivores possession of food is undoubtedly nine-tenths of the law, the tom seldom sought to steal back his own property from his by then fiercely growling, defensive sister.

The pumas remained in their wintering range until the ice breakup was over and the floodwaters had receded almost entirely in most parts of the region. Large rivers, such as the Skeena, Nass, and Kispiox, however, were still running swiftly and in places overflowing their banks. At the end of May, the mother judged that it was safe to travel. At dawn, setting out at a leisurely pace, she led the young cougars out of the valley and began to retrace her journey to Kitseguecla Lake.

Because of her persecution by Andrew Bell's guides, the cat no longer felt secure in her old haunts, and she had recently decided to take her young and go in search of a permanent range, a place where the family would be safe from human hunters and where she would not have to dispute her occupancy with another of her kind. She did not have such a haven in mind when she set out en route for Kitseguecla Lake, but, because she was familiar with the country and knew where to find many hiding places within it, she had selected this area as a place from which to start looking for a new range. Still, she was in no hurry.

10

During the first week of June, the young pumas and their mother arrived at Kitseguecla Lake after an uneventful journey along the trails they had used on their outward trek. Traveling in a leisurely way, they had rested when tired, hunted when hungry, and at times stayed for several days in particularly enjoyable locations. Eventually, as they drew closer to their goal, the mother's urge to reach the quiet lake caused her to hurry.

Several times during the last stages of their journey aircraft from Moose-skin Johnny Lake forced them to seek shelter within the deep forest, but the noise of the motors soon faded, for the Cessnas were being used merely to resupply Bell's outlying lodges in preparation for the new fishing season.

A month earlier, at about the same time that the mother puma led her son and daughter away from their winter range, Andrew Bell had returned to High Country Safaris and thereafter had kept everybody busy at headquarters; this included Taggart and Cousins, who were, much to their chagrin, too occupied to take time out to accompany the pilots on any of the trips to the lodges. Nevertheless, both guides did manage to slip away for short trips, engaging in some out-of-season hunting of bears, moose, wolves, and deer, continuing the poaching that they had done throughout the winter to supply Joe with animal parts.

Their employer, of course, was kept in ignorance of the illegal enterprise in which his two senior guides were engaged and to which they had applied themselves to such good effect that, one month after Bell had left for his California winter residence, the men had shipped their first consignment of parts and pelts, for which they had received almost three thousand dollars. To earn that amount of money, Taggart and Cousins had killed eight wolves, three black bears, two grizzlies, five lynx, one wolverine, two moose, and fifteen mule deer. Only six weeks later, they had collected another load, this time being paid four thousand dollars, their success stemming from the fact that they had set leg-hold traps around the carcasses of the animals they had killed while collecting the parts that were to make up the first shipment. They were, of course, pleased with their successes, but they were also disappointed, for Joe had been unable to send them the poisons they had requested. The virulent substances were impossible to obtain without a license, and they were not available from black-market sources because demand for them was too low to warrant the risks that would have been involved in that kind of trade.

Although winter was over, the men wanted to make up one more load of animal parts. Besides, they were fed up with the chores that had kept them more or less captive at headquarters, so they were understandably delighted when one morning Bell called them to his office and ordered them to survey the northern part of his licensed region to assess the number of animals that had survived the winter or had migrated into the territory since the spring. Bell, like all outfitters, conducted such studies every year in preparation for the hunting season, for although he could not guarantee that his clients would be able to kill the animals for which they had obtained licenses, a count of the species that inhabited his hunting fiefdom was essential if he was to maintain the success rates that he had enjoyed in the past and that featured prominently in all his advertisements and in the glossy, illustrated brochures he distributed.

A month before he decided to dispatch Taggart and Cousins on their errand, Bell had ordered his pilots to do aerial surveys, but properly conducted ground studies, he knew, are more accurate, especially when one is seeking to determine the numbers of such animals as wolves, grizzly and black bears, cougars, wolverines, lynx, and mountain goats—all greatly prized trophies.

For Taggart and Cousins, the scouting expedition was especially welcome because, when the helicopter pilot had arrived to pick up their last shipment, he had brought a message from Joe, who wanted a cougar pelt with head attached. If the guides could secure such a trophy, even if the fur was not in top condition at that season, they would receive five hundred dollars.

Mounted and leading a packhorse carrying their supplies for the two-week trip, the guides traveled slowly, covering an average of eight miles a day and sleeping each night in a new location. Rising at sunup, they spent their days studying tracks and droppings and searching for the remains of predator kills, frequently stopping to scan the country through field glasses from convenient heights.

At noon, eight days after the puma and her young had returned to their summer range, the guides reached the Kitseguecla Valley at a point half a mile south of the small lake. Pausing to scan the open country that surrounded the blue-green water, the two men were about to spur their mounts onward when movement on the far side of the valley attracted their attention. Taggart lifted his glasses, focused, and was just in time to see the young female puma as she darted into cover. The young cat had gone to the lake to drink and was returning to the family's resting place when she heard and sighted the men and their horses. Panic-stricken by their arrival, she hurried to catch up with her mother and brother, who had been resting within the trees and had not detected the intruders.

Taggart got only a fleeting glimpse of the cat, but he was able to identify her species. Lowering the glasses, he turned to Cousins. "That was a cougar, Steve! Damn! If only we'd brought one of my hounds along!"

Cousins shrugged agreement. Without a tracking dog, it is impossible to stalk a puma in such terrain.

Because the Kitseguecla Valley was at the limit of Bell's northern territory, the guides decided to interrupt their survey and return to Moose-skin Johnny Lake to tell Bell that they believed the population of grizzly bears in the region had increased dramatically since their last study of the area but that they needed a dog to get a fix on the ranges occupied by each animal.

Six days later they were back at headquarters. Although Bell agreed that they should return with a dog to complete a survey of the grizzly population—such bears commanded large guiding fees—the lodge owner decided that they should postpone the journey until July because fishing guests were already arriving and he needed the two of them to act as guides.

Taggart and Cousins were not happy with this decision, but they had to accept it. Postponing their scouting trip for almost one month meant that they would have to call in the helicopter before they had a large shipment of parts; otherwise, the summer heat would spoil some of the partly cured organs. Above all, the delay would probably mean the loss of five hundred dollars for a puma pelt and head, for it was unlikely that they would be able to catch up with the cougar they had so recently sighted after such a long delay. Taggart and Cousins did not know that the mother puma and the white tom had also been present, and they certainly were not aware that the mother cat was the very one responsible for the loss of Taggart's arm.

Because the breeze had been blowing from the pumas toward the men and their mounts, and because the mother and the white tom had been within the trees and unable to see more than a few yards in any direction, only the young female had been aware of the intruders. The puma noted her daughter's apprehension the moment she rejoined the group, but, inasmuch as the young female had often been made fearful when she had found herself alone, the cougar ignored her agitation, which, in any event, was soon replaced by normal behavior when the young female realized that neither her mother nor her brother was alarmed.

The puma had earlier decided to remain in the region for the summer. She believed it safe, and she knew that the valley and its surroundings were inhabited by many mule deer, a number of moose, and a variety of other, smaller prey animals. Had she scented Taggart and Cousins, her phenomenal memory for odors, upon which all predators depend for survival, would have allowed her to recognize her enemies. She would then have led her young to a new range.

That same night, the pumas jointly killed an aging bull moose, this being the first time that the adolescent cats had actually participated in a hunt with their mother. In fact, on her own, the puma would have been unable to subdue such a large animal, despite the fact that his hindquarters were partly crippled by arthritis, a disease that affects all wild animals that live to old age.

The three cats had picked up the bull's scent when they were a quarter of a mile downwind of it. With the mother leading the way, the pumas loped silently through the forest, heading toward the Kitseguecla River, slowing down when they were only one hundred yards from their target.

The moose was at the river's edge, chest deep in water. He was doing his best to graze on submerged eelgrasses, thrusting his scarred head under the surface, but doing so only briefly. Each time he came up for air, he carried in his mouth a small amount of weeds, but instead of eating the food right away, he had to pause to breathe, his wide nostrils quivering and making audible, puffing sounds when he exhaled and hoarse, rasping noises when he inhaled. His labored respiration, his thin body and stiffened legs, and the awkward way in which he bent his long neck to reach the water were all noted by the cougars as they sighted their quarry. The moose was obviously old and in poor condition.

The pumas now walked cautiously through a finger of trees that led to within thirty feet of the river's edge, the screen of evergreens ending only a few feet away from where the moose was trying to feed. As they approached the quarry, the cats began to stalk, their sinuous bodies crouched low as they moved slowly and carefully, their paws set on the ground with the merest whispers of sound.

The moose was entirely unaware of their presence until the three pumas reached the open riverside, when a red squirrel that was sitting high up in a white spruce, watching their advance, suddenly gave his chattering alarm cry. The startled bull turned his head toward the sound, saw the pumas, and sought to gallop away. But his ungainly body had made little more than half a turn before the cougars launched themselves.

The mother cat cleared twenty-five feet from a standing jump; the white tom, leaping almost in unison, managed to span eighteen; his sister did not jump at all. As the larger pumas were traveling through the air, the smaller female bounded forward at her best speed.

Closely followed by her son, the puma touched down as the moose completed his turn in preparation to run. She leaped again from a position so close to the bull that she actually descended on his hindquarters. Her speed and weight caused the bull to stagger. Before he could recover, the white tom was on him, securing a grip with his front paws, one on each side of the neck and just behind the back of the prey's head. The moose crashed to the ground.

The puma released her grip on the bull's hindquarters, intending to go for his throat, but the white tom forestalled her. Holding on with one spread paw, he released his grip with the other, reached out, and gripped the animal's nose, twisting the neck. He then opened his mouth wide and closed it sharply on the bull's stretched throat. The killing fangs sunk in deep.

The attack did its work swiftly. The young cougar's right upper fang pierced the bull's left carotid artery. Blood spurted into his mouth, scarlet tendrils of it squirting out around his lips, despite the pressure his jaws were exerting on the quarry's neck. The bull tried to gain his feet, but the mother cat secured a hold behind his neck, her mouth almost touching her son's clamped jaws.

The young female had meanwhile joined the fray. Dodging a back hoof launched by the moose in a spastic kick, she fastened her mouth on his uppermost thigh and began to pull backward, bracing her broad paws against the ground, front legs stiff. Held from three quarters, his blood gushing from the throat hold, the moose died within moments. His head dropped, his legs stopped kicking, excrement jetted out of him explosively. The large body quivered once; as he died, his mouth opened wide in rictus. The three pumas maintained their holds for some seconds, then they opened their jaws and stood upright.

When the tom lifted his head, his face, neck, and chest were plastered in slowly gelling scarlet, the rich color of the blood contrasting starkly with his white coat. He licked his lips, his long, coarse tongue being almost as bloody as his fur. But, as his sister made to approach the bull's protuberant stomach, evidently intending to open it, he charged her, his lips curled back to reveal red-stained fangs. The cat retreated, and her brother raked the quarry's paunch with his right paw. His extruded claws ripped the stomach wide open, and the tom immediately thrust his head into the cavity. As he ate eagerly, biting and swallowing the soft internal organs, his mother watched him and his sister, perhaps recognizing that her son and daughter had now crossed the boundary between adolescence and adulthood. During the next half hour, the three cats fed, quietly for the most part, but making occasional ripping sounds as they pulled meat from the carcass and, now and then, emitting short, raucous growls when one was approached too closely by another.

The arthritic moose was almost twenty years old when he died. His sinus cavities were filled with botfly worms, and his liver had been attacked by flukes, which are the larvae of trematode worms. Worse yet, his nervous system had been invaded by nematode larvae, and, had he not been killed by the pumas, these would soon have reached his brain. In their thousands, they would have deprived him of reason, causing him to run staggering and aimless through the wilderness, smashing into trees and rocks and charging imaginary enemies. Exhaustion would at last have brought him to his knees, but, unless predators ended his suffering, he would have lingered on, experiencing a lunatic half-life that might have lasted seven or eight days. Death by the fangs and claws of the three pumas, although violent and gory, released him quickly.

With the exception of a few mice and voles, the pumas had not eaten for almost three days. Now they gorged, each consuming some twenty pounds of meat. Afterward, assisted by the young cats, the mother pulled the heavy carcass away from the river edge and into the trees. The load exceeded her own weight four times. Once in concealment, the carcass was covered with leaves and detritus from the forest floor, after which the family walked into the shelter of a rocky outcrop and went to sleep.

While the pumas rested, a variety of small animals and birds took their fill from the moose carcass; they were soon joined by a flock of seven ravens, whose noisy descent on the mountain of food was instantly noted by the pumas. The white tom leaped to his feet and was about to charge down to eject the birds, but when his mother and sister exhibited no concern, he contented himself by lashing his tail vigorously from side to side and glaring for some seconds at the offending interlopers. Afterward, he stretched out and went to sleep.

The cat family remained near the moose carcass for the next four days, but on the morning of the fifth day, although they padded down from their shelter intending to take one more feed, they found that the meat had putrefied. Content with eating a few tentative mouthfuls, the young cats soon rose from the remains when their mother strode away. They followed her as she led them to the river for a long drink, then again when she turned around and headed for a wide valley that lay southeast of Kitseguecla Lake. There, the puma knew, she would find mule deer, mountain goats, and moose as well as other, smaller prey. Because the valley was bordered by dense forests and ringed by mountains that at midelevations were almost honeycombed by caves and tumbled rocks, the area offered shelter and concealment. All of these elements combined to offer an ideal range.

That summer, Taggart and Cousins were kept continually busy by a flood of clients at Moose-skin Johnny Lake, the majority of them lured there by widely distributed full-color brochures and by advertisements placed in leading sporting magazines in North America and Europe, extolling the quality of the hunting and fishing to be had at High Country Safaris. As well, readers were offered an opportunity to meet, and be guided by, the man whose right arm (the promotion implied) had been torn off by a ferocious puma, and clients could also make the acquaintance of Steven Cousins, "the heroic rescuer," as the media repeatedly had billed him.

Although flattered by all the attention that they constantly received, and more than happy to take the extra money they got each week for guiding those clients who specifically demanded their services, the two guides were impatient to get away from headquarters.

In previous summers, before Taggart's accident, Bell had periodically sent them to check on the horses or to scout for game animals in preparation for the autumn hunting season, which was by far the most lucrative aspect of the outfitter's business. These trips, which kept the partners away from headquarters for periods of ten days to two weeks, left them free to do much as they pleased. But now, with their sudden popularity, they were constantly occupied with clients. Two other employees had been sent to do the work that Taggart and Cousins had always deemed theirs by right of tenure and that, of course, allowed them to make extra money poaching for clients, especially while they were surveying and mapping the best hunting areas.

Had the mysterious Joe not recruited Taggart as a supplier of animal parts, Taggart and Cousins would not have greatly minded remaining at headquarters, for, in addition to the extra cash they were earning, they were treated to a great deal of admiration and, in Taggart's case, to a lot of extra whiskey. But, as time passed, they became increasingly restless, remembering the puma they had glimpsed—and especially the fee of five hundred dollars for its pelt and head—and their promise to Joe to stock up on animal parts so as to make a helicopter shipment before the start of the hunting season.

By the middle of August, both men had become irritable. Cousins was more dour than ever, replying to questions tersely and whenever possible saying nothing, merely nodding or shaking his head when a yes or no would suffice. Taggart had been bad tempered and argumentative with other staff members; he was also drinking heavily. But his cupidity prevented him from upsetting his clients. The only person with whom he felt at ease was his partner, who would listen to his complaints, limiting himself to terse replies.

Bell had noted the change in his senior guides, putting it down to their confinement at headquarters, a conclusion that was partly correct, for Taggart and Cousins were only really content when they were traveling the wilderness. But the outfitter was in business to make money, and, because he knew the guides kept their clients happy, whatever their own moods, he ignored their off-duty surliness.

Early one morning during the third week of August, when Taggart and Cousins had become so fed up that they were starting to discuss the possibility of quitting their jobs and devoting themselves full-time to the animal-parts business, Bell called them to his office and told them they were to leave the next day to check on the mounts and scout for game animals. Both men beamed at the news.

"Hey! That's sure good news, boss!" Taggart almost shouted.

Predictably, Cousins merely nodded.

Bell explained that the men he had sent on the same errand in June had not performed well.

"They don't have your experience, and after they got back, it turned out that they hadn't surveyed the northern range."

He then told the partners they could be gone as long as two weeks. They were to take a two-way radio with them to keep in touch with headquarters. "You can start south, around Burnie Lake, but don't waste too much time on the mounts," Bell said as the guides were about to leave his office, "since they were checked three weeks ago. Afterwards, head north. And I want you to do a *real good* scout for game, especially moose and grizzlies up there, above McDonell Lake."

"I maybe better take a hound along," Taggart suggested.

"Yes. I expected you to do that, but keep it in check. We don't want to spook the game."

The guides left at dawn the next morning, just as the eastern peaks were starting to become highlighted by the oranges and yellows of the hidden sun. Taggart was astride his black gelding, two of his hounds tethered to the saddle horn by long rope leads. Cousins was mounted on a roan mare. As usual, he led the packhorse, which carried large panniers containing their food and camping necessities.

Heading south along the west bank of the Thautil River, the men rode in silence, but the hounds, eager for a chase, whined intermittently as they trotted beside the gelding. An hour away from Moose-skin Johnny Lake, Cousins kneed his horse alongside Taggart's mount. "You figure one hound's not enough to chase the cat?" he asked.

"You're damned right!" Taggart replied. "The way I figure, that cat was likely sitting pretty up there for the summer. If we get near it, it'll take two hounds to tree it. Any case, maybe we'll get lucky and start up a griz."

"You tell Bell?" Cousins queried.

"Hell no! He asks later, I'll say I figured two hounds was better'n one. What's it to him, anyways?"

Cousins dropped back, and they rode in silence until noon, when they rested the horses and ate the corned beef sandwiches the cook had prepared for them.

Four hours later they reached the Burnie Lake camp. The caretaker of the otherwise deserted lodge, a garrulous old-timer who had spent his entire life in the region, was glad to see them. Leading the way into the stable, he helped them unsaddle the mounts and unload the packhorse. That done, the gear was brought into the lodge and the hounds were tied outside.

Leaving Taggart in the kitchen sharing a pint of rye whiskey with Gold Dust, as the caretaker had been dubbed years earlier, Cousins walked away to check on the remuda, a four-mile trip that took two hours to accomplish. On his return, Cousins reported to headquarters by radio, notifying Bell that all the horses were accounted for and in good condition. Tired after a long day, the guides turned in early that night.

The next morning, once again as dawn was breaking, the guides headed north. Soon after leaving the camp, they began to survey for game, a task that caused them to stop often, sometimes dismounting and leading the hounds on foot while following the spoor of bears, moose, coyotes, and wolves. In this way, mile by mile, they began to work their way toward the Kitseguecla Valley, moving slowly and consciously marking on survey maps all the locations where animals might be encountered during the hunting season.

Both guides were proud of their ability to track game and to judge the most likely ranges of a variety of large mammals. They took this task seriously, not only because they enjoyed the freedom that it gave them but also because their jobs depended upon it. Nevertheless, when after three days they had not encountered traces of pumas, they started to get impatient, lured toward the place where they had seen the young female cat in June.

On the morning of the fourth day, when they had traveled only eighteen miles, Taggart, in the act of drinking black coffee, looked up. "You know, Steve, I reckon we should hustle along up to where we saw the cat, have a go at it, and do the rest of our surveying after we get that varmint."

Cousins, starting to pack the camping gear, paused. "OK. *If* we get the cat. Case we don't, we'll have to head back anyways."

Taggart, optimistic whenever he was on a hunt, snorted into his enamel mug. "Steve, you sure can be a pain, you know? We'll get the varmint. It was there. We both saw it. I bet ten bucks we'll get it."

Four days later, in midafternoon, the men reached the Kitseguecla Valley. As they started to unpack the saddle horse and set up camp, Taggart's hounds began to whine, pulling at their leads. "They're onto something, Steve! It's got to be the cat!"

Cousins, busy with the saddle horse, noted the behavior of the dogs and nodded agreement. "What'll we do?" he asked Taggart.

"Do? Why, let's get on the trail, *like right now*! We got another three hours of daylight yet. Come on! Tether the packhorse and let's get at it!"

Five minutes later they were mounted. The dogs were unleashed and immediately dashed away, bugling loudly and continuously. Spurring their horses, Taggart and Cousins raced after the dogs, taking advantage of the flatlands to gallop at full speed. Soon, however, as they approached the forested area, the terrain began to get steep and be strewn with boulders. They had to slow down, even as the sonorous baying of the hounds became progressively faint. After some minutes, as the horses were forced to dodge standing trees and deadfalls, the guides dismounted.

"This is no damned good," said Taggart as he tied his black to a tree. "We're going to have to follow on foot."

Cousins did not reply. Leading the packhorses, which they had to take along because they camped in a new place each night, he had lagged behind. But as Taggart dismounted, he caught up. Alighting, Cousins tied his mare and the packhorse to a sapling. Then, as his partner had done, he pulled his rifle out of its saddle scabbard. The poachers set off at a brisk trot, aiming in the direction from which the now faint bugling of the hounds was issuing.

Stumbling and cursing the forest, Taggart led the way at first, but he soon began to flag. A heavy smoker, he had also been sedentary for a number of weeks, during which he had consumed too much whiskey. He was so out of condition that, after jogging for only one hundred yards, he began to gasp for breath, his face turning a deep red. He slowed to a shambling, wheezing walk.

Cousins drank very little alcohol and, although a moderate

smoker, he always kept himself fit. He was also ten years younger than Taggart and lean of body. He ran ahead, quickly disappearing from his partner's view. Moments later the baying of the hounds became high-pitched and more rapid. Their voices were issuing from a static location.

Both men stopped. Listening intently, Taggart smiled broadly, and, although panting from exertion, he shouted at Cousins. "We got it! The varmint's treed! Wait up for me . . ."

When Taggart and Cousins had arrived in the valley, the pumas were resting near the remains of a deer they had killed the night before. The mother was sprawled on a flat-topped rock, relaxed, idly monitoring the environment; her young were below her, on the forest floor. The female cat was asleep, curled up nose to tail; her brother was sitting upright, ears pricked forward as he listened to the scurrying claws of a red squirrel that was traveling in the upper branches of a tall spruce.

The puma suddenly leaped to her feet, her tail lashing from side to side, her eyes staring fixedly in the direction of Kitseguecla Lake as though she sought to penetrate the barrier of trees. She had heard the sound made by Taggart's gelding as it blew through its nostrils after topping a rise.

The white tom immediately responded to his mother's alarm. He rose, his own tail wagging spastically; he also stared toward the lake. His sister, although she lifted her head, did not appear to be alarmed. It was as though she was content to allow her mother and brother to worry about whatever influence they had detected.

Mother and son remained fixedly attentive for a few seconds. Now that they were aroused, they heard the men and their horses and hounds, even though half a mile lay between the cats and the intruders. Growling alarm, the puma turned and dashed away, closely followed by the white tom. The young female cat now became alarmed. Springing to her feet, she ran after the others at full speed.

By the time the hounds were unleashed and had begun the chase, the three cougars had traveled a quarter of a mile from their resting place. As the baying dogs dashed in pursuit, their voices spurred the cats, causing them to run faster. But they soon began to tire.

The mother, knowing the terrain, veered toward the northeast, where, half a mile away, stood Rocky Ridge, a steep, bald granite upthrust the west flank of which was strewn with large rocks and riven by sheer chasms. The puma and her son galloped toward this refuge, but the young female, in panic and lagging behind, turned west, soon reaching the river.

Bewildered, out in the open, she became confused, not knowing whether to cross the deep and fast-running stream or to turn away and make for Rocky Ridge. As she hesitated, the two hounds burst out of the forest and ran toward her, their deep bass voices further confusing her. Snarling in anger and fear, she turned to face the dogs, mouth opened wide.

The lead dog, a large black-and-tan animal, was six years old. He had chased many pumas and knew exactly what to do. Leaving his companion to worry the cat from the front, the big hound circled and came up behind the quarry. The puma turned to face him and was immediately charged by the other dog, who snapped at one of her flanks. His teeth merely grazed the cat, but the attack caused her to run. Streaking toward the nearest tall spruce, she leaped, grabbed the trunk with both front paws, and kicked herself upward with her back feet, her fast climb making loud scraping sounds and causing showers of brown, scaly bark to fall to the forest floor, harmless missiles that yet caused her pursuers to dodge away and gave the puma a chance to climb beyond their reach.

The hounds, heads lifted as they watched their quarry, began to bugle frantically, at times whining with excitement. The puma continued to climb until she was almost forty feet from the ground. At that height, feeling secure, she balanced herself on two branches, her front feet on the higher, her back paws on a lower limb. Now she stared balefully at the dogs, her mouth open in a hissing snarl.

Ten minutes later, while the hounds maintained their siege, restlessly circling the tree or jumping at it and falling backward, and as the cat continued to show her fear and hatred, Steve Cousins arrived.

The guide stopped about fifty feet from the spruce tree and looked up at the cat, which was sideways to him and offered an excellent target. Behind him, Cousins could hear his partner's lumbering progress and, although he worked the lever of his Winchester, placing a cartridge into the breach, he decided to wait until Taggart arrived, knowing that his partner would be angered if he was not given first shot at the puma.

Moments later, the puma showed signs of coming down the spruce. Cousins raised the rifle and took a deep breath as he sighted on the cougar's chest, seeking to make a heart shot. When he moved, the cougar stood still. Cousins's index finger put gentle pressure on the trigger. Even before the shot rang out, the bullet had pierced the puma's heart, and she had started to fall. The shell's staccato explosion coincided with the dull thud made by the puma's inert body when it hit the ground.

Cousins was securing the hounds with the leather leashes that he carried attached to his belt when Taggart burst out of the forest. The big man stopped, his eyes sweeping the scene. At first, gasping for breath, he could not speak, but after some moments, a time during which Cousins pulled the excited hounds away from the dead cat, Taggart swore loudly. "Son of a bitch! You couldn't wait for me, could you, you bastard! You *knew* I wanted to shoot that varmint. You *knew* that!"

Cousins stared coolly at his partner. He nodded. "Sure. I knew. The cat was going to climb down. Had to shoot. If you was in better shape, *you* could've killed it. Now, *get off my back, Walt!*"

Cousins's clipped, deliberately spaced words calmed Taggart. He well knew that Cousins was not a man to tolerate insults. In truth, and although he would never admit it, he was afraid of the younger man. Cousins turned away from Taggart, the tugging, reluctant-to-leave hounds having to follow him as he headed for the trees. Just before entering the forest, he stopped and turned to look at Taggart, who was now standing over the dead cat, one booted toe under her head, lifting. "I'm going to get the mounts. You want to start skinning, go ahead."

Taggart looked at his partner and nodded.

Cousins nodded sparingly and reentered the forest.

When Cousins returned with the horses, Taggart had already skinned the young puma. The pelt, with paws and head attached, was folded up, a blood-stained bundle that lay beside the naked and bleeding corpse. The younger man paid but scant attention to the dead animal's mutilated remains. He appeared excited as he led the mounts and the pack animal toward his partner. "There's two more cats out there, Walt," he announced.

Taggart was washing the skinning knife at the river's edge. He jumped upright, water dripping from his hands, and stared at Cousins. "Two more? How'n hell d'you know that?"

"Found two sets of tracks. Heading northeast. One set big, the other *real* big. The three cats must've been together and split up," Cousins replied.

Wiping his wet hands against the seat of his pants, Taggart, beaming, strode to the bundled hide. As he tied the trophy securely with cord, he spoke. "Get me one of the spare ropes from the packs—they're in the left one, I reckon. What we'll do is hoist this pelt up high, so critters won't get at it. Then let's get after the other cats!"

Ten minutes later, the poachers retraced their route to where Cousins had noticed the spoor, a small open area over which sediments from a rockfall had spread themselves for some distance, practically covering the grasses and small plants. In this soft medium, the tracks were elongated because the puma and her son had been running. But their prints were easily identifiable.

Hardly bothering to examine the prints, Taggart released the hounds. Eagerly, they nosed the ground and immediately picked up the scent. Dashing away while bugling in full voice, the hounds quickly disappeared among the trees. Taggart and Cousins rode after them, but, as before, the guides were soon forced to tie their horses and continue the chase on foot. This time, however, Taggart told Cousins to lead. "Go on, Steve. I'm still blown from the last run. If you've got to do it, go ahead and shoot the varmints. But, I sure hope you don't have to!"

While the young female cat was being chased and killed, the puma and her son bounded up the slopes of Rocky Ridge, both cats showing signs of exertion but persevering, spurred to the utmost effort by the baying of the dogs and, before they were halfway up the precipitous and barren slope, by the sharp report of Cousins's rifle.

When the two cougars reached 3,500 feet, they encountered a large rock slide and a scree-filled slope, its loose, slippery pieces of flaky rock impeding their passage. The tom turned right, running parallel with the scree until it ended, after which he continued to climb. But the mother puma turned left, and, although she too intended to bypass the dangerous fall and then continue the ascent of the mountain, the slide barred her way, ending at a steep cleft. The cougar could have turned back, but, in her anxiety to escape, she followed a descending pathway and soon afterward found herself on relatively flat, well-treed terrain. She reached the forest at the same time Cousins untied the horses and mounted his mare, setting off on his return to Taggart and the dead cat.

The hounds had now stopped baying, and the puma, believing that she had escaped, crawled under the full skirts of a large spruce and lay down to rest, her breath short, her mouth open as she panted. She lay quietly within her shelter for half an hour, but, as she was about to get up and return to Rocky Ridge so as to catch up with the white tom, the hounds—released again by Cousins as he took up the chase—picked up the scent and started to bay, their voices coming toward her. Springing to her feet, the puma ran into the deep forest. But she was still tired from her previous exertions; her pace became slower. The hounds began to gain rapidly on her.

After running for only about a quarter of a mile, the cat knew that the pursuing dogs would soon overtake her. She stopped and looked back, her mouth open in a silent snarl. Seeing a tall spruce, the trunk of which was bare from the ground up to a height of twenty feet, she began to climb, kicking herself up while pulling with her clawed front feet, and not stopping until she had reached the upper branches. Fifty feet from the forest floor, she stared down just as the excited hounds rushed up to her refuge, there to leap and bugle. The puma began to snarl loudly. She was still doing so when Cousins arrived.

Cousins remembered his partner's words. Since Taggart was so keen on shooting the cat, he decided to secure the hounds and take them some distance from the tree; experience told him that, when no longer so closely pressed, the animal would be less likely to leave its refuge in an effort to escape. He was right. As soon as he and the dogs had retreated fifty paces, the puma stopped snarling. She continued to glare at her enemies, eyes full of rage, ears pasted against her head, but she did not appear ready to descend.

Taggart, his face almost puce, arrived some minutes later.

He was so out of breath that he could not speak. He stood beside Cousins, gasping noisily, trying hard to regain his breath.

His partner pointed at the puma. "Go ahead, Walt, shoot the varmint."

Taggart, literally speechless, was yet able to show his rage. He stared at Cousins, his eyes blazing, and he shook his prosthetic arm at the man.

Cousins just grinned. "Hey, why don't you sit for a time, Walt? That cat'll wait for you . . . if she don't, why, guess I'll have to shoot her after all."

Taggart looked at the puma, then returned his gaze to Cousins's face. His breath was easier now. Moments later, gasping between words, he spoke. "You . . . SOB! I'll . . . shoot it . . . you'll see."

Cousins grinned again, and nodded.

In all, it took Taggart almost ten minutes to regain his breath and pulse sufficiently to ensure a clean shot.

Raising his rifle to waist level, he took careful aim, also seeking a heart shot. Seconds later the shot rang out. The puma reared and was flung against the tree trunk by the force of the bullet's impact. Then, as she died, her body went limp and began to topple downward. For a second or two it seemed as if she was going to stay in the tree, held there by the claws of her front feet, which had extruded as her nervous system gave its final convulsions. But the powerful black claws were wrenched loose by her weight. The puma pitched headfirst out of the tree, her body buffeted by the branches. She landed at the foot of the tree with a loud *thump*.

Standing on a ledge near the peak of Rocky Ridge, at the five-thousand-foot level, the white tom jumped when the shot rang out. He had been resting farther down the mountain, but he had begun to climb again as soon as he heard the baying of the hounds. He was only a few hundred yards below the rounded top of the mountain, and he soon crested it and began the descent on the far side. He knew that he was alone now. His keen nose and hearing had identified the killers, and, as he made his descent, the white puma learned to hate man.

When he reached the forested bottomlands, he ran, heading northward while keeping within the trees, paralleling the course of the Kitseguecla River. After bounding without rest for more than an hour, he stopped, climbed a rock-strewn slope, and lay down among its boulders. Here he napped for two hours. It was early afternoon when he rose, stretched, then monitored his environment.

When he detected neither the scent nor the sounds of the men and their dogs and horses, the tom set off again, padding along at an easy pace while aiming himself directly north, at times thrusting his way through underbrush without regard for the noise he was making, on other occasions loping across open areas in full view. Only when he encountered steep mountains and deep waterways did he detour.

As the puma traveled, hunger began to gnaw at him, but his desire to leave the ill-fated country in which he had grown up, and in which roamed the beings who had slaughtered his mother and sister, was greater than his need for food. So, having placed a good distance between himself and his enemies, yet anxious to find a home range where he would be safe, he kept on going, remaining within cover whenever possible but not trying to hide his presence from the senses of prey animals, which were alerted by the sounds of his passage through the tangled wilderness. In open locations the puma showed himself to moose and deer without so much as glancing in their direction. And the browsers, recognizing that he was not hunting, ignored his presence and continued to feed.

When the Kitseguecla River turned northwest, the white tom turned also, walking openly along the bank. Half an hour later, the waterway led him to a location where he detected the faint but unmistakable sounds and scent of humans. He quickly reentered the forest, although he continued to follow the river. Soon afterward he reached the place where the Kitseguecla empties its waters into those of the wide and boisterous Skeena River, at a point near the Indian community of Kitseguecla. The puma once again became afraid. He turned due north. After an hour he slowed down, then stopped. Once again he smelled and heard humans. Checking his environment with great care, he at last decided that his enemies were not nearby, and he continued north until he encountered a roadway at a place where the iron tracks of the Canadian Pacific Railway cross over the Skeena.

The white puma had never before encountered such alien terrain. From the shelter of the forest, he studied the black roadway and the iron bridge, through the center of which passed the strange, gleaming lines that curved south as they approached the water crossing and then curved north to run parallel to the roadway when they reached the far bank.

It was late afternoon. Although the sun had dropped behind the peaks, the light was full. Distrustful of the road, the bridge, and the lines, the puma decided to retreat into the wilderness and there to wait for nightfall before attempting to cross the strange things that stood between him and the northern country.

For the next five hours he lay in concealment, at times dozing but most often wide awake and ready to run should he be disturbed by his enemies. At last, as a crescent moon hung over the southern peaks, he rose and loped forward.

At the edge of the road he stopped, made nervous by a multitude of strange smells. He recognized the odor of man and the smell of gasoline, but most of the other scents were new to him.

The tom spent fifteen minutes checking the road and the railway bridge. As luck would have it, neither automobile nor train passed during that interval. Nervously, he put one front paw on the roadway. It felt smooth and warm, not unpleasant. When nothing happened, he stepped full on the blacktop and ran across it. At the bridge he stopped again, repeating the earlier experiment. In the continued absence of alarm, he dashed across the bridge and quickly disappeared into the sheltering forest.

The next morning the puma brought down a deer, and he gorged, eating twenty pounds of meat. Sated, he abandoned the carcass and continued his journey, not yet daring to lie up in order to finish the kill.

Four days later, having been forced to swim across the Kispiox River, the white tom found a new range near the headwaters of the Nass River, a vast mountain-and-lowland wilderness where moose and deer abounded and where there was no sign of human activity. Here he was destined to remain for the next fifteen months, until the urge to breed drove him away in search of a female cat.

11

Preoccupied with the task of finding a safe retreat, the white puma did not at first miss the companionship of his mother and sister, but, soon after settling in the new territory, he had felt in need of them. He became lonely and confused. Although he clearly understood that their absence was a result of the scent and sounds of humans, particularly the rifle reports, he kept looking for them, sniffing at the ground for traces of their scent and sometimes climbing to convenient heights to scan the valleys below. Initially, because of his anxiety, his hunting abilities were blunted, and hunger became a constant and unwelcome companion that gnawed at him while he disconsolately searched for his family.

Eventually, however, several weeks after the puma and her daughter had been killed, the white tom accepted his aloneness, a state natural to those of his kind in any event, even if, like his mother before him, he had had it thrust upon him brutally and ahead of time. From then on, he had adapted well to his northern refuge, pursuing without emotions the solitary life of an adult male cougar.

Undisturbed by human activity, he had at first hunted small animals, especially beavers, snowshoe hares, groundhogs, and marmots, practicing his stalking and charging skills until he was able to bring down a large mule deer buck, an animal that weighed almost four hundred pounds. After that, he sustained himself on large animals throughout the winter.

The following spring, he was able to kill a yearling moose and, the next day, a coyote that had come to disinter the covered remains.

Each experience added to his confidence. Culminating as they did just as he was reaching young adulthood, his successes made him feel that he was, indeed, the master of his range, although he was aware that his mastery had to be shared with the big wolves that inhabited the region as well as with the grizzly and black bears that between spring and late autumn roamed and hunted through the mountain country.

Soon after he became adjusted to his solitary state, a pack of eight wolves had chased him away from the carcass of a large marmot he had killed, surrounding him before he had taken his first bite and forcing him to swivel constantly to try to keep all of them in view. The moment that his back was turned to any of the pack members, they darted forward, snapping at his haunches without actually making contact. Agile as he was, no matter how quickly he turned to meet an attacker, it would dart out of his reach at the same time that another wolf charged him from the rear and snapped at his haunches.

After jousting in this way for some minutes, he became exasperated by the swift tactics of his opponents. Snarling loudly, he charged through the encircling pack and bounded away. But as soon as he realized that he was not being pursued, he stopped. Fifty feet from the wolves, he turned and sat down, facing them. The pack entirely ignored him, despite his continued growls and the lashing of his tail while he watched angrily as the marmot's body was expertly and swiftly devoured.

The white tom went hungry during the remainder of that day and all through the following night, but he had profited from the experience, realizing that he should have stood over his kill and forced the wolves to attack him. His formidably armed paws would have routed any wolf daring enough to try to steal his food. Such a tactic, he unconsciously realized, was the right one, as he was to prove later under similar conditions, when a pack sought to panic him. On that occasion he stood firm, and ten minutes after the wolves arrived they left, having made only a few tentative passes, during which they never put themselves within reach of his claws.

Nevertheless, not long after his second encounter with wolves, the white puma was again challenged and driven from his rightful prey. On an early morning in August, he killed a deer, gorged on the meat, then covered the carcass before selecting a nearby spruce and draping himself comfortably in its branches. Replete and lazy, he went to sleep, only to be awakened soon afterward by the arrival of a large male grizzly, who scented the meat and came to help himself to it.

Snarling loudly at the intruder, the tom charged headfirst down the tree, leaping into space while he was still eighteen feet from the ground. He landed sixty feet away from the bear, but as his front paws touched the forest floor, his back legs propelled him upward again, the second leap placing him within charging distance of the shaggy thief.

The puma rushed at his antagonist but stopped short when the grizzly stood his ground and indicated by a series of relatively low growls that he was more than willing to meet the cat's challenge. The tom, now undecided, continued to snarl. Not to be outdone, the bear reared up on his hind legs and uttered a ferocious roar. He stood some three yards from the puma, a seven-foot-tall monster with foul breath and great yellow tusks fully exposed, seemingly eager for a target.

The puma was not intimidated. Snarling and spitting, he was about to charge when the grizzly dropped to all fours, shook his massive head from side to side, and roared again as he began to hop up and down, using only his front feet to power each jump and keeping his back paws on the ground. This action had the effect of raising his head and shoulders, which he moved from left to right every time he jumped. The puma had started to move, but now he stopped dead in his tracks.

When the cat halted, the bear again stood upright and roared a challenge.

The tom wisely retreated.

Several months later, when the same grizzly tried to appropriate another of his kills, the tom, having gained both considerable experience and heft, drove the giant away by making fast darts at him, moving in quickly, slashing, and as swiftly jumping out of reach of the bear's massive paws. Frustrated by the elusive adversary, the grizzly gave up, leaving the scene with a left ear torn by the tom's claws.

In September trouble arrived in the white puma's range in the shape of another male puma, a six-year-old who had been driven out of his territory by a scarcity of prey. The stranger quickly encountered the first of the tom's scent stations. He ignored them.

The older cat, confident in his fighting abilities, was determined to oust the present occupant from a territory in which, his nose had soon detected, prey species were plentiful. So he advanced boldly, pausing often to spray his urine against those tree trunks and rocks that had previously been sprayed by the rightful occupant.

Not being immediately challenged, the intruder became careless. Instead of advancing in stealth, he strode nonchalantly through a pass, paused at the top of the defile to briefly survey the valley that occupied a large section of lowland, and, seeing nothing alarming, began to descend, the pitch of the scree-covered grade causing him to slip and stumble and so to travel rather more quickly than he intended. Soon afterward he reached the valley floor. There he stopped and scented the air. He immediately noted the strong odor of the occupying cat, but he continued to ignore it.

After traveling a quarter of a mile, the invader detected the scent of fresh meat. The aroma was strong—the kill was not far away. Hungry after his long trek, he hurried forward, so intent on following the smell of meat that he passed right underneath a rock shelf on which the young tom was waiting for him.

Just as the stranger was level with the ledge, the white puma leaped. The shock of the attack was intimidating, and the would-be usurper screamed in alarm; then he screamed in pain, for the tom's claws dug deeply into the skin on both of his shoulders. Yet the intruder had been fortunate, for the white puma had landed with his hind feet on the ground. Had he landed fully on top of his rival's back, his powerful claws would have flailed the skin and meat off the other cat's hindquarters.

Both pumas crashed to the ground and for some moments became a blur of interlocked, roaring frenzy in which the tom's white coat contrasted startlingly with his opponent's tawny fur. Soon after, the powerful antagonists broke apart, paused for a moment, then charged each other simultaneously.

The intruder was large, and the scars on his face and shoulders proclaimed that he had already fought several times with other males of his own kind. But the challenger was not as powerful as the white tom. Locked in each other's embrace, they fought furiously, and the wilderness echoes with their roaring and snarling, a great caterwauling that was now and then accompanied by shrill screams of rage or pain when one or the other was raked by his adversary's fully extruded claws. Then they broke apart again. But not for long. Again they charged, grappled, and rolled over and over on the forest floor, their rage making them oblivious to the bumps and scratches they were receiving from dead branches and tree trunks.

With brief respites between bouts, the two pumas fought

their contest for almost five minutes, a long time for an encounter between such powerful and well-armed adversaries. But the challenger at last realized that he was outclassed and, no doubt, that he had suffered enough. He broke away. Bleeding from a number of deep gashes on his shoulders, head, and flanks, he fled the moment he was free from the clutches of his opponent. At top speed, he raced down-valley, pursued for a short distance by the aroused tom, who had himself sustained several slashes.

After chasing his enemy for about one hundred yards, the white puma stopped, his chest heaving, his lips drawn back to reveal his bloodied fangs. He snarled loudly, his tail lashing and his eyes glaring at the retreating puma; then he cupped his right front paw and with it took several swipes at the ground, each swift blow dislodging soil and grasses that flew sideways, showering debris into the air. Seemingly content after his display, he snarled one more time and turned away, bloody rivulets staining his otherwise pristine coat.

In late November, fourteen months after his arrival in the Nass region, the white puma became restless. He was now more than two years old, a fully mature male who weighed 210 pounds and measured nine feet, one inch from the tip of his nose to the end of his three-foot-long tail. He had developed into a magnificent physical specimen; his pure white coat and the coal black markings on his face, on the tips of his ears, and on the end of his tail combined to show off to its best advantage his lithe, well-muscled body, which was further embellished by intense, greenish amber eyes that during all his waking hours constantly examined the environment with inquisitive and highly intelligent perception. Until now, the white puma had been content to remain in his own territory, but daily he became more and more unsettled, his mood unknowingly responding to the urge to breed, an arousal that he was experiencing for the first time.

Finally, in mid-December, he surrendered to his sexual needs and left his range early one morning. It had snowed during the night, the large flakes piling at high altitude to a depth of two feet but mounding to only about eight inches in the valleys. But snow was not an impediment to the puma, although when he set out he traveled along the bottomlands to avoid the steep passes. Coincidentally, by following the valleys his way led back along almost the same route he had taken to reach the Nass region.

For the next seven days he moved steadily in a southerly direction, stopping once to kill a deer on which he gorged before abandoning the kill and continuing his journey. On the eighth day he again encountered the railway bridge that spanned the Skeena River, but this time he arrived at the crossing after midnight. Recognizing the trestle, he paused only long enough to make sure that his way was clear before he dashed across the alien pass. But he was nervous. At the edge of the roadway, he stopped once more, satisfied himself that no dangers lurked nearby, and ran across the blacktop at full speed, distrusting the highway more than the bridge because it smelled strongly of humans and their synthetic, acrid chemicals.

By first light the next morning, the white puma reached the east bank of the Kitseguecla River, finding himself now in well-remembered country. He followed the waterway, traveling in a southeasterly direction, and by noon reached the south slopes of Rocky Ridge, almost at the same place that he and his mother had climbed to avoid Taggart and Cousins. Memory of those events returned in fragments.

He could not recall with clarity the pursuit, nor the separation from his mother, but he became aroused, feeling an admixture of aggression and fear, emotions that caused him to change his pace from a walk to a lope, so that he was now traveling at a rate of ten miles an hour. He maintained that speed for the next thirty minutes, until the river veered away from

Rocky Ridge and the dense spruces that ringed the Kitseguecla Valley offered him concealment.

Panting noisily, he stopped and checked his surroundings at length, using all his superb senses. Reassured, he moved forward at a slow pace until he reached the grassy meadow that surrounded Kitseguecla Lake. Pausing within the screen of trees, he again inspected the open land before he advanced to the lakeside and there stopped to drink, first using a paw to sweep away the snow and break the thin sheet of ice that coated the water. Tired from his long trek, he turned away after drinking his fill and padded to the cave where he and his family had sheltered. As he entered the darkened grotto, memory nagged at his cortex.

Despite the passage of time, his nose could still detect faint traces of his own scent and those of his mother and sister. Now he felt immediately at home, and after some moments he walked to the end of the cavern, where the roof sloped, and there he lay down, resting his chin on outstretched front paws and closing his eyes. Ignoring the demands of hunger, he went to sleep.

When the tom awakened, a gibbous moon shed yellow light over his wilderness, a glow supplemented by the flashing, almost fluorescent radiance of the aurora borealis and by a firmament sequined with countless stars. The temperature had fallen to ten degrees below zero, causing the snow to become crisp and to crunch when stepped on. But the white puma crossed the open country as silently as a ghost, walking, as his mother had done, very slowly, setting down each broad pad gently and so allowing its heat to defeat the giveaway crackling that otherwise would have announced his presence to the keen ears of prey animals.

With the infinite patience of his kind, the tom circled the lake, pausing often to sniff at the tracks left by the animals that had earlier come to the water to quench their thirsts. Some of the impressions left by the sharp, hard hooves of deer gave off fairly strong scent, but no spoor was really fresh. When he reached the south side of the lake, he entered the forest. Here he could travel at a normal pace, for the tree cover had protected the snow surface from the night freeze. But after stalking patiently for most of the night, he failed to find fresh deer scent until dawn was crimsoning the eastern peaks.

As the dim light of early morning seeped into the forest and created long shadows, the admixture of brightness and darkness hindered rather than helped vision. Hungry as he was, the puma had just decided to wait for full daylight before resuming his quest for food when his nose collected deer scent. The spoor was faint at first, but, as he followed the trail into the deep forest, the odor of deer droppings grew stronger.

He continued to follow the aerial trail, linked to it as unerringly as if they had been tied by a long and winding thread. Five hundred yards later he found the source, a mass of oval, dark brown droppings deposited beside a round depression in the snow. When he sniffed the bare ground in the middle of the thawed circle, it gave off the body scent of the deer that had used the place as a bed during the night. The animal had arisen at first light and relieved its bowels nearby before leaving to forage within the shelter of a stand of young aspens.

The puma began to stalk. Moving slowly, legs half bent to lower his height, he advanced, heading westward and going from cover to cover as he followed the scent trail rather than the clear imprints left by the quarry, for all predators hunt by scent rather than by the sight of tracks. The deer had left a line of small, sharply outlined footprints, the space between each indicating that it was walking in a leisurely way. This information was absorbed by the puma, which noted the distance between the strong odors released by each track: the longer the space between odor clusters, the faster the gait of the quarry.

When the deer had left to feed, it had at first wandered

casually, stopping here and there to browse the tips of seedling aspens, but traveling a circuitous course toward a large stand of cedars, the foliage of which was a favorite winter food.

By the time the white puma reached the buck's resting place, the quarry had already been ensconced within the cedars for more than hour and had eaten his fill. He was now lying down to chew the cud so as to fully digest his meal, unaware that the breeze was fanning his scent to the puma's keen nostrils. Traveling as slowly as he was, the puma took twenty minutes to settle himself into position for a charge. The buck continued chewing.

Seconds later, the deer was dead, its neck broken.

The cougar began to feed. Suddenly, just as he swallowed his third mouthful of warm meat, he jumped to his feet. Lashing his tail in agitation, he turned to face south, his eyes fixed on the trees but unable to see beyond the foliage. He had heard stealthy movement, but because he was positioned so that the breeze was blowing over his body, he could not detect the intruder's odor. As he was about to move away from the kill so as to lie concealed until he could identify the cause of his disturbance, a loud, prolonged scream shattered the silence of the forest. The cry, emitted suddenly, startled the puma, but before he could move it was repeated.

The tom became excited as inherent forces allowed him to recognize the calls as those made by a female of his own kind who was looking for a mate. Aroused, he started toward the wailing cat, and as he moved he began to whistle a reply, his lips pursed and slightly puckered and his whiskers arcing forward so that they almost met in front of his nose.

The female puma was seven years old. She had already given birth to five litters, of which a total of six kittens had reached adulthood. Of these, only one survived, a young female from the mother's last litter. All the others had been killed by Taggart and Cousins, either when they were guiding a hunter or when they were poaching. The cat had scented the white tom the previous day. Now she was coming to him.

As soon as she heard his whistles, she replied in kind as she hurried forward, her own breeding urges fully aroused by the male's replies to her initial, bansheelike wails.

The two pumas met in a small, cleared space within the cedar forest. The tom, brash and anxious, immediately advanced on his prospective mate and sought to initiate physical contact. To his surprise and alarm, the seductively feminine cat immediately raised a front paw, claws extruded, and smacked the white tom on the head, the blow controlled, so that the claws did little more than scratch.

The puma was astonished. He leaped backward, shaking his head as he whistled loudly but not taking his eyes off the desirable but decidedly temperamental female. Of course, he persevered. He advanced toward her again, his body crouched low in submission as he whistled a cooing, pleading series of rapid notes.

Only seconds later he was rebuffed anew, although on this occasion, half-expecting the cat's reaction, he managed to leap clear of her flashing paw before it could strike him. From a safe distance, he studied her intently. Now that she had driven him away, she became coy, purring, stretching her body languorously, and spraying her urine against the trunk of a large cedar. In the mind of the inexperienced young puma, the cat became a frustrating temptress, at one moment whistling at him in encouragement, at the next becoming a seemingly fierce antagonist who wanted no dealings with him.

Trying to understand the female's behavior, he moved some distance from her and lay down against a large, flat-sided rock. Unconsciously, but probably motivated by inherent promptings, he had made the right move, for as soon as he appeared to lose interest in her, the cat padded to him and began to lick his broad head while purring loudly.

Surprised yet delighted, the tom began to purr also. Soon afterward the pair mated, an act they repeated a number of times during the three weeks they were to spend together.

On the morning of the twenty-second day after their initial meeting, the female walked away while the tom was still feeding on a deer they had jointly killed the previous evening. The white puma, gulping down a large piece of partly frozen meat, showed no interest as his erstwhile mate left him. He remained prone by the carcass and continued to eat. Like the female, he had lost the urge to breed. Instead, his appetite dominated the immediate present. Chewing and swallowing, he watched with disinterest as the cat disappeared among the trees.

The female, padding northward at a brisk pace, was as disinterested in the tom as he was in her. Her estrus cycle was over. She was pregnant. Her immediate concern now was to find a suitable range for herself, a territory where she could give birth to her kittens the following April.

The white puma did not fare well during the remainder of that winter. Deer and moose, both of which had been plentiful in the region when the cougar was a kitten, were now scarce, overhunted by Bell's clients and, out of season, poached by Taggart and Cousins to supply antlers and hides to Joe.

Wandering continuously, even during deep-snow time, the puma kept himself alive hunting whatever animal or bird he could find. But when spring arrived he was in poor condition. He had lost almost forty pounds, a loss of muscle and body fat made evident by his hipbones—which looked as if they had been pushed upward, displacing the fur on his hindquarters—and his ribs—which could have been counted, even through his winter coat, which, in late March, had not yet started to shed. In this condition, the tom wandered southwest toward the headwaters of the Zymoetz River, following the waterway to an area of flatlands that lay east of the Hazelton Mountains, a region he reached during first light in early April, at the start of breakup.

The Zymoetz River was then in full spate, so, instead of following it, the white puma began to explore that valley, a location in which he and his mother and sister had spent some time, living well on the deer that had then been abundant. But, after searching the upper part of the valley for more than two hours, he failed to scent a single deer. Instead, as he was crossing a small creek, bounding from rock to rock to avoid the icy waters, he scented horses. The odor was well remembered and immediately associated with the presence of man.

The puma became aggressive. He lashed his tail, his lips curled back to reveal his fangs, and he snarled softly. At first he had an urge to run, but as the tantalizing scent grew stronger, he went into a stalking crouch and advanced toward it, taking care to move without sound while remaining in cover. He traveled in this way for half an hour, becoming more intense and aggressive as the odor grew stronger. When he could hear the horses, he stopped and listened for several minutes, his nose working hard as it searched for the scent of man that his memory said should be associated with the strange animals.

When he failed to detect human odor, he advanced again, but now he climbed above the valley, scrambling over rocks at first, then entering an area of lodgepole pines that grew on the east flanks of the mountains. He stopped climbing when he was three hundred feet above the valley and situated at a location where he could see the bottomlands while remaining concealed by the trees. Below him, grazing on forbs and the dried grasses left over from last year, were fourteen horses.

The mounts were those assigned to High Country Safaris' northernmost lodge, located on the east shore of McDonell Lake. Considering the coarse fodder they had been forced to consume during the last six months, they had wintered moderately well, yet all of them were suffering from malnutrition.

Staring hungrily, the white tom chose as his target an emaciated two-year-old that was about the size of a young moose and stood with drooping head some distance from his companions. The horse had suffered considerably during the winter. He limped on his right back leg; one of his ears was badly frostbitten, about half of it already putrefying; and he had a long scrape on his left flank, evidently acquired during a fall. The wound was infected and dribbling a viscous, yellow discharge.

Downwind of the horses, the puma started his descent, his eyes fixed on the target animal. The young horse continued to stand dejectedly; the others were too busy trying to find fodder to worry about anything else. The white puma reached the valley floor, crept through a tangle of dwarf juniper, and settled himself for the charge.

Rising like a phantom, the sight of which panicked the horses, he struck his target on the left shoulder with both front paws and broke his neck. Hunter and prey fell to the ground simultaneously as the other horses panicked and stampeded down-valley.

Disliking the open location that surrounded him and his kill, the cougar grasped the horse's uppermost thigh and began to drag the animal toward the junipers. Thin as he was, the dead gelding still weighed over six hundred pounds, nearly three times the weight of the cat. Walking backward while keeping his head high so as to raise slightly off the ground the hindquarters of the carcass, the puma had little difficulty dragging the animal into a juniper-screened depression. Dropping his burden, he rested for some moments, panting heavily. Later, he began to sniff the carcass, hesitant about biting into the strange prey, which he had never before encountered. But he was ravenous. He ripped open the paunch, exposing the steaming entrails, and plunged his head into the opening, searching for the lungs and kidneys, which he quickly devoured; then he ate large quantities of intestines.

Fifteen minutes later, fully sated, he covered the remains and climbed up-slope until he found a jumble of rocks. One of these, larger than a billiard table, was tilted at an angle. Underneath it was a dry shelter that was within hearing and scent distance of the kill. Curling up in the granite den, the cat went to sleep.

For the next three days and nights he remained near his kill, eating when hungry and resting under the rock, the horse's remains kept fresh by the frost that until mid-June descends in those latitudes from the higher altitudes. Early on the morning of the fourth day, he left the remains uncovered when he finished eating. He had decided to move on in search of a range where he could once again survive on his natural prey.

Sitting upright a short distance from the kill, he meticulously cleaned the blood from his paws, muzzle, and chest; then he stood up, yawned, and padded away. But he had traveled barely one hundred yards when he had to stop to move his bowels. Afterwards, although he had no intention of claiming this territory as his own, he tarried in order to cover the droppings, as usual facing into the wind so that his face and fur would not be soiled by flying bits of vegetation and soil.

Because of a low-pressure ridge in the southwest, the breeze was brisk that morning; its passage over his ear openings, as well as the noise made by tree branches as they rubbed against one another, disturbed his hearing. These things kept him from detecting the arrival of Steve Cousins until the guide had actually ridden into the valley.

Leaving his partner at the McDonell Lake lodge, Cousins had set out at dawn to check on the horses, a yearly chore for which he and Taggart were responsible and which was usually undertaken after breakup time in early June.

The partners had arrived at the northern camp the previous afternoon. They had ridden all day from Burnie Lake, where they had counted and inspected Bell's second remuda. All of these horses had survived the winter in better than usual condition because, by good fortune rather than judgment, they had been turned out on a large flatland area that was rich in the coarse but nourishing fodder known as beaver hay—a wild grass that takes root in the nutritious bottom mud of an abandoned pond after its builders have moved to a new location.

Cousins's horse picked up the puma's scent as soon as it reached the meadow. When it did so, its inherent fear of predators caused it to snort loudly. The white puma was shocked by the sound, which he immediately recognized. The horse snorted a second time and reared back suddenly, alerting its rider that something was amiss.

As the tom was moving, intending to leave the area surreptitiously, he turned his head toward the intruders. Seeing the horse and rider, the puma bolted. By now, however, Cousins had pulled his rifle out of the saddle scabbard. As usual when he and Taggart were riding the wilderness these days, the guide's weapon had a shell in the firing chamber, ready for almost instant use. Cousins was thumbing back the safety catch at the same instant that the white puma ran for cover.

Sight of the pure white mountain lion astonished the guide, causing him to delay his shot for a fraction of a second. Even so, the soft-nosed bullet struck a rock that was within inches of the puma's rump. The report came almost on the heels of a shower of splintered granite that struck the puma's right thigh. The shock of the report and the stinging pain of the granite chips made the cat leap thirty feet, a jump that landed him among boulders. Using the rocks for cover, he ran at full speed up the east flank of Howson Peak, an eight-thousand-foot, glacier-covered mountain that is part of the Hazelton chain.

In the meadow, Cousins held his rifle in his left hand while pulling back on the reins in order to control his horse. The guide had never before discharged his rifle while mounted on the palomino. Already made nervous by the scent of the puma, the horse had been startled by the gun's report so near his head and had immediately begun to buck.

Once he had his mount under control, the guide looked up-mountain and realized that he had no chance of killing the white cat. Now the usually taciturn man began to babble aloud to himself, alternately cursing and expressing wonder. "Hol-ly hell! A *white* cat! . . . *Jee-suss!* Worth a fortune . . . a *fortune*! Hell . . . just wait till Walt hears."

Cousins looked up-mountain one more time. Then, his equanimity restored, he shrugged and sat his horse calmly, debating his next move.

The white puma, meanwhile, had run at full speed up the precipitous mountain, staying in cover but having to bound from rock to rock. When he had climbed one thousand feet, he stopped within the trees, where he felt safe. Exhausted from his all-out flight, he lay down. Stretched full length on his left side, gasping for breath, the white puma felt his latent hatred of humans become fully aroused.

12

Annoyed with himself for having allowed surprise to interfere with his shooting, Cousins urged his horse toward the place where he had last seen the white puma. But the palomino had only covered a few yards when it shied violently to the left, almost unseating its rider. Busy controlling his mount, the guide did not at first notice the remains of the horse. When he did, he cursed again, this time under his breath but no less vehemently.

He was reaching for the radio that linked him to headquarters, intending to report the dead horse and the extraordinary animal that he had seen, when he realized that if he broadcast the news of a white puma, hunters would swarm over the country, every one of them eager to kill the rare cat. Thinking about these things for some moments, Cousins radioed headquarters and reported that a horse had been killed by a puma, but he made no mention of the animal's color.

When Bell was summoned to the radio room, he took the microphone from the dispatcher. "What happened to the horse?" he asked.

"Mountain lion. About three, four days ago. Most of it's been eaten. Big cat. I saw it; took a shot at it, maybe nicked it. Anyways, it took off up-mountain. Probably still going."

"Have you checked the other mounts?"

"No. Just got here. Will do. I'll call in if any more been killed. Over and out."

Ten minutes later the guide found the remuda peacefully cropping beaver hay at the far end of the large meadow.

Anxious to get back to McDonell Lake to tell his partner about the white puma, Cousins left the horse herd, at first walking his mount over the rough ground but spurring it into a brisk trot as soon as he reached the well-beaten trail that led from the meadow to the McDonell Lake lodge, a pathway estimated to be centuries old, having first been blazed by animals and later traveled by the Tlingit Indians until about the turn of the twentieth century. Since that time, the trail had reverted to the animals of the region, only rarely used by humans until Bell's northern hunting lodge was put into operation. But the passage of uncountable paws, hooves, and human feet had hardened the surface to an almost cementlike consistency that forbade all but a few hardy plants from growing on it.

Before Cousins had covered half the seven-mile distance between the meadow and the lodge, he met Taggart, the big man obviously agitated and pushing his black at a gallop along the trail. When he saw his partner, he drew rein. "I heard you on the radio. What the hell's going on?"

When Cousins explained, Taggart said roughly, "How in hell did you miss, you *jerk*?"

Cousins shrugged. "Had you been there, reckon you'd've missed too, Walt. I'm telling you, that cat is a shocker. It's white as milk, all but the face and tail markings. And *big*. Must go over two hundred!"

Taggart smiled at that. "Guess we'd better go back. You ride to Smithers, find a booth, and phone Joe. If he's busy, leave a message and the number you're calling from. It takes about five minutes for him to call back. He's mostly there. You tell him about the white cat. If he *ain't* there, leave a message about whitey anyway. Say it's his for five grand."

Taggart paused, evidently debating his next words, but when he saw that Cousins was going to interrupt, he added, "Meanwhile, I'll head back to Moose-skin and make ready. Get the dogs pumped up with a few short runs . . . and I'll tell Bell you've gone after the cat because you think you wounded it. That way, he won't miss you for a day or two."

Cousins held up his right hand, palm outward. "Hold it, Walt! That's a twenty-five-mile ride to Smithers. There and back, fifty mile. It'll take two days through that country!"

"So *what*! That white cat's worth one helluva pile of bucks! Joe'll sure want that hide. You keep going, you oughta make it back by sundown tomorrow."

Two days after leaving McDonell Lake, Cousins returned to headquarters with Joe's promise to pay five thousand dollars for the skin and head of the white puma. Because it was late when he reached Moose-skin Johnny Lake, he did not report to Bell, going instead directly to Taggart's cabin to give him the news. To the younger man's surprise, his partner responded with anger. "Damn it to hell! We should've asked double! I figured Joe'd haggle over five grand!"

Cousins shrugged. He knew his partner's cupidity. It wasn't worth a fight. Instead, exhausted from the long ride, he left Taggart, walked to his own cabin, and went to bed.

The next morning, accompanied by his partner, Cousins reported to Bell, explaining his absence with the fiction that Taggart had concocted and adding that he was now sure that he had missed the cat with his one, hasty shot. He had not, he said, found traces of blood after following the spoor for more than a mile. "I lost the tracks when the critter climbed over rocks. But Walt's hounds oughta pick up the scent," he concluded.

While the guides were still in his office, Bell contacted predator-control authorities at the region's headquarters in Prince George, 230 miles east of Smithers. Requesting out-of-season permission to eliminate the stock-killing puma, he alerted the officials that he was going to claim compensation for the dead horse under the terms established by the British Columbia government, which routinely paid the owners of livestock killed by wild predators.

Bell's intention to ask for payment for the loss was, therefore, not unusual. Neither was it unusual for the game department to consent to the out-of-season hunting of predators accused of being stock killers, although the correct procedure in such cases was for a government predator-control officer to go to the site to examine the remains of the domestic animal in order to determine whether its death was natural or the result of predation.

Because regional game and fish departments were understaffed, and because personnel were often reluctant to travel long distances in wilderness country to make such verifications, the regulations were frequently ignored. As a result, hinterland outfitters and ranchers found it expedient to blame predators for the loss of all livestock, whether an animal had indeed been attacked by wolves, pumas, bears, or coyotes or had died from starvation in winter, had fallen from a height, or had bogged down in a swamp.

After obtaining official consent, Bell ordered Taggart and Cousins to go after the puma that same day. As the partners were turning away to get ready for the hunt, the outfitter added, "I want you guys back here for the start of the fishing season. And that means you've got ten days to get that cat. Mind, I figure you should be done a lot sooner than that!"

Cousins nodded. Taggart grinned.

"Shouldn't take but a couple days to get that killer, boss," said the one-armed man as he followed his partner through the doorway.

When they left the office, the two guides walked to Taggart's cabin in silence. Then Taggart turned to Cousins. "OK, what we do—as usual—we kill the cat, then tell Bell we couldn't find it. No way he's going to get a share of the money!"

Cousins nodded agreement.

The white puma rested in a small, moss-covered opening near the den he and his siblings had occupied after their mother had moved the kittens from the waterfall cave. The cat's memory of those days was dim, but he had retained the geographic knowledge of the den and its environs, a location that was six miles west of the beaver meadow where he had killed the horse. The den site overlooked the junction made by Red Canyon Creek and the Zymoetz River. At 2,500 feet, and facing almost due south, it afforded the puma a good view of the fairly wide alluvial valley that straddled the river. Moose, deer, and other animals habitually traveled along the gently sloping corridor. Late during the previous afternoon and three days after he had been shot at by Steve Cousins, the tom had killed a deer on the north shore of Red Canyon Creek at a place one thousand feet below his den. The puma was by then ravenous, having fasted since the last meal he had taken from the remains of the horse, but because the kill site was too exposed, he had dragged the carcass into the shelter of the trees before he began to feed. Even then, despite his hunger, the memory of the rifle shot and of the hated scent of man caused him to pause repeatedly between mouthfuls in order to check his environment for signs of danger. On several occasions he rose from the kill and walked to the edge of the trees to scan the distant country, his stance and expression signaling an admixture of fear and aggression.

As a result of his frequent interruptions, the cat did not satisfy his hunger until nightfall. Then, sated after consuming more than twenty pounds of meat, he covered the remains and climbed a nearby tree. Embraced by stout branches, he slept soundly until dawn, when he returned to feed on his kill. Now, somewhat reassured by the continuing peacefulness of the wilderness, he fed without pause. When he was full, he noted that the sun was starting to climb above the eastern peaks.

He had just covered the remains and was ready to climb to the den site when he heard the hounds. The baying was faint, but he knew at once that the dogs were approaching his locality from the direction of the beaver meadow.

He stood facing the sounds, his eyes glaring, his lips peeled back in a silent snarl. He sniffed at the air. The wind was slight but blowing toward him, bringing with it the faint yet distinct odor of men, horses, and dogs.

Lashing his tail, he started down-slope, aiming toward the valley of the Zymoetz River, already having decided to make for an area where a series of ancient slides had littered the ground with rocks, scree, and broken trees, a combination that had created an impassable barrier for dogs and horses, but that could be easily negotiated by an agile puma.

The white tom ran at full speed for ten minutes; then he slowed to a walk, approaching the river above its union with Red Canyon Creek at a place where innumerable bends had become silted by the current. Here, standing at the extreme edge of a sandbank and facing a second dry bar, he paused, judged the distance, and leaped, his body forming a snowy, graceful arc as it soared over the icy stream to touch down, front paws first, on the edge of the targeted shoal. An instant later, the jump was completed when his back feet landed in a few inches of water. He sprang again, landed on the shrub-cluttered riverbank, and padded up-slope to seek concealment among the aspens that bordered the eastern side of the waterway.

As he gained shelter, the voices of the hounds became appreciably louder, and their canine scent was strong in his nostrils. He was about to bolt up-slope to take refuge among the alpine rocks, where he knew he would be safe, when he realized that he could no longer detect the odor of humans, or of their horses. Facing the baying of the hounds, he listened for the sound of galloping horses while his nose continued to search the air for their odors and, particularly, for the disagreeable scent of their riders. As he was doing these things, the voices of the dogs grew louder. They were not far off now; they had evidently outdistanced the mounted hunters and would arrive soon. But they would reach the puma without the backing of the humans.

The cat turned, looked upward. He saw a sharp rock overhang that was screened by a thick copse of young larches, their yellow-green needles newly emerged and forming a concealing, yet relatively open lattice that would hide his body but would allow him to see his enemies. The tom bounded up, following a gentle grade until he reached the base of the overhang. Here he stopped. Once more he tested the air and listened for sounds.

The hounds were about to ford the river, perhaps only a quarter of a mile away, but the breeze was still free of the odor of the hunters and their mounts. Facing the fifteen-foot-high rock, the puma leaped, his powerful hindquarters lifting him smoothly and landing him on top of the granite shelf. Arranging himself on the outcrop, head at its edge and facing the slope along which the dogs would have to travel if they were to reach him, the white puma waited, ears back, whiskers jutting forward, and tail lashing spasmodically. The muscles on his haunches tensed, bulging his silken fur. He was ready to attack from ambush.

The baying became louder. Minutes later he heard the

splashes made by the hounds as they dashed across the river. He tensed, rocking slightly from side to side on his haunches, back claws digging into the thin, mossy soil that covered the surface of the rock. As he waited, he listened, and he continued to test the air for the odors of the men and their horses. But all he could hear and smell were the dogs, their ever louder and excited baying, and the crashing of underbrush that advertised their imminent arrival.

The puma prepared himself for the charge. He raised his haunches slightly; he braced his front paws, spreading the pads; and he lowered his head, his chin barely touching the rock and lying between his front paws.

Seconds before the four hounds burst into view, the cat's tail became rigidly still. His lips peeled back, showing the canines and incisors and wrinkling the upper part of his muzzle. Yet he made no sound.

Led by Blue, Taggart's best tracking dog, the four hounds charged out of the screening aspens, noses to the ground as they headed for the slope up which the puma had traveled. When the lead dog reached the start of the grade, the white puma sprang, mouth agape, front legs stretched forward, their paws spread wide to show the great, hooked talons. A banshee wail of utter rage issued from the cat's throat as he descended on his chosen target.

The startled hounds tried to stop, but they were too late. The puma struck the lead dog. Whiplash broke the animal's neck, but the tom's paws caved in his chest, the impact hurling the inert body against the rocks. It had taken only three seconds to kill Taggart's lead dog.

Immediately afterward, and even as the remaining hounds tried to turn away, the cat reached one of them, striking him with his right front paw. The unfortunate animal sailed through the air and landed, whimpering, some six feet from its attacker. The last two dogs ran.

Snarling loudly, the white puma stood glaring at the disappearing survivors, but as soon as they were concealed by the underbrush, he turned and sniffed at the dead dog. Without pause, he picked up the carcass and began to carry it up the mountain. The second dog lay unmoving, but he continued to whimper. The puma's claws had inflicted four deep slashes on his left shoulder, and the fall had broken his right front leg.

Taggart and Cousins were still on the other side of the Zymoetz River when they saw the two escaping hounds running toward them at full speed. The guides reined their horses to a stop.

"What the . . . !" Taggart muttered, hardly able to credit what he was seeing.

Cousins, taciturn as usual, dismounted and called the dogs to his side, securing them with the rope leads that the men used while riding. "Hounds are scared, Walt. Something ain't right."

"For *damn sure* something ain't right! Mount up, let the hounds lead us to the others. Maybe these got separated from Blue and Turk."

Twenty minutes later the guides found the injured Turk. While Taggart was examining the hound's injuries, Cousins bent over the battleground and noted the signs of the scuffle. Afterward he traced the puma's tracks, which were accompanied by clear marks that had been made by the hound's trailing body.

Taggart, still squatting by the injured dog, turned to his partner. "That goddamned cat's cut up Turk's shoulder pretty bad. And busted his leg! *But where'n hell's Blue?*"

Cousins stood upright. "Blue's dead, Walt. The cat's done for him and dragged him away. Up there." As he spoke, he pointed upward, to the area of tumbled rocks and deadfall trees. "There's no way we can follow that mess."

Taggart began to curse, uttering a stream of invective until shortness of breath silenced him. Panting, he stared up-mountain, his face red, his eyes filled with rage.

"Ain't no good cussing, Walt. The cat's out of reach."

When his partner remained silent, Cousins spoke again. "We better head back to where we left the packhorse. I'll carry Turk, take him home and fix him up. Then we'll start again with the other two dogs."

"Like hell we go back! We'll trail on foot, keeping the dogs on the lead. We'll get that damned cat yet!"

"And what'll we do with Turk meanwhile?"

"Do with him? We shoot the son of a bitch! *That's* what we do with him. He ain't no good to us like he is. Anyways, he can't be much of a hound, letting the cat get him like that!"

Cousins looked at his partner and recognized that rage was clouding his thinking; he knew that the man was fond of his dogs. "You're nuts!"

Taggart was silent, frowning as he looked at the injured dog.

"Take a hold of yourself, Walt! That's a good hound and he did his best. No way am I going to let you shoot Turk! *You* can go on afoot if you want. Me, I'm taking Turk home and I'm going to fix him up!"

Taggart needed little persuading. In fact, while he was listening to Cousins, he was unconsciously stroking the injured dog's head.

"Yeah, OK. Maybe you're right. But I hate like hell to think of that mangy cat sitting up there someplace *eating* old Blue!"

"Sure, I know," Cousins replied. "But we'll get him, you'll see!"

Four thousand feet above the river valley, the white puma rested. He had taken his fill from Taggart's hound after carrying the body almost one thousand feet up the mountain. When he finished eating, he left the remains, not bothering to cover them because he did not intend to feed again on the carcass. He had not eaten dog before now, and, although he had found the meat edible, he had not greatly cared for its strong and musky taste. In any event, he was anxious to move away from the region.

The puma intended to remain at high elevation as he wandered southward while staying concealed in the alpine tree zone, which, in that region of glacier-covered peaks, reached altitudes between three thousand and four thousand feet.

Earlier, as he had been climbing upward encumbered by the hound's body, which weighed more than fifty pounds, the puma had heard his human enemies when the guides reached the scene of his attack on their dogs. But, apart from uttering a low, husky growl between jaws that were closed on the dead animal's neck, he showed no concern. The men's voices were distant, and, in any event, he felt safe, aware that the steep, rock-strewn terrain up which he was climbing would prevent pursuit. Tired and hungry when he neared the thousand-foot level, he settled down to eat despite the fact that he could still hear the faint voices of his enemies and, occasionally, the snorting of their horses. Later, as the sun was low in the west, he crossed Blackberry Creek at the four-thousand-foot level and rested once more.

An hour after sunset the white puma rose, stretched as he yawned, and then, spraying a nearby rock to advertise his ownership of the range, continued traveling southward, but now descending to take advantage of the better going offered by the lower slopes. At midnight, under a clear sky encrusted with green stars and a moon made red by the unseen sun, the tom reached Many Bear Creek. Here he stopped to drink. Afterward, he checked the area for the scent of another puma, found none, and again sprayed to announce his tenure. Crossing the creek, he turned east and continued in that direction until he reached Limonite Creek.

By now, inasmuch as he had not encountered the scent of another puma, the white tom had decided to remain in the region. He felt comfortable in it, and he recognized many of its features, although he did not remember that, as kittens, he and his sister had been led here by their mother.

At Limonite Creek he turned northeast, keeping within sight of the stream while traveling along a well-beaten but winding trail that eventually led him to the Telkwa Pass. Crossing the divide, he began to descend, still following the trail, which now ran almost due east.

During late evening, hungry after his long trek, the tom turned off the trail when he detected fresh deer scent. The odor of spoor led him north, toward Milk Creek, one of the many tributaries that feed the Telkwa River. He was about to cross the shallow stream when his keen eyes caught the movement of brush some five hundred feet below his position. He immediately began to stalk, the scent of deer now strong in his nostrils.

Half an hour later, near the place where Milk Creek joins the river, he killed a deer, a doe made barren by age and crippled by arthritis. After taking his fill, and as darkness descended, he lay down near the remains; soon he went to sleep, unaware that, only fifteen miles to the southwest, Taggart and Cousins sat in the one-armed man's cabin discussing their future plans.

Following their return to Moose-skin Johnny Lake headquarters the previous day, Cousins had treated Turk while his partner reported to Bell. Cousins, like so many men whose lives are spent in the wilderness, had acquired considerable skill in the treatment of injured animals, and the task of splinting and immobilizing the dog's broken leg had not taken long. The slashes on the hound's shoulder would certainly have been sutured had a veterinarian been available, but Cousins, lacking the proper surgical supplies, merely disinfected the wounds, which, in any event, had stopped bleeding by the time the party had returned.

Now, two days after the encounter with the white puma, the guides were again prepared to go after the prize animal. They were ready to leave at first light, although Cousins was not as enthusiastic about the hunt as his partner. "I don't reckon we're going to find that varmint in the time Bell gave us," he said.

Taggart, sipping rye whiskey from a plastic tumbler, waved his glass at the younger man. "We got the two dogs. We know where the cat was last time we saw it. We know the country. Course we'll get it!"

"Maybe. But I figure . . . by now, it could be anywhere within fifty miles from where we lost it. Sure wish we could use the Cessna!"

Taggart had finished his whiskey. He leaned forward, reaching for the bottle as he spoke. "You know darn well aircraft ain't no good at this season. That varmint's got too much green cover now. Without snow to spot its tracks, it'd be useless to fly over all that country, even if Bell agreed."

Cousins nodded. "So, where do we start to look?"

"We go back to where we lost the trail and we climb that mountain and we pick up the trail," Taggart said.

Unconvinced, but willing to go along, Cousins shrugged.

It was still dark when the guides set out the next morning, accompanied by Taggart's two hounds. As usual, Cousins trailed behind his partner, leading the packhorse. Because it was too dark for him to see, Taggart allowed his black to pick its own way along the narrow, rough trail that led from Moose-skin Johnny Lake to McDonell Lake. The horses walked slowly, but their riders were often scraped and buffeted by unseen branches that, like skeletal hands reaching for them in the darkness, stung their faces and knocked off their hats.

Dawn allowed the guides to take control of their mounts,

but the rough terrain east of the Hazelton Mountains continued to slow their travel so that, by sunrise, when they had been in the saddle for more than three hours, Taggart called a halt. They had traveled only eight miles.

"Hell," he said, lighting a cigarette. "At this rate we ain't going to reach the Zymoetz till dusk!"

Cousins shook his head. Drawing on one of his brown-paper cigarettes, he exhaled a cloud of acrid smoke before answering. "No. Trail's better up a ways, about another two miles. Reckon we'll be at the spot where the cat killed Blue by around one, two o'clock."

"You sure?"

"Yeah. I know this country, Walt."

The big man nodded. He was familiar with all the trails in Bell's southern region, but he knew that Cousins had spent considerable time in the northern range.

As the hunters plodded northwest, aiming for the place the puma had attacked the dogs, the white tom, thirty miles away, crossed the Telkwa River and continued south, a direction that within the next few hours would lead him to the Eagle Mountain cave where his mother had taken refuge after being wounded by Taggart—and where she had unwittingly caused the guide to lose his arm.

Arrived at the place where the puma had killed Blue, the guides dismounted and tethered and belled their horses. Afterward, with Cousins ahead and leading the hounds, they began to climb the mountain.

The dogs, although they were clearly able to pick up the weakened scent of the puma and of their ill-fated companion, showed by their demeanor that they were following a cold trail. Two hours later, however, after a difficult climb to two thousand feet, the hounds began to show more interest. Noticing this, Cousins accelerated and, as he was doing so, called back to his companion, who was some distance to the rear. "Scent's stronger now, Walt. I'm going ahead."

Taggart, his face almost purple from exertion, managed to yell at the younger man. "*Damn it,* Steve! You wait for me!"

Before Cousins could reply, the dogs darted forward, stretching their leads to their fullest and pulling Cousins upward while struggling to reach a thick patch of dwarf juniper. The guide, thinking the puma might be lying in ambush, pulled back on the leads, halting the dogs, but he quickly realized that if the mountain lion had been nearby, they would have been extremely excited and would have started to bugle loudly. Releasing the dogs and following them at the double, Cousins saw the reason for their increased interest.

Scattered behind the junipers were the remains of the dead hound. All that was now left of Blue were a number of yellow bones—some much chewed and cracked—a few pieces of sinew and skin, the dog's torn collar, and a scattering of chocolate brown hair. Tracks in the area showed that a variety of other mammals and birds had fed on the hound's remains.

Cousins turned away and began to descend, pulling the dogs with him. He was anxious to intercept Taggart, to prevent him from seeing what had happened to Blue and so to forestall an outburst from him.

Even so, on learning of Cousins's find, the big man swore loudly and without stopping for half a minute. After a breath-catching pause, he vowed to exact vengeance. "I tell you, Steve . . . I'm going to gut-shoot that cat and I'm going to watch it die! And *that's a fact!*"

Cousins merely nodded. After some moments he opined that the white puma had crossed the east-west divide and was probably on the far side of the mountains that run between the Zymoetz and Telkwa rivers. "I figure we should mount up and circle back to the McDonell trail. Then we'll head south to the

Telkwa. If we hit the tracks before, we follow; otherwise, I bet the cat's somewheres near the Telkwa Pass." As he finished what for him was almost a speech, Cousins lit a cigarette.

Taggart was quiet as he thought about his partner's proposal. Presently he nodded. "Yeah. Guess you're right. It's gotta cross the divide, for there ain't much to eat up there in snow country."

They camped that night at McDonell Lake and, leaving again at first light the next morning, covered the next twenty-five miles of their southward journey in under three hours, arriving at the junction of Milk Creek and the Telkwa River by eight o'clock in the morning.

Ten miles away, the white tom had found the cave and spent the night in it. But although he had explored the tunnel and den used by his mother as a refuge, he had elected to sleep in the cavern's main chamber, from where his ever-alert ears could monitor outside sounds.

He had awakened before dawn. Going outside to spray his scent over the rocks and bushes, claiming the place for himself, he smelled the strong odor of mountain goat. He followed the odor and soon located the animal, an old billy that had evidently fallen from a height and was lying dead in a rocky declivity, its body still in rigor, proclaiming that the animal had died only a few hours earlier. As a rule, the puma would have passed up a carcass he had not himself killed, but he was hungry, and the area around the cave offered no better meal. So, descending into the ravine, he fed on the cold meat. Afterwards, just as pastels of rose and purple tinted the eastern peaks, he returned to the cavern, intending to spend the daylight hours within the cool and darkened shelter.

Four hours later the baying of hounds awakened him. The bugling calls were distant, but, as he listened, he determined that the dogs were running toward his shelter. He leaped to his feet and snarled, raising his tail high. Stiff-legged, he strutted to the entrance, arched his back, and again sprayed urine over nearby rocks. He paused to listen. The baying continued to be faint. Snarling one more time, the white puma left the cave, going up-mountain and heading north, toward the Telkwa Pass.

After climbing over Eagle Mountain at a place fifteen hundred feet below the snowy peak, he began to descend. He intended to keep to the high country and so to stay out of reach of the men and their dogs, who, if they were to continue the chase, would have to take the longer, easier route to the Telkwa Pass.

By early afternoon the cat had found safe concealment two thousand feet above Limonite Creek, a location from which he could monitor the west entrance of the pass without fear of being seen or of being approached from behind. Here, tired after his arduous journey, he lay down. He was starting to get hungry, but after his distant contact with the hunters and their dogs, he preferred to wait for darkness before seeking prey.

Three hours later, the white puma heard the approach of horses. Soon afterward the mounted men and their dogs appeared at the entrance of the pass. The puma sat up, watching, his hatred rekindled.

When Taggart and Cousins stopped by Tauw Lake to discuss their plans, the puma remained immobile. When the men moved on, the cat followed. Later, he watched as they made camp.

13

Four hours after Taggart and Cousins crawled into their sleeping bags, the campfire still smoldered and an occasional short-lived flame burst out of the coals. Beyond the soft glow cast by the embers, the wilderness at ground level was an ebon mass, for the night was velvet black. But above the trees, clear skies were filled with the refulgence of uncountable stars. Cool temperatures had arrived with darkness, driving the mosquitoes to seek shelter under leaves or among shrubs and grasses.

During the last hour of his vigil, the white puma had descended the mountain slowly and in stages as he made his way toward the camp, his silent progress halted whenever the dying fire emitted one of its periodic flames. These sudden outbursts of light invariably caused the cat to freeze, and he remained unmoving for several minutes after each errant deflagration had died down anew. Patiently, he had continued to advance.

Now, at midnight, the white puma was within one hundred feet of the orange tent, downwind from the dogs and in a position to monitor the entire campsite by scent, hearing, and vision. Lying flat within the edge of the forest, the cat studied the camp. He could smell the dogs and the horses and he could hear them. He could also smell and hear Taggart and Cousins. Especially he could hear the one-armed man, who snored loudly. Snoring was a sound new to the cougar and one that at first inhibited him.

Presently, reassured, the cat moved forward in a stalk, legs bent, belly to the ground, ears flattened. He crawled yard by yard without making a sound until he was only twenty feet from the tent, facing it broadside. Here he paused, a white amorphous shape against the grass, while he monitored the camp again. It continued to be quiet.

The puma arranged himself for the charge. With his front paws stretched forward and flat against the ground, he raised his haunches and shuffled his back legs in position. Ready, he remained statue still for several seconds; then he launched, aimed at the tent and screaming his rage as he left the ground.

The impact of his body almost flattened the small tent, but, rather like a trampoline, it bounced the cougar backward. Astonished, the cat scrambled to his feet and, about to make a second charge, changed his mind when he heard the screaming and cursing coming from within the now thrashing shelter. Then a shot was fired.

The crack of the rifle, although partly muffled by the confines of the tent, caused the cat to jump in alarm at the same instant that he saw the flare from the gun muzzle reflected against the nylon. Well aware of the meaning of the rifle's sound and scent, he turned and dashed for the trees, the excited baying of the hounds spurring him to run at his best speed.

Inside the tent there was chaos. The cougar's claws had ripped a yard-long slash in one wall and broken three of the guy ropes, partially collapsing one side and half the entranceway of the shelter. Awakened so abruptly from a deep sleep by the unearthly cry of the charging puma, Taggart and Cousins had virtually exploded into uncoordinated activity when the tom's heavy body hit the tent. Struggling to free himself from his sleeping bag, Taggart had encountered his rifle with his left hand, accidentally hitting the trigger. The gun had exploded.

Still in his sleeping bag, Cousins was almost deafened by the rifle's report as the bullet whined past him, barely missing his flesh. *"Walt, you stupid bastard! You almost shot me, you damned fool!"*

Struggling to escape from the smothering nylon, Cousins found the slash made by the puma and crawled through it. Behind him, still entangled in the tent, Taggart continued to curse and thrash about. Guided by a few glowing embers, Cousins walked to the fire. Fumbling for some starter wood he had left near the makeshift hearth, he broke off small pieces and, on hands and knees, coaxed flames from the coals.

The fire cast a glow in the tent and allowed Taggart to get his bearings. Ridding himself of the sleeping bag, he followed his partner's example and crawled out through the slash made by the puma, clutching his rifle. Standing, he walked to the fire, glancing fearfully to left and right.

As Taggart reached him, Cousins had just finished pumping pressure into the gasoline lantern the guides always carried. He opened the gas flow and lit the lantern. Its bright light filled the camp's surroundings but could not penetrate beyond the trees and riverbank.

Together, while Cousins carried the lantern and Taggart held his rifle at the ready, the men walked back to the ripped tent and began examining the sandy ground. They soon found the white puma's huge paw prints and followed them back to the forest wall. They also found the place where the cat had lain in wait and the spot from which he had charged the tent.

"Christ Almighty, Steve! That cat's *hunting us*!" Taggart's usually loud voice was reduced to an awed whisper. Again he looked around, as if expecting the puma to appear out of the blackened forest.

Cousins nodded. "I think we better get the hounds. Bring them here, by the fire. We can't do anything else till daylight."

Collecting his rifle from the tent, Cousins returned to the fire and picked up the lantern. He and Taggart had started to walk toward the dogs when a long drawn, unearthly shriek filled the wilderness, a banshee wail that echoed among the mountains and seemed to surround the men. They stopped dead in their tracks.

"Oh my God!" whispered Taggart, raising his rifle to waist level.

"Jesus!" said Cousins, setting down the lantern and unslinging his rifle.

Without speaking, the two men positioned themselves back to back. Hardly had they done so when the scream came again, a primordial cry of pure rage that silenced, then caused the dogs to whine in fear.

Then there was quiet. An unnatural absence of sound in a wilderness where small, companionable noises were always present, even in the dead of night: the twittering of roosting birds, the patterings of mice and voles traveling through the underbrush, the small rustlings made by insects tunneling through dead wood. All of these had ceased. Only the gentle soughing of evergreen boughs fanned by the breeze and the crackling made by the fire dared to defy the silence commanded by the puma's voice.

Taggart and Cousins, unconsciously seeking reassurance, leaned against each other. And they clung tightly to their rifles. Safeties off, muzzles pointing at the darkened forest, the guns were ready to shoot at the phantom who had come so close to savaging the men's sleeping forms, the big, ghostly cat who had now openly declared war on them. But they could not see their enemy. Night was his amphitheater, the arena in which he was champion.

Fear virtually paralyzed the guides. They could not see beyond the flickering firelight and the circular glow of the lantern; they could not hear, and, certainly, they could not smell. The puma could be within a few yards of them. He could attack silently from any direction, and they were helpless.

Never before had the two hunters experienced such terror, never before had *they* been the hunted.

After launching his second cry, the white puma climbed Howson Mountain, passed below and between twin glacier-covered peaks, and descended on the east side, thereafter walking the lowlands along the southern section of the Telkwa River in the direction of Burnie Lake.

At dawn the following day, the cat killed a large marmot, eating almost all of it before lying up on a small, treed island that protruded above a marshy swamp near the headwaters of the Burnie River. He was now within six miles of the meadow where Bell's second horse herd ranged. Because he had never been in the region before, he was not aware that the remuda was nearby; nor did he know that High Country Safaris' third camp was located eight miles west of the southern tip of the lake and that it was to this lodge that Taggart and Cousins were even then making their way.

The guides had remained by their fire until the first light of day allowed them to see their surroundings. They had spent most of their time feeding deadwood to the blaze and cursing the puma. Throughout the night, despite the gasoline lantern, they had not dared to move more than a few feet from the campfire.

They discussed going to get the hounds, which had stopped whining soon after the last scream had spent itself in the distant wilderness. But the darkness and the continuing unnatural silence decided them against doing so. Both were afraid to leave the shelter of the fire, believing that the flames would keep the puma at bay.

Fear kept them from drawing on their own experience. No

feline predator will remain long in the vicinity of a failed strike, knowing that once a prey animal has been alerted, several hours—even days in some instances—must pass before it may again be stalked and charged with any hope of making a kill. But, instead of collecting their wits and packing up their equipment to be ready to leave at first light, Taggart and Cousins huddled by the fire until the rising sun actually showed above the eastern peaks.

Afterward, riding south along a narrow valley, the guides made plans, deciding not to mention the night's experience, fearing that a hue and cry would result and other guides would set out to kill the "man-eater." Instead, they would report that the horse killer had escaped but had been chased out of the range. For Taggart, it would take an effort of will to forgo the opportunity of regaling his soon-to-arrive fishing clients with a luridly exaggerated account of his experience with the "killer cat." But he reluctantly agreed to remain silent when Cousins pointed out that they would lose a lot of money if a widespread search for the puma was mounted.

"Even if me or you killed the cat, we'd have to share with the others. Anyways, we couldn't rightly sell the hide to Joe then," Cousins said as they neared the lodge.

Taggart, riding alongside his partner, nodded before speaking. "Yeah! Besides, Bell might refuse to hunt the varmint now, so he could offer it as a real prize to the hunters next fall. *He'd* get most of the profit."

This agreed, they radioed their story to headquarters from the third lodge, then went on to Moose-skin Johnny Lake for the start of the fishing season. Two days later the clients arrived.

Taggart's "pilgrim" was a short, stout man, an industrialist from Essen, West Germany. Judging from his attire and equipment, and, especially, from the eighteen-karat gold Rolex watch that was fastened to his left wrist by a gleaming expansion bracelet, he was obviously prosperous.

His name was Erwin Hegel, and he was visiting Canada for the first time. An avid fisherman and hunter, Hegel had read a High Country Safaris advertisement in a German magazine and, since he had to do business in Vancouver, had decided to try the fishing and, of course, the facilities of the lodge. If satisfied with both, he told Taggart, he would return in the autumn for the hunting season.

Hegel was an easy client to guide. He enjoyed large quantities of beer from two ice coolers provided by the lodge, and he listened with great interest to the guide's tall tales, being particularly intrigued by the story of the puma that had caused Taggart to lose his arm.

A few days later the weather turned cloudy and the thermometer climbed to eighty-five degrees by midmorning. Affected by the temperature, the lake trout became inactive. By noon Hegel had had enough. Red of face, with perspiration beading his forehead and soaking his shirt, the German asked Taggart to guide the boat to a shady place so that they could have lunch.

Hegel had earlier caught a three-pound smallmouth bass, and after Taggart grounded the boat on a shaded, secluded beach, he offered to grill the fish while the two men enjoyed a cold beer. After their meal, they sat on shoreline rocks, chatting. Taggart, relaxed and beery, let slip that he knew where to find a pure white puma. The news galvanized Erwin Hegel. "What? A white puma? I must have that! I can pay well for it!"

Taggart cursed himself silently. He had not intended to discuss the cat. He remained quiet for some moments, thinking. "Well, sir, it's like this, see. My partner and me, we already got an offer from a guy in Vancouver, who wants the cat's hide, head attached. And he don't care if he shoots it or we do."

"How much has he offered? Never mind, I offer you ten thousand dollars if you guide me. OK? A deal?"

The guide was staggered. In an unguarded moment he had blurted out a secret and cursed himself for doing so. Now he was being offered ten grand for the cat. Twice what Joe had agreed to pay!

"Yeah, well . . . you see, it just ain't as easy as that. First we gotta find the cat, then shoot it. And I can tell you this much, sir—that's a hard critter to get your sights on. And another thing! When me and Steve was after that varmint less'n two weeks ago, he up and charged our tent in the middle of the night. Yeah, that's a dangerous cat."

But Hegel was undeterred. Noting this, Taggart swore him to secrecy. "And we gotta keep it that way, else we'll have hundreds of guys out here trying to shoot it, you know?"

Hegel's eyes were glowing with excitement. He nodded his head. "But what happens if another hunter sees the puma?"

"Yeah, now that's a problem. You see, Mr. Hegel, me and Steve, my partner, we've agreed with our client—the one that offered *eight* thousand bucks—that *we'd* hunt the puma *out of hunting season.* We'll get it before the competition knows about it."

Taggart, having lied about the fee, went on to lie about the agreement. He and Cousins, he said, were to shoot the white puma as soon as possible, skin it, and preserve the hide and head, so that when the hunting season opened one of them could take the "client" out and, several days later, return to headquarters and claim the kill. "That'd make it legal, and he could ship the hide and head to his home in America with the proper papers," the guide concluded, adding that he and Cousins could not in good conscience break their promise to the client.

Hegel, an astute and hardheaded businessman in all other respects, took the bait. "My friend, what if *I* gave you twelve thousand dollars? Can you then not find some way to shoot the puma for me? Can you not tell your client that the puma is gone from here? That you cannot find it?"

Taggart pretended to ponder this proposal. In truth, he was

more than prepared to accept Hegel's offer, but he was not yet ready to make a firm commitment. He had to contact Joe, to see if the illegal trader would offer more than Hegel was willing to pay. But first he needed to think of an excuse that would persuade Bell to allow him to go to Smithers during the height of the fishing season. It would have to be a good pretext, for the outfitter was always reluctant to grant time off at this season. For the moment, the guide needed to play for time.

"Tell you what, Mr. Hegel. I can't promise for sure yet, but I'll talk with Steve and *maybe* we can make a deal with you. OK?"

Hegel, who knew greed when he was exposed to it, nodded assent.

Taggart offered his hand. After they had shaken, Taggart told Hegel that he thought their deal would probably go through. "But, you'd better book your hunting time with Mr. Bell right away. He's got lots of clients wanting to come out to hunt up here."

That night, Taggart and Cousins discussed Hegel's proposal. They agreed they should give Joe an opportunity to top the offer, but they did not believe the dealer would do so. If that was the case, Taggart would pretend to capitulate and promise to sell the puma's skin and head to Joe for five thousand dollars, as per their deal. They would, nevertheless, promise the cat to Hegel. And if he came up with the right amount of cash, he would get the prized trophy.

"We just tell Joe later that we couldn't shoot the cat and that Hegel got lucky and bagged it. Ain't nothing he can do about that," Taggart said.

"I hope Joe don't figure on cutting us out of the parts business, Walt."

"Hell, I don't figure he can! We've got him on that one. He sure can't turn us in. And if he tried to get someone else, we could turn *him* in. No. I don't reckon it'd ever come to that. Joe wants our parts pretty bad. And, let's face it, we done him pretty good until now."

Three days before Hegel was to leave High Country Safaris for Vancouver, where he had several business deals to attend to, Taggart entered Bell's office at seven in the morning and told him that he had been up most of the night, unable to sleep because of a raging toothache. This statement was half true, for, always thorough when manufacturing excuses, the big man had stayed up late drinking a considerable amount of whiskey.

Looking at him, Bell saw a haggard individual with bloodshot eyes, a day's growth of beard adding age to his face. He believed the excuse and arranged to have Taggart flown to Smithers so he could see a dentist. An hour later, Taggart arrived in the town, found a dentist, and submitted with trepidation to the drilling and filling of two molars, which had needed attention for some time but which, in the absence of pain, Taggart had neglected.

Later, when the local anesthetic had worn off sufficiently to allow him to talk coherently and without drooling, he called Joe's number. He was in luck. Joe was immediately available.

As expected, Joe was adamant. He had, he said, accepted Cousins's offer in good faith and had already made arrangements to resell the finished hide and head for eight thousand dollars. Joe claimed that he was making very little profit out of the deal. He was going ahead with it only because the buyer was a good client.

"Just don't get fancy with me on this one, pal! I've dealt fair with you, and I expect the same treatment from you guys. *I want that white lion!*"

Taggart offered reassurances. If they could shoot the puma,

Joe would get it for the originally agreed price. "Only trouble could be that we can't shoot it before the hunting season. Then maybe you'd have to wait for winter. OK?"

"OK. But no funny business, Taggart. I got a long arm, you know?"

Hanging up the telephone, Taggart was about to turn to leave the booth when he pursed his lips and blew a raspberry at the instrument. "Sure, pal! You're gonna come here and break my good arm, right? I'd like to see you try that, buster!"

Back at Moose-skin Johnny Lake, Taggart told the German he had a deal, and the next day, his last until he returned for the hunting season, Hegel paid Bell's extra fee for Taggart to take him riding.

The two men had traveled for several hours, stopping for lunch on the shore of the Telkwa River, at its junction with Milk Creek. Afterward, Taggart took Hegel to the cave on Eagle Mountain where the puma had caused him to lose his arm. Hegel took dozens of photographs, several inside the cavern with Taggart hunkering beside the crevice out of which the puma had leaped, the prosthetic arm well in evidence.

The next day Hegel was flown to Vancouver. Soon after his departure, one of the guides from Bell's third camp radioed headquarters to advise that another horse had been killed by a puma. The guide, whose job it was to check on the remuda from time to time, reported that the kill had probably taken place four or five days earlier. The tracks left by the cat, he said, were larger than any he had ever seen. Taggart and Cousins were again sent to track down and kill the offending animal, but this time Bell ordered them to continue the hunt.

"That horse killer's got to be stopped," the outfitter stressed. "You keep at it until you've got the cat, or until the hunting season. I'm surprised you didn't get it last time. You don't usually screw up on a hunt."

Taggart was offended by what he felt was a slight to his

abilities as a tracker and hunter. "We'll get the sucker, all right, boss. But this cat's different. It don't tree, it keeps to the high ground, and it attacks the hounds. If we could use one of the Cessnas, we would soon get it."

Bell shook his head. "I need all the aircraft; you know that. Besides, an air spotter can't see much at this time of year."

Taggart had bought two dogs to replace Blue and the still convalescing Turk. Both new trackers were experienced. One, a female named Queen, was, in fact, Blue's sister; she was considered an excellent cougar hound. The other, called Moose because of his size, was younger but had participated in several hunts. Queen had immediately become Taggart's favorite, not only because she resembled her brother but because on a recent trial she had proved herself eager and untiring.

Four days after Hegel had gone to Vancouver, the hunters left Moose-skin Johnny Lake at first light, covering the twenty miles to the Burnie Lake meadow in under five hours. There they located the remains of the horse and started the hounds on the old spoor. It led them south along the east bank of the Burnie River, which they followed for twelve miles without noting undue excitement among the dogs, all of which continued to nose the spoor while indicating by their behavior that the trail was old.

In early afternoon, soon after the guides had forded a small creek that tumbled down from Herd Mountain, the four hounds became excited. Queen, raising her tail high, began to bugle and to pull against her tether, the other end of which was attached to Taggart's saddle.

Cousins, riding behind his partner, led the packhorse and the other dogs. As the trail they were following became narrower and more thickly brush covered, the younger guide called a halt. "Wait up, Walt. I'll tie the packhorse here, it's getting too tangled to lead her."

As he waited, Taggart scanned the trail, which appeared to

become steep several hundred yards ahead, in an area where large boulders and deadfall trees indicated a relatively recent landslide. Queen, meanwhile, was straining at her lead and whining, eager to be let loose. Her companions, attached to Cousins's saddle, were equally anxious.

Having secured the pack animal, Cousins mounted his horse. As he did so, Taggart suggested that the dogs should be turned loose, but his partner disagreed. "Reckon we should wait a bit. I'd like to see what's ahead, up there, past them rocks."

Taggart nodded, kneeing his horse forward. The group followed the white puma's trail, the men carrying their unsheathed rifles, the dogs becoming more and more excited as they advanced. Five hundred yards up the trail, lying flat on an outcropping of rock, the white puma watched his pursuers, his stance denoting his hatred of these relentless enemies. To get to his vantage, the cat had detoured, climbing upward and away from the track, then circling back until he found the granite shelf that stood some twenty feet above the trail at a place where it was made narrow by a sudden drop-off, a steep, downward slope over which grew shrubby, second-growth alpine firs.

The tom's position was ideal for an ambush. He had chosen it deliberately some time after he had become aware that he was again being pursued. He was now employing the same hunting techniques he would have used had he been seeking to bring down a large prey animal. His pursuers had to pass below the outcrop, but just far enough away from it to allow the puma to leap downward upon one of his enemies. When he struck with his outstretched front paws, he knew that the quarry would be thrust violently over the edge and would then roll downward and into the concealment of the full-skirted young firs. He knew also that he would continue his own momentum and would follow the prey, but his descent would be controlled.

He waited, an immobile nemesis whose white coat was hardly visible from the trail and whose pursuers, guided by the dogs, would be so engrossed with the scent spoor that they would be unlikely to look upward.

Ten minutes passed. Taggart and Cousins were silent, each staring straight ahead, riding with slack reins and rifles at the ready. The hunters approached the ambush station, Taggart in the lead with Queen pulling at her tether. Within a few yards of the puma's hiding place, the black horse, perhaps sensing danger, snorted, but it obeyed when Taggart heel-kicked it.

The puma sprang. Uttering another of its unearthly, hate-filled screams, it soared off the ridge, front legs outstretched, the great paws spread, talons jutting out like black sickles.

Taggart's black had bucked just before the puma launched himself. Almost unseated, Taggart grabbed at the reins with his prosthetic arm, missed, and, as the puma shrieked, he dropped his rifle and screamed when he saw the charging white fury that was almost on top of him. But the gelding, by bucking when it did, had put its rider just out of range of the puma's formidable front paws, which struck the black horse's rump. The impact knocked Taggart out of the saddle and almost caused the gelding to fall over the edge. It screamed as the cat's talons raked its back.

Having missed, the puma sailed past the horse and landed some twenty feet down the slope. Alighting with his usual sure-footedness, he sprang away, clearing thirty feet. Landing, he leaped again and disappeared in the trees before Cousins could get his own horse under sufficient control to think about shooting.

The dogs became terrified as soon as they heard the puma's scream. The three tied to Cousins's saddle tugged hard on their ropes, further unsettling the guide, while Queen, secured to Taggart's saddle, was almost trampled by the excited horse.

Cousins was as afraid as he had been during the puma's night attack. He fired a shot down the slope, hoping that it would intimidate the cat. Then, getting his horse under control and dismounting, he tied the horse to a sapling and went looking for his partner.

Taggart lay sprawled on his back. He was unconscious and bleeding from a cut on his forehead.

Before attending to him, Cousins secured the black horse, which was prancing excitedly near Taggart's recumbent form, blood seeping down its left flank from three claw slashes on its rump. When the gelding was tethered, the guide took Taggart's canteen from its saddle pouch and walked to the injured man. Squatting and thrusting an arm under Taggart's head, he dribbled water over his face, talking as he did so. "Come on, Walt. I know you ain't hurt bad. You just banged your head. Come on!"

Taggart opened his eyes as Cousins was dabbing the blood away from the head injury.

"How're you doing?" Cousins asked.

"I'm OK. Got a damned good headache, though. That son-of-a-bitching cat! It's done it again. Did you get a shot at it?" Taggart sat up as he spoke.

"I fired a shot, but just to scare it. Couldn't see it. Can you stand?"

Helped by his partner, Taggart struggled to his feet. Blood still dribbled from his cut, but the injury was not serious. Cousins took the first-aid kit from one of his saddlebags and removed a small bottle of iodine, pouring some on a ball of cotton batting and dabbing at the cut. Taggart yelled, tried to jerk his head away, but Cousins held on and finished swabbing the wound, then peeled the protective tabs from a Band-Aid and applied it to the cut. "There. You should be fine now. Want a drink?"

"I sure as hell do, but not water. I got a half quart of rye in my saddlebag. Get it!"

Taggart uncapped the bottle, took a long swallow, rubbed

his lips, spat on the ground, took another swallow. He belched, then handed the bottle to Cousins, who took a quick swig, then went to check on Taggart's horse.

The black had three long but shallow scratches on his rump. Cousins wiped away the blood and cleaned the injuries with hydrogen peroxide. Ten minutes later the crestfallen guides mounted up and headed for headquarters.

14

On the day the cat jumped Taggart, Erwin Hegel was attending an evening reception in Vancouver, an affair conducted by British Columbian industrialists seeking wider trade relations with Europe. Hegel, who represented a German consortium interested in establishing a craft-paper pulp mill in Canada, was seated at a dinner table with Canadian and Finnish pulp mill specialists, two of whom had just invited him to visit a northern British Columbia community where, some years earlier, a large facility had been established with Canadian and Finnish capital.

"The autumn would be a good time to go north," said the Canadian. "And, if you like hunting, I'm sure something could be arranged for you. There's lots of game up there."

Hegel, his deal with Taggart still very much on his mind, explained that he was already booked for the autumn. The German had consumed a good amount of alcohol at a predinner reception and had continued drinking during the meal. Now, over cognac and coffee, he was feeling the effects of the evening. A man accustomed to heavy drinking, he was not entirely intoxicated, but his speech was slightly slurred, and he suffered few inhibitions. When the Canadian asked him why he could not put off his projected hunting trip with Bell's High Country

Safaris, he gave his audience a conspiratorial smile and blurted out that he was going to hunt a unique animal. Pressed, he told of the white puma.

His four dinner companions were polite, but they assured him that such an animal did not exist. None present had ever heard of a white puma. Hegel, irked by their disbelief, insisted that there was, indeed, such a cougar in the Hazelton Range. Three of his companions smiled, shook their heads. The fourth, himself an avid big-game hunter, said, "Herr Hegel, you are being fooled by that guide. I assure you that no white puma has ever been known to live in British Columbia. I'll tell you what, will you be satisfied if I ask Trevor Burns? He's over there, at the press table. Trevor writes business news, but he's a keen hunter and also writes a magazine column on hunting in British Columbia."

Burns, hearing his name and noting that he was being beckoned by the speaker, rose and walked over to Hegel's table. He listened to Hegel's story without interrupting and, unlike the German's companions, without signs of skepticism. When Hegel concluded, Burns asked, "What's the guide's name?"

On being told, the newsman showed excitement. He remembered the reports of Taggart's injury. "Well, white pumas *have* been known," he said. "Very few, but the records show that two were shot in Oregon before the turn of the century. Yes, it's possible for one to be in British Columbia. That surely would be some trophy worth having!"

Hegel was too muddled by alcohol to realize that he had now, almost literally, let the cat out of the bag.

Early the next afternoon, at Moose-skin Johnny Lake, Bell called Cousins to his office. "How's Walt?" he asked when the guide entered.

"He's OK. Got a bit of a headache, and, I guess, a bruise or two, but he's good. He's lucky. That cat almost did for him!"

Bell nodded, looked at some notes he had made on scratch paper, then looked up. "Right. Now, what do you know about a white puma that's supposed to be in our territory?"

Cousins was completely taken aback by the question. "I, ah . . . well, I guess not much" was the confused reply.

"That means that you *do* know about a white cat, right?"

"Yeah, I guess I—we, that is, Walt and me—we know about it. Yeah."

"And how is it that *I* didn't know about it until I got a radio call from some goddamned reporter in Vancouver?"

Cousins was stunned by this news. "Huh?"

"You heard me, Cousins! A reporter from Vancouver radioed in and wanted to know about the cat and about you and Taggart. *How come?*"

"Jeez, boss! *I don't know!*"

"Well, you'd better make it your business to tell me what's been going on with you and Taggart. The way I heard it, that German that Walt guided got snapped at a dinner in Vancouver and boasted he was going to come here in the fall to shoot a white puma. He told this reporter, that guy Burns, who writes for the *Hunt B.C.* magazine, and he radioed to ask me about the cat and to tell me that you and Taggart were going to guide Hegel, that you two were the only ones to have seen the white puma. So, talk!"

Cousins had no alternative, but he held back on the dealings with Joe and Hegel, explaining that he and Taggart had wanted to keep the cat a secret because they were afraid other hunters from outside the region would come to try to horn in.

Bell was not fooled. Knowing Taggart, he realized the big man must have made a side deal with Hegel, probably for a large sum, and so the two guides were reserving the puma for the German. What he did not know was that the animal in question was the one that had killed two of his horses and had attacked Taggart.

"Well, the secret's out now, so you two smart asses can't go through with whatever deal you cooked up with the German. Burns wants me to radio back to him to confirm or deny the story. I'm going to confirm it. And I'm going to advertise it for the coming season. That way we'll *all* profit. Having an albino cat in our territory will bring big-game hunters in here from all over!"

Bell had already decided to increase his rates for the season. Now he could charge even more to those hunters who wanted to be guided by Taggart and Cousins. And most would, since they were the only guides who had so far seen the cat and knew the range on which the animal had settled.

"OK, Steve, go and tell Taggart the news. By rights I should fire you both, but the way things have turned out, you and your crafty partner are going to make me some extra money. Oh, don't worry," Bell said as he noted the look that had come over Cousins's face. "You guys are going to be pretty popular guides, and *I'm* going to charge extra for your services. Like before, you'll get a share. Now beat it and get some work done."

Later that afternoon, Burns radioed for confirmation or denial of the story and Bell, seeing an opportunity for free publicity, confirmed the existence of a white puma in his licensed territory. Believing that he was lying to increase the publicity value of the affair, but unknowingly reporting the truth, Bell added that it was the white puma that only the day before had attacked Taggart, injuring him and his horse. "This is a dangerous animal," Bell told Burns. "Apart from going after Taggart, it has also killed two of my horses, it has killed Taggart's best tracking dog, and it has badly mauled another of his hounds. We have a right to hunt it out of season. If by any chance we don't kill it before the season opens, it will surely will be brought down at that time."

Bell had no intention of going after the puma out of hunting season. He would lose a lot of bookings by doing that. But he believed his statement would get front-page treatment. He was right. The print and electronic media pounced on the news once Burns made it public.

Television film crews once again flew to Moose-skin Johnny Lake to interview Taggart, Cousins, and Bell. Although the one-armed guide enjoyed being the hero of the hour and was more than willing to talk about himself and his adventures, in the privacy of his cabin he berated his partner for admitting to the presence of the white puma. "You really screwed up! We sure as hell can't get twelve thousand bucks now. You and that big-mouth pilgrim sure messed it all up."

Cousins shrugged. As far as he was concerned, once Hegel had told his story, the damage had been done. "But we still got a chance. Bell wants us to go and scout for the cat after the newspeople booger off. Well, we do that." Cousins smiled. "But, if we find it, we shoot it. And we tell Bell we can't find it. That way, we still got the hide and head. And we can keep the deal with the German."

"You're right. But what if we can't find it?"

"We'll be no worse off. We can still take Hegel on the hunt. Maybe we'll get lucky anyways."

One week later, when all the newspeople had left, Bell ordered the guides to go and look for the puma. "But don't shoot it! Just find its range. I want that cat alive for the hunting season," the outfitter said.

The white puma had traveled south, once again climbing over the mountains, for he was well aware by now that neither the men nor their dogs could track him in the high country. From Herd Mountain he worked his way due south, now and then having to descend into the lowlands, but always climbing as soon as he had crossed from one mountain to the other.

Ignoring hunger, the puma loped almost nonstop for three days and four nights, until he descended Nanika Mountain and at dawn reached the northern end of Morice Lake. Padding along the shoreline while continuing to head in a southerly direction, he reached the Morice River. Here he was forced to swim for almost a quarter of a mile in order to get to the lake's far shoreline near McBride Creek. By noon he'd reached the swampy, well-wooded region that lies between McBride Lake and the Nanika River. He killed a deer that afternoon. Later, having failed to detect any trace of human presence within the cloistered forests, he settled down, aware that prey animals were plentiful.

Taggart and Cousins spent the next ten days searching for the white puma in the wilderness that lies between Herd Mountain, Burnie Lake, and Howson Mountain, a rugged, isolated region encompassing more than 250 square miles. The only trace of the cat they encountered was the white tom's old trail, which led them to the place he had attacked Taggart.

Discouraged, with supplies running short, the guides abandoned the area on the tenth day, returning to Camp Three to restock their provisions and report to Bell, half-expecting the outfitter to order them to return to headquarters. "No," said Bell in response to Taggart's question. "You stay on the trail. Try farther north. I think you should follow the Zymoetz up to Red Canyon Creek, then head east. While you're at it, you might as well check on the horses up there. If you haven't cut any sign by the time you reach the horse meadow, head for Kitseguecla Lake. And if by then you've still not found the cat, come on back. I can't keep you guys out there forever!"

For the next eight days the guides continued to comb the country without results, reaching Kitseguecla Lake three weeks after they had left headquarters. Their midmorning arrival almost exactly coincided with the appearance over Moose-skin Johnny Lake of a single-engine, float-equipped Aeronca, which circled the headquarters site three times before touching down.

The pilot cut his engine as the two-seater slowed to a virtual stop one hundred yards from the mooring beach. While the plane was still moving, a man and a woman climbed out of the cockpit, each carrying a paddle, and descended on the floats, the pilot alighting on the left, his passenger on the right. Working together, they paddled the light aircraft to Bell's dock, there to be greeted by the outfitter, who believed that more publicity was coming his way.

"Hi! Welcome to High Country Safaris," he shouted jovially as he advanced, right hand extended. "I'm Andrew Bell, the owner."

The pilot stepped forward and shook the extended hand as he introduced himself. "I'm David Carew," he said. Then, nodding toward his companion, he added, "This is Heather Lansing."

The woman, a slim, tanned brunette in her late twenties, stepped forward and shook Bell's hand. "Mr. Bell, I am the president of the Canadian Conservation Alliance, from Vancouver. David Carew is a biologist who acts as our scientific adviser. We've come to talk to you about the white puma that has been reported in this area."

Bell's smile of welcome faded. He looked from Lansing to Carew, then, ignoring the woman, he turned to the man. "There's not a lot to talk about, mister. Yes, there's a white cat hereabouts. Yes, it has killed stock, and one dog, and hurt another, and attacked and injured one of my guides. And, yes, we're sure going to shoot it, sooner or later."

Carew smiled, but made no reply. He and Lansing just stood

there. Bell was puzzled at first. He looked at Carew, then at Lansing. After some moments it became clear to him that Carew was not going to reply, that by his silence he was pointedly telling Bell to address himself to Lansing. Scowling, Bell faced the woman. "So, apart from being a nature freak, you're a libber as well? OK. You heard what I told your bodyguard, or whatever he is. That's it. Now get going. You're trespassing on private property."

"You are wrong on several counts," Lansing replied, her tone level, her gaze penetrating. "First, *Doctor* Carew is a biologist and not my bodyguard—I don't require one of those. Second, we are not trespassing on private property. This is government land and you are licensed to hunt on it, but you cannot evict us or anyone else. Third, although I do consider myself to be liberated, in this instance, since I addressed myself to you, David quite properly refrained from replying to your rude and obvious attempt to exclude me from the conversation."

Bell was infuriated. "Listen, *lady*! I haven't got time to stand here listening to your yapping. Just tell me what you want and then get the hell out of here!"

"Thank you. What I want to tell you is that my group would like to invite you to help us preserve the white puma. It is a unique animal and should be allowed to live and—who knows?—to pass on its genes to future generations of white mountain lions."

The outfitter stared at Heather Lansing, his mouth open in astonishment. *"Are you out of your cotton-picking mind, lady?* Here I've got a unique cat that's going to bring me more hunter clients than I've ever had in any other season . . . and you've got the *gall* to ask me to help you save it?"

Bell looked at Lansing as if he believed her to be totally insane. Then, looking at Carew, he added, "Get that toy plane turned around and get out of here. Like right now!"

Lansing and Carew remained calm. Carew looked at his companion and nodded, silently suggesting that she should reply.

"Well, Mr. Bell, we will leave, but rest assured that you are going to be hearing from us. *And* you will see us again. I promise you, that if you kill that puma, you will regret it!"

Not waiting for a reply, the couple turned and walked to the Aeronca. They climbed on the pontoons and pushed away from the shore. Soon afterward they were airborne on a return course to Vancouver.

At Kitseguecla Lake, Taggart turned his horse around, aiming for the trail to Moose-skin Johnny Lake. "Well, that's it!" the big man said, swinging in the saddle to face his partner. "The varmint's disappeared. If we don't find tracks between here and Moose-skin, I reckon it'll be because it left the country."

Cousins shook his head. "Maybe it's holed up someplace we haven't searched, Walt. The way I figure, the cat's pretty cute. It has to know we're after it. Could be it's south, just waiting till we're tired of looking for it."

"Maybe so," Taggart replied. "Don't matter none just now. We gotta head for Moose-skin."

"Yeah," Cousins agreed. "Reckon you're right."

For the next two hours the frustrated hunters rode in silence, Taggart, as usual, leading the way.

Reaching Hankin Lake, a small body of water some eight miles from their starting point, Taggart called a halt. "Let's take a break," he said, stepping out of the saddle and lighting a cigarette.

Cousins reached for tobacco and the brown cigarette papers he used and rolled himself a smoke. He had just inhaled the first puff when his belt radio beeped. He lifted the unit and opened the circuit, acknowledging the call.

Bell's angry voice emerged from the radio's speaker. "Get yourselves back here just as soon as you can!" he ordered. "I just got a visit from a couple of nature freaks who want to save the white cat. I got to talk to you. What's your location now?"

Cousins reported that they were south of Kitseguecla Lake and already heading for headquarters. "Well, get here as fast as you can. Over and out," Bell replied.

"Hell," said Taggart. "I'd figured on staying the night at McDonell, taking a rest. My arse is getting sore!"

"Yeah. Me too," replied Cousins. "But I reckon we'd better keep on going. The boss sounded real pissed."

While the guides were heading back to headquarters, the white puma was becoming greatly aroused by a scent being fanned toward him from the direction of McBride Lake. The odor was familiar. He remembered the female with whom he had mated. But this scent, although much like that given off by his first mate, was subtly different. One characteristic of it, however, was the same—the cat's sex hormones, which wafted his way and drew him inexorably. He started to trail the aroma.

The young female cougar had also scented the tom. She was in estrus, ready for her first mating. She was shorter and much lighter than the male, and her burnished coat displayed the characteristic colors of her kind.

When she heard the tom's cooing low whistle, she was padding through a cedar thicket some five hundred feet from where the white puma had stopped, his head held high, upper lip wrinkled as he siphoned her alluring odor. The female stopped also. She lifted her head the better to sniff the male's scent. An instant later she opened her mouth and cried her banshee wail, a love call that halted all the animals within its hearing and even seemed able to still the fluttering of the aspen leaves.

The tom, galvanized by the shriek, whistled his own subdued love call. The cat screamed again as she advanced.

Soon they met. The female, now coy, rejected the tom's initial advances by biting his shoulder and scratching his rump as he turned away. Afterward, she sprayed her urine over nearby bushes as the tom, now experienced, observed her and sniffed from a safe distance. When she was finished, he whistled; then he sprayed, aiming his rear at the only rock to be found in the swampy terrain, a monolithic granite cube that rose from the very edge of the swamp.

For two hours they danced, growled, sprayed, and called, each eager for the other's attentions. Then, in midafternoon, they mated.

For the next four weeks they remained together. At the end of that time, the white tom left the valley.

Bell emerged from his office as Taggart and Cousins rode into headquarters. "Take care of the animals," the outfitter ordered. "When you're done, come to the office."

Twenty minutes later, sitting in front of Bell's desk, the guides heard about Lansing and Carew. "You know what that means," Bell concluded. "So, after you rest for a couple of days, you're going back out there and you're going to find that confounded cat, if it really exists. Then you're going to map the area and keep tabs on it, if need be, until the hunting season opens six weeks from now, OK?"

Taggart and Cousins were secretly delighted by these orders. Nodding agreement to Bell's instructions, they were about to leave when Bell stopped them. "While you're surveying, plot the location of any other cats in our region," he instructed. "I've decided to call the fish and game people in Victoria and ask them to declare open season on *all* cougars in our region. I'm sure they'll agree . . . I've some influence there, you know. Then I'll phone a number of good clients and offer them a chance to come and hunt mountain lions ahead of the season. The white cat will be the big draw. Hell, boys, we're going to have one damned good season this year."

When the guides left his office, Bell telephoned Victoria and had little difficulty persuading the authorities to agree to an open season. Politically, the outfitters had a lot of clout around Victoria's Parliament buildings, for they employed local people as guides and in other capacities and were thought to contribute to the economic well-being of isolated northern regions. Besides, the hunters, especially those coming from Europe and the United States, spent a great deal of money in the province.

The day after High Country Safaris received its open season permit, the media featured the story, the news having been routinely picked up by reporters assigned to cover government events. One prominent daily featured the story on its front page, leading the account with a description of the white puma and listing the number of attacks that this "killer cat" had already launched against Taggart and Cousins as well as on the horses and hounds. The article also made reference to a young male puma that some years earlier had wandered into a suburb of Vancouver and had been shotgunned to death by a government conservation officer, who had later stated that the animal was dangerous, which was why he had not been about to seek to immobilize it by using a dart gun to inject it with a tranquilizer. Dipping further into the past, the writer dredged up the stories of two boys who had been killed by pumas, one in 1924, in Okanogan County, Washington, and the other in southern British Columbia in the 1940s.

The writer, who was the newspaper's outdoors reporter and himself an avid big-game hunter, concluded that the British Columbian authorities had been wise to declare open season on pumas in the region and, especially, on the white killer. A sidebar to the main story on an inside page featured Andrew Bell's operation and described in more general terms the business of other outfitters, giving an account of the income generated by nonresident and resident hunters in areas of British Columbia that were otherwise economically depressed. It wasn't long before most newspapers in British Columbia and a good many outside the province carried stories about what some referred to as "the Great Puma Hunt," while radio and television stations sought to outdo each other and the print medium.

Meanwhile, Heather Lansing and David Carew mounted their own campaign, condemning the open season and, especially, calling for full protection for the white puma. Until she had become outraged by the government's management of the province's wildlife, Lansing had been employed as a copywriter for a large advertising company in Vancouver and had not given too much thought to the question of conservation. But when government biologists began shooting wolves from the air and poisoning them on the ground with the infamous compound 1080, twenty-eight-year-old Heather Lansing determined to work toward changing a system that, she now firmly believed, was rooted in medieval superstitions and perpetuated by human greed.

By means of a poll that she personally designed and supervised, she discovered that those who were opposed to the hunting of animals for sport and to the inhumane poisoning of predators that occasionally kill domestic livestock far outnumbered those who favored such killings. It was then that Lansing gave up her job and founded the Canadian Conservation Alliance, devoting half of her time to conservation and half to working as a free-lance copywriter, her days beginning at 7:00 A.M. and not ending until late evening.

Starting out virtually alone—except for the help of a few close and like-minded friends who donated time as volunteers—Lansing nursed her neophyte organization, which grew from seven individuals to a membership of over five thousand in two years. She worked hard, was expert at getting media attention, was articulate when addressing public meetings, and was totally dedicated to the conservation cause. At the end of this time, the Canadian Conservation Alliance was supported by donations and had its own board of directors. Lansing was elected its executive director at a modest salary and became able to devote all of her time to the alliance's affairs.

The year before she visited Andrew Bell, she had been approached by David Carew, who had taught biology in Seattle at the University of Washington, then had decided to go into business for himself as a conservation consultant. For a year he had been doing some work for the state government and some for the government of British Columbia, as well as for industry and municipalities. Years earlier, when he was nineteen years old, Carew had been drafted and, in mid-1970, not long before he was due to finish his tour in Vietnam, he had received several wounds, one of them serious enough to necessitate his return to the States. Recovered, he had gone back to school, studying biology at the University of Washington until he received his doctorate. Now, at age thirty-six, after reading about Heather Lansing's organization, he decided to join, offering his services as a consultant free of charge and, because he owned the Aeronca, flying Lansing and other CCA members on various assignments.

In just two years the alliance had expanded its membership beyond British Columbia to other parts of Canada and the United States. It had also become a thorn in the side of the Ministry of the Environment and, particularly, of its game and fish branch. Now, it seemed the CCA was going to become at least as big a thorn in the side of Andrew Bell.

After they had been widely interviewed by reporters who sought their comments regarding the open season on pumas, Lansing, Carew, and the four other members who made up the organization's executive staff held a strategy meeting in the dingy two-room offices that acted as their headquarters. The meeting lasted two hours. At the end, the conservationists were agreed on a plan they hoped would capture the media's attention and enable them to save the white puma and persuade British Columbia's Ministry of the Environment to rescind the open-season program.

15

After leaving his mate in the swampy region near McBride Lake, the white puma loped south, following the Morice Lake shoreline until he reached the Atna River and turned north, intending to return to the Zymoetz River but traveling in a leisurely way and stopping to rest for a few days whenever he made a kill. It took him sixteen days to arrive at the headwaters of the Clore River, a waterway that drains the Burnie and veers west some six miles south of the Zymoetz.

He arrived in midafternoon during the second week of July, just as an unseasonal heat wave enveloped the region and caused its many glaciers to pour icy waters into the lowlands. Hot and pestered by biting flies, the puma swam across the Clore and climbed up the south slope of Pillar Mountain until he reached the four-thousand-foot elevation, where ice patches still lingered to cool the ninety-degree heat and flies were absent.

Here he stopped, first drinking from a small, icy pond, then lying down in the shelter of a large patch of mountain huckleberry bushes, a screen that stood somewhat more than three feet but allowed him to see the distant valley lands when he chose to sit up and peer through the interstices of the thin trunks and branches. He was not, of course, aware of the controversy he was then causing, yet he was more than usually cautious, knowing that he was approaching the domain of his human enemies.

Tired and hungry, for he had not eaten during the last three days, he had earlier been tempted to hunt in daylight before seeking height and concealment, but prudence had urged him to forgo food in favor of safety. Lean in the belly but resolutely ignoring the pangs of hunger, he closed his eyes and went to sleep as soon as he lay down in the shelter of the huckleberries.

At eight in the evening he awakened to see that the sun, a huge orange disk, was hanging over the Dog's Ears Peaks, a series of triangular alps that lay some distance to the southwest. Stretching in the prone position, he rolled onto his back, his legs fully extended, claws extruded. He yawned, his mouth gaping, breath emerging from it audibly. Next he leaped to his feet, tail twitching, and he bowed, his front paws reaching forward, then scratching at the ground as they were retracted, the claws making a series of furrows among the shrubs and turning up yellowish soil and chips of ancient granite. Afterward, standing relaxed, he gazed down, an alabaster being waiting for the sun to hide its glowing face behind the western mountains.

Presently, as twilight came to cast shadows over the wilderness, the white puma began to descend, traveling in short leaps at an angle to the slope and soon entering the tree line, an area where grew an admixture of Engelmann spruces, alpine firs, and lodgepole pines. At first, most of these evergreens were somewhat stunted by altitude, but as the cat continued his descent the evergreens rose straight and to their full height. Here he stopped and checked his environment. He detected the faint scent of deer.

Orienting himself to the odor trail, he continued down-slope, walking in a half crouch, moving very slowly and stepping with great care.

Half an hour later he killed a mule deer in a lowland, marshy place near the junction of the Clore and Burnie rivers. The kill site was twenty miles from Bell's southernmost hunting lodge.

Erwin Hegel stood outside the Burnie Lake lodge waiting for Cousins and Taggart to bring up the horses and the hounds. The temperature was in the nineties, and Hegel's normally florid face was beet red; perspiration dripped down his cheeks and beaded his forehead. In his arms he cradled an expensive Manlicher Shoenauer carbine chambered to accept .375-caliber, 300-grain Magnum superspeed bullets.

Taggart, a gun lover, smiled widely. "Hey, that's some kind of gun! What's the caliber?"

On being told, he whistled. "Well, that gun'll come in real handy if we gotta knock down some trees!" he joked.

Hegel gave Taggart a frozen glance. "I am not interested in trees, Mr. Taggart. Only in the white puma."

The German's terse reply angered Taggart, but Cousins, recognizing the signs of an impending explosion, interjected. "He's joking, Mr. Hegel. That's a great weapon you've got."

Hegel acknowledged the joke with a bleak smile.

Ten minutes later, equipped for two weeks in the wilds, the party left the lodge.

Three weeks after the open season had been declared, no puma had been located by any of the High Country Safaris guides, nor by any of a number of local hunters who had been quick to take advantage of the open season and whose presence in his licensed territory was a thorn in Bell's side. He now regretted having spoken so freely to the press. Adding to the outfitter's annoyance were the conservationists now moving freely in the region.

David Carew had flown in two young men and had helped them set up a base camp beside Kitseguecla Lake. Because of the limited capacity of his small aircraft, Carew had made three trips to the lake to ferry in the passengers and all their supplies. Afterward he had remained at the camp for two days, flying the conservationists, one at a time, over the region to reconnoiter the area and allow them to orient their topographic maps with the features of the terrain.

Coincidentally, the camp was set up near the cave in which the mother puma had once sheltered with the white tom and his sister. The conservationists had used the anterior part of the cavern as a storeroom for nonperishable items of equipment, including several cases of canned goods; Carew had flown in enough food to last for one month. The cave also sheltered a battery radio.

When he was sure that the Kitseguecla camp was properly set up, Carew returned to Vancouver to pick up Heather Lansing. Jamming as many supplies as he could into the small cargo space of the aircraft, Carew then headed for Atna Lake. There, on a small, treed island at the eastern end of the lake, he and his passenger unloaded. This was to be headquarters, a base from which Lansing could contact her Vancouver office and communicate with the other camps, and, of course, from which she could travel through the southern part of Bell's Burnie Lake lodge region.

Leaving Lansing to set up camp, Carew took off again, returning to Vancouver to pick up more supplies and another volunteer, a twenty-four-year-old graduate biologist named Linda

Delacroix, who was to be Lansing's partner at the camp. Carew had next landed two other volunteer conservationists on the shores of a small unnamed lake three miles south of Burnie Lake. Finally, after making one more trip, he returned to Atna Lake to join Lansing and Delacroix.

The Canadian Conservation Alliance now had six of its members deployed in Bell's territory. All were determined to start interfering with the hunters as soon as possible. Carew, the seventh member of the group, was to act as liaison between the camps and, in his aircraft, as spotter.

Having become aware of the Aeronca's repeated flyovers in his region, Bell had sent out a spotter aircraft of his own. By the time that Carew returned to Atna Lake after supplying the last camp, the outfitter knew exactly where each party was located and how many conservationists were now in the region. He was greatly annoyed: he had come to think of the territory as his domain—a sort of personal fiefdom in which his word had always been law—but he well knew he did not have the authority to evict the intruders. He had already petitioned the Victoria headquarters of the game and fish department to order the conservationists to leave the region. But the officials, embarrassed by the negative publicity generated by the decision to declare open season on pumas, had firmly refused.

"Look, Mr. Bell," an official had remarked, "we have given you an open season on the mountain lions, and we have granted you a considerable extension of your licensed hunting territory. Both actions are justified, but I'm afraid that is all we can do for you. In fact, the minister of the environment himself has ruled on this. Of course, if those people were to do harm to your business, well . . . you'd no doubt be justified in taking appropriate—and, of course, *legal*—action on your own behalf. Do you get my meaning?"

"Yeah," Bell had said to himself after the conversation, "I sure *do* take your meaning!"

One way or another, Bell was determined to rid himself of those whom he deemed trespassers before the regular hunting season opened. He expected a lot of wealthy clients, and he didn't want a bunch of bleeding hearts interfering with his profits.

Before Taggart and Cousins had set out with Hegel, the outfitter had taken the guides aside and promised them a bonus if, as he phrased it, "those bloody activists discover that the land licensed to High Country Safaris won't tolerate their shenanigans. Since the German's booked for three weeks and has paid top dollar, you'll have to look after him," Bell added. "But just as soon as you guys get back, I want you to *persuade* that libber bitch and her hangers-on to get the hell off *my* property!"

"You care how it's done, boss?" Taggart had asked.

"No, I *don't* care! Just don't kill anyone. And no witnesses. Get one at a time!"

Hegel and his guides were only a few miles west of Burnie Lake when Carew's Aeronca flew over the party, the aircraft descending to within two hundred feet of the ground as it approached the riders. Taggart, in the lead, shook his prosthetic arm at the approaching plane, cursing loudly as he looked up, his left hand seeking the holstered rifle. Before he could grab the gun butt, however, the little two-seater began to climb again, turning southwestward as it gained height.

Hegel had seen Taggart's hand go to his gun. The move alarmed the German. "Mr. Taggart," he called, kneeing his horse forward to get closer to the burly guide. "I do not like to think that you would shoot at that aeroplane! If you plan to do that, then I cannot continue with you."

Taggart turned, grinning. "Nah! I ain't about to shoot at that kite. Just to scare the pilot a bit. Don't you worry, mister."

In the Aeronca, Lansing leaned toward Carew, speaking loudly to compensate for the noise of the motor. "That big man was reaching for his rifle, David. When you banked, I got a picture of him. If it comes out, we can send it to the media! That was great!"

Carew looked at her, smiled, and nodded. "I saw the move," he said. "I wondered if you'd notice. I don't think he'd have dared shoot, but I didn't waste time down there."

Carew and Lansing had been flying their first reconnaissance of the entire region and following the Burnie River when they had spotted the hunting party. Carew had been keeping the aircraft immediately above the water and in the center of the long valley, holding to an altitude of five hundred feet as they traveled but descending to within two hundred feet when they detected animals or, as they had just done, when they sighted Taggart and his party.

Lansing occasionally photographed the ground with a 35-millimeter Canon that was fitted with a 200-millimeter telephoto lens. She also had a video camera, but with the Canon in hand when she had seen the hunters, she'd only had time to take one still picture of the guide as he was reaching for his rifle.

Not long after they had passed Hegel and the guides, Lansing, using powerful field glasses to search the valley, saw a flash of white some distance ahead of the Aeronca. A *moving* flash of white! "My God, David! I just saw it. I *saw* the white puma, down there, in that small meadow! It seemed to be near that swampy part—see? Straight ahead. If you dip the nose, you'll get a good view!"

Doing as his companion suggested, Carew saw the junction of two rivers and a creek. In between the waterways there was a clear area and a marshy section that sloped toward the water. But Carew failed to see the puma. "I see the marsh. But I don't see a white cougar."

"No. It moved like a streak of light. I think it headed south. In any case, it disappeared in the trees. Let's fly over that part."

Lansing was looking at her topographic map as she spoke. "David, see that tall peak? Way over, to your left? I'm pretty sure that the puma was heading in that direction."

Carew turned the aircraft.

"That's it. You're heading right for it. The map says it's sixty-one hundred and three feet tall. It's called Hope Peak. The one before it doesn't have a name. It's five thousand feet high. See?"

"Yeah, I see. But Hope Peak's covered in ice. The cat won't be going up that. Maybe we should circle and see if we can get another look at it."

Carew swung the aircraft toward the east, then turned south again, intending to climb and make a pass over the lesser of the two peaks. As the Aeronca approached the mountains, Lansing, scanning the terrain through the binoculars, noticed a small open area, perhaps a few acres of scree that had sprawled into a declivity at the foot of a steep, slide-scarred ridge. Focusing the glasses, she saw movement. Seconds later she saw the puma, a beautifully lithe and milky shape that flashed across the scree and dashed into the trees. It appeared to be traveling on a southerly course.

This time, Carew also saw the puma. Even after the animal had disappeared within the trees, the pilot's eyes remained fixed on the evergreens, trying to catch another glimpse of the magnificent cat.

Lansing dropped the glasses and reached for the video camera, which she thrust out of her window. She remained poised, camera ready, as she scanned the terrain. When it became obvious that the puma had found deep shelter, she withdrew the camera and turned to her companion, her eyes glowing with excitement. "He's *lovely*, David! *Gorgeous!*"

Carew smiled, nodded. Then, "Hey, how do you know it's a male?"

"Well, I *don't* know. But I think of it as a male!"

"Whatever its sex, I think we'd better do a bit of faking. If we follow, that bunch back there will maybe guess we've spotted the puma. What do you say we turn around, fly toward Pillar Peak, and do some circling between the mountain and the river?"

"Yes, let's do that! They'll believe we've spotted the puma."

Carew turned the Aeronca and within minutes was flying fairly wide circles over the Clore River, staying between Pillar Peak on the northeast and Nimbus Mountain on the southwest. A quarter of an hour later, as Carew was about to suggest that they return to Atna Lake, he saw the hunters. Even from a height of three hundred feet and a distance of a quarter of a mile, he was able to note that the party was hurrying. Taggart, in the lead, was spurring his mount; Hegel was some distance behind him, and Cousins farther back. The four hounds, still attached to the second guide's saddle, were jumping excitedly, evidently infected by the excitement of the humans. It was clear that humans and hounds were convinced a puma was somewhere in the river valley.

"Now, David! Let's get out of here. Make as if we've been surprised."

Carew nodded. Gunning the motor, he raised the aircraft's nose and headed south, soon to disappear between Hope Peak and Dog's Ears Peaks.

On the ground, Taggart again raised his prosthetic arm and shook it at the aircraft. Watching the guide through the field glasses, Lansing could see that he was laughing and yelling something to his companions.

"Those stupid jerks just showed us a cat," Taggart called, reining his mount to a stop.

Cousins rode up to him, leading the four hounds. The dogs were quiet now, showing no interest in the trail. "I don't know, Walt. The hounds ain't acting like there's a cat hereabouts."

"No. But the plane was farther over, down there, where the Burnie meets the Clore, maybe two miles ahead when it saw us and turned to have a look," replied the big man, greatly overestimating the distance.

The party rode west, the horses going slowly at first because the terrain sloped steeply toward the waterways. When, about twenty minutes later, the hunters neared the place where the white puma had made his kill the previous night, the hounds began to strain on their leads, baying loudly. They had the cat's scent.

"Here we go! Let them loose, Steve," said Taggart.

Hegel, riding just behind the one-armed guide, pulled his rifle out of the saddle holster, worked the action to put a shell in the chamber, and set the safety catch. His hands trembled slightly as he held the gun across his saddle.

As soon as Cousins released the dogs, they raced away, tails held up and curving over their backs. Within minutes they had found the remains of the puma's kill and begun circling it, sniffing and baying. Then the lead hound picked up the cat's trail and began to follow it, only to be halted by an almost perpendicular granite cliff that stretched north and south for several hundred yards. It was part of the northeast flank of Nimbus Mountain. About two thousand feet above the location, the trees ended and the scree and ice began. The puma had easily scaled the cliff, but the hounds, although they tried repeatedly, kept sliding down the incline.

Taggart began to curse, but Cousins, remembering that the Aeronca had been circling the river valley some distance ahead of the kill site, dismounted and leashed the dogs, pulling them away from their excited labors and tying them to his saddle.

"The way I figure, Walt, the cat climbed up here, turned northwest, and kept going past Pillar Mountain. Why else would that plane have been circling?"

"Damn, I reckon you're right. Sure, the conservation freaks spotted the cat and circled it. When they saw us, they took off quick, trying to pretend they'd seen nothing. OK, let's ride."

They set off at a good pace, soon having to ford a creek to cross over to the north side of the Clore River. But after traveling for eight miles, the hounds had failed to pick up a scent. Cousins, who had used his field glasses to watch the Aeronca, was sure they were still within the circle flown by the aircraft. But apart from one hundred yards or so of shrubs and grasses that covered each bank of the river, dense stands of spruces rose up-mountain, cutting visibility to zero. "Well, either that aircraft fooled us into following it into this country, or the cat was higher up. Any which way you look at it, *we* can't follow the critter. So . . . what'll we do now?"

Taggart cursed. Looking around, he shrugged. "I guess we'd better get going, find us a campsite, and settle down for the rest of the day. Tomorrow, early, we'll try again. There ain't much we can do now, it being afternoon and all."

In camp, Lansing briefed Linda Delacroix, describing the white puma and the hunters who were on its trail. "I think that by flying in circles, we put the hunters off the track," she said. "The question is, what do we do next?"

Carew had been studying the map of the region. "It seems to me that we ought to try and locate the puma. First, though, we should do a flyover and locate the hunters. If we can find their camp, at least we'll know if they're near the cat," he said.

Delacroix also had a map. She had marked the locations where the puma was sighted as well as the area circled by the aircraft and later approached by the hunters. "We still have good light. Why don't we fly out now, David?" she suggested.

Carew looked at Lansing, who nodded. "OK. Let's refuel and take off."

Soon afterward, with Delacroix in the seat beside him this time, Carew took off from the lake on a direct course for Pillar Peak, fourteen air miles away. Shortly after crossing the Burnie River, Carew saw a thin tendril of smoke rising from about ten miles north of his position. The pilot nudged his companion and pointed. "Smoke. Dead ahead," he said.

When the Aeronca was less than a mile from the hunters, Delacroix picked up the field glasses, leaned close to the windshield, and focused. A moment later she lowered them and turned to Carew. "That's them, I guess. They've camped. There's three guys, four horses, and some dogs; four, I think, but they're tied near the bush and I can't make them out too well."

Carew nodded, continuing to fly toward the smoke. Moments later, he turned to his companion. "We'll be right over them soon. I'm dropping to two hundred feet. When I say *now*, I'll tip the nose down so you can use the video. Get ready."

Through the telephoto zoom, Delacroix was able to positively identify the party. The camera's focus changed automatically as the aircraft approached the camp. She soon noticed Taggart's prosthetic arm, for the big man was standing and looking directly at the Aeronca. Then Cousins, who had been crouched in front of the campfire, rose to his feet and lifted the field glasses that hung from his neck, focusing them on the aircraft.

"The thin man is watching *us* now, David," Delacroix noted.

"Yeah, I can see that. Let's swing away." Carew began to

turn the aircraft as he spoke. "Get your map and plot their position."

Scanning the topograhic chart, Delacroix soon located the campsite. "They're southwest of Howson Peak, camped on the shore of Miners Creek, near a marshy area. It looks like the creek is a tributary of the Kitnayakwa River, which flows into the Zymoetz," she said.

Carew banked the aircraft away from the camp and headed west before answering his companion. "OK. We know where they are. Looks like they've set up a base camp. That's logical. From the camp, they can ride through the valleys and passes to search for the cat. Let's go back to base and make plans."

As the sun was setting that evening, the three conservationists sat beside a small fire on the island's north shore. They had eaten supper, a relatively spartan yet nourishing meal consisting of instant potatoes, freeze-dried vegetables, and fresh-caught rainbow trout. Now they were plotting strategy.

"I'm convinced the puma was headed south," Lansing was saying as she poured herself a second cup of instant tea. "And looking at the map while you two were searching for the hunters, it seemed to me that a likely place for the puma would be somewhere southeast of Dog's Ears Peaks, in a little valley where there are three small lakes. Here, look."

Spreading the map, she showed Carew and Delacroix the tracings she had made. The three lakes formed the middle of a triangle between Dog's Ears Peaks, Hope Peak, and Corona Peak. The area was filled with streams, and the valley was accessible on foot via the lowland passes and valleys that lay between them and Atna Lake.

"From the map, I calculate that the lakes are between eight

and ten miles from the west end of our lake. It shouldn't take longer than four or five hours to hike in from here."

Carew interrupted. "That's quite a walk, Heather. There's nowhere there for the plane to land, so whoever goes will have to carry supplies, the small pup tent, and a radio. Could be a problem to explore that country on foot."

Holding her finger on the map, Lansing looked at Carew. "*I'm* going in there! Linda can stay here and coordinate, and you can fly over now and then. If I need supplies, you can drop them. You *did* bring those little parachutes?"

"Yeah, I brought them, but that's some trip you're contemplating. What happens if you get hurt? And what do you do if you find the puma?"

Lansing's mouth set stubbornly. "I'm *going*, David! I have this feeling . . . the puma's there. I just *know* he is! And don't forget, I've climbed a lot of mountains. I *know* what I'm doing. I'm going, and that's all there is to it!"

Carew and Delacroix looked at each other. Both knew Lansing; they recognized her determination. Delacroix nodded at Carew, signaling that they should not continue to object.

"You're one stubborn woman, Heather! But, OK. Only *I'm* walking in with you. I'll carry extra supplies and help you make camp. Then I'll head back."

"Look who's talking about a long walk now!" Lansing said. "All right. If you think you're up to a twenty-mile walk in one day."

Carew laughed, shook his head. "No, I'm not. I'll pack a sleeping bag and ground sheet, and I'll sleep along the trail back. I figure that once we get there, you'll be set up in about an hour. Then I'll head back. If we leave at first light tomorrow, we should reach the lakes by no later than ten o'clock. If I leave you at noon, I can be halfway back before I get too tuckered to keep going. I'll camp for the night and be back early the day after. Linda can hold things down here while we're gone, and we can keep in touch by radio. OK?"

Lansing and Delacroix nodded agreement.

"Well, if that's settled," Delacroix said, "I suggest we turn in early. Tomorrow's going to be a hard day for the two of you. But there's one thing I've got to say. According to reports, that puma is dangerous. Maybe the media exaggerated, but there seems no doubt that it attacked the two guides. If you find its territory, what if it attacks you, Heather? Or you, David? And what about grizzlies?"

Carew made to reply, but Lansing spoke first. "I'm not convinced that what the guides reported was true. In any case, we have a good supply of bear bangers and the road flares. And I guess I can take the air horn. That's enough to frighten grizzlies, pumas, or whatever. But I'm *quite sure* that animal won't attack us if we go in peace!"

Lansing and Carew left at daybreak the next morning, using the aircraft to taxi to the far side of the lake so they could save themselves a two-mile walk and, on arrival, anchoring the plane in shallow water, securing it additionally with a line to the shore. So as not to isolate Delacroix on the small island, Carew had inflated the two-passenger rubber raft they'd brought with them. Equipped with oarlocks, the sturdy craft could be rowed by one person, or, like a somewhat clumsy canoe, it could be paddled by two. In the raft, Delacroix could quickly cross the narrow channel that separated the island from the lakeshore, a journey she planned to make that day in order to explore Morice Lake's southernmost, finger-shaped bay and its surrounding country.

Carew and Lansing donned their packs. Carew carried a large canvas pack fitted with a leather tumpline strap that rested on his forehead and eased the weight. In the pack he carried a radio, his own rations and sleeping gear, a package of road flares, and extra food supplies for Lansing, a load that weighed some sixty pounds. Lansing carried a modern, tube-framed rucksack made of nylon, a bag smaller than Carew's but weighing nearly forty pounds nonetheless. Burdened as they were, the conservationists soon realized that the journey they had undertaken was going to be challenging.

As they stepped away from the lake, they immediately felt the pull of their loads. Both were fit and accustomed to physical activity, but it had been some time since they had hiked a long distance while carrying heavy packs.

"Just as well we left early," Carew commented as they trudged up a slope. "If it gets as hot as it was yesterday, by noon we're going to have to rest up for at least three hours."

"You're right," Lansing said, stopping to adjust a strap that was already cutting into one shoulder. "I think we should walk as fast as we can for an hour, rest for ten minutes, and do the same again. Maybe we'll get most of the way before noon."

Adhering to this plan, they trudged on, the perspiration soaking their clothing and dripping into their eyes, despite the headbands they wore. Between 6:00 that morning, when they left Atna Lake, and 10:30, when they were too tired to go on, they covered something more than six miles, despite their loads, the heat, and terrain that at times forced them to climb several hundred feet before they were again able to descend to the narrow valleys that led circuitously to the three small lakes.

Lying exhausted in the shade of a thick stand of aspens and with a cool breeze fanning downward from the summit of Corona Mountain to compensate for the heat, they went to sleep, heads resting on their packs. An hour passed. Carew's and Lansing's heads were covered by nets to ward off the biting flies, and they were wearing light cloth gloves. A breeze stirred the treetops, filling the forest with susurrus that occasionally was punctuated by a snap when a forest dweller stepped on a dry and rotting branch.

During the first fifteen minutes of her sleep, Lansing had several times been awakened by those percussive little sounds and by the calls of the birds, but she soon learned to tune them out and entered into deep sleep. Now, as another such breaking branch announced animal movement, she and her companion continued to slumber.

Moments later, a black bear approached Lansing's pack cautiously. Lured by the scent of food, the yearling female was at the same time daunted by the variety of other aromas that emanated from the recumbent figures. The bear had never before encountered humans, but she sensed that these strange beings were alive and, perhaps, dangerous. Still, the tantalizing smell of beef jerky and dehydrated chicken soup drew her on. Step by step, pausing often and ready to bolt, she advanced. At last she was within reach of the pack. As she thrust her head forward, her black nose made contact with the nylon. The aroma that entered the bear's nostrils was too tempting to be denied. She pushed harder, opening her mouth at the same time.

Lansing awakened with a start. She raised herself on her elbows and turned her head. For a split second neither the bear nor the woman seemed to credit what their eyes were telegraphing to their brains. Then Lansing sat bolt upright, screaming. The bear huffed loudly and began to dash away, but one of her paws landed on Carew's head. Already awakened by Lansing's cry, but unaware of its cause, Carew gave a yell of his own as the bear's sharp claws scratched his scalp through his bush hat, dislodging the headgear and, with it, the fly net. As Carew and Lansing leaped to their feet, the young bear ran at full speed, dashing between the boles of the trees as she sought refuge in the dense evergreens that grew only a little distance up-slope.

The conservationists realized the cause of their disturbance almost at the same time. They looked at each other, frowns creasing their foreheads. Then Carew suddenly burst out laughing. Lansing, responding to his guffaws, began to giggle nervously. Afterward, Carew felt his scalp. The bear's claws had not drawn blood.

They resumed their journey, walking more slowly because of the noon heat but feeling somehow elated by the brief encounter with the young bear.

"You know," Lansing said, "I'm sure that the bear was more scared of us than we were of it."

"Maybe so," Carew replied. "But, for a couple of seconds, when it stepped on my head, I reckon I was probably as scared as it was. I'm glad it happened, though. It emphasizes the need to keep your food supplies suspended high from a tree branch."

16

Lansing was awakened at dawn by the call of a varied thrush.

The bird sat in a tree near the orange pup tent, perhaps drawn by the color of the material, which, to the jealously territorial songster, may have looked like a large, competing male of its own species. The repeated quavering, high-pitched whistles ended with a pause but were quickly followed by a short low note. Then the song was repeated, again and again.

Stretching and yawning, Lansing remembered last night's fears. At first, sitting before a small campfire drinking hot tea, she had been fascinated by the arrival of dusk and by the sleepy voices of roosting birds. Later, when darkness had limited her vision to a few feet around the flickering halo of light cast by the flames, she had begun to feel uncomfortable. And lonely.

Carew had helped set up her camp on the shores of the southernmost lake. During midafternoon he had cut up a supply of firewood. And he had tossed a rope over an outreaching branch of a tall dead cottonwood, a limb that was strong enough to support the weight of her food pack but too small for a black bear to climb and too far from the trunk for a raider to reach the supplies with an outstretched paw. That done, he had left her.

Alone, but confident in her abilities to carry out the task that she had set for herself, Lansing had gathered up her compass, map, camera, and binoculars and gone to explore her immediate surroundings, walking first of all to the other two lakes and later climbing to the two-thousand-foot elevation, to scan the country through field glasses. She had returned to her camp as the sun was setting.

Relaxed and content during supper and while doing her chores, Lansing had devoted no thought to the possibility of danger. But when full darkness had arrived and small noises echoed within the forest that surrounded her on three sides, she'd begun to feel nervous.

Remembering the bear that had investigated her food pack, she could not help wondering what she would do if an adult black bear were to arrive at her camp during the night, drawn by the smell of her cooking. Or worse, a grizzly. Such an animal could tear her thin shelter to shreds with one swipe of its massive paw before she could reach for the air horn or light a highway flare.

Thinking about such things while trying to force her eyes to see beyond the dancing firelight, she realized that she was on the verge of panic. She had always been an active woman; she loved the mountains and had climbed many of them. She was fit and strong, and she was a determined person. Now, facing stark fear for the first time in her life, she drew on her resources.

She stood, turned her back on the fire, and looked up. The sky, blue-black and filled with countless stars, greeted her and gave her a sense of majesty, of inner peace. She smiled, turning back to the fire. Carefully, using a three-cell flashlight to guide her work, she shoveled lakeshore sand on the flames, covering the fire until it was quite extinguished.

Finished, she walked to her tent without benefit of light. She was, she thought, emulating the white puma, copying as best she could in her own, unspecialized way the behavior of that wonderful animal—walking in the dark, seeing the night sky as he would see it, feeling confidence in her own ability to survive, as he must feel confident in *his* survival prowess. Entering her tent, she undressed and crawled into her sleeping bag. Five minutes later, thinking of her glimpses of the wraithlike white puma, she fell asleep.

This morning, attended by the cheery call of the thrush as she emerged from her sleeping bag and began to dress, Lansing could hardly believe that she was the same woman who last night had sat frightened in front of the fire. Today she felt confident, exhilarated. More than that, she felt that she belonged in the wilderness, that, although alone, she was not alone, for she had become a part of this pristine sylvan world; she was in tune with the wild and could now sense its pulse. Most of all—and although she admitted to herself that it was a preposterous thought—she believed that the wilderness respected her presence; that, somehow, the beings who lived in this alpine kingdom knew who she was and why she was here. Especially the white puma! Although she knew that she had no valid reason for thinking about him as she did, Lansing, a pragmatic woman in most other respects, felt that she and the white puma were mystically united. It was, she thought, as though they were one in spirit.

Humming quietly, she walked to the water's edge, a small plastic basin in her left hand, her sponge bag in her right. Kneeling, she dipped the bowl into the icy lake water, withdrawing it full; then she rose and carried the water some distance from the shoreline. She removed all her clothes and washed herself, sponging every part of her body despite the shivers and goose bumps that covered her fair skin. Chilled as much by the water as by the coolness of the alpine morning, she toweled herself briskly; then, her skin dry and glowing, she dressed. Afterward, refreshed and continuing to feel exhilarated, she built a new fire, boiled water for tea, and ate a bowlful of dry trail rations, a mixture that consisted of nuts, sunflower seeds, soya beans, raw oats, raisins, and dried fruits.

One hour after awakening, Lansing prepared herself for the trail. Binoculars and camera hung from her neck; a haversack that contained the map of the region, a compass, the flares, and the air horn was slung over one shoulder; and a bag of trail rations was tied to her belt, which also supported a small hand ax. Now she was ready for her first day of exploration. But before setting out she radioed base, giving Delacroix the coordinates of the route that she proposed to take. She learned that Carew had not yet returned to Atna Lake but had checked in and expected to arrive within the next two hours.

Returning the radio to her tent—it was too heavy and cumbersome to carry on a day trip, she felt—Lansing left the campsite. Soon she began to climb, aiming herself in the westerly direction, toward the Dog's Ears Peaks. She planned to pass below the eight-thousand-foot glaciered alps at the four-thousand-foot level. From there, according to the map, she would encounter a defile that descended between the Dog's Ears and Hope Mountain to lead into the region where the white puma had last been seen.

The direct distance from her campsite to the start of the pass was two and a quarter miles, but the ascent, although covered in evergreens, which offered themselves for purchase, was almost precipitous in some places and in others was studded with fallen trees or tumbled rocks. Thus Lansing had to make frequent detours and, in the end, cover nearly five miles in five hours before she reached her goal.

It was eleven in the morning as, tired, hot, and thirsty, she sat down on a mossy rock, took a few sips of water from her canteen, and gazed downward. Only then did she realize that what the map had shown as a pass, while it did give access to the lowlands that lay to the north of Hope Mountain, appeared to be very narrow and quite steep, at least for that part of its descent visible from her vantage. What lay farther down was covered by serried ranks of evergreens, but beyond the trees she could see the meandering Clore River and a small open area on its east bank. Orienting her map, she concluded that the river was some three miles from where she sat.

She put the binoculars to her eyes and focused on the open area just in time to see a smallish brown shape emerge into the open. She was unable to identify it at first, but when the newcomer stopped, threw up its head, and yipped, the melancholy thrice-repeated cry reaching her faintly, she realized it was a coyote. Having called, the little wild dog trotted toward the river and stopped. It appeared to be eating something it had found lying there. Probably the remains of an old kill, Lansing reasoned.

She continued to watch. A few minutes later, another coyote emerged from the trees, stopped, looked around, and joined its companion. Movement in the top branches of an aspen that grew near the kill site attracted Lansing's attention. Focusing on the tree, she saw three large ravens sitting side by side on a swaying branch. The birds were preening. They had evidently fed on the carrion and then settled down to clean their shiny ebony feathers.

Lansing began her descent. At first, the journey down-slope was steep but free of detour-causing obstacles and was much easier than her climb had been. But after progressing for half a mile, she found herself enshrouded in evergreens, tall trees growing so close to each other that the bottom branches, all of them dead and dry, had become partially interlaced. The ancient game trail that snaked toward the bottomlands ran through the center of the forest. Four or five feet from the ground, the path was clear of obstructions, the dead branches having been broken off by generations of passing animals. Above that height, Lansing found that she must either stoop low or, using her belt hatchet, chop off the spiky branches that at times scratched her face and constantly threatened to tear off her hat and head net. The map could not have prepared her for such a habitat, but, determined to reach the lowlands, she persevered. And, despite her difficulties, she made relatively good time.

After an hour of uncomfortable travel, she was relieved when the land sloped more gently and its rocky nature prevented the trees from crowding together. She judged she had now reached the halfway point and was at an altitude of about two thousand feet. The trees that grew in this area were red cedars and white spruces, in some places mixing together and in others growing in small pure stands. Passing around a large granite boulder, she stumbled. Looking down, she saw puma tracks and realized that she had tripped over the animal's fecal mound. She picked up a dead stick and, snapping it in half, began to spread the mound. The fecal matter was soft and odorous, telling her that it had been deposited not long before, last night perhaps, she thought, her heart pounding rapidly.

Staring round eyed, she spoke softly to herself. "My God! Have I found him already?"

In reality, Heather Lansing had not found the white puma. *He* had found Heather Lansing.

The tom had become aware of the human presence in his range when Lansing began her descent of the pass. He had been resting within the heavy forest a short distance above where he had built his territorial mound. When the woman's scent first reached his nose, the cat lifted his head, took several deep sniffs, and pricked his ears forward. Without conscious effort, he immediately isolated every one of a variety of smells that emanated from the intruder's person, and he easily identified her sex from the minute amounts of hormonal discharges present on her skin, exudations so tenuous that a human nose could not have detected them had it been within an inch of her body.

The cat as quickly noted the other smells. Some were strong in his nostrils, such as the scent of the soap she had used to wash herself that morning and the woodsmoke from her fire, brewed tea, toothpaste, and the hair shampoo she had used two days earlier. And lipstick.

Lansing didn't know—as the majority of humans do not—that she presented a scent signature that was as uniquely her own as her fingerprints. The puma had no difficulty reading her olfactory signals. Just as a male moth, given the right wind conditions, can smell the scent pheromones of a sexually receptive female of his species across one mile, so the cat could get the scent of prey, an enemy, or another puma, from at least as far away. In fact, his nose was capable of picking up odors at a much greater distance than his ears were capable of detecting sounds, although his hearing was also acute.

Because survival so often depends on an animal's ability to *recognize* odors, the puma never forgot smells and unconsciously categorized them as being either important or unimportant. Within his own range, he knew the meaning of the odor of the different soils, of the various trees and plants, of the animals and birds, of the waters of lakes and rivers and creeks. Similarly, he had become intimate with the odors of Taggart and Cousins, with those of their dogs and their horses, and with the smell of the exhaust of those aircraft used by Bell and his pilots.

When the tom detected Lansing's presence, he became puzzled by her scent. In most respects it was unlike the smell of Taggart or Cousins, yet it was similar. This realization almost caused him to spring to his feet to gain height and thereby place himself out of reach of his enemies. But as he continued to sniff, he picked up only a faint trace of a scent that, when strongly emitted, was always associated with aggression and fear: the odor of adrenaline. During normal metabolism adrenaline is exuded in minute amounts; at times of aggression or anxiety, it floods the bloodstream and is then excreted in large quantities. Lansing was relaxed, at peace with herself and with the environment, so she metabolized normally; her body odor telegraphed neutrality.

Curious, the cat rose and began to follow the scent spoor. When he had shortened the distance between himself and Lansing to less than half a mile, his ears picked up the small sounds that she made as she walked over a thick carpet of evergreen needles. The tom now detoured, climbing up-slope, circling, but keeping downwind of the woman.

By the time she stumbled over the fecal mound, the white puma was above her and only thirty yards away, crouched beside a fern-encrusted boulder. From this vantage, he had a clear view of her. Remaining absolutely still, he watched as she probed into his mound, and when she began to follow his pugmarks, backtracking because the forward spoor disappeared a few yards from the mound, he waited until she became concealed by the trees. Then he began to follow her.

Lansing walked slowly, stopping occasionally to photograph the spoor. She well realized she was actually going the wrong way, yet she hoped that she would eventually find a partially consumed kill to which the cat might return that evening. But she was to be disappointed. Half an hour after she had encountered the tracks, she lost them in a rocky area.

"Darn! He must have come down through those rocks . . . ," she muttered as she looked around. She turned and faced her back trail. She was bitterly disappointed, and she blamed herself for what she considered her failure as a tracker. She was on the verge of tears as she tried to decide what she should do next.

The cat had stopped twenty yards from his quarry. He became a statue. Despite his white coat, he blended perfectly with the rocks and underbrush that surrounded him. When he heard Lansing's voice, he was startled, and curious. He realized immediately that it was quite unlike the harsh tones of Taggart and Cousins. Like the woman that he was watching, he became undecided. His hatred of the men had at first urged him to attack the lone and helpless being that had invaded his domain, yet she was so obviously at peace, so *interesting*. Immobile again after his brief start, he continued to watch her, now intensely curious.

Lansing remained standing. She was almost as still as the cat. She could not formulate a plan of action, and frustration added to her disappointment. "Damn, damn, damn," she muttered in a small voice.

She took a step forward to a nearby rock, then sat brooding. Suddenly, she laughed aloud. The explosive sounds startled the puma. He jumped. The movement attracted Lansing's eyes. She saw the cat for just an instant, a white form partly shrouded by bushes and fern fronds, head turned toward her and amber eyes fixed on hers. Then, like a wraith, he was gone. At one instant he had been looking at her, at the next, with an incredibly swift movement, he had swung away and disappeared, making hardly a sound.

"Oh, my God!"

Lansing remained rooted to the rock. She stared round eyed at the place in the forest where the white puma had stood but seconds earlier. Unaware that she was doing so, she spoke again. "I found him. I really did . . . *I found him!*" Then, in a surprised tone, "Or *did* I? I guess he found me! I was right . . . he *knows* me! He *knows* I mean him no harm!"

Euphoric and not really conscious of her actions, Lansing rose and began to climb, following the route over which she had descended, her mind full of her experience, seeing again and again the magnificent animal that had been studying her, his white coat shining silver as it cast off reflected light.

It was not until an hour later, as she approached the heavily treed section of the defile, that she was calm enough to consider a future course of action. Entering the heavy forest, but now making better time because of the pruning of dead branches that she had done on her way down, she admitted to herself that she really didn't know what to do. At first, she thought she ought to stay in the area and hope the cat would search her out anew. But she discarded that idea when she realized that she did not have enough food. Or any shelter. Then, too, Carew and Delacroix would become worried if she did not make contact with them that evening, as she had promised. Her failure to do so would bring Carew to the region, and the noise of his aircraft would probably disturb the puma.

As she climbed, she made up her mind. She would return to her little camp as fast as she could, radio the Atna Lake camp, and have her companions walk in the next day with more supplies and another pup tent. The three of them could then stay in the area for at least a few days and look for the white puma.

By the time she reached her tent, exhausted from her long journey, Lansing realized her hasty plan was a bad one. The presence of the conservationists in Bell's territory was intended to discourage the killing of *all* pumas, not just the white one. And Carew, especially, had to keep flying, looking for hunters and advising the ground crews. The group could not afford to have three of its members engaged in the search for one cat, even though this was the most spectacular animal that had ever been seen in British Columbia.

Taggart, followed by Hegel and Cousins, led the way across one of the many creeks that flow into the Burnie River. When they reached the far side, they veered toward the northwest. The hunters had been searching for the puma since soon after sunrise that morning, first exploring the area east of Pillar Mountain, then crossing the river at its shallowest point north of Hope Peak, and eventually reaching a place where the white tom had made a kill three days earlier.

On arrival, the dogs sniffed at the meager remains and at the puma's old tracks and those of a number of scavenging animals, but they showed little excitement and, as they had the day before, gave up as soon as the trail led them to the rocky outcrop.

The men reined their mounts. "There's no use checking the Clore again," Cousins noted while he rolled one of his brown cigarettes.

"Nah," said Taggart. "We gave that a real good going-over. Seems like that damned cat just sprouted wings and flew off!"

Cousins lit his smoke, smiled at his partner. "You know, Walt, maybe you're dead right. Maybe that cat did sort of fly away," he said.

Hegel and Taggart looked at him. Taggart shrugged, believing his partner was joking. But the German questioned the guide. "Meaning what, Mr. Cousins?"

"We can't find the cat down here, and we sure know it climbed that rock face. Well, I reckon it went up-mountain." Cousins said, pointing toward Dog's Ears Peaks.

"Maybe you're right," Taggart said, frowning over his map. "But that's kind of a climb. And through a lot of timber. I don't reckon the nags can make it up through there."

Cousins nodded. He was looking at his own map. "The pass is narrow, all right. What say we ride up as far as we can, then have a go on foot?"

"Will the puma attack our horses?" Hegel asked.

"Don't reckon so," Cousins replied. "We ain't picked up his scent, so if he's around these parts, he's gotta be ahead of us."

"Anyways," Taggart added, "the dogs'll let us know if he's around."

The sun was already sinking toward the western peaks and, because of the lateness of the day, it was agreed that the party would camp for the night and resume the hunt in the morning. Hegel, a comfort-loving man, was not thrilled by the prospect of a night under the stars, despite the well-insulated sleeping bags that were lashed to the saddles.

"You'll be OK, Mr. Hegel," Taggart said. "We got lots of grub, and there are tarps to spread over the bags should it turn to rain. Which it won't, judging from that red sky."

Lansing had already told Carew about her encounter with the puma. Now they were discussing their plans.

"I've got to stay out here, David. I'm pretty sure I'll meet him again. And I wouldn't want to miss that. What do you think? Over."

"Agreed, but you're going to need more supplies." Carew paused. "Do you remember that small lake, the one south of Pat Peak that we stopped at on the way in? Over."

"Yes, David. I've got it on the map. Coordinates fifty-four degrees four minutes north and one hundred twenty-eight degrees fifty-one minutes west. Over."

"Yeah, that's it. OK. By seven tomorrow morning I'll fly in and leave a food cache for you at the north end of the lake. I'll hang the stuff in a couple of trees, wrapped in canvas. You can walk in—it looks to be less than four miles from your camp—and ferry back the supplies as you need them. We'll pack canned stuff and dehydrated foods, and lots of crackers and whole wheat cookies. Can you handle that? Over."

Lansing agreed. She could make as many trips as needed over the next several days. Carew then suggested that he fly over the region, maintaining height while in the area where she had seen the puma, but dropping low if he saw the hunters. He would report back to Delacroix while he flew, so she could liaise with Lansing.

"I know the radio is extra weight, Heather," Carew said. "But you'd better carry it with you from now on. And take along the spare batteries. Over."

Lansing protested, but Carew was firm. "Listen, we're worried about you in there alone. The cat didn't attack you, but it just might at another time. And what about bears, or if you fall and hurt yourself, or if those guys find you in there? No, Heather. You've *got* to take the radio. Otherwise, Linda and I will come and join you. And that would mess up our entire operation. Over."

Lansing reluctantly agreed. Later, sitting before her small fire, she concluded that Carew was right. Apart from considerations of safety, the radio meant he could alert her to developments in her area when he flew over, and she could relay information to him through Delacroix or directly if he was actually in the air in her vicinity.

That night she turned in early, intending to be up at four in the morning and to leave for the drop-zone lake at first light. Her last thoughts before she fell asleep were focused on the white puma.

Lansing had been sleeping for several hours when the puma thrust his head and shoulders out of the screening forest and stared at her small tent. While his eyes examined the shelter and the few objects she had set up in her camping area, his nose was busy with the many unnatural smells that permeated the small lakeside clearing. A few of them reminded him of the hunters, especially the acrid odor of the campfire and of the leather that came from the woman's boots and from some of her equipment. These airborne signals at first caused him to flatten his ears and to open his mouth in a silent snarl. But Lansing's personal fragrances were more alluring; they piqued his curiosity and caused his ears to project forward and his mouth to close. He was particularly fascinated by her female body odors, which were so like and yet so *un*like those emitted by a female of his own species.

Apart from those first moments when he was reminded of his enemies, the puma did not feel aggressively disposed toward the strange being that had suddenly appeared in his range. To the contrary. He was greatly interested in her. Unlike a female puma, which, outside of the breeding season, would have attacked him on sight, the woman had already demonstrated that her intentions were neutral. Now, as he walked toward the tent without making a sound, her deep, regular breathing told him that she was sleeping. Cautious, but irresistibly drawn to the orange shelter, he advanced until his nose was within twelve inches of the nylon. He stood in a half crouch at a slight angle to the tent's doorway. He continued to listen and to sniff. Then he began to purr.

Lansing awakened. Sleep-bemused and not knowing why she had been aroused, she sat up; as she did so, the material of her sleeping bag rustled. The faint noises startled the cat. Rising on his hind legs and swinging his body away from the tent, he bounded off, his pads whispering in the sand. In seconds he disappeared within the trees.

Lansing heard him leave, but the disturbance he created was so slight that she mistook it for the passage of a rodent, perhaps a vole or a white-footed mouse, both of which at times skittered up and down her tent. She went back to sleep.

The white puma traveled up-mountain, his pace unhurried, his passage through the forest almost totally silent. He was now hunting.

An hour later, when he was halfway down the pass, he killed a mule deer buck on the sandy shore of an alpine creek that trundled down the lower slopes of Hope Mountain. He spent the next half hour feeding. When he had eaten his fill, he dragged the carcass across the sand to a nearby shrubby area and covered it with leaves and soil. That done, he climbed for five hundred feet to a rocky knoll. From there he commanded a view of the pass.

17

Lansing's alarm awakened her at four o'clock, as the first faint blush of dawn silhouetted the eastern peaks. This morning she made do with a quick wash, after which she dressed, drank some water, fastened the bag of trail rations to her belt, and, with camera and binoculars around her neck, prepared to leave for Pat Peak and the lake where Carew would land her reserve supplies. By the time she was ready, the glow of the unseen sun had filtered into the lowlands; it was then that she noticed the puma's tracks. The large pugmarks ran in a straight line from the forest edge to her campfire and all the way to her tent.

"Oh my God!" she muttered breathlessly. "He visited me during the night!"

Reentering the tent, she took a small flash unit from a carryall, fixed it to the camera, and returned outside. She photographed all the tracks, including several long ruts in the sand, just outside the tent's entrance, that had been made as the puma wheeled away after being startled by the rustling of her sleeping bag. Looking at these, she remembered waking up, now realizing that it had been the puma that had roused her from sleep.

Discovery of the tracks immediately altered Lansing's plans. The supplies that Carew would bring, she knew, would be hoisted from a tree. They could wait. Now it was important for her to contact Atna Lake, to report her findings. That done, she would try to find the puma.

Picking up the radio, she called the base. Delacroix replied. "I'm not making the trip for supplies today, Linda. I had a *real* surprise last night. *He* came to visit me while I was asleep. He left his tracks right up to the tent. Is David still there? Over."

Carew came on the air. "Say no more, Heather! I'll fly over and look for the opposition. I'll call you later. Take the radio with you. Over."

Lansing immediately understood. The conservationists knew that the High Country Safaris people carried radios. Somebody might be monitoring their transmission.

"OK. I understand," she replied. "But you'd better not fly over me. Over."

"I won't, don't worry. I'll visit you this afternoon after the resupply, about four o'clock. On foot!" Carew replied. "Over and out."

Excited, but not quite sure how to begin her search, Lansing put the radio in a shoulder satchel. As an afterthought, she reached into the carryall and took out of it a one-pound package of finely ground chili pepper. She had brought the pepper with her after having been told that if dogs were given a sniff of it, the resulting irritation blocked their sense of smell for at least an hour but would not otherwise harm them. She probably would not need the chili, she thought as she tied the tent doorway. But if the hunters and their dogs came her way, she would no doubt hear the baying and could then sprinkle pepper on the ground, especially over the scent mound she had found, or any other that she might encounter.

Beginning at the campfire, she started to follow the puma's tracks, but a short time later she lost the trail within the forest. Frustrated, she determined to continue, now bringing to her aid the studies she had done in the past of the ways animals walk and of the tracks they leave in suitable ground. She knew that the space between the tracks of the advancing limbs represented the animal's stride and remained relatively constant.

Crouching over the spoor, she took a six-foot metal tape from her pocket and began measuring, soon learning that each of the puma's walking strides covered between fourteen and sixteen inches of ground. That done, she chopped down a sapling alder and shortened it to sixteen inches. Then she placed a notch two inches behind the leading end.

Moving to the last noticeable stride tracks and facing the direction in which the puma had walked, she laid the stick on the ground, one end in between the pugmarks. Now, by crouching and looking to the left of the forward end of the stick, she found the place where the cat's left hind foot had bruised the grasses.

In this way, with infinite patience, Lansing followed the puma. Two hours later, however, having covered only some three hundred yards, she gave up. She was hot, fly bitten, and cramped from so much stooping. And she was more frustrated than ever. She sat on a rock and took a drink from her canteen before eating some trail rations. And she tried to think like a puma.

Innumerable questions chased each other in her mind. Why had the cat visited her camp? Where did he go after he ran away? He evidently had decided to walk down the trail, but why? Should she go down the pass? Should she climb higher in the hope of seeing him below her, in the pass? Was he now sleeping somewhere? Had he made a kill? If so, could she find it and stand vigil near it for when he returned to eat again?

In the end, she realized she could not answer any of her questions. Forcing herself to calm down, she decided to descend the pass, estimating that she was five miles from the small clearing where she had seen the coyotes eating carrion that, she guessed, was the remains of one of the puma's kills.

It was now eight o'clock, and the sun was well above the peaks when she set off. She had no way of knowing that Taggart, Cousins, and Hegel were at the same time leaving their night camp and guiding their horses toward the defile.

Carew loaded the Aeronca with extra supplies, which he intended to land on the Pat Peak Lake during early afternoon. Before he took off, he and Delacroix discussed strategy.

"After I check with the other camps this morning, David, don't you think it would be a good idea to call Vancouver and issue a press statement? I mean, we've not been here long, but we now know that there really *is* a white puma. The other camps haven't yet reported any activity in their areas, and it seems to me that the real action is here."

Carew agreed.

"OK then," said Delacroix. "I'll write another press release after talking with the camps. Meanwhile, if you see anything, you can call me. I expect to contact Vancouver by about eleven o'clock. Can you fly over Kitseguecla and the Burnie camps to check their surroundings? So far, nothing much has been happening near them. A couple of guides near Kitseguecla, and the German's party near Burnie."

"Yeah. I don't think there's too many pumas in this whole region. It's the white one that Bell's boys are after. I'll check the other camps, in any case," Carew answered.

Delacroix helped him push the aircraft away from the shore. Moments later, after taxiing into position, Carew lifted the Aeronca off the water.

Lansing walked slowly. Every few minutes she stopped, remained still, and scanned the surrounding forest, listening as intently as she knew how and even trying to isolate and identify scents. But apart from the songs of the birds, the sound of the alpine wind in the trees, and the occasional rustle made by a mouse disturbed by her presence, she could detect nothing, no trace of the white puma.

When she had been traveling for half an hour, she reached the halfway point of the pass, the place where the spruces crowded together. Stopping here and again examining her surroundings, she saw a tunnellike trail that she had not noticed the previous day. The feral pathway led in a westerly direction, and its headroom allowed her to walk upright. On impulse, she turned into it and soon found herself climbing a gentle slope.

Walking carefully and, as before, pausing often, she had negotiated about two hundred yards of the gloomy passage when the tightly packed spruces abruptly gave way to a mixture of aspen, birch, and Sitka alders and the understory became carpeted by small plants and ferns. Within this unexpected parklike glade, she heard the gurgling sounds of flowing water. Walking faster, she came to the rock-strewn east bank of a fast-flowing mountain creek. Orienting her map, she noted that this was one of the Clore River's many feeder streams. It began at the five-thousand-foot level of Dog's Ears Peaks, where blue-ice glaciers leaked crystal water between spring and early autumn.

As she approached the creek, she noticed that, because of a sharp bend, the floodwaters had scattered rocks and other debris on the east bank but had spared the west bank. For the most part it was carpeted by fine sands in which grew horsetail rushes and, in damp areas, patches of wild ginger, their purplish brown flowers hugging the sand and almost entirely hidden by the huge leaves.

To get a better view of the far shore, Lansing scrambled up a large boulder. As she was about to raise the field glasses to study the country above the creek, she saw the mound. It rose near the trees, about one hundred yards from the water's edge. It was unmistakably a puma's covered kill!

Lansing stared, her mouth open, her heart beating so fast she could almost hear it.

She put the glasses to her eyes and began to scan the sand, immediately seeing a maze of cat tracks. Studying the area, she was able to piece together the puma's behavior. He must have been lying in ambush among the shrubbery that crept down to the edge of the sand about one hundred yards from where she was then standing. The prey—a deer, she decided, judging by a series of tracks that were noticeable in the sand—had approached the stream, no doubt thirsty. The puma had charged. She could see his tracks, the disturbed sand. He had caught the deer as it was turning away from the water and brought it down.

The signs of the struggle were clear. So was a large, brownish patch of sun-dried blood where the greatest disturbance had occurred. The drag marks of the carcass were also clear. The cat had evidently lifted the dead animal by the neck or by its front quarters and carried it to its present location, for Lansing could see twin narrow trails in the sand, lines made by the hind hooves of the deer.

Releasing the binoculars and picking up the camera, Lansing exchanged the standard objective for a 200-millimeter telephoto lens. She systematically photographed the evidence. Then, cutting a stout sapling as a balance stick, she probed the water, finding that it was only a few inches deep a yard from the bank. Entering the frigid stream, she advanced, prodding for depth with the stick when not using it to help her keep her balance against the fast current.

The creek at this location was some fifteen feet wide. As she waded, it got deeper. When she was midway across, the water reached her thighs, numbing her legs. It must have been only a few degrees above freezing. Now she felt the full thrust of the flow. If she hadn't had the stick, the current would have knocked her down.

The ordeal lasted only a few minutes, but when she reached

the sandy bank and stepped clear of the water, Lansing felt as if she had been wading in ice for an hour. Fortunately, the sun was high overhead and the temperature, even at that altitude, was in the high seventies. The heat began to comfort her almost immediately. She removed boots, socks, and jeans and spread them on a bush to dry. Then she exchanged camera lenses again and started to take close-up photographs. Beginning at the kill site and following the cat's spoor, she found the place he had lain in wait, a patch of ground where the ferns and grasses had been flattened to the contours of the animal's body. During all this, she was so intent on her work that she paid little attention to the flies that were feasting on her legs.

She was about to photograph the drag marks and the covered remains when she saw that the back trail from the ambush site led to the creek bank farther down the pass. Investigating, she found that as the cat climbed he had kept to the sandy bank, no doubt because it contained only sparse vegetation and allowed for easier, more silent walking.

Lansing followed the spoor for the next half hour, covering about half a mile. By then the flies were pestering her unmercifully, and, although the sand conditions appeared to continue for some distance downward, she postponed further exploration in order to return to the kill site and dress herself.

An hour and a half had elapsed since she'd crossed the creek, and her boots and clothing, although still damp, were dry enough to wear and to protect her limbs and feet from the flies. Fully clothed again, she put new film in the camera and continued to take pictures, working toward the kill. As she was about to fire the shutter, she heard a low growl.

Startled, she raised her head.

She saw him!

He was standing on a pinnacle of granite thirty feet high and immediately above her. She could see his head and shoulders, his chest, and his legs down to the huge velvet pads whose toes were gripping the edge of his platform. His mouth was slightly open, his lips peeled back, revealing the great ivory fangs and the red tongue on which a drop of translucent saliva was gathered.

Lansing was transfixed. She stood rock still, staring into the slanting yellow eyes, too astonished to feel fear or excitement. As she watched, the white puma opened his mouth a little wider and growled again. From the volume of sound, she realized that the cat was not fully aroused.

He was warning her to stay away from his kill!

Moving slowly, she stepped backward. When she had taken five paces, the puma closed his mouth. He continued to stare at her, but his demeanor had changed. He seemed to be studying her, curious rather than belligerent.

Lansing belatedly remembered her camera. The puma was framed against a backdrop of evergreens, and sunlight had turned his pure white coat to luminous silver. She lifted the camera, focused, and took a picture. The puma flinched slightly at the click of the shutter but otherwise remained calm.

With hands trembling from excitement, Lansing removed the standard lens and fastened the telephoto to the camera, all the while watching the magnificent animal. He continued as before, a burnished, living sculpture who appeared to show almost as much interest in the woman as she did in him. Lifting the camera, she again focused and pressed the firing button.

This time the puma did not flinch. He continued to stare at the perplexing being that had come into his world, a creature much like his enemies, yet unlike them, a peaceable entity, whose intimate odors intrigued him.

Lansing took another picture. She sat down on a nearby rock, put away her equipment, and simply looked at the white puma. The cat stared back for some moments. Then, with consummate grace, he lay down. His front legs protruded over the rock shelf, his wrists bent, the great paws hanging limply. Moments later, without taking his gaze off Lansing, he laid his broad head on his legs, his eyes, an amber shade now in the reflected light, and his toffee-colored nose contrasting with his white chest and the anthracite markings around his muzzle.

The woman and the puma appraised each other in peace and in companionable silence, the animal unmoving except for the slight tremors of his flanks that accompanied his breathing; the human, although relaxed, shivering from time to time, little tremors of body and hands that bespoke her excitement.

Lansing only half-believed what she was seeing. She thought at times that she must be asleep, dreaming of this encounter. On an impulse, she began to talk to the white tom, her voice soft, using endearing terms, almost as though she were talking to a lover, or to a loved child. The puma's ears, which had been held low and to the sides, sprang upright, and he lifted his head, turning it slightly to look at her with intense, fiery eyes.

"I am looking right into the *wild*," Lansing said in her mind. Aloud, she said, "You are simply wonderful! You are the loveliest being I have ever seen. You are *gorgeous*. I truly love you."

In response, the white puma yawned. He opened the pink cavern of his mouth wide, arched his tongue, and gaped, his impressive teeth reflecting sunlight. When he finished, he closed his mouth with an audible snap. And he began to purr, a sound not unlike that of a domestic cat, but *loud*, carrying to Lansing clearly.

She cried for joy. But she continued to talk to him, her voice made husky by emotion, the tears running down her cheeks and dripping on her shirt.

The puma abruptly stopped purring. He turned his head, facing down the canyon. Suddenly, with incredible speed, he sprang to his feet and disappeared.

Lansing was startled by the swift action. She turned her head, looking down the defile, but saw nothing unusual. As she stood, not quite knowing what she should do, she heard the faint baying of hounds. "So *that's* what made him run!" she exclaimed aloud.

She looked at her watch. It was half past one. Carew, she believed, would be in the air, not too far away, she hoped. She took the radio out of her satchel, switched it on, and began to call. Delacroix answered. Carew was at Kitseguecla Lake, out of range of Lansing's radio.

"Get in touch with him, Linda. It's urgent! I'm *very* near the *special project,* but the hunting party is coming up the pass." She gave Delacroix her coordinates. Delacroix would contact Carew.

Lansing used her binoculars to search up-mountain for the puma, but he had disappeared. Because the terrain was too steep for the hounds to follow, she felt confident that the cat would elude the hunters. But she was angry.

She began to stride down the slope, hurrying along the trail the puma had climbed before he made his kill. The baying, although closer, was still distant, but she began to jog. Twice she stumbled and almost fell, yet, determined, she continued for twenty minutes, until she arrived at the end of the sand, after which the puma's tracks were no longer visible.

Now she turned, facing uphill, and thrust her hand in the satchel. Taking out the package of chili pepper and opening it, she began to sprinkle the pungent condiment into the puma's tracks, covering them with a fine, red blush as she followed the trail.

When she had traveled two hundred yards, and the bag of pepper was almost half empty, she scattered chili across the trail over an area several feet wide. Then she returned to the place of the puma's kill and settled herself on a granite shelf seven or eight feet from the ground. From here, about ten yards south of the mounded remains, she could see the creek.

With her back against the rock and her legs stretched out, Lansing used the radio. Carew answered her after the second call, his voice faint, but his words understandable. "Hi, Heather. I've just taken off from Kitseguecla. What are your coordinates? Over."

Lansing acknowledged and gave her coordinates.

"OK. I'll be in your area in about twenty minutes. What's happening? Over."

"The hunters are climbing the pass. They're after *him.* I guess there's no point in hiding behind words now. I've peppered the tracks, so there should be some sort of reaction soon. The hounds are getting closer, but they haven't reached the peppered tracks yet. The cat took off up-mountain. Over."

"I don't like what you're telling me, Heather. Leave your radio on receive. I'll talk every few minutes, so they won't figure you're on your own. If you have a problem, switch off and on twice. I'll answer immediately. Those guys are going to be pretty mad at you. Out."

Barely one mile after entering the pass, the hunters had been forced to dismount and tie up their horses, choosing a place where scree had prevented the growth of mature trees, but where there were enough widely spaced saplings to secure the animals, each far enough away from its neighbors to prevent entanglement.

Cousins, fitter and more agile, led the way. Hegel walked behind him. Taggart, leading the dogs at this stage of their foray, brought up the rear. By prior agreement the men did not talk. The only sounds of their presence were made by the panting dogs, the tread of boots on the uneven, rocky ground, and the hard breathing of Hegel and Taggart. Two miles up the pass, Cousins stopped, knowing from experience that the client as well as his partner would need a rest.

Taggart and the German immediately sat down, the guide choosing a downed tree and Hegel sitting on a mossy boulder.

The dogs, anxious to keep going, tugged at their leads until Taggart yanked them backward. *"Sit!"* he growled at them.

Cousins rolled himself a smoke, lit it, and walked a little way up the trail. A couple of hundred yards ahead he saw the densely packed trees and noticed the opening that Lansing had made. He returned to his companions. "Someone's been up here in the last day or two. There's a pass been cut through the trees up yonder."

"Cut?" asked Taggart. "Like with an ax, you mean?"

"Yeah. You know what spruces are like when they grow packed. Someone's hacked off the dead limbs about head height."

"Damn it!" growled Taggart, standing up. "Let's get on up there. Maybe those conservation freaks have been messing around up there."

Before the party moved on, Cousins took charge of the two best dogs. Fifteen minutes later the hunters were still moving through the spruces. Taggart and Cousins were taller than Lansing and were slowed by having to keep ducking their heads.

Suddenly, the two lead hounds began to pull at their leashes while baying loudly, noses to the ground.

"They're on it," shouted Taggart.

The big man slipped the leashes from his dogs. Cousins did the same. The hounds, tails curving stiffly over their hindquarters, began to run, their hoarse voices louder than ever, their noses almost touching the trail. In moments they were out of sight.

Half a mile ahead, the excited dogs had raced across the creek and were approaching the first chili-treated tracks. They could actually smell the pepper, although the scent was weak. But the odor of the puma was strong in their nostrils. They started to bugle, the deep, bell-like call that signals a fresh spoor. The hunters increased their strides. Soon they reached the water.

The chill water hit Hegel and Taggart hard, but Cousins,

who had dashed across without giving it a thought, reached a bend in the trail and called back to his lagging companions. "You'd better get a move on. The hounds've got a good scent, by the sound of that bugling."

Suddenly, the dogs stopped bugling. The men halted in their tracks, bewildered by the sudden silence.

"What's going on, Steve?" Taggart called. "I never heard them stop like that when they were on a good bugling trail."

Cousins didn't have an answer to his partner's question. Leaving the others behind, he trotted uphill, his carbine in his right hand. He ran without stopping for two hundred yards. Then, gasping for breath, he slowed to a walk and at last halted, leaning against a tree and trying hard to control his breathing, his heart hammering so hard that its rhythm almost deafened him. Still winded, but at least breathing less stertorously, he became aware of a completely unexpected noise. The hounds were whining. And, he thought, they were all whining at the same time.

Alarmed, for the hounds had never behaved in such a manner, he forced himself to walk upward, striding as fast as he could. Still hemmed in by the serried ranks of spruces, which restricted his vision to only a few yards ahead, he became increasingly alarmed as the whining grew in volume. Now he noted that some of the dogs were also yelping intermittently. Putting on a spurt, he at last emerged from the trees and came in sight of the sandy shore.

What he saw stopped him in his tracks. The four hounds were rolling over and over, pawing at their faces and rubbing their noses in the sand. Oblivious of his presence, even after he called to them sharply, the dogs seemed in extreme distress.

Cousins ran toward them and, with difficulty, was able to restrain one and force its head up. The animal's eyes were watering, and fluid was discharging from its nose. He released the dog, grabbed another. It showed the same symptoms.

As he was reaching for the lead hound, which seemed to be more affected than its companions, he saw, a few feet ahead, one of the puma's undisturbed tracks. It was then he noticed the red powder that covered it and was spilled all around it. He bent low and sniffed. His nose immediately began to burn, and he started to sneeze, his eyes watering. Blowing his nose and wiping his eyes, he found that he could endure the discomfort. He had not, after all, sniffed up much of the powder. He wet his finger, dabbed at the powder, and tasted it gingerly.

Cousins was no cook, but he had tasted chili. He now knew what ailed the dogs. For some moments he was nonplussed. "How in hell did that stuff get in the tracks?" he muttered as he watched the contortions of the dogs, which were less agitated now.

From below he heard Taggart and Hegel as they brushed against dead spruce branches. At the same time he heard the as yet distant droning of an aircraft engine. "That's it!" He uttered the words like an expletive. "*Those damned conservationists!* They've done this!"

Without waiting for his companions, Cousins continued to run uphill, keeping alongside the tracks and looking down at them. He saw that the chili was in all the pugmarks, and he was furious. He knew the dogs' irritation would soon pass, but they were now useless for tracking and would probably take several hours to recover their sense of smell.

Anger made him open his rifle's breech and ram a shell into the firing position without afterward putting on the safety catch. It was something he had never before forgotten to do.

On her rocky perch, Lansing had been monitoring the guide's progress from the sounds he was making as he climbed.

When he worked the action of his rifle, she heard the metallic noise and realized that he was near. She became apprehensive and thought about calling Carew, but changed her mind. The guide would hear her speak. Then she got angry. She would not allow those men to spook her. Sitting quietly, she waited.

Cousins was out of breath when he reached the open area above which Lansing was sitting. He did not see her at first; his attention was focused on the mound that concealed the deer's remains, which he had immediately recognized for what it was. He cursed and started toward it. At the same moment, Carew's voice crackled from the radio in Lansing's hand.

Startled, Cousins looked up, saw Lansing, and simultaneously took a step backward. His foot hit the puma's scent mound, and he stumbled. The rifle slipped out of his fingers, bounced on a nearby rock, and discharged.

The bullet hit Lansing's right thigh.

She screamed as she switched her radio to send. *"David! My God, David, I've been shot!"* she called, grabbing at her leg with her right hand and switching the radio to receive without the usual Over signal.

"How bad is it? Over!" Carew replied, his voice calm, but belying his feelings.

"I don't think it's too bad, David. But it really, really *hurts*! It's my thigh . . . I guess about between the knee and the hip. I can move the leg, so I guess the bone isn't broken. Over."

"OK, Heather. Stay calm. Use the first-aid dressing you've got in your pack. If the bleeding won't stop, use the surgical tubing—there's some in the first-aid kit also—to make a tourniquet *above* the wound. Preferably at the femoral artery, if you can find it. Meanwhile, I'll call Linda so she can report this, and we'll get a helicopter in there to lift you out. Over."

During the few moments Carew and Lansing had been talking, Cousins had stood below the woman's rock perch, his mouth agape, his expression one of horror. Punching the palm of his left hand with his right fist, he ignored Taggart's shouts, which reached him only faintly, muttering the while: "Oh Christ . . . Oh Christ . . . Oh Christ . . ."

Lansing gingerly felt the bullet wound. Blood stained her jeans, but careful probing led her to believe the injury was superficial. She acknowledged Carew's call, telling him she did not think the wound serious enough for her to be lifted out by helicopter and asking him to stay on the air for a while. Then she switched off her radio and looked at Cousins. "You shot me, *you bloody fool*! Instead of standing there cursing, get up here and help me."

The guide, continuing to pound one hand with the other, looked up. "Jeez, lady! It was an accident. You *know* it was an accident. Anyways, you got no darned business in here, interfering with our hunt."

Lansing, rummaging in her bag for the first-aid kit, replied without looking up. "Never mind all that now. *Get up here!*" she shouted.

Cousins started to move toward her rocky elevation. He took one hesitant step, then another. Suddenly, from somewhere above and behind Lansing, the deep, menacing growl of an enraged mountain lion burst on the silence. Almost in the same instant, the white puma's body appeared as if in flight. The cat was so fast, Lansing was barely aware of its leap.

Cousins was looking upward, his legs frozen in the stride position. From below, the cat loomed huge. Its great mouth was open wide, the ivory fangs gleaming in the sunlight. Immobilized, the guide saw the dreadful, lethal paws aiming at him, enormous curved black claws reaching for him, just as the puma's body was passing only a few feet over the woman.

Lansing looked up and momentarily saw the spread front paws and the black talons. An instant later, the cat's milky underparts flashed blurrily across her vision. Instinctively, she screamed at the puma. *"No! Don't do it!"*

Perhaps it was the unexpected sound of the woman's now shrill voice that caused the puma to land short of his target, instead of striking Cousins in midleap. Perhaps the highly intelligent animal understood the meaning of Lansing's cry. Whatever the reasons for his subsequent actions, the cat remained crouched for a split second after he had landed, his fierce gaze fixed on the man's eyes. Then, less than ten feet from the mesmerized Cousins, he lifted off again, seemingly intending to launch himself at his now defenseless enemy.

Lansing screamed again. *"No!"*

The white puma shifted slightly in flight. Instead of hitting the man squarely with his lethal paws, he gave Cousins a hard blow with his right shoulder before touching down in the water, and immediately thereafter leaping across the creek. When he landed on the far side, the white puma turned to look briefly at Lansing, then ran into the trees and disappeared.

Hit by more than two hundred pounds of swiftly traveling cat, Cousins was hurled off his feet and seemed to fly through the air before alighting in the water with a great splash. There, on his back and partly submerged, he struggled to sit up, a task made difficult by the current.

At that moment, Taggart appeared. Earlier, the rifle report had startled him and, leaving Hegel with the sneezing, nose-rubbing hounds, he had hurried up the pass. Now, panting, his normally florid face almost purple, he stopped, mouth agape with astonishment at sight of his partner wallowing in the stream. "What in the name of hell you doing, Steve? You gone loco? Was it you fired the shot?"

Cousins struggled to his feet but had difficulty walking toward the shore. He did not reply to Taggart's questions. He was still in shock, his face white. He knew that he had just met death, that he had survived the encounter by a miracle.

"Yes, *sir!*" Lansing called. "It was your friend that fired his gun. And *I* was the target. That man *shot* me!"

Taggart whipped his head up. He stared at Lansing, his eyes round. "Wha . . . what's that you say?" Shaking his head, he turned to look at Cousins, who was just reaching the bank. "Did you shoot that woman?"

Cousins, still visibly shaken, was yet spurred to words by Lansing's accusation. "My gun did. It was an accident. I stumbled and the damned gun slipped outa my hand and went off. I didn't mean the lady no harm."

Taggart was silent. Still short of breath, he looked from Cousins to Lansing, then back at Cousins. He tipped his hat back and scratched his head. He looked at Lansing again. "And was it *you* that spread that there red pepper in the cat's tracks, so my hounds'd get a snootful?" he asked, his voice sharp.

"That was me! And I'll keep on doing it so long as you keep trying to kill pumas."

Taggart made a noise not unlike the growl of an animal. He may have been trying to clear his throat, or to find words with which to reply to Lansing, but speech did not immediately emerge from his open mouth. He stayed silent for perhaps half a minute, then, shaking his head as though he had just come out of a trance, he looked at Lansing. "I wouldn't be so uppity, I was you, lady. You're out here alone. People can get to disappear awful sudden in this country."

"None of that, Walt! You try hurting her, you're gonna have to settle with me first! Anyways, I'm climbing up there. She needs help."

Cousins, dripping wet and bareheaded, was unsteady on his feet, his shoulder aching from the blow delivered by the puma. But he felt he had to make amends to the woman. He had been careless. If he had set the safety catch, the gun would not have discharged. Slowly and painfully, he climbed to Lansing's ledge, paused to relax for some moments, then unsheathed his hunting knife. He bent over her leg. "Look, ma'am, I'm gonna have to slit the pant leg right down to the end, so we can bandage the hurt. OK?"

Lansing nodded agreement, surprised by the change in the man. He had been so aggressive earlier. Now he sounded so mild and sympathetic. And he seemed really to regret having wounded her.

Lifting the denim with his left hand, the guide inserted the end of his sharp knife into the bullet tear and started running the blade down toward the ankle. Lansing flinched; the pull of the material and the journeying knife caused her pain.

Cousins muttered apologies, then added, "Can you lift up your leg some, ma'am, so's I can see the wound?"

Lansing did so. Bending her knee, she brought her heel back, lifting her thigh off the ground. The movement hurt only a little, but the wound began to bleed more copiously.

Cousins, noting the first-aid kit in Lansing's hand, took it from her, lifted the lid, and saw a small bottle of hydrogen peroxide and a package of cotton batting. He took both items from the container, made a swab from the batting, soaked it with peroxide, and used it to wipe away the blood, pinching together the edges of the torn flesh to stanch the bleeding. Lansing leaned forward to look at the injury. So did Cousins.

"Just a glancing slash, lady. Won't need no stitching." As he spoke, the guide found a package of sterile gauze in the kit and placed it over the injury. On top of this he made a pad of cotton batting. When he'd fastened the dressing with surgical tape he looked at Lansing. "D'you think you can stand?"

"Yes. I'm sure I can. Your rifle is a bad shot, mister," she replied. Then, "Anyway, thanks for patching me up."

Cousins gave her one of his rare smiles and shrugged his shoulders. "I owe you, lady. And I ain't paid my debt yet. Not by a long shot! Need a hand to get up?" As he spoke, Cousins looked down. He was searching in one of the capacious leg pockets of his army surplus pants.

Refusing his help, but supporting herself against the rock, Lansing stood up without much difficulty. A moment later, she began to flex her leg. It was sore, but she felt sure she could walk back to her camp if she did so in easy stages, perhaps with the aid of a stick.

When the guide withdrew his hand from the pocket, it held a small flat can. Removing the lid, he took out a large needle and a coil of strong twine. He showed the items to Lansing. "If you stand still, I'll cobble up the cut in your pant leg. I ain't much of a hand at sewing, but I reckon it'll be better sewed up rough than to let the flies get at you." He paused. "Oh, ah . . . the name's Cousins, ma'am. Steve Cousins."

Lansing acknowledged the man's name with a small smile and agreed to the sewing.

Taggart had stood silent during all this time. He was confused by his partner's seeming change of attitude. Now he realized he had no idea how Cousins had come to be floundering in the creek. But before he could ask, Hegel, followed by the four disconsolate hounds, emerged from among the trees.

Hegel looked distressed. He was red in the face from the unaccustomed exertion, but he was also frightened. The behavior of the dogs, the rifle shot, and the sound of the aircraft, which was still circling overhead, had convinced him that serious trouble was afoot. He did not want to become involved in any wilderness feuds, yet it seemed to him that was exactly what he was doing. In truth, he was just about fed up with the hunt. It was not at all what he had envisioned.

When he had first heard about the white puma, he had yearned to shoot the animal for a trophy. He had thought only of the fait accompli and of the compliments that he would get when his hunting friends saw the white cat spread in front of the fireplace in his den, a large room with walls covered by the mounted heads of a variety of mammals, and the floor displaying a number of skins that bore further testimony to his hunting prowess. But things were not turning out as he had imagined. Not even by half!

Hegel had always hunted comfortably in the past. Hunting the white puma would have been simple, a matter of riding about the wilderness for a day or two while the guides worked him into position for his shot. Instead, he had been dragged through this dreary and unforgiving wilderness, his skin itching from dozens of fly bites, his only companions two uncouth men who did not seem to know what they were doing. Not only had they been unable to find the white puma but they had been unable to find *any* pumas. And he was paying a lot of money for all of this failure and discomfort!

Emerging from the forest, he was stunned by the sight of Cousins inexplicably sewing up a woman's pant leg! It was crazy! And Taggart—he had left him alone in the forest, left the dogs, which were sick. It was really crazy.

Annoyance and distress made Hegel speak in German. *"Was machen Sie, Herr Taggart? Was ist los?"*

"Say what?" replied Taggart.

"Ich haben . . . Oh. I mean, what is going on here? Who is that woman? And what's wrong with the dogs?"

"Them's a lot of questions, Mr. Hegel, and I ain't too sure myself what the hell's going on. Maybe when Steve's done fussing, we can get some things straightened out. *Right, Steve!"* Taggart spoke angrily, scowling and looking first at the German, then up at Lansing and Cousins, who ignored him, leaving him to gape in silence.

The Aeronca's motor broke the silence. Then Lansing's radio beeped. She switched it on and spoke. "Yes, David? Over."

"Heather, what in blazes is going on down there? Over."

"Right now, Mr. Cousins is helping me. The wound is not

at all serious. He dressed it for me. I can stand and walk, and the pain is quite bearable. The German and the big man are here, with the dogs. Over."

"OK, what's next? Over."

Before Lansing could answer, Taggart, who had climbed up to the rock, yelled into the radio. "Never mind what *she* wants to do, you bastard! What about the pepper she put in the tracks so's my hounds got their snoots boogered!"

Carew did not answer him. Instead, he spoke to Lansing. "Do you want to report the shooting as an accident, or as an attack? Over."

Cousins, who had just snipped off the last thread at the cuff of Lansing's pant leg, stood upright and looked at her. "It was an *accident.* You know that, don't you? You ain't going to get me in trouble, are you?"

Lansing shook her head. "It really *was* an accident, David. I don't want you to report it at all. OK? Over."

"Right. If that's what you want. Over."

Cousins smiled at Lansing, nodded thanks.

"Listen, David," she said into the radio. "I can manage the walk back to camp. You land on Pat Peak Lake, spend the night there, and then come and join me. Over." She did not mention the white puma, and Carew understood.

"OK. I'll land in about ten minutes, but I won't spend the night there. I can make it to your camp in about the time it will take you to get there. And I'll bring some penicillin. But are you sure you can manage to walk that far? Over."

Before Lansing could reply, Cousins leaned forward, reaching for the radio and smiling slightly. Lansing passed him the set. "Mister, this is Steve Cousins. It was my gun that hurt the lady, so I reckon I'll make sure she gets to her camp OK. You ain't got no need to fuss about *that.* Over."

Carew acknowledged and signed off just as Taggart began to yell at his partner. The big man was furious. "You stupid jerk!" he screamed. "You figure on us helping *her*! You're nuts! Let her make her own way. And if she don't get there . . . well, so much the better!"

"Cool it, Walt!" Cousins, his eyes cold as granite chips, spoke quietly. He jumped down from the rock shelf and approached Taggart. "That woman could've put me in for a lot of hurt with the law if she'd a notion to lie. But she didn't. And she told the pilot not even to report the *accident.* So you just cool it, partner. If she needs help getting back to her camp, she's got it from me!"

This was a long speech for Cousins, and it impressed Taggart. But what had the greatest effect on the big man was the look in those eyes. The younger man was normally quiet, not given to outbursts of temper, but Taggart knew it did not pay to push Steve Cousins.

"OK, OK, Steve. Whatever you say."

Hegel now interrupted. "I must tell you both that I will return to Moose-skin Johnny Lake. Then I fly to Vancouver. I have had enough of this hunting."

Cousins shrugged.

Taggart, because he now saw a chance of shooting the puma and selling it to Joe, smiled. "Yeah, we understand. But you won't get a refund from the boss, you know?"

The German nodded.

Taggart turned to Cousins. "Now, buster! Tell me how come you wound up sitting on your duff in that creek?"

Cousins looked up. He read apprehension in Lansing's face. Giving her what he hoped was a meaningful stare, he turned to Taggart. "I stumbled and fell backwards into the creek. That's when I dropped the rifle and it went off. I reckon I was pretty damn careless. I didn't set the safety."

Taggart roared with laughter, bending forward and gleefully slapping his thigh with his left hand. "I'll be darned! You wait till the boys hear about that! Cousins trips over his own feet, falls in a creek, and shoots a conservationist! Man, oh man . . . that'll buy me a drink or two, I'll wager!"

Lansing stared at Cousins in utter surprise. He had lied. Why, she wondered. Why had this hunter lied? And why was he now showing her so much consideration when not an hour ago he had been so angry with her?

18

They were walking up the pass. Lansing used the stick that Cousins had cut for her. The guide carried her gear and helped her when the going got difficult. Arriving almost at the crest of the pass, Lansing stopped, her breath near gasping. Cousins, walking some yards ahead, did not at first realize she had halted. When he did, he turned, at once noting her labored breathing and the way she was leaning on the stick. "Are you all right, ma'am?"

"Yes, but I guess I'm a bit worn out."

"Sure," said Cousins. "And you've every right to be. I gotta tell you, ma'am, you're sure some gutsy lady."

Lansing smiled. She was still puzzled by this man. Catching her breath, she asked him, "Why didn't you tell your partner that the white puma attacked you and threw you in the creek?"

Cousins, standing with his back against a tree, did not immediately reply. He looked at Lansing quizzically and hitched up his belt, a wide strap of leather that was studded with cartridge pouches. Then, looking away as if he were embarrassed, he spoke. "Don't rightly know, ma'am. I saw him all stretched out, reaching for me with them big paws and them black hooks, and I reckoned I was done for."

Cousins was silent as he rolled another of his endless supply of brown cigarettes. He lit the smoke, looked at Lansing, then stared into the distance. Exhaling an acrid cloudlet, he spoke again. "But when you yelled at him the second time, I *swear*, ma'am, I saw him twist his body, like he flicked his shoulders left, away from me. Like he understood what you'd yelled. After, with Walt, I don't know . . . I kinda thought . . . well, I guess I figured that maybe it weren't right to kill that cat."

Lansing looked at the man in astonishment. He continued to stare into space, as if he were ashamed of confessing a weakness. She remained silent, sensing that he had more to say. She was right.

"I can't figure it. He could've killed me, but he didn't. He turned, I know he did. *I saw him turn away*. But I can't believe it. Never reckoned an animal could think. And I sure never figured that it could understand words. I just don't know, ma'am."

Lansing waited. Would this laconic man say more?

Cousins turned his head, looking directly into her eyes. "Reckon I'm done hunting. I just don't reckon I can go and kill animals if they can *think*. It ain't right!"

Amazement and delight mingled in Lansing's face. Then she felt sorrow for the man. He was obviously deeply torn. His words rang true, but what would such a man do to earn a living? For the first time she began to understand a bit about people like Cousins, and, yes, even his partner, the gross, one-armed despoiler. "If you don't guide anymore, Steve, what will you do? How will you earn a living?"

Cousins, still looking at her, shrugged. "Don't know, ma'am. Maybe I can go logging. Hire out as a teamster. I know horses good. I don't know. But I ain't going guiding no more. That's for sure!"

Rested, Lansing started to walk again. Cousins moved ahead, leading the way at a moderate pace and turning around every now and then to make sure that the woman was keeping up.

They traveled in silence until they heard Carew's aircraft approaching, coming from the north.

"Will you switch on the radio, please?" Lansing called to her companion.

Cousins took the instrument out of the satchel and did as he had been asked, picking up the last part of Carew's transmission. ". . . in five minutes. Over."

Cousins gave Lansing the radio. She asked the biologist to repeat.

"I said I would be landing on Pat Peak Lake in five minutes. How are you making out, and what's your camp ETA? Over."

"I'm fine, David. The leg's a bit sore, and I'm tired, but OK. We're on the down-slope side now and should reach camp in about an hour. Over."

Carew acknowledged her message and said he would walk to her camp immediately after landing; when he signed "Over," Cousins took the radio. "This is Cousins. If you need a hand, you can wait and I'll walk in. Reckon I can be there an hour after leaving the lady's camp. Over."

"No, thanks, I can manage this time around. Maybe you can give me a hand in the morning. Over and out."

They arrived at the camp just as the sun was reaching for the western peaks. Lansing, tired and in some pain, entered her tent and lay down on her sleeping bag. Outside, Cousins started to gather firewood.

As he worked, the guide thought about the white puma, marveling at the animal's seeming ability to understand human words. After a lifetime in the backwoods of British Columbia, during which he had learned the ways of the wilderness and of its natural inhabitants, Cousins had never felt emotion when trapping or killing animals. He had always taken them for granted. But now, suddenly, he found himself fascinated by a mammal for its own sake. Except for horses and dogs, which he held in high esteem, he had never considered that animals were sentient beings capable of reasoning, of loving in their own ways, and of feeling pain.

An hour later, as he was returning to the camp carrying on his shoulder a large dead log that he intended to cut up for firewood, Cousins still could not quite believe that the puma had obeyed the woman's command. Yet of one thing he was very sure; the charging cat had deliberately avoided striking him with its paws.

Unaware that Lansing was standing by the tent watching him, Cousins dumped the long trunk on the ground, then straightened up and stood still, staring at the lake water. "If he'd hit me with them paws," he muttered aloud, "I wouldn't be standing here now. He'd like to have broke my neck."

"Well, Steve, I for one am very glad that you were not hurt," Lansing said.

Cousins whipped around, his face scarlet. He looked, thought Lansing, like a small boy caught with his hand in the cookie jar. "Uh . . . guess you kinda startled me, ma'am. Didn't know you was about."

Before Lansing could reply, Carew hailed the camp, his voice loud.

"Hi, David," Lansing called.

Cousins, using Lansing's eighteen-inch bow saw, busied himself by cutting up the log, but he had not yet sawed off the first round when Carew entered the small clearing, a large pack on his back and a three-foot bow saw in his right hand.

Seeing the guide working with the small tool, Carew walked over to him and offered the larger one. "Here, this should get the job done a bit faster," he said.

Cousins smiled and took the proffered saw.

"Good to see you again, David," Lansing said, giving him a hug. "Good to see the supplies, too!"

The first item to emerge from the biologist's tumpline pack was a two-man nylon pup tent. Throwing it on the ground, he addressed Cousins. "It seemed a good idea to bring along a second tent. I wasn't sure you'd be here, but I'm glad now that I picked up the two-man job."

When all the supplies were unpacked and the second tent erected, Carew took a small plastic pill bottle from his first-aid kit. Opening the lid, he took Lansing's hand and shook one white tablet into her palm. "Penicillin," he said. "Take it right now. You get another one in the morning and another one again tomorrow evening."

After supper, the three of them sat by the campfire and talked about the day's events. Delacroix, Carew told Lansing, had been in contact with Vancouver and had learned that a number of conservation groups in British Columbia, elsewhere in Canada, and even in the state of Washington were now protesting the hunt for the white puma. "Linda says that the Ministry of Natural Resources has also received a flood of calls and letters from individuals protesting the hunt. She thinks the government may be about to cancel the open season."

Cousins listened in silence. After a time, he looked at Carew and said, "I reckon Bell got kinda greedy. He sure got himself a sweet deal, getting that extension to his license. And he's been making a potful of bucks."

The guide rolled a cigarette, licked it closed, and lit it. He was quiet for some moments. "D'you reckon it'd do any good if I was to speak to your conservation outfit about what's going on out here? Like, about poaching, and scouting for game from the air, and using two-way radios to lead hunters right up to the kill? Stuff like that?"

Lansing and Carew looked at each other, surprise on their faces. Lansing answered. "It would do a *lot* of good, Steve. Would you do that?"

Cousins did not answer immediately. He puffed on his cigarette, staring into the dancing firelight. "Yeah. I'd do that. I been thinking a whole lot since that cat flew at me. He could've killed me easy. But when you yelled at him, I know darned well he listened to you. I don't understand it. Ain't never seen the like. But I'm sure he listened to you, ma'am. I guess I owe you my life.

"But that ain't all. That ain't all, not by a long shot. I don't know, but now I reckon that killing animals for money, and babying those pilgrims what come from all over to shoot things . . . well, I reckon it ain't right."

Carew looked hard at the man. Did he mean what he was saying? It seemed inconceivable that this inveterate hunter and, the biologist strongly suspected, longtime poacher would suddenly reform. But he let the matter drop for the moment.

As they sat by the fire, Lansing told about the day's events, beginning with finding the puma tracks outside her tent. She told of her discovery of the cat's kill and scent mound, and, her eyes shining at the memory, she told of her momentous encounter with the animal and of their quiet time together. "Before the hounds started to bay, he just lay there, relaxed, looking at me. He was simply magnificent. There's no doubt at all that he was friendly."

"You still think of it as a male, but you don't know that for sure, do you?" Carew asked.

Cousins interrupted. "Maybe *she* don't, but *I* sure do. Apart from his size—and he's real big—when he was flying toward me, all stretched out like he was, I could *see* he was a male."

"Well," said Carew. "As a biologist, I must say the puma's behavior was unusual, to put it mildly. But I find it even more surprising that he was still near you when Steve showed up . . ."

Cousins again interrupted. "Near! You ain't kidding! I saw that cat pop up from behind a big slab of rock maybe fifteen feet from the lady's back. That cat hadn't run off, no sir. Not hardly. Another thing, it seemed to me he stuck around because of the lady. He acted like she was his mate—excuse me, ma'am, but he did, you know?"

Carew had been writing furiously, making notes. The biologist already had visions of publishing a paper after he'd studied the puma at greater length, if that should turn out to be possible. He probably would not get to see the cat on his own, but, with Lansing along, he believed his chances would be excellent. At that moment he was inclined to agree with Cousins. It was likely that, in some strange way, the animal related to Heather Lansing simply because she *was* female. This, however, did not have any bearing on the puma's behavior when he'd charged Cousins.

"OK, Steve, it's your turn now. And, please, give it to me straight. You and your partner claimed that a puma attacked your tent and that before that, the white cat, or another of his kind, killed one of your hounds and mauled another. Did those things really happen?"

"They sure did! No doubt about that. They happened. And it *was* the white cat. I can show you the track of his right hind foot, which is missing a bit from the outside toe."

Both Lansing and Carew looked surprised. Neither one of them had noted such a significant identification mark.

"You've had lots of experience with pumas. Did you ever know of one that attacked its hunters, or killed dogs?" Carew asked.

"Nope. Never did. Nor did we ever know but one other cat what wouldn't tree."

"How do you account for the behavior of this particular mountain lion, then?"

"Can't. This cat's different, is all."

Deferring to Lansing's injury, the trio remained in camp the next day. Meanwhile, unknown to them, an angry Andrew Bell was facing Hegel and Taggart at the headquarters of High Country Safaris. The first thing that morning, the outfitter had talked with Taggart alone, learning of the previous day's events. Then he asked Hegel to come to his office. "You know, Mr. Hegel, I can't force you to continue this hunt. But our agreement clearly states that if for any reason a client has got to abandon the hunt and elects to be flown out of our facilities, payment will not be refunded."

Hegel shrugged, nodded, and then asked when he could be flown to Smithers so that he could get a flight to Vancouver. Glad to see the last of the bothersome client, Bell sent for his chief pilot and instructed him to take the German to Smithers as soon as Hegel was ready to leave.

Alone again with Taggart, Bell continued his questioning, especially asking the guide if he was sure that the woman had been wounded by Cousins's rifle.

"I reckon so, boss. We heard the shot. But when we got there, I didn't see no injury. Nor no blood. Steve was sewing up a long tear in her jeans. Like he was some kind of freaking mother hen! And he owned up that he'd fallen on his keister in the creek and dropped his gun and it fired on account of he hadn't set the safety—the bloody fool! I tell you, boss, Steve's gone strange."

Just then there was a radio call for Bell. He went to the communications room and sat in front of the powerful set. The caller was a senior official in the department of game and fish.

"I'm sorry to have to tell you, Mr. Bell, that the Ministry of Natural Resources has reconsidered its decision to grant you an open season on mountain lions. As of now, the regular hunting regulations are in force."

Bell, enraged, protested, but he was interrupted with more bad news. "There is another matter, Mr. Bell. The extra licensed territory that we granted you *on a provisional basis* has been revoked . . ."

"What! Listen, you SOB! What about the lodges I built? The costs! What about that? Hey!"

"Yes, we are aware that you spent money on those lodges because of the extension of your range. Frankly, we are somewhat embarrassed. The extension should never have been granted. So, the government is prepared to compensate you in full—in return for a quitclaim from you, of course. I think it would be best if you got your lawyer to talk to us about the matter, Mr. Bell. It would also be useful if you could come to Victoria to discuss a couple of other things."

"What other things?"

"Well, they're better not discussed on the air. Can you fly in to see us?"

"You bet your life I can! Like first thing tomorrow morning!"

"Excellent. We'll expect you here at, say ten thirty A.M. Is that convenient? Oh, by the way, if you've got anybody out hunting puma right now, you'd better recall them. And no hunting in the canceled territories, right?"

"Yeah!" Bell shouted into the microphone.

Striding back into his office, where Taggart sat smoking, Bell pounded his desktop with his fist. *"Now, Taggart, what the hell have you and Cousins been up to?"*

"Been up to, boss? Why, nothing other than baby-sit that fat German."

"Then why, by all that's holy, did those bastards in Victoria *cancel the open season on pumas as well as my new territory licenses?* Answer me *that*, Taggart!"

The guide stood, cigarette in hand, mouth hanging open. He was as stunned by the news as Bell had been. He shook his head. "Boss, I don't know! Honest! I don't know!"

Bell, almost apoplectic, smashed the desk again. "Well, by God, I'm going to Victoria in the morning to find out just what this is all about. Those bastards are torpedoing my business!

Jesus Christ! I went into debt to expand, now they're cutting me off at the knees!"

"What'll you do, boss?"

"Damned if I know! Where the hell is Cousins, anyway?"

"I don't know. Last we spoke, he was going to help the libber to her camp. When I chewed her out, Steve . . . be damned if he didn't turn on me. You know, the sucker can get plenty mean when he's riled up. I let it go."

"OK, get hold of Jack. Tell him to fire up the small Cessna and you two go find that woman's camp. When you've got it spotted, come on back, saddle up a horse, and go see what's going on. Take a spare horse, saddled, so if you find Cousins he can ride back with you. Those conservationists have been up to something and Steve may know what it's about. I want him here tomorrow so I can talk to him. I'll radio from Victoria."

Taggart nodded and left the office. Bell told the office manager he was going to Victoria. "While I'm gone, make sure that Taggart finds Cousins. I have to know what's going on. And when you bring in the other guides and hunters, question them. I'll call you from Victoria before I have my meeting with those SOBs."

"How long will you be away?" asked the manager.

"I don't know. A day, maybe two, probably. Have someone keep a radio watch from now until eight o'clock tonight and from then on from eight in the morning to eight P.M. until I get back."

"What's happening?"

"Trouble, that's what. I don't know why yet, but, by God, I'm sure going to find out." As he left the building, Bell slammed the door.

At midmorning, while Bell was flying to Smithers, Cousins was returning to camp with an armful of dry firewood, which he dumped just inside the trees. Then he went to speak to Carew, who, having photographed the puma's slightly deformed rear track, was measuring all the other pugmarks. He was some distance from the tents. "I got a bad feeling," Cousins announced.

Carew, on his hunkers, looked up after jotting some figures in a notebook. "What about?" he asked.

"These tents can easy be spotted from the air. Wouldn't surprise me none if Bell didn't send a scout plane to look for the camp. I reckon we should move the tents into the trees. There's a big enough opening just inside the bush, over there," Cousins said, pointing to where he had dropped the wood. "There's space for both tents and we can have a fire, too, but the tops of the trees around the opening will hide the camp."

"Why would anyone be looking for us, Steve?"

"You don't know Bell. He can be real mean when he's crossed. And Walt can get pretty mad, too. Could be nothing'll happen, but I figure we should be ready if it does. Anyways, if they spot the camp, they'll figure out we're here because we reckon the cat's around here someplace."

Carew stood and delivered a playful punch to Cousins's shoulder. "Now I *know* you're on our side, Steve. I'm sorry, but I wasn't sure if we could really trust you."

Cousins looked hard at Carew, shrugged, but did not reply.

Lansing, emerging from her tent in time to hear Carew's words, called angrily, "David! I *knew* we could trust Steve from the moment he defended me from Taggart. If you'd asked me about your doubts, I would have put them to rest. Steve's *with* us!"

Cousins smiled. Before Carew could say anything, he spoke to them both. "It's OK, ma'am. Reckon it's natural for Mr. Carew to feel like he did. No sweat. I understand."

"Well, Heather's right, Steve. I owe you an apology. I'm sorry."

"And while we're about it," Lansing interjected, "let's get rid of this ma'am and mister stuff. I'm Heather, and he's David. Oh, by the way, Steve, David's not a mister, in any case, he's a *doctor*."

Cousins smiled again, but he looked surprised. "A doctor? Reckon your wound's in good hands then, ma'am . . . uh . . . Heather?"

Carew and Lansing laughed.

"I'm not that kind of doctor, Steve. I'm a doctor of biology. It means I study animals."

"Well, reckon we're about even then, Dave. I study animals, too. Done it all my life."

An hour later the camp had been moved into the forest and all signs of their presence had been eradicated from the lakeside site.

In early afternoon, they heard the drone of an aircraft. Cousins, who had been sitting on a log smoking a cigarette, jumped to his feet and ran to the edge of the trees. Taking care to remain within cover, he scanned the skies. Presently he saw Bell's small twin-engine Cessna. It was flying low and at its slowest safe speed. The aircraft did three passes, then gained height and headed south. Cousins returned to the camp. "I'd make book that Jack Kent is piloting that plane and that Walt is sitting next to him," he noted.

"Well, they're going south, so they're going to spot my Aeronca," Carew said. "But that twin prop can't land on the lake, it needs a lot more room."

The arrival of the search aircraft caused Carew to worry. He knew that as soon as his Aeronca was spotted, Taggart and the pilot would conclude that they were in the region. "We've got a lot to think about, so I vote that we start right now. It's almost two o'clock, the time for Linda to switch on. I think we ought to call her, give her our news, and find out if anything unusual has been occurring in the last twenty-four hours."

Delacroix had been anxiously waiting for two o'clock. She had earlier called conservation headquarters in Vancouver and had learned that Bell's open season had been rescinded and his license rights to the expanded hunting territory canceled. The news was already being carried by the media.

When Carew called, Delacroix almost babbled as she gave him the information. "You know, the white puma is a *celebrity*. The media is clamoring for pictures, and you should hear the protests against the hunt! Headquarters played me part of a tape of a rally in Vancouver. They say that *thousands* turned out! And the written protests have flooded the department of game and fish. *We've won!* Oh, I'm so excited, I almost forgot. A Dr. Lightfoot, at game and fish, wants to talk to you, David, as soon as possible. He said it was really important that you should fly to Victoria because he doesn't want to discuss it over the radio. And he'd like Heather to go also, if possible. I'm supposed to call back and tell him when you'll go and whether or not Heather will be with you. Over."

Carew acknowledged her news, but said he'd call again in fifteen minutes. "I want to talk things over with Heather. Over and out."

While Cousins excused himself and went to gather more wood for the fire, Carew and Lansing talked quietly, debating whether to ask Cousins to stay in the region on a full-time basis as the puma's protector, an idea that had come to Carew the previous evening when, he told Lansing, he had decided to seek a grant from the university to study the animal.

"You know, field studies are not continuous. If I get the grant—and I'm pretty sure I will under the circumstances—I'll probably spend six or eight weeks in here during late summer and autumn, and a month or so in winter for this year. We'll need someone here full-time to protect the animal. Indeed, we could probably use two caretakers. But, before I apply, I want to at least catch a glimpse of the cat. To do that, I'll need you to help. The cat obviously trusts you and those who are with you, or he would have probably killed Steve."

Lansing readily agreed to help. She had, she said, budgeted for at least a month when they set out to interfere with the hunt, so it would be no problem for her to remain with Carew and Cousins.

"Who is Dr. Lightfoot, David? And why does he want to see us?"

"He's a biologist with the game and fish people, a senior man. As to what he wants, I don't know. I would guess it's to do with the white cat. We should go, in any case. I know John. He's a good biologist."

They were silent for a while. Then Lansing asked, "Do you think you can get funds for a puma protector, David?"

"I believe so. This is a unique opportunity to study the first white puma known in British Columbia. The animal is different in more than color. We have proof of this in that he wouldn't tree, that he attacked his hunters and killed and injured their dogs. Yes, I feel I can get funds. The question is, would Steve accept if I do?"

"Ask him, David. There he comes now."

Cousins was startled by the offer. Several minutes passed before he answered. "Reckon I would. But only if I can make a deal with Walt."

"A deal with Walt?" Carew asked. "What kind of deal?"

"It's like this. You know me and Walt have been partners a long time. He's often ornery, he drinks too much, and he's a greedy SOB. But, no matter what, we're partners. I gotta talk to him to get him to agree not to try and kill the cat. If he does, I'll take the job if your grant pans out."

"But why do you want his word? And will he keep it?" Lansing asked.

"Yeah. He'll keep it. I know he will. Why do I want it? First, I wouldn't want to have to fight Walt if I caught him trying for the cat. Then, him and me, we'll always be partners, even if I'm looking after the cat and he's guiding for Bell. So I got to talk to him."

Carew understood. He was about to agree to the proposal when Cousins spoke again. "There's another thing I got to talk to Walt about. And to you."

"What's that?"

"It's been bugging me since I met up with you guys. Maybe you'll not want me when I tell you, but I reckon I just gotta tell anyways!"

Cousins now confessed about the poaching he and Taggart had done on their own in the past and, in more recent times, the poaching they had done for Joe and his animal-parts business. He described the shack that he and Taggart had built, the way they contacted Joe, the helicopter pickups, and the fact that Joe was willing to pay five thousand dollars for the white puma's hide and head.

Lansing and Carew were stunned into silence.

Presently, Lansing got up, walked to where Cousins was standing, and, without giving a hint as to her intentions, reached out with both hands and gripped the guide's face. She drew his head down toward her own and kissed him full on the mouth, releasing him at the same time.

Cousins went red in the face. He took a step backward, staring at Lansing as if she had suddenly gone crazy. "Huh . . . why'd you do that, ma'am?"

"Because you're a good man."

Carew walked over and offered his hand. They shook.

"I agree with Heather, Steve. Telling us what you did took guts. And, I must tell you, it may yet take even more guts to deal with the problem. We have to report Joe and his organization. You understand that?"

Cousins did understand. But he was adamant that Taggart be left out of it.

"I ain't snitching on Walt. There's no way I'm snitching on him. But I'll talk."

Carew was confident that they could get the authorities to agree not to prosecute Cousins in exchange for his full confession. As for Taggart, they decided that Cousins would use the radio to call Bell's headquarters and arrange a meeting with the big man.

At six o'clock, Cousins reached Taggart.

"Steve?" Taggart, as usual, felt he had to bellow into the microphone. "Where in hell's name are you, you jerk?"

Placating Taggart by his lack of aggression, Cousins learned that Bell was in Vancouver.

He asked Taggart to wait a moment. Shutting off the mike, he turned to Carew. "Bell's away. Can you fly me to Moose-skin in the morning so's I can talk to Walt?"

"I think you'd better wait until we get back from Victoria. We'll leave in the morning and come straight back tomorrow evening. How about you meet with Walt the next day?" Carew suggested.

Heather Lansing, David Carew, and Steven Cousins sat opposite Dr. John Lightfoot, chief biologist of the game and fish department. The four had been talking for more than an hour, and now, responding to a knock at his door, Lightfoot rose and opened it.

The man who entered was in his fifties, a tall, somewhat stooped figure whose once black hair was heavily streaked with gray. He was the department's head of law enforcement, a veteran officer who had joined the ministry years earlier when, as a sergeant, he'd changed his occupation at the time the provincial police force was disbanded and its duties taken over by the Royal Canadian Mounted Police. Deciding against an offer to join the Mounties, Charlie Morgan had entered the department. He'd become a district game warden and been posted to the West Kootenay region. Later, he was made chief warden with a wider area of responsibility. More recently, he had been promoted to head of the enforcement section. Morgan was a field man first and foremost, and he was a staunch advocate of conservation, a subject over which he often clashed with his superiors.

Now, after he was introduced to Lightfoot's visitors, he listened without interruption while first Carew and then Cousins talked about affairs in the Cassiar District, the region in which the white puma lived and in which Bell operated his outfitting business.

Carew, with occasional comments from Lansing, explained what they and their group had been doing since word had first leaked about the presence of a white puma within the vast territory encompassed by the Morice Provincial Forest. Then he related their experiences following Lansing's accident, explaining that although it had been Cousins's gun that had inflicted the wound, the shooting had been entirely accidental and the injury slight.

At this point, Lansing began to speak. "You may wonder why the shooting wasn't reported. We all knew that such accidents *should* be reported to the police, but I voted against doing so at the time because I was far more concerned about the fate of the white puma. After all, I was not badly hurt and the injury had been taken care of by Mr. Cousins. Afterwards, in my camp, Mr. Cousins had no reservation about helping us protect the puma."

Although the somewhat dour Morgan asked a number of leading questions, in the end he expressed his satisfaction with the conduct of all concerned. Then he turned to Lightfoot. "None of our laws have been broken, according to what these folks have stated, so why am I here, John?"

Lightfoot, looking at Cousins, said, "For two reasons. One deals with a matter of routine enforcement. But I'll get to that later. The other is more serious."

Lightfoot paused and looked at a scratch pad before continuing. "There's something going on in that country that most definitely concerns your department, Charlie. But the information was given to me in confidence by Mr. Cousins. If he talks to you, he will do so only under certain conditions."

"I don't like making deals," Morgan said. "And I sure don't like making deals when I don't know what laws, if any, have been broken."

Lightfoot turned to Cousins, a question in his glance. Cousins nodded.

"OK. I have given my word to Mr. Cousins that I will respect his confidence. He refuses to talk otherwise. But he *has* authorized me—at my insistence, I may add—to tell you that although he has been involved, what we are dealing with is *not* the prosecution of one, shall we say, pawn, but rather the unmasking of a highly organized, well-funded ring of poachers who operate an international export business of animal parts and are at this moment active in British Columbia and Alberta. The principals in this affair are all Americans."

Morgan, his gaze intent, leaned forward in his chair. "I *know* about that ring. They work out of Washington State. The U.S. Fish and Wildlife enforcement chief on the West Coast contacted me three, four months ago. But the FWS don't know who runs the operation and where exactly it is run from. That's one of the reasons the deputy minister asked Andrew Bell to come in after I told him I've suspected that guides in the region have been involved in the operation. Twice last winter we got word of a helicopter flying in and out of the general area."

He turned to look at Cousins. "If you can help us nail these swine, there's no question but that we'll protect you as a source. You have my word on that."

Cousins nodded. "OK, this is how it works."

David Carew interrupted.

"No, Steve. I trust these gentlemen, but I don't think you should incriminate yourself without a written guarantee. Immunity from prosecution. Maybe we should get a lawyer for you."

Lansing looked at Morgan, expecting a protest. But the man was smiling. "No problem with that. It's reasonable. Who's your lawyer?"

"That *is* a problem," replied Carew. "He's in Vancouver."

Morgan nodded. He thought for a moment. "Let me make a suggestion. If I get you a written guarantee from the head of our legal department, signed by him, by me, and by Dr. Lightfoot and dated today, will that do?"

They agreed that it would do fine.

As good as his word, Morgan telephoned the lawyer, explained what was needed, and hung up. Agreement had been reached.

"Right, the paperwork is being done. Should be here in about an hour. Now, what about that other matter?" he asked the biologist.

Lightfoot pointed to Carew. "It may be better for Dr. Carew to explain."

"Well, Heather is really the one who should speak. She's not only the president of CCA, but she founded the organization. We've discussed the needs in the field, so she should take it from here."

Lansing did not need a second invitation. She began by describing her first meeting with Bell, then told about the deployment of conservationists in strategic areas of the territory, from that point on describing all the events as they had transpired.

When she had finished, noting that Morgan was going to speak, she held up her hand.

"On arrival at the island airport, I phoned my office in Vancouver while David was phoning the university. We are now actively fund-raising. I'll talk about that in a minute, gentlemen," she said, sweeping both men with a glance.

"First, I must tell you that we have a guarantee of *some* funding from both the university and the CCA for a long-range study of the white puma *and* for the employment of a man whose job it will be to protect the animal from poachers. David and I believe we have enough funding for the field studies, but we need more money to pay the protector."

Morgan had listened intently, his face impassive. "Well, Miss Lansing, if a 'protector' is needed, he will have to be authorized by my department. In consultation with others in the ministry, I must add. As you probably know, we have provision for hiring deputy conservation officers. I think that Dr. Lightfoot and I can probably arrange for the hire of another. The question is: who can we find in that region? There's not too many men up there, and I suspect that of the very few who *are* available, most would be unsuitable and, in any event, unwilling to spend so much time in the wilderness."

Lansing looked at Carew. They smiled at each other. "Well, as it happens, we've got an ideal candidate for the job," said Carew.

"Oh? Who?" asked Morgan.

"Mr. Cousins," said Carew.

Morgan slapped his thigh. "I'll be darned!" he exclaimed. "I don't know. It *could* work. It used to be said in Britain that the best game warden was a reformed poacher! But we'll have to check Mr. Cousins's background."

Turning to Cousins, he asked, "You want to do this, Mr. Cousins?"

"Yeah. I do."

"You know you'll have to take an oath?"

"No, but that's OK, I know lots of 'em!"

The laughter didn't last long.

"No, not that kind. You'll have to sign a document stating that you will perform your duties according to law and that you will be faithful to the service."

"OK."

It was agreed that the documentation would be prepared within the next few days and sent to the game and fish department's Smithers office, where Cousins could take the oath of service and sign whatever papers were necessary.

Before leaving the office, Cousins, aware that he would have to remain in the region on an almost full-time basis, wanted to know where he would live.

"The way things are, you'll probably have one of Bell's lodges as your headquarters. The ministry has agreed to buy them from him," Morgan said.

"Then the best would be at Burnie Lake. It ain't grand, but it'll do. And it's in the cat's range," Cousins said.

At noon on the day after the meeting in Victoria, Cousins arrived at Taggart's cabin, opened the door without knocking, and entered to find his partner sitting at a table cluttered with dishes. The big man was drinking beer. "You stupid dog turd!" he greeted Cousins. "I've been worrying about you since I last saw you sucking up to that libber, and here you are, bold as brass and with a simper on your face."

Cousins merely shrugged. "You done cussing me, Walt?" he asked as he put the finishing touches on a brown cigarette.

"Done cussing you? I'd like to break your scrawny neck!"

Cousins lit his smoke, looked at his partner.

"Whatever's right, Walt. If you think you should and you want to try, why, just go right ahead. If not, listen up, I've got something to say to you."

"Spit it out of your craw, then!"

"Right, Walt. First off, I got to tell you I'm quitting Bell. I'm going to be a deputy conservation officer."

Taggart was too astonished to speak.

Cousins smoked, waiting.

"Are you out of your cotton-picking mind!" Taggart did not shout. He roared.

"Nope," said Cousins. "I'm in my right mind, Walt. And you better listen good, or you're gonna be in deep trouble."

"What in hell are you talking about?"

"Now, Walt, you know that getting riled up don't do no good with me. Listen up, you no-account cripple!" Cousins spoke quietly.

Instead of getting angry, Taggart sat down on his bunk and nodded. "OK, weasel face. Talk to me."

"Walt, the business with Joe is done. So's the poaching for clients. The enforcement guys of the game department in Victoria know all about the parts smuggling and they got a pretty good idea about the poaching by us and other guides out here."

Cousins then told Taggart about his trip to Victoria and his meeting with Morgan. Taggart did not try to interrupt, but his face flushed and his eyes reflected intense anger.

"I ain't nuts about crossing Joe. He's a bad mother! But it's him or us. I kept you out of it, and you'd better stay out of it from here on. The enforcement guys will be checking pretty good," Cousins concluded.

"You weaseling little bastard!" Taggart yelled, jumping to his feet. "You cover your own arse and drop me right in the muck. Some partner!"

Cousins looked at his burly friend. "Not so. I took a chance.

I could've been charged. But you didn't hear me good: *I kept you out of it,* you stupid jerk!"

Taggart reached for his beer, took a swallow, began pacing.

"Walt, we've done pretty good over the past three, four years. I know you got a good bit of cash put away, so, listen up. It's time to quit!"

"You stay out of my business, Cousins. What in hell do you know about how much cash I got? You get mixed up with conservationists, next thing you turn on your partner and you rat on him. You son of a bitch, I've half a mind to put a bullet through your head!"

Cousins smiled. "Quit being a jerk, Walt. You and me, we've been partners for a long time. I know you good, you hardheaded SOB, and I know you don't mean half of what you say. I won't be guiding for Bell, but I'll still be around, and I reckon you and me, why, we'll always be partners."

"How'n hell do you figure that? You'll be some kind of a cop!"

"I'll be me, Walt. I've agreed to watch over the white cat, and I will. But that's all. You give me your word you won't try for that cat, and we'll stay buddies."

Taggart's temper outbursts never lasted long. Now, sipping his beer, he visibly cooled down. Seeing this, Cousins told him about his encounter with Lansing and the puma, especially about his belief that the animal had deliberately avoided him when Lansing had called. "It's hard to believe, I know. But that cat *thinks.* He understood Heather. He could've killed me easy and got clean away. But he didn't. He swerved and just banged me into the creek."

"So that's how come you ended up in the water! You little weasel, you sure kept that quiet. I'll be damned . . ."

Taggart paced some more. Then, "I got to admit, apart from being white like he is, there's something different about that cat. Maybe it's right to leave him be. Yeah, OK. You got my word."

"That's settled then. But listen, Walt, if you keep on poaching, they'll get you. That guy, Morgan, he's serious about enforcement. And he had a pretty good idea of what's been going on out here. He'll get you sure if you keep on."

"Yeah. For a while now, I've wondered how long it'd last. But you're right. I've got a few bucks saved up. I guess I'll keep guiding for Bell and forget about the rest of it. But, now and then, I'm still going to get a deer or moose out of season. You know we can't hunt when the pilgrims are all over."

"If you hunt for meat, I don't think anyone'll bother you, Walt. Not me, anyways. My job will be to look after the white cat. That'll be my turf, so you stay out of it!"

"What, not even for a visit?"

"For a visit, sure. But leave your gun at home."

A week later, Cousins was sworn in and received a shiny badge that said DEPUTY CONSERVATION OFFICER. The words ran in a half circle; beneath them was the official emblem of British Columbia. Afterward, he had to sign documents relating to his duties and his pay, which would be two hundred dollars a week, a modest sum but adequate, especially because the Burnie Lake lodge had been assigned to him, free of charge, as his home and base. In addition, he had been issued a radio and a tent for use when he had to remain in the wilderness.

The next day Taggart helped move Cousins's belongings, an event that did not at first go smoothly, for Bell was outraged by what he considered Cousins's desertion as well as by the reduction of his hunting territory. In the end, however, he could only tell Taggart that he would dock his pay for the time spent helping Cousins.

Once Cousins was comfortably installed, Carew, Lansing, and Delacroix flew to Burnie Lake and were greeted at the landing by Cousins and Taggart, who was staying on for a few days.

The visitors were bearing the necessities for a party, but before the festivities went into full swing, Carew called a meeting. He was anxious to begin studying the white puma and was worried about a couple of things. For one, the smell of Cousins and his horses might cause the cat to attack them or anybody else who accompanied them, with the notable exception of Lansing. For another, because the animal had been harassed by aircraft, it would not be productive to try to establish its territorial boundaries using the Aeronca. "But if we use dogs to track him, the cat will almost certainly go after them."

Taggart interrupted. "I reckon I could lend you my Susie. But you'd have to keep her on a lead. Suze's got a real good nose, but she don't bay worth a darn, and when she does, it's only if she's with the others. Alone, on a lead, I reckon she won't do more than follow a fresh track."

"It might work," Carew said. "But are you sure about lending us the dog, Walt?"

"What's done is done. Steve's got a stake in this, so I'll help him. I ain't helping you none."

"Fair enough," said Carew, smiling. He appreciated the man's candor.

"But the puma will scent one dog as easily as three or four. Won't he try to kill Susie?" Lansing asked.

"I don't think so. So far, the cat has only attacked dogs when they have been in hot pursuit of him. If Susie is kept on a lead, and we don't press him, it's unlikely that he'll attack," Carew said. "Still, if Susie won't bay, how will we know that she's on a track?"

"You just gotta watch her tail and the way she pulls at the lead," Taggart replied.

"How does that work?" Lansing asked.

"When she's sniffing for a scent but ain't found one, her tail's sort of at half hitch. But when she finds a good sniff, up goes her tail and she starts to pull hard."

Difficult as it would be, it was finally decided to stable the horses and to use only the one dog. Carew would pick up Cousins when necessary and fly him to whatever lake was nearest the puma's last sighting. From there, they would walk.

Cousins suggested they build small bivouac shelters in strategic locations in the range. "We can stock up with dry grub and canned stuff and we can sleep out if we're on a track."

All agreed. At last, it seemed, they had a manageable plan. But Carew had one last suggestion. "Here's what I think, Heather. If Steve and I each loan you a shirt, could you wear one for a couple of days and then give it back *unwashed.* The same with socks?"

Taggart and Cousins looked at Carew. Was he losing his mind? Lansing understood.

"Sure. That's an idea. I put my scent on clothing that you guys can wear when you're looking for the cat, right?"

"Exactly," Carew said.

Cousins grinned, but when Lansing went further and suggested that Carew and he dab some of her perfume on their skin and use her brand of deodorant, he adamantly refused. In the end, Lansing suggested a compromise acceptable to Cousins. He would dab some perfume on his hat, and Susie, the hound, would be treated with deodorant.

"Good idea!" said Carew, who had earlier been in close proximity to the quite odorous hounds.

Carew, assisted by Cousins and Lansing, who had decided not to return to Vancouver for a time, spent the remainder of the summer studying the white puma, his territory, the kills he made, and the relationships that existed between him and the other animals of the wilderness, especially the predators—the wolves, bears, wolverines, coyotes, and bobcats. Although interested in the study of the animal and its total environment, Carew was especially intrigued by odors, particularly as these affected the puma's relationship with the humans he had accepted. Clearly, Carew's scent scheme, which he and Cousins had put into effect during the first two weeks of their search, had worked. They had sighted the cat on three occasions without incurring his wrath, although they got quite close to him.

It soon became evident that while the white puma tolerated the human males within his territory, his interest in Lansing continued as before. Whenever the woman was alone in an area where his fresh tracks abounded, the puma revealed himself to her. As the summer wore on, the relationship between Lansing and the cat grew apace. By mid-August, she had sat within a dozen paces of him on a number of occasions. Always he remained relaxed, his loud motorlike purr filling his surroundings with feral yet peaceful sound.

By early September, Lansing was due to leave the wilderness, and the camp had to be dismantled. Carew flew to Vancouver with some of the excess supplies and equipment. Returning to Atna Lake, he found Lansing agog with excitement. "David!" she called to him as soon as he stood onshore. "You will never guess! Yesterday evening, while I was sitting watching the sunset, I saw movement on the mainland shore. I couldn't believe my eyes, David. Out of the bush came a female puma followed by three kittens. And, David, *one of the kittens is pure white!* The puma has a son or daughter just like him!"

A field biologist and naturalist, R. D. Lawrence has made his home in Canada for more than thirty-five years. While his fieldwork has taken him to four continents, much of it has been done in the Canadian wilderness—including one ten-month stint in British Columbia's Selkirk Mountains where, in total isolation, he staked out and then observed a puma through three seasons of its life.

Mr. Lawrence is the author of twenty previous books, among them: *In Praise of Wolves, The North Runner, Secret Go the Wolves,* and *The Zoo That Never Was.* Born in Spain of a Spanish mother and an English father, Mr. Lawrence saw service in the Spanish Civil War and in World War II before returning to his family in England to complete his education. After some years as a journalist, he emigrated to Canada, eventually homesteading in the area of Lake of the Woods, Ontario. There he took up the work for which he is best known: studying nature and exploring the wilderness. In 1961 he returned to journalism, and in 1973 he purchased wild land in Ontario's Haliburton Highlands. There, with his wife, Sharon, and their two timber wolves, Tundra and Taiga, he rescues and rehabilitates wild animals. He is currently at work on a memoir, *The Green Trees Beyond,* which promises to be as interesting as the extraordinary life it records.

The text of *The White Puma* was composed in the typeface Weiss by Creative Graphics, Inc., of Allentown, Pennsylvania. It was printed and bound by The Book Press, Inc., Brattleboro, Vermont.